RITA® Award-winning author

Catherine Mann

presents a thrilling novel in her bestselling series
WINGMEN WARRIORS.

The men of this C-17 squadron are on a new,
dangerous endeavor to rescue hostages from the
war-torn country of Rubistan. But this time, these
rugged air force pilots are confronting their enemy
with a tough squad of Army Rangers and a hot-shot
group of Navy SEALs.

Bound together by the bonds of military
brotherhood, the stakes are high for three men
in particular. As they find their lives involved in
a mission like no other, they also find their hearts
embroiled in a battle with three strong-willed
women who will present a challenge they never
expected.

* * *

"Catherine Mann is one of the hottest rising
stars around!"
—*New York Times* bestselling author Lori Foster

ANYTHING ANYWHERE ANYTIME

Catherine Mann

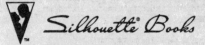

Published by Silhouette Books
America's Publisher of Contemporary Romance

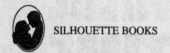 SILHOUETTE BOOKS

ANYTHING, ANYWHERE, ANYTIME

ISBN 0-373-21815-X

Copyright © 2004 by Catherine Mann

All rights reserved. Except for use in any review, the reproduction
or utilization of this work in whole or in part in any form by any
electronic, mechanical or other means, now known or hereafter
invented, including xerography, photocopying and recording, or in
any information storage or retrieval system, is forbidden without
the written permission of the editorial office, Silhouette Books,
233 Broadway, New York, NY 10279 U.S.A.

All characters in this book have no existence outside the imagination of the
author and have no relation whatsoever to anyone bearing the same
name or names. They are not even distantly inspired by any individual
known or unknown to the author, and all incidents are pure invention.

This edition published by arrangement with Harlequin Books S.A.

® and TM are trademarks of Harlequin Books S.A., used under
license. Trademarks indicated with ® are registered in the United States
Patent and Trademark Office, the Canadian Trade Marks Office and in
other countries.

Visit Silhouette at www.eHarlequin.com

Printed in U.S.A.

In memory of Corporal Dave Woomer, USMC and 2nd Lieutenant Al Taft, USAF, as well as all our fallen patriots who died while safeguarding our freedom. Your sacrifice is not forgotten.

ACKNOWLEDGMENTS

Many thanks to my editor, Melissa Jeglinski,
my agent, Barbara Collins Rosenberg, and my
critique partner, Joanne Rock. I appreciate more than
you could know the unfaltering encouragement and
guidance. You ladies totally rock!

Endless appreciation to those who patiently
answered my million military questions:
The Reverend Todd Morrison, former
Army mechanized infantry officer, my brother-in-law
and dear friend. And a great big thanks
for introducing me to Rob!
First Lieutenant Brad "Baby Doc" Mooney, USAF,
former Army Ranger medic.
Thank you for explaining the importance
of the hoo-uh.
Jim Fowler, former Navy diving and salvage officer.
Thanks bunches for the Navy details
during those long phone calls, cousin.
And of course, all my love to my husband,
Lieutenant Colonel Robert "Wanna" Mann, USAF.
Thank you for always being there for me with
anything, anywhere, anytime!

Chapter 1

Major Jack "Cobra" Korba, USAF, had mastered butting heads with mountains by the fifth grade when he discovered his ability to make people laugh. But right now he suspected there wasn't a knock-knock joke on earth that could offer much help against the 6500-foot rocky peak screaming toward his windscreen at three hundred knots.

"High terrain. Coming thirty degrees left," Jack clipped through the headset to his copilot.

Adrenaline crackled inside him like the popping flickers of light across his night-vision goggles—NVGs. The gear strapped to his helmet narrowed his vision into a neon-green tunnel.

"Copy that, Cobra, thirty degrees left," affirmed his copilot, Captain Derek "Rodeo" Washington.

The C-17 cranked left, massive cargo plane hugging craggy landscape. Desert dunes and jagged ridges whipped past in an emerald kaleidoscope haze.

He lived to fly. But today he flew as lead pilot for this mission so that others might live. One person in particular.

Rodeo ran his hands along the dimly lit control panel checking readings while Jack gripped the stick. No steering yoke like with older cargo planes, the Air Force's C-17 boasted the stick and grace of a fighter jet despite its hulking size.

Four more C-17s packed with Army Rangers trailed behind in formation. Total night swallowed them, no lights on the wings or ground. Only minimal illumination on the instrument panel guided them through the roller-coaster pass in their low-level flight.

Hazardous as hell to fly with NVGs, but necessary for stealthy penetration into enemy territory to offload cargo holds full of Airborne Rangers—the final phase of the mission to seize a Middle Eastern terrorist camp. Aside from having ties to 9/11, the radical faction had assassinated the ambassador to Rubistan and taken three American hostages.

Jack worked the rudder pedals, refusing to allow the need for vengeance to chink his concentration. Mountains to the left and right posed a constant threat outweighed by the benefits of masking them from detection by enemy radar. Visually, dark aircraft blended with the thrusting backdrop of sand and rock. Sound reflected off the mountains until pinpointing a plane's locale became all but impossible.

Hell, yeah, the protection from enemy ground-to-air missiles offered a hefty payoff to counterbalance the perils of weaving 174 feet of hurtling metal through a serpentine pass. At night.

All the more reason to nail this final training run over the Nevada desert. Soon to be a Middle Eastern desert. He contained the anticipation. Had to stay focused. Training missions could prove as deadly as the real deal.

Rodeo keyed up his mike. "Sixty seconds to turn point. Right turn three-zero-five degrees. Climb to 3700 feet. High terrain this leg. Peak, right side of corridor, 4900 feet. Stand by to turn."

"Copy, co." Jack's gloved hand clenched around the throttle, nudging it forward. "Heading three-zero-five. Climb to 3700."

Clipped numbers and confirmed calls zipped back and forth, every contingency considered. Jack hoped. Damn but did he ever hope since this was their last chance to work out any bugs.

Dust swirled in a murky haze from the 40,440 pounds of thrust from each of the four jet engines powering the C-17 past the arching peak. He steadied each breath in time with his heartbeat. Only a week until the three American hostages would be rescued. Only a week until Monica's sister would be free.

Major Monica Hyatt—the one mountain of will he couldn't move. His heart rate kicked an extra beat ahead of his breaths.

And God knows he'd tried to sway her to the point of screwing up their relationship so damned bad there was no going back. Probably for the best given that when Monica discovered he'd kept the plans for this mission from her, his flight surgeon ex-lover would likely take a scalpel to him.

Only by the grace of God and connections in D.C. had he managed to land himself in the position of primary planner as well as lead pilot. Having Monica in his biscuits was a distraction he couldn't afford right now. Not that she was speaking to him, anyway.

"Cobra, check right."

Mountains dipped beyond his windscreen. Jack roped in his thoughts. The weight of lives in the plane, as well as on the ground in that camp overseas pressed on his shoulders heavier than the bulky NVGs anchored to his helmet. "Copy, co. Got it visually."

Jack angled through a saddle dip where a valley divided crests into a stretch of desert waiting to welcome the aerial assault from rangers offloaded into the drop zone. Low and slow. He eased back on the throttle.

Keep cool. Laid-back but steady, his lifetime mantra.

Time to offload the troopers from the 75th Ranger Regiment. Jack thumbed the mike button to signal the loadmaster. "Tag, level at 3800 feet."

"Roger, Major. Level at 3800 feet. Ready when you are."

The loadmaster snapped through the checklist calls and confirmations until control panel lights signaled dual doors opening with the loadmaster, Tag, orchestrating. Tag, a looming silent mystery around the squadron and a magician in the air, off-loaded cargo with a swift efficiency that resembled a disappearing act.

Fifty-five seconds later, one hundred and two paratroopers from his plane split the inky sky. Jack's grip around the stick loosened. The boulders on his shoulders crumbled. Sure the C-17s still had to return to base for a no-lights landing, but it was only their butts on the line now.

He shrugged through the tension.

With pressure easing, piddly ass concerns trickled over him like the sweat down his back. Such as the fact that his arm hurt like a son of a bitch from the immunizations required for a deployment to the Middle East. His hand slid up to rub the sore inoculation site.

Rodeo nodded toward his arm. "You okay, Cobra? They pumped us full of more crap than normal for this one. Damned morphing virus strains."

"This new anthrax shot feels like the time I picked up one of my sisters' curling irons while it was still plugged in." And it wasn't as if he could call on his favorite flight surgeon for TLC anymore. "Sometimes it's tough to tell which is worse, the shot or the disease."

"You'll survive. My mama used to dose me up with every inoculation the minute it cleared the FDA, sometimes before." A military brat, Rodeo had grown up around the world, moving with his Army medic mother. The guy could party in four languages and never left a friend alone in a bar fight.

A wingman to trust.

Why then did he trust Rodeo with his life in the air, but hadn't told a man he considered his best friend about the mess with Monica? "Doesn't seem your mama stunted your growth."

Rodeo's deep chuckles rumbled through the interphone without arguing. No need since his wiry height spoke for itself. "Made any plans to kill time before we ship out?"

"Me. My pillow. One-on-one for twelve hours straight." Jack pushed the throttle forward, climbing into the opaque sky.

"Don't hand me that hangdog crap. Let's head down into Vegas and hit one of the casinos' all-you-can-eat setup before we're stuck with a week of that mess hall shit on a shingle. Crusty was telling me the Rio's got this kick-butt Carnival World

Buffet.'' He kissed his gloved fingertips. "Everything from sushi for me to those cheeseburgers you love. Too bad Crusty's already over in Rubistan. He's always up for food.''

Vegas? Irritation and memories chewed his hide. "Thanks for the offer, but my bed has a kick-butt pillow that won't take me a half hour of driving to find.''

If he could sleep the night through without dreams of Monica—or nightmares about her sister who'd been taken hostage simply because she wanted to feed a few hungry peasants.

Guilt slugged him and not for the first time. He'd used those same damned connections in D.C. to wrangle an introduction for Monica's sister with the Rubistanian ambassador. Bingo, her team with the IFB—International Food Bank—had been granted entrée into Rubistan.

All because he'd wanted to impress Monica.

No matter how many times logic told him Sydney Hyatt would have found her way over there with or without him, the guilt stayed.

"Come on, Cobra. What's up with you? We've got a week in Rubistan and then hell only knows how long in Germany afterward.''

Jack grunted, running out of excuses and not in any hurry to share, even with Rodeo.

"Ah, I get it.'' Rodeo nodded, his hands running over the dim neon glow of the control panel as he noted altimeter settings and airspeed. "You've al-

ready got something lined up, maybe someone to
meet you on that pillow. Korba, for a hairy, ugly
son of a bitch, you sure score a lot.''

He wanted off this subject. Now. ''Not tonight,
pal. I'm taking my hairy self to bed.''

''Yeah, right. What's your secret?''

Jack upped the throttle again, bringing him closer
to his pillow and the end of this chat. ''I start with
calling a woman by the right name.''

''Ah, hell.'' Rodeo's curse rode a laugh. ''Then
I'm totally screwed.''

The headset echoed with laughter from Tag in
back, Rodeo's call sign no great secret. His first had
been ''George,'' a link to his last name Washington
until word leaked that Rodeo had a reputation for
shouting the wrong woman's name during sex. Ru-
mor had it one offended babe of the week bucked
him off and onto his bare ass in under eight seconds—rodeo style.

Minutes after the tale hit the Officer's Club,
somebody tapped a keg for a new naming ceremony
and ''Rodeo'' was born. A funny-as-hell moniker
if it weren't for the fact that Jack suspected Rodeo
always called out the same woman's name. Something Rodeo had never shared any more than Jack
felt compelled to spill about Monica.

Sympathy knocked with a reminder of how close
he could come to being in the same position. Bare
butt on cold tile.

Sweat iced on his back. ''How about after we

wrap things up overseas and get back home to Charleston, let's take some time off? Hang out. No women. I've got a line on some tickets to a Braves' game if you're in for a road trip over to Atlanta.''

And damn it, he would not think about how much Monica enjoyed ball games, as at ease in jeans and a ponytail as in her flight suit and a French braid.

"Sounds like a plan." Rodeo smirked beneath the NVGs, his teeth a mocking green grin. "Well, hope you enjoy your date tonight with your... pillow."

"I'm sure I will."

When he completed this mission, he could clear the slate and move on. Celibacy was a pain in the ass, not to mention other body parts. Much longer and he'd be qualified for a call sign change to "Blue."

Problem was, he didn't want anyone else. But if he didn't get his head on straight again, he would alienate everyone around him. What the hell happened to his normal boots steady, laid-back, keeping it cool?

Cracked desert heaved and rolled with rocky outcroppings leading back to Nellis AFB, the location hosting final mission rehearsal as all the combatants from different bases came together. The city lights of Vegas stayed well out of sight in their route chosen for NVGs.

Vegas. That must be what had him on edge, too

many dark-cloud memories of his last trip here with Monica. They'd been so damned jazzed over landing a joint TDY—Temporary Duty. Then the news of her sister's capture had come through and everything spiraled out of control in a flat spin—unrecoverable.

Ridiculous to think for a second Monica would hang all over him in gratitude once she found out he'd taken on the upcoming mission to save her sister. Clinging vine wasn't her gig. Fine by him. He'd never wanted her to change.

Much.

Hell, no, he didn't expect gratitude complete with waterworks and hot, thank-you sex. Well, okay, yeah he would give his left nut to have Monica naked in his bed again. He was human. Male. Alive.

But he didn't want her taking him back out of gratitude. Rescuing the hostages was the right thing to do. It was his job. His mission. His calling. He would do the same for anyone's sister, mother, daughter—be they from the United States or Timbuktu.

Still, he couldn't stop the bitter surge of satisfaction in knowing that once he finished, he would damn well be imprinted on Monica Hyatt's memory, if not her life, as she'd been imprinted on his.

Only one more week and he would be free to sleep without hellish nightmares or tempting dreams. He could erase her name from his brain and off his mouth. Because no way did he intend to tap a keg for a call sign change to "Rodeo Two."

In two minutes flat Monica Hyatt talked her way past the cleaning lady outside Jack Korba's room at the Warrior Inn VOQ—Visiting Officer's Quarters. Piece of cake, since she'd changed into her flight suit after flying in on a commercial airline from Charleston.

Facing Jack again, however, would be tougher and more embarrassing than taping Band-Aids over her nipples for the bathing suit competition in the Miss Texas pageant.

She'd been first runner-up for Miss Texas. She wouldn't accept anything but a win today with the stakes a helluva lot higher than scholarship money for medical school.

Monica clicked the door closed behind her. The thud of her combat boots against industrial carpet echoed a lonely tattoo in the empty room. The need to bawl her eyes out clogged her throat, her nose, her head. She couldn't afford the luxury. She didn't lose it often, so when she did, all the bottled emotions overflowed.

And since her sister's capture, she'd been containing a flood in a Ziploc bag.

Slinging her green military bag to rest on the foot of the bed, she paced off restless energy, tugged the spread smooth again. Straightened a lampshade. With each heavy thump of her boots, she reminded

herself she was in control, a combat veteran. Sure
she might have only taken the Air Force contract
as a way to pay her way through med school when
the pageant gig flopped. But the minute she'd put
on the uniform, she knew.

It fit.

As a flight surgeon she treated the aviators, spe-
cializing in ailments induced by aerospace stresses
to the body. A challenging way to serve her country
while fulfilling her dream of being a doctor. Sometimes she broke into a sweat over how close she'd
come to missing her niche. Of course, her high
school guidance counselor in Red Branch, Texas,
never mentioned combat boots as an option to grad-
uating senior girls.

She'd just never expected to lace those boots in
defense of her own family.

Monica stacked loose coins on the oak dresser,
avoided touching Jack's wadded-up T-shirt trailing
over the edge and tamped down images of what her
sister must have endured during three and a half
months of captivity. Her baby sister who splashed
in puddles and forgot her lunch box.

Unshed tears burned like alcohol on an open
wound.

Don't think. Her feet carried her to the minifridge
where she helped herself to a bottled water beside
a half gallon of milk. Her eyes grazed over Jack's
predictable box of Froot Loops on top of the refrigerator. A smile tickled as she thought of how he

hated mornings, always carting along a quick breakfast to bypass the extra time to find a mess hall or restaurant.

Picking up the open box, she traced the toucan. Jack would pop a rivet when he found her in his room, but no way in hell did she intend for this confrontation to go public. Especially with so much other baggage between them that could well start spewing once words flew. Meeting him alone in a room with a bed might not be the wisest course of action, but there were precious few private options.

Ironic as hell in a base that controlled some of the stealthiest of test projects. The perfect place for practice runs of the covert ops Jack planned for rescuing her sister.

A plan of which he hadn't shared one damned detail.

Her knees folding under her, she sagged to the edge of the bed, cereal box clutched to her belly. She'd suffered too many extra days of fear when he could have reassured her. She'd only stumbled onto a hint of the mission by accident when a squadron member assumed she must know because of her sister's involvement. One sentence of breached security necessitated a briefing on the whole plan.

Now she knew. Jack was the lead pilot and primary planner for a joint forces rescue operation into Rubistan—the Air Force dropping in SEALs to secure the hostages, then offloading Rangers to seize the terrorist compound.

And he hadn't told her. The betrayal cut deep.

For God's sake, it was her sister out there. Sydney, her blood, her responsibility since their mother had hauled ass to greener pastures, ironically found in the middle of the damned desert with some Omar Sharif look-alike. The same desert that had lured her sister on a crusade to feed starving babies and find answers about why her own mother had abandoned her children.

As if the answers weren't clear enough.

Their mother had picked the prestige and cash of being one of four wives to a Middle Eastern, oil-rich royal instead of staying with her two daughters in a pissant tiny Texas town where their father fit hubcaps on an assembly line. No surprise. How many times had she listened to her mother's favored fairy tales about a man to swoop her off her feet? As if it didn't slice into her daughter knowing Daddy wasn't cast in the role of that love-ya-forever prince.

Love. The smell of fruity Os teased her nostrils from the open box.

Sure Jack used to say he loved her. At least ten times a day. But then Jack also loved his airplane. His grandmama. Roller coasters. Elvis. A double cheeseburger with the works, hold the pickles, because he *hated* pickles, hated them with as much passion as he loved that cheeseburger.

Most of all, Jack Korba loved the emotional charge of a challenge. More important, he had the laid-back patience to wait. And win.

Every time Jack said he loved her, she read in his sleepy-lidded eyes the burning drive to *win* her response. Maybe if she'd accepted his first date offer, his interest would have fizzled. Instead she'd said no to the squadron player. He'd asked again. And again, until she'd finally accepted.

I love you, Mon, he'd repeated hundreds of times, determination firing his eyes.

Sure as she knew Jack Korba hated pickles and loved to kiss his way down her spine, she realized if she ever answered him, the challenge would be gone. He would walk. And she resented him for that. Even as she wanted him and enjoyed the way he made her smile, which made her want him all the more.

And he'd used those feelings to manipulate her. How many times did he have to twist her heart around before she got over him?

She dropped the cereal box to the floor before it weakened her with breakfast-in-bed-with-Jack memories. He bulldozed his way over weakness with slow determination and a loose-hipped strut.

Stay strong and hang tough, she reminded herself. Resolve kicked up a notch. She could keep thinking about the way he left her out of the loop and resisting him might not be so difficult after all.

Monica picked fuzz balls off the cheap, polyester

bedspread. She wouldn't be conquered by a Pos-
turepedic stretch of box springs any more than by
six feet two inches of tempting Greek testosterone.

Hints of leather and sweat uniquely Jack whispered up. Around her. Invading her senses. The
tickle of nerves in her stomach tingled into heat
pooling lower.

She sat straighter, cross-legged on the bed. It was
only a weak moment brought on by too much worry
over her sister. Just as during the night in Vegas
three and a half months ago. Except this time she
would know to keep her guard up around Jack.

Focus and forge ahead like in the pageant bathing
suit competition. Eyes straight, head tall regardless
of how exposed she felt with those Band-Aids
sealed on her nipples. Surely she'd faced the worst
with Jack.

Too bad she couldn't escape one simple fact.
While slapping those Band-Aids on had been mor-
tifying and uncomfortable...

The pain had been nothing compared to peeling
them off.

Five minutes and he could peel off his flight suit.

Jack stared down the long corridor of the Warrior
Inn to his room, debrief for their night flight completed by sunrise. Plans and test runs were finished,
even the Army Rangers had begun to straggle back
into billeting for sleep. Nothing he could do now

but pray like hell they pulled off their three-part plan.

Anything. Anywhere. Anytime. Like the squadron motto stitched on the patch stuck to his sleeve, he would unleash it all to bring an end to this.

Loping ahead, Jack nodded without speaking as he angled past other **crew dogs** milling—Joker and Tag with Rodeo. He **just wanted** to crawl under the sheets alone in his nice quiet room and rack until time to leave for Rubistan.

An ADVON team—advanced echelon—led by Captain Daniel "Crusty" Baker had already deployed to set up their temporary base in an old airport donated by the Rubistanian government. The Rubistans were working like hell to diffuse tense U.S. relations with political distance from the terrorist faction. If not for Rubistan's slack security once the captured terrorist leader had been deported from the States, Ammar al-Khayr would still be in custody rather than back in power.

Jack chewed on a curse. Practice runs might be done, but he would rehearse it in his head at least a hundred more times because failing was not an option.

He would lead a formation of cargo planes into Rubistan under the guise of transporting humanitarian relief to NGO workers. Once there, he would drop SEALs deep in-country to recon intel for a couple of days. Then the SEALs would slip in to secure the hostages just before five hundred Rangers rained from the sky to seize the terrorist camp.

Piece of cake, right?

Hell.

Rounding the corner, Jack slowed, nodded to the senior officer lumbering toward him in the narrow corridor. No salute necessary indoors, a fact his aching arm appreciated. "Morning, sir."

"Korba." Colonel Drew Cullen nodded in return. While Jack had planned the mission, everyone would report to Cullen, the Ranger Regimental Commander from Ft. Benning, Georgia.

Jack started to pass, but Cullen pulled up short. "Hold on a minute, Korba."

"Yes, sir?"

Sun, sand and duty had carved lines in the Colonel's face, marking every one of his years in the field. Even with below-the-zone promotions, the guy had to be in his early forties. Cullen reached into the front pocket of his camouflage BDU—Battle Dress Uniform—and pulled out a roll of LifeSavers candies. "Have one."

Turning him down seemed in bad form. "Uh, sure. Thank you, sir."

Weathered lines softened with a smile. "I'm celebrating my first grandkid."

Grandkid? Jack thumbed a lime LifeSaver free. God, this guy wasn't even ten years older and already had a grandchild before Jack got started on children. Of course he would have been knee-deep in a family if Tina hadn't died from a fluke heart attack during childbirth. Fifteen years had eased the pain over losing his wife and stillborn son until he managed to walk through days at a time without thinking of them.

Then moments like this brought it up front again. "Girl or boy?"

"Baby girl."

"Congratulations, sir." Jack popped the Life-Saver into his mouth to blunt the sour aftertaste of memories with lime. Monica always ordered lime—not lemon—in her water.

Hell. Both Monica and Tina crowded his brain when he preferred to think of neither. Oblivion worked better.

His pillow called to him louder than ever. "See you tomorrow morning, Colonel."

"Sleep well, Major."

Jack pivoted on his boot heel, stopping just shy of ramming the cleaning cart. The uniformed maid smiled, steadying a tottering pyramid of toilet paper rolls. "Sir, I went ahead and let your wife into your room. I hope that was all right."

Wife?

He didn't need three guesses as to who'd tracked him down. Steady ground shifted under him. Too much Monica in his present and Tina in his past cycled through his head when he was too dog-tired to fight it.

"Your *wife?*" Rodeo slid up like a bogey from

his six o'clock and slugged him on the arm. The sore arm. "Knew you were holding out on me, Cobra."

Jack winced, massaged his bicep. "I'm not—"

"Who is it?" Rodeo lounged a shoulder against the wall, his flight suit creaseless in spite of the sweaty hours crammed in a crew compartment. Somehow the guy made even military issue shout Armani. "The chick at the registration desk? Or that hot lieutenant from the weather shop? Ah, hell, who cares? I'm just glad you're in the saddle again, man." Rodeo stared back with somber brown eyes as dark as his skin.

So much for the great wall of deception about his screwed-up relationship. "I'm fine. Just need to sleep. Alone." Understatement of the century. "But thanks. Once this crap's over with and we're in Charleston again, I owe ya that Braves' game."

Rodeo nodded, his fist swinging back for a farewell slug.

Jack held up a hand. "Lay off the arm, bud."

"Wimp."

"Ass." Jack grinned. "Catch ya later."

Rodeo cut into the milling crowd, booming, "Hey, Joker, ever been to the Rio?"

Jack's gaze homed in on his room number. For five seconds he even considered finding another place to sleep. Except his "wife" was here for a reason. And he needed her diverted and safely tucked away before he left.

Jack swiped his room card through, pushed open the door to find…Monica.

Yeah, that cleaning service woman was dead on target. Thanks to a drunken mistake in the Elvis Chapel of Love three and a half months ago, Jack was once again a married man, this time to Major Monica "Hippocrates" Hyatt.

And his wife waited in his bed, long legs folded and silky caramel hair calling a man to bury his face deep as he buried his body deeper.

"Hello, Jack."

Two words, spoken in a sandpaper drawl packed with perpetual hints of morning bedroom voice, and his body went on high alert. What the hell was it about her? Seven months hadn't given him the answer, and still he couldn't stop asking himself the question, a damned fine excuse to stare at her.

Not delicately pretty like Tina, or bombshell-knockout like some of the other women he'd dated, so much as…arresting. Full lips and the slash of strong, high cheekbones lent her an almost exotic air in spite of her all-American Texas twang.

And she was here. From the rare stillness in his normally restless new *wife,* he predicted trouble. He wanted to think it was screwed-up bad luck that had brought her to Nellis, but he didn't believe in coincidence.

Somehow she'd found out about the mission. Ah, hell.

"Jack?" She extended her legs in front of her, one at a damn time in a never-ending stretch.

His eyes locked on with radar precision while his Johnson twitched a howdy-do in response. Apparently all of him wasn't dog-tired. Of course, he'd have to be dead not to want her. Problem was, keeping people from ending up dead depended on him keeping his mind on his mission and his Johnson in his shorts.

Helmet bag dangling from his hand, Jack kicked the door closed behind him. "Hey, babe, enticing as it is to finally have my wife in my bed three and a half months after the wedding, the King's too damned tired to break into a chorus of 'Are You Lonesome Tonight.'"

Chapter 2

Eyes too full of hot Jack Korba, Monica thought a verse of "Devil in Disguise" might be more appropriate.

"Babe? Hey, *babe?*" She straightened, restrained the urge to throw a pillow at him, blinked back shock that he would spur her on purpose with a piggish remark. "God bless it, Jack, you know diminutives like that really piss me off."

The fact that she still wanted him pissed her off even more. But then emotions never came in measured doses around this man—or for him. He laughed, loved, argued, laughed again with a robustness reflected in his large-boned body.

Even his exhaustion came in full force. He

shrugged, slinging his helmet bag onto the dresser. "Told you I was tired."

Her fingers itched to comb through his jet-black hair, thick even when cropped short with military precision. Sweat from wearing his helmet too long brought a hint of curl above his ears, along his brow.

A look much like during sex.

He never called her babe then, always groaning her name with an intensity that raised goose bumps even at the whispered memory. So why throw a match on gasoline with the babe comment now?

Because he wanted to distract her. Fatigue must be kicking hard for him to resort to something so transparent.

Nice try, Jack. Not gonna work. "We need to talk."

"No shit. And we will." Two lazy strides brought him beside the bed. Close. Too close, yet not close enough. "In four weeks, at the lawyer's office, just like your summons told me. I have the date on my calendar. Shouldn't be tough to dissolve drunken vows said in front of a preacher wearing white leather fringe and a bad wig."

Her husband—for now—dropped into the bedside chair. Unlaced his boots one at a time and let them fall to the floor. Thud. Thud.

Kind of like her heart. Her hands fisted in the bedspread to keep from reaching to smooth away the weary lines creasing the hard angles of his face.

Monica swung her legs over the edge of the mattress. "That's not why I'm here."

"Uh-huh." Standing, he gripped the zipper tab on his flight suit and tugged.

Gulp. Toeing off on the floor, she inched down the side of the bed. Away. "Uh, Jack..."

Broad shoulders shrugged out of the green uniform.

"Jack!"

One leg, two legs, flight suit free. For a guy who usually moved slow, he shucked his clothes fast, leaving lots of Jack with his back to her while he wore nothing but shamrock shorts and a black T-shirt.

"What the hell are you doing?"

"Getting undressed," he shot over his shoulder, gripping the hem of his T-shirt and starting the upward sweep. "Feel free to keep talking."

If she could unpaste her tongue from the roof of her mouth. Heel, hormones. Heel now, damn it.

His shirt went up and off, revealing bronzed man and the cut of shoulder blades. She shook with the need to stand, wrap her arms around his waist and lean her cheek against his bare back. What she wouldn't give to soak up the warm comfort of his skin against hers. To inhale the spicy musk of sweat and Jack.

His thumbs hooked on his boxers.

She bolted to her feet and spun away. Palms flat on the window ledge, she stared at the canvas of heavy blue curtains blocking early morning sun. Counted to ten while straightening the part in the coarse fabric. Then to twenty while evening out the cord pulls.

He always did this to her, damn him. Muddled her world by never acting as she expected. Like with the rescue mission. Part of her wanted to kiss every inch of his beard-stubbled face in gratitude, while the rest of her wanted to scream in frustration because he hadn't told her.

Fears for her sister quivered through her, threatened to spill free, but she contained them with an airtight will. Ziploc tight. She'd looked for comfort in Jack's arms before and landed herself in an Elvis wedding chapel, for God's sake.

How humiliating. And yet the humiliation was nothing in comparison to the burn of betrayal. He'd known how she'd felt about waiting to be sure before committing. She'd shared her deepest fears with this man and yet he'd pushed her the minute she'd let her guard down.

Not again.

Bracing herself for the image of him—naked— she turned, finding a tanned back and taut flank moving toward the bathroom.

Gulp.

"Jack, will you please be reasonable." And could her voice please, please not crack next time she tried to talk?

"Mon, I'm taking a shower." Muscles flexed

and rippled as he continued walking away. "And in case you were wondering, you're not invited."

"I wasn't—" The bathroom door clicked closed. She steamed. "—wondering."

Damn, that man chapped her hide.

She stood alone, cinder block walls closing in like a cell. A cell with Froot Loops. She scooped the box off the floor and folded down the bag inside before replacing it on top of the minifridge. The shower started, louder, shooshed a different tune with the intrusion of a body.

Options?

Wait. Leave. Go after him. All stunk.

She should have stood her ground in the first place. So what if he stripped bare-ass naked in front of her? She'd seen him before. Often.

Her hand gravitated to his flight suit slung over the back of the chair. With one finger she traced the patch on his sleeve still warm from his body. *Anything. Anywhere. Anytime.* His squadron motto encompassed well a larger-than-life man when she was a down-to-earth woman.

Monica nudged his boots straight, correcting their haphazard landing on the carpet. She should have blocked the path into the bathroom and made him talk. Would have served him right to battle it out all vulnerable in the nude.

Except she'd wager Jack Korba had never been vulnerable for one second of his slow-walking life. Her hand fell away from his uniform. Even at times when anyone else would have looked like an idiot, he managed to laugh it off. Nothing rattled him.

Not even losing her.

And that hurt. Which chapped her hide even more.

Monica swiped the wrinkles out of her own flight suit. If he wanted to play the bravado game, then fine. Her boots weren't all that steady under her, but her resolve was strong enough to compensate.

Praying the bathroom door wasn't locked, Monica strode across the room. Wouldn't that take the oomph out of her game to be stuck rattling the knob? Ugh!

She twisted. Turned. The door gave way. So did a sigh. Up and out her mouth air went before she could snatch it back.

The tinted-glass doors muted her view but left a picture no less appealing as Jack worked soap across his chest. He whittled away her resistance on a good day and today her defenses ranked low. Her mouth dried, worse than peanut butter sticking to the roof of her mouth.

His scrubbing slowed with an awareness that she'd joined him, but he didn't speak. Finally he resumed his bathing. The dinky cubicle crackled with the knowledge that a few short months ago she would have held his washcloth. Hell, her *body* would have been his washcloth as she rubbed herself against him to work up a lather and more.

Monica closed the toilet lid and plopped her hormone-riddled self down on the john before she fell on her face. Or on him. "Just so you're clear, I'm not here about the divorce." Man, that last word bit on the way out. "I know about your mission to Rubistan, and no way in hell are you dodging this conversation even if you stay in there until you're a prune. The best you did with your shower stunt was buy yourself ten extra minutes, tops."

"I'm sorry I didn't know my bathroom was cleared for classified discussions."

Always quick with a comeback. Another sigh slipped, exasperated this time, but just as frequent as the turned-on sighs around Jack.

She shifted, fidgeted, stared at herself in the mirror as if her reflection above Jack's twisted tube of toothpaste might offer aid. She couldn't afford to misstep, and she wasn't giving up. Still, it hurt that he could be so unmoved by seeing her when she had a lump in her throat the size of a gauze roll.

Her reflection blinked back at her. She frowned. Cocked her head to the side...something niggling, not right about the mirror. She reached. Touched. Found.

No steam.

A smile creased her oh-so-clear reflection. He'd been in the shower for at least five minutes and the mirror was fog-free. Well, hell. He wasn't unaffected by her after all.

Jack was taking a cold shower.

* * *

The Rubistanian desert was cold at night, and Yasmine Halibiz hated being cold. Standing outside the temporary military installation, she wrapped an arm around her waist. Pitiful protection against the plunging temperatures.

For once she missed the stifling robes that had been mandatory garb for women in her country. Western clothing might be more flattering to the figure, but it definitely did not help fight a chilly breeze against the back.

Cooking rated low on her list of preferences, as well, but hacking up a beheaded goat carcass proved a small sacrifice in exchange for keeping herself alive.

Stars, sand and rock stretched for miles with a reminder she could not survive on her own. Yasmine scraped the blade of the butcher knife against the block, swiping entrails into a bin on the ground, then the remaining roasts into an industrial-size bucket. Hefting up the meat, she made her way back toward the kitchen door leading into the converted airport soon to be overflowing with American soldiers.

A small team had already arrived, military personnel sent in as—what did they call it?—an advance element. People to ready the cooking facilities. Set up security. All of which offered her time to ease into her role as a local girl hired as a mess hall cook, the perfect task to bring her into contact with the American contingent so she could select the best target.

Her arms straining, she shuffled up the cement steps toward the light slanting through an open door. The weight competed with the grit in her sandals to rub blisters and irritation. She did not doubt her ability to pick wisely. She had spent the first seventeen years of her life covered in public, often having to gauge other females as friend or foe by only their eyes.

The cultural customs might have loosened, but even six years later, her skills stayed honed. Good and evil scripted across the eyes if only a person looked. Not many looked, always too busy running or dreaming.

She had no dreams. Just a goal. Survival.

Her sandals slapped the tile floor inside, echoing with the mingled languages and bustle of activity in the cavernous kitchen. She stifled a rebellious smile over the pleasure of making noise with her shoes. Of course she could still move with stealth if she chose, a hard-learned legacy, especially during the past year.

Yasmine slung the goat roasts onto the counter beside a steaming pot of boiling water. One by one, she pitched the clammy meat hanks into the roiling cauldron. She had her orders from her uncle. She knew the price if she failed. She shivered even as the steam popped sweat along her brow.

Jamming a long-handled spoon into the water,

she stirred, her gaze skipping from worker to worker until it landed on a lone serviceman with his head stuck in the pantry. Military. Air Force. She would have to establish a connection with someone. Certainly she could not be lucky enough to settle the issue with her first try.

Women made their own luck.

Wearing a wrinkled desert-tan flight suit, the man backed out of the pantry empty-handed and frowning. Her mind categorized him.

Messy. Careless even? But no, sharp intelligence lurked beneath his uncombed hair. As if he sensed her evaluation, he shoved a hand along his head. His wedding ring flashed. Ah, a safer male to approach, perhaps.

Except not all men honored vows.

And she most definitely did not want to fend off questing hands. So she tested him. With just a shy smile.

Not interested, his eyes broadcast.

The wedding ring seemed to glow brighter. She sighed her relief. Maybe he would be a safe contact after all, even if he was a *man.* And the fact that she did not find his boyish looks attractive only added to his appeal as a potential target.

No formal name scrolled across the name tag on his flight suit, just one of those irreverent call signs Americans seemed to enjoy so. *Crusty.*

Crusty? Yasmine resisted the urge to roll her eyes. His poor wife.

He stepped closer. Close enough for her to look past the easy smile, deeper into his eyes to find…anger. Hatred. The desire for vengeance.

She backed against the stove. Steam soaked her dress, but she did not dare move.

He reached past to select a sugared fig off the counter beside her. "Do you speak English?"

Not that she would be admitting just yet. Why should she make it easier for him to trap her?

She frowned, feigning dim-witted confusion.

"All right, we can speak this way, then." He switched to Arabic with too much ease.

This one would bear watching. She discounted him as an option for contact. But who? Already her mind scanned for possibilities while time trickled away.

She spun to stir her pot and gave him her back.

The man, Crusty, eased into her line of sight for another fig. "I'd like to ask you a few questions about this place." His tone left no room for negotiation.

"May I ask for what reason, sir?" she answered in her native tongue. Dim-witted humility did not sit well with her. But she had learned to curb her temper and mouth in the year since her parents' deaths in a flu epidemic had thrust her from pampered protection into a nightmare. Selecting a peppermill from the shelf above, she speckled the sheen of fat bubbling to the top of the pot.

"It's standard procedure for a representative

from military intelligence to interface with locals during a deployment.''

Military intelligence? Nerves churned like the roiling stew. She reassessed her assumption that he was merely one of those arrogant fliers and searched for a convenient kitchen accident that would take her away. ''I have bread to make.''

And she pitied the people who would eat it.

''Well, the thing is, if I don't talk to you, you might not get to stay on. That is if you want to continue working here.''

Her eyes flew to the bubbling goat. ''Of course.''

Yet, if he was truly military intelligence, then he would have already seen her falsified papers—and could catch her in a misstep.

''What was your name again?''

''Bahijah Faris.'' A lie.

''And your parents?''

''Dead.'' Truth. Pain sliced in clean, relentless swipes, but she would not let it win. She rolled through her borrowed identity. ''I live with my brother and his wives. Money is very limited, so I must help.''

If only the real Bahijah had been bright enough to carry this off. Of course if Uncle Ammar had been smarter, he would not have sent his niece. How stupid to think she would be loyal to him—a man who was nothing more than a fourth cousin interested only in the inheritance of anyone with whom he could claim even a distant relationship.

Ridiculous since everyone in this small country was related somehow. Too bad Ammar had slipped away from justice once before.

She hated stupid mistakes. Of course, babbling stupidity could well drive *this* man away. "Faris is a very old and honored name here. It means 'wounded soldier on horseback,' which my grandfather says—"

"Where does your brother live?" His mouth smiled. His eyes didn't.

"Outside the capital."

"What are you here to do?"

Boil up goat and horse meat for servicemen who are told they are eating beef, you ignorant male. "I am on the cooking staff."

A pride-pinching duty given her true status, not that she could let that show.

She wiped her hands on her apron. "I need to collect the vegetables now or there won't be an evening meal."

The flyer intelligence contact scooped up a handful of dates and backed away. "By all means, then, don't let me keep you."

Making tracks toward the pantry, she scanned the sparse crowd. Searching. She would need to find another candidate, soon. And if her uncle's information was correct, she would have many, many more men to choose from by the week's end. Failure was not an option.

Only survival.

* * *

How much torture could one guy survive in a single night?

Icy shower pellets stung Jack's skin. Talk about caught between a rock and a hard place. Stay in the shower until his Johnson succumbed to terminal shrinkage or step out there and explain to Monica exactly why she wasn't going on the mission to Rubistan. Either way, he was dead meat.

At least the cold water worked enough numbing magic so he didn't have to face her with his Johnson saluting.

Jack opened the shower door. Monica's gaze flicked him like a brief brush of a flame before shifting away. She thrust a towel at him.

"Thanks." He tied it around his waist before grabbing a second towel and scrubbing his head.

"I don't want to fight with you anymore. I just want to get my sister back."

He peered at her through the fluffy white folds. The pain staining her eyes threatened to level him.

Draping the towel around his neck, he clutched the ends to keep from gripping her shoulders to pull her to him. "You'll see her soon. Just be patient a while longer."

"Oh, Jack, you know I don't do patient well, never have."

Her early graduation from college and med school attested to that. At thirty-four years old,

Monica always lived life on fast-forward while he took his time.

Images blindsided him of how impatient she could be while he took his time stroking her to the edge, holding back. *Now, Jack. Now.* Her husky drawl reached to him through vivid memories.

Space. Pronto. He angled past her and out of the too damned small bathroom. Fishing in the top drawer, he yanked black sweats free. What a dumb-ass idea to strip down. What had he expected to accomplish?

Her joining him.

He hitched the sweats over his hips. "How did you find out about the mission?"

Monica glided into the room, her walk an intriguing mix of military precision cut by a hint of a sway. She stopped beside him, arms behind her back, palms flattened against the wall as she leaned.

"Joker came in to update his flight physical for immunizations." She hooked a stray hair behind her ear. "He thought I knew, so he wasn't guarded in what he said. Once I looked at what he was being given and did some digging around for a few days, I figured it out. Or at least enough where…"

"You had to be briefed in on the rest." Damn. He jerked a T-shirt over his head, tried not to wince at the pull to his arm.

"Are you okay?"

"Fine."

"Anthrax immunizations hurt, don't they?"

"A little." A lot. He worked his arm in a circle and stayed silent. Snagging his box of Froot Loops, he frowned at the neatly folded bag before tearing it open to toss back a handful.

"You can take one dose of Motrin, you know, without going off flying status."

"Uh-huh," he grunted, munching.

"Damn flyboys, always afraid of medicines and then they're big babies about the pain."

A self-deprecating smile snuck free. Yeah, she knew her job and patients well. "You'll be sorry to hear, but I think I'll live."

He reached for another scoop of cereal.

She grabbed his wrist to stop him, held his gaze as firmly. "That's not funny, Jack. Regardless of what we've been through, you know it would hurt me if something happened to you."

So Monica still had feelings for him. Damned silly to launch into one of his grandma's Kleistos dances over a simple comment. Not that he was asking for anything from Monica anymore, right?

Only fifteen minutes alone with her and already he'd peeled away all his clothes and half his resolve. He didn't know what he felt around this woman, and she didn't seem inclined to give them time to figure it out. He jerked his hand free and ate his Froot Loops before she could seal his bag closed again. And he didn't doubt for a minute she'd done it the first time. If a man wanted to eat his cereal stale, big damn deal. He crunched.

"So, Jack? Do you want to replace one of the other doctors with me, or can you justify adding another flight surgeon to the roster?"

"Not going to happen. Against regs for you to fly with me since we're married." He jammed his cereal box back on the refrigerator, top open. If she didn't want to be his wife, she could keep her cereal-sealing hands to herself.

"You really underestimate me, don't you?"

Ambush ahead. He scrambled for a recovery but she beat him to the end of the runway.

"I'll be in a different plane." She unzipped the top of her military bag and dug inside. "And if we're chitchatting about the fuzzy edges of conflict of interest, you haven't said a word about Blake Gardner's SEAL platoon running one leg of the mission."

He blinked. She couldn't be planning to unpack and stay in his room. What was she talking about anyhow? Blake Gardner?

"The boy's club in action, huh?" She yanked out a clothespin. "You can rescue my sister. Blake can help his old girlfriend. But I'm supposed to sit back and wait when she's my own flesh and blood."

"It's dangerous." And Gardner was in his own personal hell over not being able to stop Sydney from going. A hell Jack had no interest in visiting because of Monica.

Stalking back to the refrigerator, she snapped the

clip on his cereal bag and closed the box lid so damned predictably he wanted to laugh. It sure as shit beat shouting.

"Get real, Jack. Are you going to follow me around for the rest of my Air Force career—and make no mistake, this is a career for me. Are you going to work your Korba magic and charm all my superiors into slotting me on only the safe missions? Step out of the Dark Ages and join the modern world."

Her eyes narrowed, jade depths just as intense and potentially hazardous as those NVG views. "What's really going on here? You've never had a problem with my job before. Quit pulling this smoke-and-mirrors garbage and talk to me."

"We're married," he repeated.

"So? Husbands and wives can't work together? Sure I'm not supposed to fly over on your plane since we're married. Not that anyone knows to call you on it. But I'll ride on one of the other jets, anyway."

He stepped closer until his dominant Greek nose almost touched the pert tip of hers. "I don't want you there."

Pain flashed for a whole second—a damned tidal wave of emotion from Monica—before she doused the spark. Well, fine. He hurt, too. Not that it stopped him from wanting to wipe away her worry.

"I can understand that, Jack, but you know how

damned scared I've been for my sister these past months."

Ah, shit. If she went soft on him, he was toast. His easygoing pop may not have taught him much, but his father had been rock-firm on one point. A man never hurt a woman. "I'm doing my best to end that fear for you."

"I know. But I don't understand why you kept this nugget of hope from me. You've never been a petty man."

She shamed him, but damn it, he had reasons— good ones. Like security. And not raising her hopes for them to fall.

He wouldn't fail. "If it had been as simple as just telling you, then hell, yeah, I'd have let you know. Except you would have insisted on a slot from the start—just like you're doing now." The truth pushed through, good thing since nothing else gained him ground. "Shit, Mon, after what went down between us in Vegas... I can't spend the next week dancing around land mines." He stepped closer. "You know how it is whenever we're in the same room."

She stilled. The air conditioner hummed in the silence between them, need riding the breeze and dulling the edges of pain until the pull between them increased. Swelled. Demanded attention. He could have her. He knew it. The defensiveness in her eyes broadcast she knew it, too.

He couldn't allow himself to take that step forward, a move that would hurt her, both of them, even more. "Don't push this. Plans are in place. Don't. Push."

"I have to. You'll figure out how to work with me around the same way I'll manage to work with you every day after the divorce is final." Her hand fell to his arm, hotter than the flaming immunization site. "Jack, for three and a half months I've tried not to think about what could be happening to Sydney. But still, possibilities smoke through my brain in this toxic black cloud." Her fingers tightened. "You know what these people are capable of. We all know what Ammar al-Khayr is capable of."

Vulnerability from the strongest woman he knew leveled his defenses faster than a SCUD missile. That her younger sister had to be there at all blasted everything else inside him to dust. He studied the floor, his bare feet, anything but Monica's eyes.

"I know you'll get her out of that hellhole, Jack."

Her faith rang clear. She might doubt him in other arenas, but not here at least. Of course he couldn't fault her for questioning him in the relationship department. Pop's advice didn't stop him from screwing up more than once. Which put him right back between that rock and hard place, wanting more time, while not wanting to hurt her again.

"Monica, you've said you trust me to get her. So we should put this on hold—"

"Please let me be there when you pull her out.

Not some stranger. At the very least, she'll need a basic physical. She'll have to give an accounting of what..." Her voice cracked.

He swallowed, or tried to, anyway, a tough-as-hell proposition with all Monica's pain clogging the air.

"Please, Jack, don't make her talk to a stranger."

Finally he sucked in air, only to find Monica's pain rode the gulp and seared his insides.

"Damn it, Jack, I'll do anything to be there when they bring my sister in." She gripped his arm. "Anything."

Anything.

His eyes snapped up to hers. The word sizzled between them with a promise of a mind-bending, all-day release from a long three and a half months apart.

Anything. Anywhere. Anytime. His squadron motto mocked from the patch on his flight suit sleeve.

How many times had she whispered those words in his ear?

He could tell she damned well remembered, too. Her emerald-green eyes glinted, pupils widening. With heat. Passion. Just like they did when he filled her. Deeper.

No way could he move forward, fling her on the bed and take her up on the offer. He might get fuzzy on relationship nuances, but this one was pretty damned clear. It would be wrong to take her.

However, if she made a genuine move in his direction? Exhaustion fell away faster than paratroopers from a cargo deck.

Monica blinked, protective shields shuttering her eyes again. "You can put that thought right out of your head, Jack Korba. I don't care what the patch on your flight suit says." She threw down her gauntlet, giving no quarter, her determination leveling him and firing him up all at once. "Nothing, nowhere, no time are you getting me back in your bed."

Chapter 3

Whoops.

Monica stifled a wince. She'd just challenged Jack Korba. Damn. Damn. Damn. God bless it, the man thrived on challenges and had patience in spades.

She watched his dark eyes narrow, flick with quicksilver determination. He may not have moved an inch closer to her, but anticipation sparked from him.

The way she saw it, she had three choices. Cry, because Jack puddled when a woman wept. Hell, he'd even married her because of a crying jag gone way wrong last time they'd been in Nevada.

Okay, no tears.

But her second option of retreating from his VOQ room and away from that bed equated to wholesale surrender. He would follow her every step, anyway. Which left only one choice. Hold her ground and face him down.

For Sydney.

Sydney, in many ways her child as well as her sister. She'd brought her up more than any of the string of live-in lovers her father had paraded through their lives in hopes of giving his girls a replacement mama.

Those women may have bought frilly dresses and styled pretty pigtails. But Monica had read Sydney *Charlotte's Web* and explained about periods. Nothing would keep her from being there for Sydney now. Not even the risk of having her heart broken by this man. Again.

Monica stepped closer. Her boots tucked between Jack's bare feet with a hint of intimacy. "I would do it, you know."

"What?" His fists clenched against his thighs, but he didn't touch her.

He didn't have to.

"I would have sex with you again if that's the price to be there for my sister. But it wouldn't be in a bed. And it wouldn't be making love." As much as her body screamed for release, her eyes stung at the loss of the tenderness he brought, as well. "Besides, we both know you won't go that route and use me." A truth that made her want him all the more. "We may be an atomic mix in the relationship department, but you're a good man, Jack."

"Shit."

"You don't scare me."

"Then you're not as smart as you think." He crowded her with his bulk and fresh-washed scent. "Do you realize how close I am to snapping? Just being in this room together has me thinking about finding you waiting for me six months ago when I landed in Germany. And five months ago when we got stranded in the Azores with a busted plane and two full days in a VOQ with nothing to do but order delivery food and make use of the bed, the floor, the shower."

She swayed, three and a half months of being without him chipping away at her with the reminder that they would never make more memories in the shower. On the floor. The bed.

He cupped her shoulders, steadied her while rocking her control. "You remember, too."

"Of course I do." That and more. Not that she planned to throw those images out there in a tangle of arms and legs and so much want.

How could she not remember with his scent and hands all over her? Knew she would continue to remember, ache even after his hands and scent slid away. His breath fanned over her, his mouth right there for the taking. Recalling his kisses, anticipating more, was almost as arousing as having them.

She allowed herself the bittersweet pleasure—the risk—of touching him, cupping his face. "My going along to Rubistan is the right thing. Make it work, Jack."

His bristly jaw flexed under her palm. Stubborn, stubborn man.

Her hands fell away. She forced herself to think of how much she'd hurt him by not being the kind of woman he needed although she wanted more than anything to languish in the memory of smiles they'd shared. "Okay, you want to play the tough guy role? Fine. I've been hanging with the big boys long enough to play just as rough." She backed up but not down. "I'm going to Rubistan. No matter what. If I have to take leave and fly on a civilian airline, I'll make my way over there to my sister."

She hadn't hauled herself out of Red Branch, Texas, by giving up every time someone told her she set her objectives too high. Maybe she was a little like her mama after all, just with different, more practical goals.

Reaching past Jack and doing her damnedest to keep her breasts from brushing the implacable hulk of man in front of her, she hefted her duffel off the end of the bed.

Jack tore her bag from her hands and pitched it on the floor. "Damn it, Monica, you're going to get yourself killed flying off half-cocked."

Something in his tone tugged at her more than his words. Right or wrong in his assumptions on her ability to protect herself, he really was concerned about her. "I understand you're worried about my being there. I worry about you, too."

He mumbled, "You have a damned odd way of showing it."

She deserved that. Even at her angriest, she realized he'd been hurt, too. If only she'd held firm to her refusal when he'd first asked her out, followed her gut that told her fireworks could blow up in a girl's hand sometimes. But he'd been persistent and charming and so full of determination she'd thought maybe…just maybe she could have practicality *and* dreams. "You drive me insane, Jack, no question. But you still get to me, too."

His eyes rose, slowly, brown heating to black. "Are you trying to talk *me* into *your* bed?"

Probably. She shook her head. "Sorry, and I really do mean that, but no. I'm trying to make a point. We might be history, but we also *have* history. And because of that, yes, there's still a lingering…attraction. Even some feelings. But that history also means you know I'm dead serious about going to Rubistan. Won't you worry less knowing I'm under the military's protective umbrella?"

She'd won. She could see it in his eyes—angry but resigned. Scrubbing his hands over his face, into his hair, he dropped to the foot of the bed.

He really was exhausted, sore from shots and

weary in his heart over her sister, too. Over the end
of their relationship, as well?

Out of the blue a memory filtered through the
anger and pain, of the times he'd rubbed her feet
after a long surgery. How could she have forgotten
that?

His hands slid from his face to clasp loosely between his knees while he studied the patternless carpet. ''I'll start the paperwork this morning. You'll
have orders in hand by close of business.''

Victory mingled with a chilly twist of loss as she
stared at his weary broad shoulders that, because of
her, wouldn't be resting anytime soon. ''Jack,
thank—''

Slowly he looked up, eyes hard, unrelenting.
''Don't thank me. I have conditions.''

Uh-oh. He wouldn't actually ask her to sleep
with him after all? Dread and, damn it, arousal
pulsed through her.

''You don't leave my side while we're there.''

''I'm not sharing quarters—''

''Fine.''

Man, he gave that part up easily. She punted
aside ridiculous disappointment. ''What do you
mean, exactly?''

''Whenever I'm on the ground and awake, you're
right there with me. And no Lone Ranger crap riding in to save your sister solo. You're only there as
a part of the medical team to assess the hostages

and tend any wounded afterward. We have medics for the battlefield.''

Her toes curled in her boots. His conditions chafed since they wouldn't have applied to anyone else, but this was his show. He made the rules. ''Okay. Anything else?''

Jack stood, took one step, another, until he stopped chest to chest with her in the small room. A single deep breath would press her aching breasts to him. What had she just committed herself to?

''Jack?'' She pushed his name free, not sure if she was asking or begging.

''That's it, Monica.'' His mouth pulled up at the corners in a slow smile that creased his eyes without reaching them. ''Now get the hell out of my room, because we both know it wouldn't take much effort for me to talk you into this bed after all.''

Inching away to grab her bag, she didn't even consider answering. No need since, damn his sexy smile and tender sweet foot massages, he spoke the total truth.

''Crew, feet wet,'' Jack called through his headset. ''Crossing out of U.S. airspace.''

The Atlantic rippled below and ahead of him, the mission under way with Monica on the roster and flying in the plane behind him. Her voice filled the radio waves as she spoke with one of the other planes in formation. Filled his ears. His mind.

They hadn't been alone together in the thirty-six

hours following their confrontation. Not that it made any difference since she'd blasted back into his life.

Multiple voices drifted through the headset, calls from his crew, from other planes in formation. Just his luck, he had the radio toggled up to Monica's frequency. While she wasn't a pilot, as a flight surgeon she could ride up front in the jump seat, complete with helmet and headset, had in fact flown with him often in the past.

Before he made the dumb-ass, drunken mistake of marrying her.

Now she flew with Joker's crew. Talked. Her sandpaper drawl riding radio waves. Exchanging crew dog camaraderie and laughing at something Joker said. Irritation—ah, hell, who was he kidding—jealousy chewed his hide. Joker, for crying out loud, the least funny man on earth, his call sign a sarcastic commentary on his somber mood.

Already she was a great big distraction and they hadn't set foot in Rubistan.

Jack scanned the altimeter, adjusted his airspeed to compensate for a headwind as clouds dusted his windscreen. At least he'd salvaged something from the conversation with Monica. Hell, yeah, he preferred to keep her away from Rubistan, but he didn't doubt for a minute she would go with or without him.

So he was stuck with her.

He'd wanted more time after their impulsive

quickie wedding to see where things went, but not this way. Monica had insisted staying married would make a further mockery of what should be sacred vows. Well, she had him there.

Problem was, he hadn't wanted something more than a one-night stand with a woman in a damned long time. He found the idea of wanting Monica again—and again—difficult to cut loose.

No question she packed a hefty dose of brains under that silky head of hair. However, she underestimated his patience and persistence. He intended to use this time to the fullest to settle things once and for all.

He stifled a laugh. Great. He couldn't win her over with roses, restaurants and European settings at his disposal. How the hell did he expect to rekindle sputtering feelings in the middle of the desert with mess hall chow and humpbacked camels for ambience?

"How's your 'wife,' man?" Rodeo piped in from the copilot's seat on private interphone.

Jack's hand clenched around the stick. Damned lucky he didn't shoot them off course and more than lucky they were on the secured interphone so Monica couldn't hear them. Just in time, he remembered his buddy was only referring to the maid's reference. "You're a riot."

"Come on, Cobra. Details. I'm going through a dry spell. Your love life's all that's carrying me through."

"Then you're in hurting shape, my man."

"Ah-hh." Rodeo nodded, reaching into his flight bag, pulling out a shrink-wrapped deli package. "You're doing that honorable no-kiss-and-tell thing." He unwrapped the plastic from around his lunch, exposing a corner of a pita bulging with sprouts.

Sprouts? Pita? The guy liked gourmet, but in bulky, meaty helpings. "Nothing to tell. When did you start eating rabbit food?"

"Since Lilly at the Rio's cigar bar offered to make me some at her place." Grinning, he tore off a corner.

"Going through a dry spell, my ass."

Rodeo smirked.

"Lilly? Way to go hanging on to her name."

"Wrote it on my hand," he answered between bites.

Jack snorted, grateful for the shift into safer conversational territory.

Sun glinted off the windscreen, puffy clouds stroking the sky without a hint of murky threats. Perfect weather and atmosphere for flying. No challenge. Boring. He flicked on autopilot.

Rodeo chewed through half his pita. "Coulda knocked me flat when I saw Hyatt walk into the briefing room."

Damn. The guy had a radar lock on the subject. Jack shadowed the moving stick with his hand and stayed silent.

"I thought for sure that woman waiting for you would be someone else. I mean, hell, whatever happened in Vegas a few months ago seemed to end it. Could detonate bombs with the looks you two throw at each other the few times you actually stay in the same room together."

"Okay, okay. I get the picture." She couldn't stand the sight of him. Like he needed a reminder of that. Much more of this and he would be ready to surrender and sign the divorce papers now.

Jack's gaze drifted to the multifunction display. The formation of planes blipped a reminder of how he'd failed to keep her in the States. Good thing that while he could hear her voice on the open frequency, she couldn't hear the private interphone discussion. Even so, time to redirect Rodeo's mental radar. "Like who?"

"Who what?"

"Who did you think was waiting for me?"

Adjusting the five-point harness belting him to the seat, Rodeo settled in for his recounting. "Well, at first I decided she was probably military, because of where we were. Then I remembered how that stripper from Barcelona worked her way into your room last year."

"That was your room."

"Oh, yeah. What about the British kindergarten teacher, uh, what was her name?"

"Elizabeth."

"Yeah, her. Damn, you're good with names. Anyhow, *she* sure as shit wasn't waiting for me."

Jack couldn't even remember what she looked like anymore since Monica's full lips and green eyes congested his mind. "Haven't seen her in eleven months."

"Well, if Doc's back in the picture and tossing around that 'wife' word—" Rodeo swiped a stray sprout off his flight suit "—guess somebody should tell the Elizabeths waiting around air shows looking for a flyboy that you're off the circuit for good. I'll have to hang with Joker, and hell, he's no fun. If he ever smiled, his face would crack."

Yet Joker seemed a damned laugh a minute talking to Monica.

Jack shrugged through tension kinks. Damn it, making her laugh was his role. Even if his humor was MIA these days. "You can hold off on corralling Joker to be your designated driver. Monica and I are not back together."

God, if she sniffed out the least hint he planned to use this time to get under her skin for a second chance, she'd run like hell. Figured when he finally opted to drop back into the world of serious relationships, he picked the most skittish woman in the free world.

"Ah, so the two of you just hung out and chatted about old times in that room all by yourselves with a big ole bed."

Sadly, yes. "She wanted on this flight for obvious reasons regarding her sister. Was pissed at me for not including her.'' Understatement. ''End of story.''

Humor faded from Rodeo's eyes. ''Hey, man, that blows. No wonder you're cranky as hell. You know what? Why wait till the Braves' game to party? I've got a line on this great club in Germany, positively crawling with pilot groupies who can't wait to climb all over a guy in a flight suit. We'll be stopping over on our way back for at least a couple of days.''

''No thanks.'' Depending on how things shook down with Monica, he'd either be a very happy, sated man or ready for a three-day drinking binge— his first since the night after Tina's funeral.

Which said more about Monica's importance in his life than he wanted to admit. He flicked off autopilot. ''Rodeo, if you're ready to log some flight time, I'd like to step in back to check in with Colonel Cullen about new satellite feed images on the drop zone.''

Rodeo wadded his empty lunch sack. ''No problem.''

Jack's grip tightened around the stick as he waggled it lightly. ''Ready, Rodeo, do you have the jet?''

The copilot wiggled the stick in tandem response to signify control. ''Copy, Cobra. I've got the jet.''

''Be back in a few.'' He reached to unplug his headset. Monica's voice echoed again. His hand paused. Her voice swirled around in his ears and head until she might as well have been sitting next to him.

And she wasn't doing anything more than talking with a Ranger medic in one of the other planes about…what?

"Roger that," she answered. "Apply the butterfly bandages and I'll check it out once we land."

Jack thumbed the radio call button. "Budweiser two-five, this is Budweiser two-one. Is there a problem? Over."

Monica's wry laugh cut the airwaves. "No problem, Cobra. A private popped the canister on his gas mask filter and cut his hand. Doesn't sound too bad, though. I'll let you know after I see him. Over."

Over. Yeah, it sure looked that way for them.

The airwaves crackled, Monica-free. Not that it helped. It didn't matter whether she was in his plane, another plane or across the damn ocean. She was in him, with him.

Jack unbuckled and shoved up from his seat. Tucking around and into the stairwell, he gave himself a mental head-thunk. Their showdown after the wedding—once they'd sobered up—had left him positive they were through, certain enough to confirm her appointment with an attorney on the first date they were both scheduled to be back home at Charleston AFB.

Except he wasn't like her, able to segment his

life and feelings into neat Ziploc bags or folded
packages with clips. He didn't know what the hell
he was feeling, except that so much spun inside him
along with her voice that he wanted time to let it
all settle out.

Boot thuds echoed down the last step, the belly
of the plane sprawling, the metal cavern packed full
of communications equipment and paratroopers in
DCUs—desert camouflage uniforms. He had two
weeks with Monica either to figure out what went
wrong and fix it so they stood a chance of her being
Monica *Korba*. Or decide how to put Monica *Hyatt*
out of his head.

Clear mind-set. Simple enough.

Except somehow either task seemed tougher to
accomplish than dodging antiaircraft fire while offloading a cargo hold of Rangers into a terrorist
compound.

Clearing the last step in the aircraft stairwell,
Monica stared out the yawning opening as the ramp
lowered to unload the paratroopers onto the tarmac
in Rubistan. That same widening portal offered a
crystal-clear view of Jack's C-17 parked a few
yards away. Tip to tail, 174 feet long with 169 feet
of wingspan, it dominated the landscape with its
impressive power and size much the same way Jack
filled her mind.

She ducked through the side hatch to the stairs
leading out into the blinding desert sun. A mild

blast from the eighty-degree spring day hit her,
preferable to the frigid temps of night or sweltering
heats of high noon.

Slowly the decrepit airfield came into focus. Oil
stains mottled the cracked parking area. Gritty wind
howled across the endless expanse of desert and
rock with gusts not daunted in the least by the two-
story main building. Sand scraped against peeling
paint while the sun baked until the color had blurred
to nondescript beige with time. Built in the fifties
perhaps, the abandoned terminal extended with
rusted hangars spoking off to the sides.

Functional.

Gripping the handrail, she descended, feet finally
hitting asphalt. She blinked until her eyes finished
adjusting. Rubistan, where her sister waited not
more than two hundred miles away. Her boots
itched to storm the compound now, to save her sister from one more minute of hell. Not wise, of
course.

She needed some of Jack's patience. And if that
failed her, she'd lose herself in work. She plowed
through the press of people. Surely the medivac
team monitoring in-processing could use an extra
pair of hands. Monica threaded through the crowd
streaming from the back of the cargo planes, Army
troopers in tan DCUs mixed with crew dogs in desert-tan flight suits.

Jack.

His flight suit might be covering every inch of

him, but her memory blazed with the image of him striding away from her. Naked. Muscle and man. Once her man.

Bodies jostled around her in an organized pandemonium of sweat and voices, gear and guns. Problem was, she genuinely liked the guy. How could she not? Funny, hot, too damned courageous for his own good.

If only he could apply his attention to detail in the workplace to a relationship, but in day-to-day life, details rolled over him. Problems? What problems? For Jack, they simply didn't exist. Will it so, smile, and problems took care of themselves.

Except life had taught her differently. Life was tough. Keeping it on track was even tougher. She'd been working her tail off since she was nine years old when her mama walked out the door, leaving her behind with two-year-old Sydney.

Daddy's union-wage-purchased, three-bedroom tract house hadn't stood a chance against a big black Mercedes cruising into town. The guy in the back seat was foreign, which was enough for Mama. She'd always been certain overseas meant better, even tried to hook her kids' names on those dreams.

Monica thanked God seven times a day for the fact that Daddy hadn't listened to Mama when it came time to fill out birth certificates. He'd vowed he must have been so excited over his first baby he just goofed. He'd *meant* to write Monaco, he would add with a wink to Monica.

Next pregnancy, Mama wised up and chose a more conventional name to house her dream. Sydney—for fantasies of Outback rogues.

Fantasies? Reality scraped against Monica in grainy gusts that filled her mouth until she wanted to spit.

A beige hangar with rusted rivets gaped open with the advance team and security forces waiting to escort troops, some to barracks, some to receive additional vaccinations. Her cue to hightail it forward. Troops divided, most pouring toward the airport entrances, a hundred others toward the hangar. Bringing up the rear, a private shuffled forward, CD player in hand, headphones sealed to his ears and two butterfly bandages on his fingers.

Monica tapped his shoulder. "Hey, Private Santuci?"

The private slid his earphones down around his neck, heavy-metal music pulsing through. "Hello, Major." He saluted with his bandaged hand.

"Glad you kept your fingers in place. Make sure you stop by and see me after the rest of your immunizations before you head off to your quarters so I can make sure you don't need stitches."

"Yes, ma'am, but mess hall first—" the dark-haired soldier rubbed his belly "—then quarters. I'm a growing boy." All six feet four inches of Army soldier grinned.

"I promise not to take long."

"Thanks, ma'am." He saluted with his bandaged hand again before replacing his earphones to pass time in line. His gaze strayed longingly toward the entrance to the mess hall like a kid ready for McDonald's.

Apparently he'd never eaten here before.

Except for the uniform, he actually looked more like a kid on his way to the golden arches to super size his meal, maybe twenty-one at the most. Hell, he even had acne on his chin. And yet he was a trained warrior, ready to put his life on the line for her sister.

The notion humbled her.

"Is he okay?"

Monica jumped, turned, found Jack, not that she needed to look. Of course she did, anyway, finding the sun showcased the hint of curl in his dark hair after hours under a headset.

She folded her arms over her chest. "Minor cut, nothing that should keep him off duty."

"Good."

Jack's face filled her eyes, so very mature with the hardened angles of years and strength. She tore her gaze down and away to the open hangar with tables manned by medic personnel. "I really need to get to work."

"Okay, then." He adjusted his M-9 in the holster on his survival vest. "Don't let me stop you."

"I'll catch up with you later." She charged past.

A long shadow slanted in front of her. Following. Swallowing her. "Jack! Why don't you go ahead to the mess hall and I'll find you later?"

He smiled. Shrugged. "Remember our deal back at Nellis? I'm gonna be stuck to you like a flight suit at high noon."

The smile didn't fool her or dilute the set of his stubborn jaw. "Okay. Fine. Keep up."

She walked faster. Her extra shadow kept pace into the hangar, looming while she talked to the doctor in charge and set up her station at a table with a folding chair for patients. God, she needed him gone before he sliced through her weary resistance like that metal through Santuci's fingers.

She pivoted, sighed. "Please, Jack, I'm here. I'm safe. You can step back at least a couple of feet. I need to tend to my patients, which I can't do with you hovering over me. So unless you need another anthrax shot?"

He paled. "Nope. All set," he asserted quickly. "Already had my first two in the series and won't need the third for another three months."

"Big baby." Stifling a grin, she turned away, reorganizing her medicine bottles in alphabetical order. "Go help someone else. You'll still be able to see me and keep track of my personal safety."

"Mon, you should know I'm not the kind to leave the little woman to fend for herself."

"Little woman?" Anger whipped her around to face him.

He grinned. Just grinned that sexy, unrepentant smile. And damn it, she couldn't help but smile in return. He always could charm her out of a mood, all the more reason to keep her distance. "You are so bad."

"I know. I'm in need of reform. Wanna spank me?"

And then other times he wasn't so charming. "Oh, yes," she said through gritted teeth. "I definitely want to."

Reaching over her tray of bottles and syringes, she whipped a pair of latex gloves from a box. Bumped elbows with her hardheaded hubby. She looked up to snap again.

But couldn't push more angry words free.

Deep brown eyes met hers. So close. The din around her faded from a roar to a dull hum. He raised his hand, took his time, as always, which gave her plenty of time to pull away. She didn't.

Jack tucked a straggling strand of hair behind her ear. "How did it go so wrong?"

Heavy silence settled between them while voices swelled again. Humvees revved outside. An intercom system barked sporadic tinny announcements.

A cleared throat snipped the tension, if not the longing.

Monica peered beyond Jack to find Colonel Drew Cullen waiting with folder in hand. A welcome distraction.

In-processing showed no favors to rank. The

colonel in charge dropped into the folding chair. Colonel Cullen, who'd probably once worn earphones around his neck but now wore lines of life, worries, work. Lines like the ones recently added to Jack's face.

Had she put them there? How many more would she add before their divorce was final?

Divorce. The thought of cutting him out of her life stung like a needle in her chest. Not that Jack showed signs of leaving her side anytime soon.

Monica turned her back on him so she could concentrate on prepping the next injection. "Roll up your sleeve, Colonel. This one's going to burn a bit."

If only life gave warnings before owies.

"Just get to it, Major." Cullen grinned, a few years falling away until he looked a little less foreboding. He crooked his arm until his bicep bulged.

"Relax, Colonel—" she snapped her glove then tapped his flexed muscle "—and it will hurt less."

Jack growled, low and soft and totally predatory. Good God. Thank heaven either the Colonel didn't notice or pretended well. Sheesh, she hadn't even noticed that Colonel Cullen actually was rather hunky until Jack started with the Cro-Magnon growl.

She swabbed, jabbed.

"Well, what do ya know?" The Colonel smiled as she pulled the needle free and swabbed again.

"The third shot in the series doesn't hurt as much as the— Son of a bitch!"

Colonel Cullen winced when the burn apparently kicked in, popped a LifeSaver in his mouth.

She stretched a Band-Aid across his skin. "Sorry about that, Colonel."

Jack dipped into her sight line. "You didn't call him a baby."

Monica peeled off her gloves. "He outranks me."

"Wise move, Major." Hand extending, the Colonel offered his roll of LifeSavers. "Here, Korba. Candy for your boo-boo."

Jack snorted—but took the candy. "Thanks, sir."

Boys.

Cullen unrolled his DCU sleeve. "Korba, meet me in the chow hall after you unload your gear and we can talk more about the satellite images of the drop zone."

Thank God for senior officers and their orders. Now Jack would have to leave.

"Yes, sir." Jack called over his shoulder to Monica, "See you in the mess hall?"

"If you're still there when I'm finished."

"I'll be there." His words echoed clear, the rafters throwing them back at her a couple more times for good measure.

Watching Jack's long legs swallow distance with lazy strides, she didn't doubt him for a minute. She knew the guy well enough to expect his persistence, but she didn't understand why. He couldn't envision how they would mend their differences any more than she could. He just expected great sex—okay, awesome sex—to smooth the way during his wait-and-see mode of solving their problems. Not enough of a reassurance for her, especially when Jack had blinders about her narrowing his field of vision more effectively than NVGs.

She restacked the foil squares of alcohol swabs, prepping for the next patient.

Did she love him? Well, if she ascribed to the Jack Korba theory that love was a good cheeseburger and an Elvis tune, then sure. She loved him. But the part of her that was so damned scared of being like her mama thought there should be more to love than that.

Except who the hell was she to judge when she didn't even know what love was? Certainly not her mother's dreams that hurt innocent children. Or her father's obsession with a lost woman that drained his spirit and broke other women along the way. She'd even spent four years dating, then engaged to a man she'd thought she loved, only to lose him in the end when they broke up.

She didn't want to be hurt again, and God, she didn't want to hurt Jack any more than she already had. She was right to walk away.

So why could she swear she heard Santuci's headphones pulsing with "Heartbreak Hotel"?

Damn.

Chapter 4

"Damnation!" Colonel Drew Cullen gulped down half a bottle of lukewarm water to wash away the crappy beef stew. Twenty years of Army mess halls and seventeen years of bachelorhood since his divorce should have made any food palatable. Apparently not. "What the hell did they put in this? Goat guts?"

Across the table, Jack Korba paused midbite. "Goat? Probably." He spooned the stringy meat to his mouth, winced, shrugged. "Could be horse, though. Seems like that's what we ate during Afghanistan."

"Probably the same damned batch from then." Drew jammed a LifeSaver in his mouth, sucked, subduing the curse he really wanted to spit out faster than the vile stew. He was getting too old for this shit.

The orange LifeSaver melted. Drew smiled. Victory.

Another day won in his personal cussing-cutback campaign. He was a grandfather now, after all, goddamn it. He may have done a piss-poor job being much of a role model for his daughter, but he'd do better by his granddaughter.

Starting with less crass language.

Of course twenty rough-talking years in the Army trenches couldn't be undone in a day. Hell, no. He figured he'd take it a step at a time. Address one letter of the alphabet a month.

April: eliminate "F" words.

Since he'd been reading up on all those child psychology books he never made time for twenty-one years ago, he knew modified behavior deserved a reward—like a LifeSaver for every time he swallowed back any curse starting with "F."

Drew stared into the bowl of mushy potatoes bobbing in grease. He sucked harder on the taste of orange while the clatter of dishes and conversation swelled from soldiers, aircrew and a lone table of SEALs filling the dining area. Not surprising the food blew monkey chunks in a place with dust and drab the decor of choice.

Spartan, but serviceable. Like his life and place back at Ft. Benning.

A month ago the stew wouldn't have bothered him. But a month ago he hadn't been a grandfather suddenly realizing he'd never been much of a father, too married to the military. Was he going soft?

Scanning the packed tables, he watched the hungry troops, more his kids than his own blood. Kids who kept an M-16 close by even at lunch.

His troops shoveled the stew so fast he prayed they wouldn't be doubled over with stomach cramps later. At least they were all drinking plenty of water, which may have had something to do with the young local woman passing out refills and snagging their lonely eyes with her hip swishing.

Trouble.

He assessed her as a potential problem. Attractive kid, probably about his daughter's age. A tomato-red scarf with bursts of white flowers in the print covered most of her dark hair in a surprise splash of color, but left her pretty little face free to smile at all the men sniffing after her. Not much to her, but more than enough to wreak serious mayhem among his men.

Damn. Just what he needed, his captains and lieutenants restraining troops from a girl angling for a green card. As if this place didn't have enough uproar brewing. Hell, the locals were already clamoring at the gates for food rations and medical aid— part of the deal with the Rubistans in exchange for free rein to use this shithole airport.

With crappy stew.

Age might be softening his language, but nothing else. If she stirred trouble, out she went. He could still eat the goat slop and do his job. Hell, he'd already logged through a discussion on the drop zone pictures before even finishing a bowl of…that.

Drew glanced over at Korba, a top-notch operational planner, even if he was a little rough around the edges. "While you were in a cushy mess hall during Afghanistan, flyboy, I was in a canvas tent eating MREs." He took refuge in the comfortable camaraderie of good-natured rivalry between the services. Shoveling another spoonful of the questionable substance into his mouth, he yearned for one of those tiny Tabasco sauce bottles packed with the Meals Ready to Eat. "Although gotta admit, an MRE tastes better than this."

Korba swiped coarse bread around the bowl to scoop up the last bite. "Wouldn't doubt it, sir."

"Of course once we cracked open those MREs, the wind started blowing and filled the damn things with sand." He gulped the last swig of water, scouted for a refill, found the woman trying to capture the attention of a young Private First Class. "After how much time we've spent over here, I feel like I've got an extra five pounds of grit embedded in this old body."

"Old?" Korba tipped back his chair. "No doubt you'll be running circles around most of us during the rest of your ten years in the service."

Drew stayed silent. Hauled another bite up to his mouth.

Korba's chair legs thudded to a landing. "You're getting out at twenty?"

"Who the hell knows? It's possible." At forty-two, he'd still have time to start another career. Doing…what?

His attention snagged on the woman sidling closer to the young private. Her dress swished like a small dark cloud drifting with each sway of her hips. The young PFC—Santuci, maybe?—pulled his earphones off his head, white bandage on his hand glaring in the bald overhead light. A single look at the flirty bat of eyelashes and Santuci smiled.

Where the hell was the boy's lieutenant? Homesick soldiers made too easy a target. Hell, they didn't even have to be across the ocean to be lonely. He'd been an ROTC student, taken in by a woman hunting for a way out of her hometown. Any officer would do for her. He'd just bitten first.

He and Glenna had lasted all of three years and one kid before she moved on to a civilian guy with a smoother veneer and higher pay grade. "Some days I think it would be nice to wake up without sand in my shorts, to spend some time playing with my granddaughter. Other days I figure I'll die with a rifle in my hands because I'm a bachelor soldier at heart. Know what I mean?"

"Afraid I do."

Korba twisted open another bottle of the water, reached into his front pocket and pulled out a thin pack of NutraSweet Kool-Aid. The powder spread a cherry-red stain and scent. Two quick shakes of the bottle and he gulped half while Drew kept a steady lock on the young love in action across the crowded dining hall.

The private pointed as if giving directions. The petite woman stared back at him without talking, studying him, before nodding. Her head tucked, she moved on.

Relief and a chuckle kicked through him. He'd turned into a cynical old bastard.

Leaning across the table, Drew tapped Korba's bottle of Kool-Aid. "Wish I'd thought of that during Desert Storm while we were stuck out there eating sand for six months."

"Here ya go, sir." Jack whipped out a purple packet and skidded it across the table.

"You could make a mint selling that over here if you bring more."

"Hope I won't need it again."

Quiet settled between them, heavy with the unspoken knowledge of the inevitability of another battle on another day in another place. A soldier's mission. Meanwhile, focus on *this* victory. Tomorrow would come gunning soon enough.

Korba scraped back his chair. "Well, sir, I need to hook up with Doc Hyatt on a few points and it looks like she's through with the vaccines now."

Drew flipped his wrist to check his watch. "It's about time to sleep, anyway. See you tomorrow at the mobile command center?"

"Roger that, sir," Korba shot over his shoulder already rounding the corner of the table.

Drew wadded up his napkin, pitched it on top of his half-eaten stew. Thumbing up the edge of the grape Kool-Aid, he smacked it against his hand idly and hunted for the girl pushing the water cart. Damn, but a man could dehydrate before she made it over.

Scanning four tables down, he found her. Talking again. This time with the copilot Derek Washington—Rodeo. The copilot's wide smile flashed across his coffee-toned skin. Her hands fluttered through the air with the same gestures as if asking for directions like before with Santuci.

Exactly the same gestures.

Like a concocted excuse to talk.

His brain shifted to military mode, never too far of a shuffle. The Air Force's Office of Special Investigations—OSI—would have checked her out. But shit happened. Stuff got past. Losing some of his men to suicide bombers in Iraq had left indelible suspicion.

He assessed her more closely, this time as a possible terrorist threat. Black dress, Western clothes, but not stylish. Length almost to her ankles. Could be hiding a knife or gun strapped to her thigh. The dress nipped at her waist, snug enough for him to

ascertain no explosives were strapped to her chest.
No, he could clearly discern the outline of her
small, high breasts.

Breasts?

F—uh, hell. LifeSaver. Lemon.

Self-disgust roiled through him like another bite
of that godawful stew. He was old enough to be her
father. Some fine damned example he was setting
for his troops.

Libido reined, he eased back in his chair, flicked
the edge of the Kool-Aid packet. Tap. Tap. Tap.
Waited. Watched. Seemed like she was settling in
for the kill with the copilot Rodeo. The man could
handle himself, but it still made for sticky politics
to mix with locals.

Both backed away from each other. Tough day
for the home team.

Almost amused, Drew watched her walk, stroll,
assess, definitely on the make. No one else seemed
to notice. She was actually fairly good at the game.
Admiration spiked for someone who might have
made a challenging adversary with a few years' sea-
soning. He'd just been around longer, seen more
than anyone else in the room. Been taken in once
himself by Glenna. His smile faded.

The woman paused, in front of Korba this time.
For about half a second before giving him a wide
berth. Smart girl. In spite of his grins and jokes,
Korba was an edgy bastard she'd be wise not to
tangle with.

She was out of her depth here. Amusing, but sad, too, how far she would go.

Not heart-tugging enough for him to sacrifice one of his men for her.

The sixteen SEALs rose as one into a human barricade blocking the woman from sight. The SEAL wall, packing M-4s along with their meal trays, moved to reveal empty air where the woman had been before. Damn.

Of course he would just check in with the AD-VON team later, notify Captain Baker to keep an eye on her. Tucking the grape Kool-Aid pack in his pocket, Drew stood, kicked back his chair, more than ready to dump this meal and find his bed.

The hair bristled on the back of his neck in a battlefield instinct he knew better than to ignore. He'd been targeted. He scoped. Found nothing.

Tray in hand, he pivoted. "Damnation!"

He stopped short of slamming into the water cart. And the woman. How the hell had she crept up on him? That she could catch him unaware scared the shit out of him more than an M-16 jammed in his face.

Women moved softly here. A fact worth remembering.

"Sorry, ma'am." He barked the apology, already making his way past.

"There is no need for you to apologize."

Shoulder to shoulder, he paused, the melodic echo of her accented words catching him as unaware as her silent tread. Dark eyes stared back up at him. Eyes as black as the night sky seen from a bedroll on a moonless evening.

Moonless evening? Hell. Apparently some damned poet had taken up residence in his head while he'd gone soft reading all that baby psychology mumbo jumbo.

Returning his tray to the table, Drew waited for her to play out her bogus request for directions. And waited while she stared back, searching. Desolation muddied her eyes beneath the bright splash of color from her sun-scorched scarf. Fast. Then gone. But no mistaking it. This woman was desperate.

And determined.

No room for sympathy. Sympathy in the battle-field got a man gut shot.

Three soundless footsteps brought her around in front of him as she stared deeper into his eyes. Closer. Close enough for him to catch her scent— soap, incense and a sultry, smoky smell that did things to his insides he had no damn business feeling for a woman this young. He was not some horny teenager for God's sake.

Let this desperate lady find another mark. And when she did, he'd have no choice but to boot her out so they could all rest easier.

He debated whether to get her name now when speaking might encourage her outrageous behavior. Or to find her name himself through the intel contact.

And then she moved. "Pardon me, sir."

She tucked to the side again to pass him after all.

Irritation nipped his ego. Hell's bells, he'd been pitched into the reject heap with Santuci, Korba and Washington. He shook off the notion. Damned ridiculous when he was too old for someone like her, anyway. With any luck, the woman was just looking for the latrines and was too scared or embarrassed to ask.

Air whispered, smoky, soapy, spicy, as she passed. Her cool hand brushed his, twisted that gut awareness into a painful knot worse than taking a bullet. Shit. Shoulder to shoulder again, she hesitated long enough to slide her hand in his.

She squeezed.

Then she was gone. So fast that even with battle-honed reflexes he didn't have time to react. Damned if he wasn't standing stunned stupid like some teenage boy after his first peek at a dirty magazine.

The woman may have left, but the brand of her cool touch stayed. He tamped down an unwelcome heat pumping through him with a very mature ferocity bearing no resemblance to horny teenage hormones. He clenched his fingers to strangle away the feel of her hand there. Closed his fist around...

A piece of paper?

The slip crumpled, crackled in his grip. He'd received—and ignored—room numbers scrawled on napkins before, but this wasn't some dive bar in Bangkok. His fingers unfurled. The paper mushroomed open like an exploding bomb. Fragmented lines became bold handwriting, words without a room number in sight.

Help me. I seek asylum in the United States.

Jack figured ambushing Monica would work best.

Lounging against the mess hall wall, he waited for her to nab her meal tray and pick her seat. A wall of windows baked the room with unrelenting rays that trickled a fresh layer of sweat over his body. His shower would have to wait.

She would just have to put up with his presence like they agreed in their deal. And maybe he wanted to look at her. Talk to her. He'd missed her these past months.

His own damn fault.

He could almost hear his father chuckling, followed by a thump on the back for his son who'd landed in trouble. *Nothing like your priestly brother, are you, my boy?*

His father didn't mean it as an insult or a compliment. There were just clearly defined roles in his family. Tony was the good kid. Jack was the wild one. And each, in his own way, was supposed to look out for their two sisters. Tony, with morality checks. Jack, by kicking ass.

Monica peeled off from the chow line and strode toward an empty end of a table, far from people and conversation.

Too bad, Mon. Pushing away from the corner, Jack dusted the flaking plaster off his arm and plowed through the clutch of personnel dumping trays and grabbing extra water bottles on their way out.

He dropped into the chair beside Monica. "Everything go okay with the vaccines?"

Smooth, Romeo. Damn, but he could use a little of Tony's sensitive oratory skills at the moment.

She startled. "Jesus, Jack. You sure do know how to sneak up on a person."

Not half as stealthy as that little number who'd almost hit on him a couple of minutes ago. But one Korba scowl worthy of his old man woken up from a nap had sent the local flirt-bunny scuttling in the other direction. Just what he needed, Monica wigging out over some imagined encounter. "Still wanna spank me?"

That earned him a smile. Ooh-rah.

"Too exhausted." She moved her spoon from her bowl to her mouth in automated rhythm.

Silence settled, uncomfortable when once they could have sat beside each other for hours without talking. Four months ago he would have followed her to her room, tugged her boots off and rubbed her feet. She always thought he was doing her some big damned favor. Little did she know how much those pretty feet of hers turned him on. The rest of her was so tough, but her feet were soft. Slim. Delicate bones and arches masked by combat boots.

The contrast yanked him inside out even now.

Maybe it also had something to do with the fact that he'd finally found the one thing she needed from him. Call him a knuckle-dragger, but if he wasn't kicking ass for a woman, he wasn't sure of his role.

"Monica?" a masculine voice rumbled above the din of diners and clanking dishes.

She glanced over her shoulder, up to the Navy Petty Officer in fatigues standing behind her, an oversize blond farm boy whose cowlick defied even a buzz cut to swirl into a left part—Blake Gardner, her sister's ex-boyfriend. Defensiveness fell away from Monica in sheets, a feat Jack wished he'd been able to make happen.

Springing to her toes, she threw her arms around the Navy SEAL's thick neck. "God, it's good to see you."

Fraternization be damned, the enlisted SEAL hugged her back. "You, too, Monica. You, too."

Jack winced at the stab of jealousy. A self-centered thought, considering the blond wonder god standing in front of him was currently living in his own personal hell since Sydney Hyatt had been taken.

They pulled apart. Monica's smile wobbled. Gardner didn't have a smile at all, not that Jack could blame him. He couldn't even stomach thoughts of Monica being in her sister's place. "Have a seat, man."

"Thank you, sir." Gardner tugged out the metal chair beside Monica.

"Call me Jack."

"Sure," Gardner answered without complying to the request. He canted forward, forearms bulging beneath his rolled-up uniform sleeves as if the building frustration from inaction strained at his skin. "And I do mean thank you."

Jack nodded once in return. No more needed to be said, and doing so would only throw baggage out there in front of Monica he didn't want examined. Women didn't understand and a part of him didn't want Monica exposed to the primal rage that pummeled a man when someone threatened his woman.

His woman? Hell, the prickly Monica who battled over being called babe would have the Cro-Magnon label out in a heartbeat.

But this wasn't about him right now. And it wasn't about Monica, either. Jack angled closer. "She's okay."

Gardner flattened his hands on the yellowed laminate covering the table. Fingers splayed with veins bulging as the man stayed quiet.

"We've got daily satellite images fed in. Hell, you'll be looking at them when we brief up your team for your drop. We would know if things had gone to shit in there. She's alive."

"For now." His fingers curved into fists.

Monica squeezed his forearm. "And she'll damn well stay that way."

Gardner's fists relaxed and he leaned back. Lines smoothed from his face, the unspoken code in place again.

Men didn't indulge in emotional crap. Men acted. Kicked ass. And that terrorist compound had a serious ass kicking coming its way very shortly. Don't dwell on what couldn't be controlled.

Gardner reached into his pocket for a pack of gum, folded a piece into his mouth as he looked around the mess hall. "Damn, you Air Force pukes got a cushy life. Maybe that's why one Navy SEAL can whoop any Chair Force dude's butt."

Oh, yeah. And men also razzed each other. None of the warm, fuzzy emotional garbage.

Monica elbowed him. "Great, when you boys tussle, I work overtime patching you both up."

Jack shrugged. "No problem, Gardner. You can feel free to hike home. Won't bother me to skip out on flying through antiaircraft fire. I'll have an extra beer waiting for you."

They shared a laugh. Rivalry between the branches was a common, welcome routine because in the end game, their combined forces were essential to survival. But the predictability of an old jab felt damned good in a world flipped to hell.

Hearing Monica laugh felt even better. And right now he didn't even care who made her laugh, as long as those dark circles faded from beneath her eyes.

Gardner pushed back from the table, secured his M-4, as lethal as the Army Ranger's M-16 but smaller, more compact. "Time for me to turn in. Just wanted to say hi to Monica." He ground down on his chewing gum, jaw clenching. "It'll be good for Sydney to have you here—after."

She just nodded. Sunlight through the wall of windows glinted on her unblinking eyes.

While Gardner strode away, Jack waited for the I-told-you-so about being there for Sydney. But it didn't come. Monica picked up her spoon again and started eating the crappy goat stew.

Likely exhaustion stemmed her smart comeback. But a part of him insisted it was something a helluva lot more daunting.

That maybe she didn't even care enough about him anymore to fight.

Shoveling food into her mouth even though grief killed her taste buds, Monica wished she didn't care so much. About her sister. About Jack. Even about Blake Gardner walking away with pain radiating from him in waves her doctor spirit couldn't miss.

God, but exhaustion made a person maudlin. That had to be the reason for the sense of impending doom when she should be rejoicing over how soon she would be seeing her sister.

From the sleeve of his flight suit, Jack whipped out a pack of Kool-Aid. "Are you okay?"

"Better than Sydney."

"You know, Mon…" He paused, reaching for her water bottle and tipping her favorite flavor inside. Green bloomed within the bottle. "This isn't a 'whose pain is worse' game."

He passed her the drink, waited until she sipped before releasing her gaze.

Why did he have to be so nice right now with the Kool-Aid, like those foot-rubbing moments? "I know. Sorry for snapping. I do better when I don't think about it."

"That, I can understand." He propped his beard-peppered cheek on one fist. "Hashing through what-ifs is fine if it brings about a decisive plan of action. But talking just for the negligible benefits of an emotional catharsis? Hell, what good is that?"

The words bubbled in spite of her. "I just get so damned mad." She stopped short. "Ah, hell. There goes your theory about staying quiet. Guess I can't help but discuss it. Woman thing." She tipped back her water bottle.

Lime exploded along senses she'd thought numb seconds before. Kind of like a dose of Jack did.

"At least you're speaking to me. Hell, Mon, I'll discuss those damned doilies my grandma loves to spread all over the house if it will keep you talking. And you have every right to want to tear Ammar al-Khayr apart yourself."

"I don't mean him." Her fingers fiddled with the fork, flipped it, bent a twisted tine back into shape.

"Although I wouldn't turn down the chance to plant a land mine under his feet."

The fork clattered to the table. Monica's shaking hands fell to her lap. "Her. I get angry at my sister, which is the dumbest damned thing. But she shouldn't have been here at all, Jack. Blake warned her what could happen and she just insisted it was her job, risks and all." Her fingers twisted, twined, tore the napkin into bits she wadded in her fist. "You're probably laughing right now thinking how you gave me the same warning."

"I would never laugh at you."

"But you're thinking it."

"I'm not so entrenched in the Dark Ages I can't see the difference." A half smile kicked up. "Don't get me wrong. I still don't want you here, but I understand that you're trained to protect yourself."

"I'm not reckless, Jack." She pitched her shredded napkin on her tray.

"Hearing you say that doesn't stop me from worrying."

Intensity hummed under his lazy demeanor, threatening to swallow her whole in a luscious lime haze of thoughtfulness mixed with dogged determination to get his way.

Her eyes fell to the straightened fork, shifted to the torn napkin. Well, hell. She'd cleaned up one mess, only to make another. The story of her life. "How could she not understand how precious her life is?"

He rested his hand beside hers. Not over it. Not touching. But there. Close. She didn't move, except for a twitch of her pointer finger, an involuntary movement toward him as her instincts overrode her intellect.

Finally he had time with her and he wasn't pressing his case as she would have expected. She told herself it had more to do with exhaustion than the fact he felt sorry for her—the woman who'd punted him out of her life.

Then his hands slid away with the moment. "Sleep deprivation has a way of making us all turn morbid without solving a thing."

He rose, waiting for her to join him, and she didn't argue. She'd accepted his presence just as he would have to accept they would be parting at her door in a few minutes.

Her hand fell on his arm. "Thank you, Jack."

He stopped, suddenly didn't look at all tired, that slumberous bedroom gaze of his having nothing to do with sleep.

She waited for the move. The Jack Korba push. Instead, he simply smiled. "Always glad to lend an ear."

"No. I mean for—" she waved to encompass the room of soldiers and dust and focus on a mission "—for all of this."

"I don't want your gratitude. I would be here even if your sister wasn't one of the hostages."

"I know. And thank you for that, too."

Her eyes held his, then flicked away to settle beyond him on a cluster of uniforms encircling a female figure pushing a cart of water bottles. The woman moved with an odd familiarity. Incredulity niggled at Monica.

No. It couldn't be.

The slight figure ditched her cart and hustled toward the hall, turning sideways at the last second. Her very familiar face flashed in full view aided by the stark bulb overhead.

"What's wrong?" Jack's question barely penetrated.

She couldn't answer. Couldn't process what she was seeing.

"Mon, snap out of it."

She forced her mouth to move. "Oh, God. What is she doing here?"

"She who?" He glanced over his shoulder. "The water girl? She's probably drawing a beat on some other lonely bastard."

"It's my sister." She forced the words past numb lips.

His head swung back around fast enough for whiplash. "Monica, Sydney's still in the camp. I looked at satellite feed with Colonel Cullen in the mobile command center while we were airborne."

Shock shifted to anger. Of all the times for a family reunion. "No. Not Sydney. My other sister, Yasmine."

Her half sister from their mother's second marriage. A prickly, spoiled brat who'd resented every rare minute of their mother's annual visits to see the two children she'd abandoned.

Jack pivoted on his boot heel toward the woman darting around a corner, Colonel Cullen making tracks toward her with a battlefield march. Monica stifled a semihysterical bubble of laughter. She'd prayed so damned hard to see her sister soon, and apparently her prayers had taken a downward swoop for darker forces to answer, bringing Yasmine.

Not a Hyatt, but a sister all the same.

Chapter 5

Sydney Hyatt curled up on the cot, back flat against the cement wall in her cell. Her home for months, such as it was.

Three beds with thin mattresses for her and her fellow hostages were wedged in corners, a toilet in the other corner. Metal shelves leaned, creaky, their possessions on display for easy search. This place sucked, but at least it was familiar.

The first month of captivity, she and her two NGO co-workers had been shuffled to so many different locations, she no longer had any clue where they were. Other than the middle of the desert with an occasional tease of a salty gulf breeze.

Inconvenient for a woman who needed to escape. Soon.

Beyond their door, a staticky television jabbered while guards laughed. Across the cell, Kayla and Phillip sat cross-legged on a cot, silently playing cards. They'd all but rubbed the numbers off the deck.

Sydney battled to keep her eyes open, unwilling to surrender to the vulnerability of unconsciousness. Sporadic gunfire from what she guessed were night-training maneuvers often interrupted their sleep, but the weariness seemed tougher to contain lately.

Her body demanded rest. Her mind fought the lethargy of waning hope. Chill remaining from the desert night seeped through the pocked plaster, a relief from the sun creeping up the horizon. Beyond the welcome cooling, she appreciated the brief respite from watching over her shoulder.

Wind whistled through the lone window high on the wall while Jeeps roared out of sight below in opposing directions. Although "window" seemed a generous description for the thin rectangular opening near the ceiling that showed only the purity of a cloudless sky. A blessing perhaps that she didn't have to view the depravity of the terrorist training camp any more often than during her late-afternoon, twenty-minute walks.

Hitching the dingy sheet up to her waist in spite of the heat, she listened to the steady click of Kayla and Phillip snapping down spades. The shoosh of shuffling cards. More clicks. Monotony offered a temporary liberation.

She needed to tell them about her plans soon, but she couldn't give them too much time to think. To fear. To break and talk.

Still, she couldn't leave them behind to bear the brunt of the fury that would come from her attempt to escape. Staying would have to be their choice, these dear friends now bonded to her through experience into a family that had nothing to do with blood relations.

She wouldn't blame them for laughing in her face. After all, what did she have? A couple of sharpened forks buried with a handful of pills hoarded from her early days in captivity. Her captors didn't offer much in the way of drugs to prisoners.

Certainly not for medicinal purposes.

Only enough to dope them into submission. But she'd saved it all in the hope of using them on her guards one day. She'd gritted through the pain of a broken ankle. Pretended to be docile. Sometimes more difficult than others.

Nausea swelled with memories. She swallowed both down.

Would Phillip and Kayla be willing to attempt escape with her or give her away? Too well she knew family wasn't always loyal.

She couldn't afford to wait much longer for a miraculous rescue. How naive to think Blake would come charging in. Her job bred familiarity with the maze of diplomatic channels required even to bring food into this country. He couldn't dial up his SEAL team buddies for a quick swoop in to scoop her out.

And she knew it was killing him inside that he couldn't. Forget that they'd broken up before she'd left the country, unable to reconcile their conflicting ideologies, the pacifist and the warrior. How damned inconvenient. Heartbreaking. And over. Blake, her dear friend who had once been her lover.

Not that sex was high on her list of favorite topics now.

Memories seared through, more persistent this time, of brutal hands claiming her body in an act of domination and humiliation inflicted on each of the hostages. She tried to remind herself that being raped had nothing to do with sex and everything to do with violence. Sometimes that helped. Other times not. And it wasn't something any of the three of them were ready to talk about.

Refusing to think about it was easier, especially as time passed without further repeats. Once certain the three NGO workers weren't CIA, their captors pretty much left them alone except for the occasional taunt, slap or punch served up with horse-meat on rice.

She'd lived through the hell. Survived. If nothing else, she'd learned these past months that the child who'd always depended on her sister's protection was a survivor after all.

Flipping to her back, Sydney stared out the thin window, eyes focused on the sky, and allowed herself to entertain the near-painful dream of seeing her sister again. Of course practical Monica would have already guessed what happened to her since her capture. But the growing proof of the incident would kill her overresponsible big sister. She tried not to worry about Monica, who always worried enough for ten people.

And there was plenty to worry about, increasing in size with each day that passed.

Rolling onto her side again, Sydney tucked her knees to her chest in a protective shield that wouldn't mask the truth from her friends or her captors much longer. Under the cover of the dingy sheet, she slid her hand to her belly, cupped the curve that would soon decide her fate for her if she didn't take charge of it herself. Because if Ammar al-Khayr found out about this baby, biologically his child, he would kill her.

Or worse yet, never let her go.

Yasmine threaded through the crowd of diners, unwilling to be caught just yet. Yes, she wanted the kind-eyed soldier with a penchant for fruit-flavored candy to apprehend her. Eventually. Once she had reached a more secluded location.

She could hear his footsteps thudding a steady pace behind her. Closer. Louder. Or was that her heart? Not that it mattered either way. She shivered in anticipation, steadied her breathing. This was the man with goodness in him she'd been hoping to find. One search into his eyes as clear blue as the endless desert sky upon sunrise and she'd known.

He was her contact. A conduit for her goal. One with cerulean eyes that soothed and stirred her all at once.

Seconds after she saw the goodness, she found more. Felt more, something akin to the crackle of a dry lightning storm across windswept dunes. But she could deal with that. She would deal with it, because nothing was more important than staying alive.

Yasmine darted from the stifling dining area into a near-deserted corridor, past faded framed posters of the Rubistanian countryside. Away from the crowd. Down a narrow side hall.

A hand clamped around her arm. Hard, thick fingers. Her heart tripped along with her feet. Please, please, she hoped she hadn't misjudged this man.

Panting, she righted her step. Her back pressed to the wall. The frame cut into her waist, a minor intrusion compared to the icy gaze digging into her soul through her eyes.

"Don't move."

Her vision filled with desert camouflage uniform and honed man towering over her, an M-16 hooked on his shoulder and pistol in his web belt holster. She focused on his blue eyes instead. "Will you release my arm, please?"

"Not until I'm convinced you aren't going to gut me or blow me up."

Fear and indignation prickled. Suicide bombers made things more difficult for everyone, sewing the seeds of distrust against even the innocent.

He touched her.

Shock stilled her. His hands roved her arms in bold swipes that left the air suddenly thick and heavy. He moved up to her shoulders, down her back to her waist.

Along her legs.

Heat rushed to her face and to other parts of her until she fought not to fidget under his search. Never had she been stroked this way, but understood she had surrendered a certain hold on her rights by pressing the note into his palm. Her mind clouded with a haze, pleasurable, urgent.

Frightening.

"Please," she whispered. "If someone witnesses this…"

His hands brushed her belly just below her breasts once before he stepped away, his search complete, no weapon discovered since she did not have one. Why would she? How useless to expect her negligible strength could outmaneuver any of these armed men. Especially one this large. She would outthink him instead.

Once she stopped seeing spots in front of her eyes.

Her uncle expected her to ferret information, to

discover if this was truly a deployment to assist with the distribution of humanitarian aid, something that happened often in her country. Or was it another American mission to destroy secret training camps in their endless war on terrorism. Since Ammar might well have other spies in place here, she would have to tread this double game warily if she wanted out of the country in one piece.

The soldier with sea-blue eyes and mountainous shoulders dusted his hands along the mottled tan print of his uniform pants as if he sought to clean away the feel of her. "Who are you?"

"I am Bahijah Faris, not that it matters. You have my note. Did I not express myself correctly?" She knew full well she had. Thanks to her American mother, Yasmine spoke English almost as fluently as Arabic. "I seek asylum in the United States. And you are?"

"The wrong man for you to play your flirting games with, little girl. So let's hope you're being straight up now." His fingers banded her arm again.

She shivered, but refused to be daunted by his threats. She'd heard worse.

He charged forward, propelling her down the abandoned corridor stacked with crates. Apparently the sensitive soul she found in his eyes was housed by a brusque exterior. Of course, many men were afraid to show anything that might be perceived as weakness. "Little girl? I think you misunderstand. I am twenty-three years old, well of age by your country's standards, unmarried, without ties to this place, so there is no reason for me to be denied my wish.''

"I'll keep that in mind, Methuselah,'' he barked, boots thumping cadence down the split-tile floor.

"Where are we going?'' She doubled her pace to match his long-legged strides without tripping.

"To headquarters for you to speak with our military counterintelligence personnel about your request.''

Military security? Her blood chilled with every step deeper into the building toward the inner offices. She stopped. "Please wait.'' She panted, from racing feet and heart. "I do not want to speak with them. I want to talk to you.''

"Too bad. That's not how things work here.''

"But I chose you. I trust you. I have no reason to trust them.'' Her attempt to leave the country after her parents' deaths in the flu epidemic had been foiled by a mole in the American embassy to Rubistan, another spy loyal to Ammar.

"Well, your choosing ended once you placed that note in my hand. We have procedures.'' He stared down at her, disbelief slipping past the hard mask. "Did you expect me to tuck you in a suitcase for a trip over the border?''

She sniffed back indignation. He didn't need to make her sound foolish. But now was not the time to roll out her diploma. "Actually, yes, I expected

something very much like that. It has been done
before, so there is no need to mock me.''

"Well, put away your Samsonite luggage, lady,
because it's not going to be done today.''

How dare he treat her like a truculent child? If
grief aged a person, then she had many years on
anyone here.

"Wait," she demanded, desperation shaving the
edge off her original intent to appear ditzy and
humble.

"What now?" His words rode an exasperated
sigh.

Apparently this man did not respect youth, so she
pulled herself taller to make use of every bit of her
five feet, two inches of height while attempting to
add years and command to her voice. "We need to
speak first before you dump me into the hands of
your security persons.''

His brows slammed down. "Listen up, I've had
just about enough of this Queen of Sheba shit. I
don't take orders from you. You made an irrevo-
cable step back there when you put that note in my
hand. Do you want to go with dignity? Or do I call
security forces to 'escort' you? Your choice.''

Time to switch tactics again. Temper never
worked with men, anyway. She lowered her gaze,
peered up through her lashes. "I'll do anything.''

His eyes narrowed, exasperation hardening to a
cold mask, no sign of warmth in those ice-blue

eyes. Oh, my. She was out of her depth, but that didn't mean she would stop swimming.

She slowed her words to give her brain time to restart, and clarified, "I will cook for you."

He winced.

Her stew.

Wrong suggestion and time was short. Desperation grew. "I'll clean for you, watch your children."

"Considering you and my daughter are about the same damned age, that's not much of an offer."

Same age as his daughter? She studied him again, took in his sandy brown hair, the handsome angles of his face perfect enough for some Hollywood poster except for sun-strengthened lines that made him all the more attractive in her eyes. "That is not possible."

He snorted. "Trumped-up flattery may have worked on one of those privates back in the mess hall, but you picked wrong in coming on to me if you expect that kind of eye-batting crap to win me over. I respect one thing. Honesty. Now let's go."

Honesty? Uh-oh. But since he would not find out her real name, no need to worry.

The grip of his hand on her elbow certainly didn't indicate any failing age. Besides, in her culture, women often married men far older. Age equated with wisdom, wealth, power. Safety.

Marriage?

That was the last thing on her mind. Never again

did she want to be under anyone's control. Without question, marriage signified a loss of rights in any culture.

And she only had seconds left to persuade him to keep embassy officials uninvolved. "Do you not realize what will happen to me if it gets out that I attempted to defect? Word will leak, make no mistake, if you carry this to others. It always does. There are no secrets from the warlords here. There must be something I can do to earn your assistance. I have money."

Money spoke all languages. Every one of those hungry Rubistans shouting at the gate was a threat to her security here. Any of them would sell her out for a jug of water and a few slices of bread.

"Sheba—" a rusty laugh scratched free and tickled her senses "—if you saw my paycheck, you'd know I'm not in this line of work for the money. None of us are."

Full fear bloomed. She'd been so certain of her plan. Her mind scrambled for a recovery, options, prepared answers to shield her connection to Ammar at all costs. "Please. If we keep this between the two of us, then if I am returned to my hell, at least I will be allowed to live."

His hand gentled on her elbow and his beautiful blue eyes filled with compassion. Relief rippled through her like the oasis near her childhood home. She had not been wrong. Others might be misled by the rugged exterior that housed this man's soul, but she saw his understanding of her pain, her fears, even if he did not fully know their root.

His shoulders braced, spread the uniform tight across a chest so broad surely no one could topple him. "There may be a host of reasons why we put on this uniform, but I can tell you it doesn't stand for lies or dishonor. You will be safe. You will be protected. And if it is truly your wish, you will receive asylum."

If it was truly her wish?

The oasis within her dried right up to reveal the cracked reality of her precarious position. She had been so preoccupied with the honesty in his eyes, she'd forgotten that wisdom could be a double-edged sword.

She searched for a suitable response, all the while wondering why she had not taken the easier route in opting for one of those naive young soldiers. Fast-approaching footsteps provided the perfect diversion, one she grasped with greedy hands, turning toward the noise.

Fate swiped her like a lion's paw.

From around the corner her sister appeared, nearing, a man in a flight suit at her side, the scowling male without a hint of softness in his eyes she had quickly sidestepped back in the dining hall. Fate was a fickle creature to bring Monica here now.

But then, fate had not been kind to her lately.

Monica, the oh-so-perfect one who would never have to resort to eyelash-batting or goat-roasting to maintain her safety, strode toward her with unflappable confidence. Unable to stop herself, Yasmine stepped back, hating the minute show of weakness. Yet she stepped again, flush against her blue-eyed soldier's rock-solid chest.

And she had thought his *hands* felt good.

Part of her wanted to leap forward before the heat of him scorched her further. Another part couldn't resist the temptation to burrow closer against his solid strength...

Oh, my.

And against his unmistakably steely arousal.

Jack sprawled in the unrelenting steel of the office chair and watched the interrogation under way. While Yasmine Halibiz, alias Bahijah Faris, might be the focus of the interview, he had a few questions himself for Monica later. But they would have to wait until his anger quieted to a dull roar.

He tried to wrap his brain around the facts. The diminutive Middle Eastern babe being interrogated by the counterintelligence contingent was Monica's sister. Half sister, anyway. The resemblance was there when he looked closer, same nose, same stubborn chin, the whole package a smaller, softer version of Monica's strong features.

And she hadn't bothered to tell him. Anger exploded in pockets of secondary blasts within him. He didn't get deep-down angry often. He was now. At himself as well as Monica because he couldn't escape the knowledge that he hadn't told her about Tina, either.

Monica was right. They really were screwed up in the relationship department.

It wasn't like they'd been so busy having sex 24/7 that they never talked. Apparently they just hadn't discussed anything important. Now he was getting critical background information about his "wife" from a cold interrogation by the OSI.

The sparse office with a dirty window bounced echoes of voices and rustling papers, too many people packed in the contained space. Yasmine Halibiz sat on one side of the table, her sister beside her but not in any comforting-family-member sort of way. The two women never looked at each other, hadn't even touched beyond the stiff-as-hell hello in the hall. Nothing like effusive reunions in the Korba clan that left a person with aching ribs from all the hugs.

Colonel Cullen didn't appear much happier, glaring, silent, leaning against the wall with arms folded over his chest, hand clutching his LMR—Land Mobile Radio. His top lip curled as if someone had overturned the latrine.

They all listened while two men conducted the interview. Special Agent Maxwell Keagan, a civilian employee in the Air Force Office of Special Investigation, peppered her with questions. Captain Daniel "Crusty" Baker, head of the advance element setup team, passed paperwork to Keagan one sheaf at a time in a subtle message to the woman to keep her story clean.

No one would guess from Crusty's apparent calm and carelessly rumpled flight suit that he had as much at stake here as the rest of them since his father—the Ambassador to Rubistan—had recently been assassinated. And to think months ago Jack had gone to Crusty for those connections to help Sydney find her way here.

A powder keg of guilt rested beneath his anger.

"Why use the fake name?" Keagan asked with deceptive disinterest. His unconventional air could be mistaken for slackness—casual khakis, a purple polo, spiked hair.

Would Yasmine Halibiz look deeper and find the honed agent with a CIA background prior to signing on with the Air Force's OSI?

"If I had applied here with my real name—" her eyes didn't shift away, but she blinked fast, too fast "—members of my family would have objected to my leaving. So I used Bahijah Faris's name, with her permission. Her family needs the money I offered. They are a large family and her sister has a baby on the way."

The questions droned on while Jack studied the two men quizzing Yasmine. He'd always been able to tackle anything he set his mind to until Monica. What secret were guys like Baker and Keagan holding back from the rest of the bachelor population?

Baker was cross-eyed ecstatic with his wife,

while Keagan was downright sappy since he got an engagement ring on copilot Darcy Renshaw's finger. For that matter, how did Keagan make the career thing work with his fiancée in their mutual Air Force workplace?

He'd definitely have to buy the guy a beer and pump him for information.

Keagan slid another form from the folder. "If you wanted to defect, why didn't you do so on any of the trips you made to the States with your mother?"

That "mother" word sent Monica's spine straighter than an at-attention airman. As pissed as he was, he couldn't turn away from her when she was vulnerable—a rare event.

Behind her and away from prying eyes, Jack gripped the back of her chair, stroked a slow reassurance with one knuckle between her shoulder blades. She bristled under his touch, shot him a warning glare, but nothing more. If she spoke, the others would know. She had to accept his comfort.

"Because I did not want to leave my mother here alone," Yasmine continued. "Because I was a child then. Because life became…difficult for me after she died. Any number of reasons, none of which matter now. I am requesting asylum, and as the daughter of a former citizen of the United States, it is my understanding this request should be fairly simple to accommodate."

Max Keagan thumbed through a folder without

looking up. "Why not just call one of your sisters?"

"I haven't been free to move since my mother and father died."

Monica's pain radiated from her until his finger burned. He didn't know what the hell was up with this Middle-Eastern mini-Monica in front of him, but if she hurt his wife, she'd be serving up that goat stew in prison.

Monica's brain echoed with Yasmine's words in this endless interview. Former citizen. Their mother. No longer alive.

Even a year after her mother's death, the loss stabbed. As long as her mother lived, there was hope of…what? Reconciliation? Some kind of inner peace over something she couldn't find her way through to forgiving?

She tried to remind herself this poised young woman wasn't the same spoiled brat who traveled to the States once a year during their mother's annual two-week treks to see her other daughters. Somehow those trips hurt worse than if they'd never seen her again. During the first year after their mother's defection, she'd woven tortured tales of how their mother couldn't return home. Wasn't allowed. A bedtime story that conversely frightened and sustained them…

Until their mother came to visit. And left again.

The next year, bringing a new baby girl with her. Again leaving of her own free will.

As a confused teenager, it had been easy to hate the spoiled brat their mother chose to keep with her. As an adult, Monica found her feelings for Yasmine more complex. But even with the tempering of years, they'd never been what anyone would deem as "close."

Yasmine pinned her with an accusatory glare. "Even if I had been allowed to call, I have no reason to trust that Monica would be willing to help me."

Monica let herself soak up Jack's soothing touch for two exhales before forging ahead. "Well, ouch, Yas, that stings worse than when you tried to rip out one of my earrings."

"I was four at the time. As I recall, Sydney had hold of the other earring."

Monica gasped. How could Yasmine be so cruel as to mention Sydney offhandedly?

Or did she not know about the kidnapping? Information didn't flow freely here.

Keagan snapped the file closed. "All a moot point now, anyway. We can't release her back into the community in case her request is valid."

And couldn't risk her sharing anything she may have seen or heard.

Yasmine's haughty jaw dropped open. "Everything is all right? I will be leaving for the United States?"

Keagan turned to the commanding officer. "Colonel?"

Placing his LMR on the corner of the desk, stone-faced Colonel Cullen blinked slowly, assessing. "There are State Department channels we need to process through. Beyond that, we don't have a disposable number of pilots on hand to ferry people back and forth. She'll have to wait until we've completed our mission here, and she'll be under house arrest until we go."

Yasmine's brown eyes flashed with fear, fast then gone. "Which means what exactly?"

"You're free to walk around the compound, but you may not leave."

"And I will be watched?"

Silence spoke louder than any affirmation.

"Thank you." Her chin dipped in a regal-princess nod at odds with her dowdy dress and faded red scarf. "Where will I sleep?"

Colonel Cullen's eyes snapped up, then away. "You can bunk with your sister."

"No!" Monica and Yasmine answered simultaneously.

Monica flushed. Silence returned, broken only by the voices building outside the foggy window beside the Colonel.

Jack palmed Monica's back. "Personally, I prefer my flight surgeon not be dead on her feet when she treats me, which is why Doc Hyatt got private quarters in the first place, unlike the rest of the crew dogs bunking double. A roommate would be disruptive enough even without the guard. Don't we have another room, even a closet available?''

Thank you, Jack.

Keagan dropped the file on the desk. ''We can't put her in the luggage return hangar with all the Colonel's soldiers.''

Crusty leafed through papers on a clipboard. ''There's a storage closet we were using for extra bedrolls. We could stack those in the hall instead and set up a cot for her.''

Relief sighed from Yasmine so loudly Monica wanted to laugh. Needed to laugh. Except life just wasn't that damned funny lately.

Yasmine rose, slowly, with an imperialistic poise that would have no doubt propelled her beyond a first-runner-up slot at the Miss Texas competition. ''I should return to the kitchen.''

A truck backfired outside. Once again?

Oh, God, a shot. Not a truck.

''Down! Shooter,'' someone shouted, inside or outside.

Pop. The window shattered, sending glass and military personnel flying. Another bullet whistled past.

No time to think. Training assumed control. Monica launched toward her sister. Saw the Colonel tackle her first.

Monica hit the ground. Hard. Jack? Where was Jack?

His arm hooked around her waist. "Quit worrying about your sister. She's fine."

He jerked Monica as he rolled. Toward the wall. Under the table and out of the line of fire.

Her heart thudded against his. Another shot took out the jagged edge of pane. Glass spewed inside. Shards tinkled along with shouts and gunfire.

Then nothing. Just barked orders but no more shots.

Still pinning Yasmine, Colonel Cullen reached for his radio on the desk corner. Already the LMR squawked reassurance—only a hungry local trying to steal a box of rations.

Monica sagged against Jack. Adrenaline gushed from her pores in the aftermath. The irony of it struck her like a stray bullet.

They were nowhere near the terrorist compound. It was just a regular sunny day in Rubistan…interspersed with the occasional gunfire. And to think her mother left Red Branch, Texas, for *this*.

Jack eased his weight off her, his arm sliding until his hand rested just below her breasts in the tangle, his leg moving in what turned into a firm, hot nudge between her legs that left her hotter. He stopped. His eyes widened with realization. Accidental positioning, sure. But no less potent.

She couldn't move, couldn't find air or space or anything but his face filling her vision. And the hell of it was, she found the hold of his stare just as captivating as the warm corded thigh between her legs.

Ten minutes ago she would have sworn she couldn't remember the sound of her mother's voice. But right now, Mama whispered through her head sure as a surprise honeysuckle spring breeze in the middle of the desert.

Sugar, this is exactly why I left Red Branch, Texas.

Chapter 6

Two hours and one disarmed local rioter later, Jack flattened a hand against the closed door outside Monica's quarters. He should go to bed. He would go to bed.

As soon as he looked at her again and reassured himself she was alive and not full of bullets.

Being a military spouse sure sucked sometimes—even when the marriage was a freaking farce. He'd sometimes wondered how Tina would have handled his combat missions. He'd never considered what it would feel like to be on the other end of the worry. Yeah, it *definitely* sucked, especially given he already understood how damned bad it cut being the one left behind by death.

One look and he would leave her alone.

A dumb-ass decision when his anger still crackled inside him, adding an extra blue tinge to the flame from his fear of losing her. Permanently.

Too many emotions fired, but then he'd never been one to play it safe. No question, the hungry look in her eyes when she'd stared up at him from their clinch on the floor had been anything but safe.

With two knuckles, he rapped twice. "It's me."

"Come on in." Monica's husky Texas drawl sucker punched him right through the shabby tin door. "It's unlocked."

Unlocked? He'd address that later when he wasn't mad and she wasn't in defensive mode. And when he could stop remembering the world of want in her eyes earlier.

He swung wide the door to the office converted into sleeping quarters. A desk, a couple of chairs and a shelf littered a corner by a door open to a tiny private toilet and shower stall. A thin cot stretched against the other wall with barely enough room for a restless night. But big enough if the two of them were absolutely in sync, the way he and Monica had always been in bed.

Eyes off the cot, pal.

Her military bag lay open on the desk to reveal neat stacks of clothes. Ziplocs sealed each toiletry from an accidental spill. Orderly. Clean. His germ-nut doctor-wife all but lived with antibacterial soap holstered to her hip.

The only time she got good and messy, sweaty and relaxed, was during a ball game. And sex.

Don't look at the bed.

Instead he studied the straight curve of her spine as she leaned against the windowpane. Silky caramel-brown hair fell free just past her at-attention shoulders, a few waves crimping it after being contained in a French braid. More than air, he wanted to kiss his way up her spine, under her aloe-scented strands to her neck, coax her head to fall forward and that stiff posture of hers to go limp and languid.

Time to shut down those thoughts or soon he would be stiffer than her spine. "You should have that window blacked out so you can sleep during the day when you need to."

"Sure. Later." Monica traced a finger along the pane, drawing circles in the dirt. "I'm sorry for not explaining about Yasmine before."

At the ring of her honest regret, some of his anger deflated. Who was he to toss stones when he hadn't told her about Tina? "We all have our secrets."

He still wasn't sure why he hadn't told Monica, and now sure as hell wasn't the time to bring it up. Of course, he never talked about Tina, and it had been so damned long ago. Still, no question in his mind, wife number two would be pissed to learn there'd been a wife number one she never knew about. Another hole to dig himself out of.

Damn. They were one messed-up couple.

He sauntered across the room. Stopped at the other side of the window. Looked at her while she looked at the world where her mother once lived, where both her sisters lived now. He waited, since patience seemed to be his one trump card around her.

Monica's slim finger slowed on the glass. Without a word she ducked around him, riffled through her duffel bag and pulled out a pack of antibacterial wipes. He almost smiled at the predictability, but her need to tidy her world seemed somehow sad right now.

After she cleaned her fingers, she swiped the disposable cloth over the window for a clearer view, flatted her palm over the pane as if to reach through to something outside. "How can a mother abandon her children like that? Regardless of whether she loved us or not, she was responsible. Even a dog stays with her puppies until they can fend for themselves." Her hand fell from the smudged view of endless sand mottled by rippling heat. "Of course, I guess she figured it out in time for Yasmine."

Monica paused, crinkling her nose in self-disgust. "Eww. Sibling rivalry sounds so juvenile."

He'd learned early not to pick sides in his sisters' battles, and *they* loved each other. The animosity between Monica and Yasmine bore no resemblance to any family relationship he'd witnessed. "She doesn't make it easy for you."

"Thanks." A wry smile flickered as she pitched

the dirty paper cloth into the trash. "Even if you're sucking up, I still enjoyed hearing that."

"I aim to please."

She snorted. "Still angling for that spanking, are you?"

"Monica."

"Yeah?"

"We don't have to laugh right now."

Her head fell forward, hair sliding to shield her face and emotions. "Thank you."

He'd seen her. She was okay. He should go. He needed sleep. His boots wouldn't move.

With a toss of her hair, she looked up again. "I don't want to be one of those people who blames their parents for everything. I'm an adult. I make my own decisions."

"Yes, ma'am, you do."

"Then why can't I let this go?"

Finally she'd given him an opening and he sure as hell didn't want to screw it up. Not just because he wanted more from her, but because it was tearing him up to see her indomitable spirit bent.

He scrounged for what his brother would say and came up dry. Hell, he'd just have to go with his gut and pray. "When I was a kid, we always spent summer days with Grandma Korba. Me, my brother Tony and our sisters. Our parents both had to work to keep the dry-cleaning business in the black. Child care was too expensive, and of course

Grandma Korba…well, she said she'd watch us and nobody argued with her.''

Monica smiled that gorgeous grin that made her perfect high cheekbones all the more prominent, exotic. ''I think I would like her.''

She would. If they ever met.

He left the statement unspoken. ''Every summer, Grandma allots five days for her pilgrimage.''

''Pilgrimage?''

''To Graceland.''

Monica poked him in the gut with one finger. ''You're making this up.''

Jack raised his hands in surrender. ''Believe me, no way would I make up anything this out-there. She would stuff all four of us in her green Pinto and leave Chicago behind for Tennessee. Now in order to afford the nights in a motel, she packed her own food. A jug of Kool-Aid, loaf of bread, peanut butter, jelly, and cereal for breakfast.''

He smiled at the warmth of the memory and at the pleasure of sucking Monica in until she wasn't looking out the window anymore. ''Frosted Flakes were messy if you ate 'em dry, so we saved those for the motel and cracked open the Froot Loops first. We'd pass that box around and around. By the time we hit the Tennessee state line, we were fighting over the prize at the bottom of the box.''

She laughed, smiled, lighter. ''I thought you said we weren't going to laugh?''

''Well, what can I say? I'm me.'' He hooked his

hands on his hips to keep from touching her. "And I still love Froot Loops and the King, thanks to those summers. But I don't like small cars. Or even small planes, for that matter, after being wedged between Tony and one of my sisters for five hundred miles."

Distance be damned. He let himself slide a hand behind her neck, cup it with firm insistence as he made his point. "Childhood affects us. Good and bad, nobody's fault. There's just no way around it."

She flicked his zipper tab with one finger. "Since my childhood's a walking advertisement against marriage, you're shooting yourself in the foot here with this argument."

Maybe. Maybe not. "Yeah, I know. But I learned something in Vegas a few months ago."

"Never drink tequila with a girl from Red Branch, Texas, unless you're prepared to say 'I do'?"

He definitely didn't feel like laughing over that one. "Not funny, Mon."

She released his zipper and let her hand rest on his chest. "Then what, Jack?"

"I only want you if you want me, too." A truth he'd only just realized himself and it definitely scared the laugh right out of him.

Her fingers fisted against his heart, green eyes full of weakness he could exploit. "It's not that I don't want you."

"Stop." He tapped her mouth closed. "We don't

have to do this now. As a matter of fact, I'm mighty damn sure we shouldn't.''

''Why did you come in here, then? I can tell you're still pissed with me over the Yasmine thing.''

He shrugged, walked over to her neat-as-a-pin duffel. His fingers played with a Ziploc full of cotton balls beside another bag sealing up facial cleanser. While his anger might have deflated, it hadn't disappeared, even with fault on both sides.

Damn. He was tired. Tired of measuring his words around her. Tired of holding back and wondering and waiting—a helluva statement on his frustrated state of mind given he considered himself one of the most patient men on the planet.

As much as he ached to have Monica, some days he wasn't sure he wanted to be with a woman he had to fight every step of the way. Love had been so damned easy with Tina. Simply there. Uncomplicated.

Still, here he was, unable to walk away.

The part of him that had been gut punched over the image of Monica with a bullet in her belly wanted to shake her up, make her just as out of control as he felt. A damned selfish wish when he'd just spent the past ten minutes calming her down.

He needed to get the hell out of her room before he lost precious ground by thinking with his Johnson instead of his brain. Keep strategy in place and remember this woman did not respond well to being chased. He wanted more than just sex from her this time—or nothing at all.

He dropped the sack of cotton balls. "Enough talking for one day. You need sleep and so do I. I'm outta here."

Jack started for the door. Monica's hand shot out, gripped his arm, stopping him. He pivoted, his brain only giving him a one-second warning that Monica intended to kiss him.

Yasmine clicked the door closed to her "closet room." No footsteps retreated. Her military escort stayed outside, as ordered. A guard should make her feel more secure. Being in the compound should make her feel safer.

It didn't. Nothing would as long as Ammar stayed alive.

She whipped the scarf from her head, folded it into her bag with the others she always kept with her. Her splashes of color in a dark world.

All of two steps took her to her cot. She unrolled the sleeping bag, wafting free a scent she was quickly coming to identify as musty military. If only Monica had not been deployed here. She'd scoured the rosters Ammar had pilfered from his embassy mole and nowhere had she seen Monica's name. At least she would have stood a chance appealing to Sydney, not that she'd heard from her in a year.

Monica wouldn't have landed herself in this

mess. But then if Monica's glances at the scary-faced, hairy Major were anything to judge by, Monica wasn't getting everything she wanted these days, either.

Yasmine flopped back onto the bed—nothing like her luxurious room growing up, but a fair sight better than her recent accommodations. Persistence sometimes beat brains. Monica might be smarter, but Yasmine knew she had grown stronger, more determined.

Reaching the States would help. Ammar feared entering the U.S. since his capture during his last trip there. His escape had not been easy.

If only it had been fatal.

Ruminating accomplished nothing, however. She was stuck with the here and now—and getting out of Rubistan before anyone discovered her distant relation to a known terrorist.

They were right to distrust her. She was not overly certain she could withstand the pressure Ammar might exert on her to obtain his will. She had almost forgotten what it felt like not to be afraid—until that brief moment when she'd stared into sky-blue eyes and fear faded.

Only the eyes, the man, remained.

Rising to sit on the edge, she pulled the pins from her twisted bun, one at a time placing them in her lap until her hair slithered halfway down her back. Air brushed through the strands, over her head in a sensuous glide heightened by the fact that no one had touched her with even familial affection in so long.

Except when the Colonel had touched her. And the sensation rivaled the glorious freedom of fresh air against her uncovered scalp.

A day ago she would have been content with the closet. Now she did not want to stay here. She did not want to be shuffled off to security personnel with eyes she could not trust. She wanted Colonel Cullen's protection.

And he wanted her. Her knowledge of male-female relationships had been limited, but she knew enough so that one brush against him told her he desired her.

Yet he confused her, too. Most men would have exploited the attraction. He seemed repelled by it because of the silly age factor, unlucky for her when she had been given to believe all American males coveted a—what was it called?—trophy wife. Not that she was looking to be a wife. She had her own plans for a career and life in the States, not as lofty as her doctor-soldier sister. But solid plans.

Once she got the hell out of Rubistan.

What should have been a help—the Colonel's attraction—would actually be a hindrance. Having been reminded what it felt like to be free of fear, she couldn't let him slip away just yet. Simple enough to circumvent his concerns, because she did not intend to be shuffled aside. Ditching a few military security personnel would be simple enough after a year of evading Ammar's spies.

If Ammar came hunting for her, she fully intended to have Colonel Cullen at her side. And to achieve that, she needed to plaster herself to *his* side.

Monica froze. What the hell was she thinking, plastering her mouth to Jack's?

But oh, my, it felt so good. So right. Even just a simple thank-you kiss thickened her blood to syrup in her veins. Their attraction had never been in question and this quick lip-lock proved it. A lip-lock getting longer by the moment.

He gripped her shoulders. *Yes.* More. Have him take control, then she wouldn't need to think or choose.

Jack moved her away, their lips holding until the last…second. *No,* her body cried at the loss.

His fingers dug into her skin. "Monica, you're giving me whiplash here. What the hell was that for?"

Maple syrup. Definitely maple, still pulsing need through her veins and into her brain until rational thought slowed and emotions overflowed. "Froot Loops."

"What?"

"Because you gave me a beautiful Froot Loop story even though I gave you half-truths about my family. I should have told you about Yasmine, but

I didn't. And I'm truly sorry. I know you're still mad at me, and you have reason. Still, you came in here to check up on me.''

His hands slid down her arms in a caress soon to end. Indecision drifted through his eyes, rare for Jack, as if he wanted to say something more. His fingers hooked on hers held.

Whatever he'd been thinking about saying blew away from his expression. ''Ah, hell.''

He jerked her forward. Not that she put up any resistance. Their mouths met, open and hungry and so very familiar with just the right slant, taste and stroke to bring instant arousal. Her hands took their time exploring every inch of muscled shoulders until she looped her arms around his neck and held on before her knees became as weak as her will around this man.

She knew this was wrong and that she would regret it later, but with her emotions in chaos, the reliability of passion with Jack brought comfort. Her face stung with the bittersweet abrasion of his sandpaper beard against her tender skin.

Temporary forgetfulness rode the surge of nerve-tingling pleasure from her breasts against unyielding chest, his erection hard against her stomach. Nerves and heat throbbed, gathered lower until Monica backed toward her cot, one step, two with Jack's saunter rolling his hips against her in a sensuous promise. She let her knees fold, not too difficult at all. Jack's arms held her upright.

Her eyes fluttered open as she eased her mouth from his. "I thought you said you wanted me if I wanted you. Well, you can be sure I want you very much right now."

His hands slid up her arms to her locked grip behind his neck. In spite of her whimper of denial, he untwined her hold on him. "I'll probably kick myself later. But as tempting as it is to take you up on your offer, I wasn't talking about wanting this from you."

Something so deep and sad shifted in his choc-olate-brown eyes that she ached to cup his bristly jaw in comfort. Started to do just that when he lifted her hands in his.

He kissed her closed fingers before releasing her. "Don't forget to lock up after me."

The door clicked closed behind him, and without the support of his shoulders beneath her hands, her knees finally gave way. She sagged to the edge of her cot, rattled to her roots by how much she still wanted him, and not just on a sexual level, but for foot rubs and Froot Loops.

And he'd walked out on her.

She'd been ready and more than willing to give him everything, and still he'd left. Her conscience niggled with the reminder she wasn't giving him everything. Just her body, and that hadn't worked for them in the months past.

God, she was too tired and confused to sort through it all. She fell back, head on her pillow and stared through the cleared circle on her window-pane. Her sister waited out there. She needed to focus on that, couldn't deal with anything more. So she watched the sun climb on the same horizon her sister watched, and tried to pretend the connection held something more than a surreal television-screen quality.

Inside the C-17 mobile command post, Blake Gardner stared at the screen filled with black-and-white satellite feed from a recent flight of the Predator unmanned spy drone shooting images of the terrorist camp. He watched for Sydney to appear. Had seen the same footage countless times and still his heart drummed in his chest.

The inactivity of this waiting game was killing him. He'd chosen the Navy, specifically the SEALs, for his branch of service because he'd never been able to sit idle for ten seconds since childhood. A trait that worked well for him when growing up on his uncle's farm.

But it bit right now. While his work as a SEAL often put him into play early in any joint military action, there was no way around the teeth-grinding wait this time.

He folded a fresh piece of gum into his mouth right on top of the old one and chewed out his frustration with spearmint rather than the nicotine buzz he used to get from dipping. After thirty-six hours' more planning at this godforsaken air base, they would finally launch into the next phase, bringing him that much closer to where Sydney waited for rescue. Waited for *him?*

A low hum of activity circled around him even though he stayed silent. Flatbed pallets down the center track of the cargo hold carried all the high-tech computer systems of any bunker command center.

Colonel Cullen clipped through last-minute questions for Korba's crew, calling for counterintelligence affirmations from OSI Agent Max Keagan and ADVON leader Captain Baker. They'd worked most of the night, would finish up soon, then sleep through the rest of the day for their night flight.

Sydney had to know he wouldn't leave her in there. If he'd needed to infiltrate alone, he would have done it for her. But he understood enough about his job and his fellow team buddies to know. This was better. Even if the extra wait was killing him, slowly, each day a whittling knife-swipe against his soul.

Not much longer. The HAHO—high altitude, high opening—drop with oxygen masks would allow them to maneuver their glide for nearly an hour over the gulf waters into the area around the coastal training camp. Then two more days to recon for additional intelligence before the rescue and Ranger drop.

The image focused on the portion of the compound where the NGO hostages were allowed out once a day. Studying their schedule was critical. He stopped breathing, knowing what the screen would show…now.

Three figures were escorted into the small fenced-in patch of sand. One man. Two women.

Cutting-edge technology from the Predator fed in a digital image as clear as any television screen. Yet even if it had been the less-detailed satellite images, he would have known in his gut which one was Sydney. The same gut that had carried him through ops in the bowels of Baghdad—missions she and he had bitterly disagreed on.

Guilt turned him into a pummeled workout bag. He should have fought harder at talking her out of coming here. Except he couldn't talk her out of her job, her calling, any more than she could talk him out of his. They both had the same goal. Peace. And two diametrically opposed ideologies on how to get there.

He'd given up on a second chance at building the family with Sydney that neither of them had ever had growing up. But he sure as hell wasn't giving up on her.

Blake leaned closer on his forearms, wanting like hell to crawl through the screen to get her. Even knowing it was old footage he'd memorized didn't stop him from looking again, like staring at her framed photo that once perched on his dresser beside the picture of his uncle who'd taken him in as a teen after his parents died.

Again he studied her hunched posture. Arms wrapped around her waist? The now-familiar twist closed his throat, just as powerful as the first time he'd seen the satellite feed. She wasn't a woman easily bowed. What pain was she hiding?

The image faded to static.

A discreet cough pulled him back to the cavernous belly of the plane. Too many eyes pinned him with a sympathy he didn't want. Couldn't handle.

Colonel Cullen rose from his seat. "One last point before we break for chow." His controlled, quiet tones rumbled with authority on a roll. "It hasn't escaped my notice that this mission is rife with conflict of interest. Now, I let this slide because you all happen to be the best available for the mission."

The Colonel's steely gaze swept Korba, Baker.

Him. Of course the Colonel couldn't argue that this Afghanistan-seasoned SEAL platoon from Virginia was anything but the number-one choice.

"But if I find any of you allowing your personal agendas to risk the life of even one of my men, I will smack you down so hard and so fast, your children will be born dizzy." The steady stare of a commander held the air captive for five seconds. "Is that understood?"

Blake nodded without checking to see if the others did, as well. He couldn't risk anyone finding something in his eyes. He had a few contingency plans of his own, but since his life would be the only one at risk, Colonel Cullen had nothing to worry about.

Chapter 7

Drew was worried.

Clanking down the side hatch steps of the C-17 mobile command unit, he blinked back the glare of the sun and gnawing frustration. There were too many agendas running on this airfield for his comfort level. And still, even without those outside elements, he would have chosen exactly this joint team for the mission.

If only they could keep personal issues clear of the battlefield.

He would have to trust what twenty years of service hammered into him. Training assumed control of a soldier in combat. It had to.

M-16 on his shoulder weighing with welcome

familiarity, Drew cleared the last step onto the heated tarmac, the gritty breeze barely broken by the smattering of palm trees. Only April and the place was already roasting like the inside of an oven. The stretch of cracked cement sizzled with activity. A few feet away, a loadmaster supervised the tie-down of food and medical supplies into a C-17 scheduled to land in a rural community. A contingent of Rangers would meet up with the IFB aid workers to disperse the rations—his men wearing different patches on their uniforms to keep their other mission covert.

Would Yasmine Halibiz notice the overabundance of troops?

God knows the woman seemed to be all over everywhere. Everywhere being right under his feet. His nose. Right in front of his eyes with that tempting smile of hers every time he turned around.

Like now.

She waited across the tarmac under a palm tree beside the empty hangar where he'd received his inoculations. Her military escort shuffled impatiently a few yards away, eyeing her, eyeing the planes. But she kept her distance from the flight line as ordered.

She wore her customary black dress, today with a yellow scarf. The tail over her shoulder fluttered like a kite in the wind.

Damned if he hadn't been anticipating finding out what ridiculous scarf she would choose from the minute he announced a chow break. And double damned if her haughty little ways and dry sense of humor weren't starting to wear him down like sand in his boots on a hundred-mile trek when there was nothing he could do.

Apparently he needed to listen to his own lecture about conflict of interest since this woman was also a sister to one of those hostages.

He marched past her.

"Colonel Cullen?"

"Good morning, ma'am." He nodded and kept right on marching.

"Colonel Cullen." She fell into step behind him, her sandals whispering faster along the asphalt while her words carried on the dry wind. "If I could just have a moment of your time. There is something we really need to discuss."

"You'll have to check with my sergeant about my schedule."

"I have noticed you are reluctant to speak with me," she said louder as the space increased between his long strides and her shorter ones. "Could it be because you are attracted to me?"

Drew stopped. Pulled an about-face. Choked on a cough and wondered if the sun was baking his brain. "Good God, woman, would you keep it down?"

Ignoring her wasn't working. But no way did he intend to have this conversation out in the open when God only knew what she might say next. He searched, found, allocated an empty hangar for a more secluded locale to stop this train wreck in the making. He gave her guard a high sign, relinquishing him from duty for a few moments.

Drew gripped Yasmine's arm and jerked her into the dim sanctuary of the abandoned hangar. "Why in the hell would you think I'm—" he longed for a LifeSaver "—attracted to you?"

She stared at him. Just stared through an extended silence broken only by a bird flapping around the webbing of metal beams overhead. In her eyes he could read the memory of him flattening her to the floor during the shooting. Before that, of her backing into him and smack-dab on the erection he'd been fighting to will away.

Damn it all, even the memory of her tight little bottom nestled against him had him throbbing back into a world of want. He'd never been more grateful for his DCUs that kept him well covered. "I thought women over here were sheltered."

"We are. That doesn't mean we are ignorant. And of course I had an American mother who wanted to be certain her daughter made—what do you call them?—informed decisions."

She hesitated, tipping her head to the side. How the hell anyone could look regal in a yellow scarf with goddamned daisies on it boggled his mind. "Well, there's no decision to be made here. You need to stop following me."

"I understand that this physical reaction of yours

makes you uncomfortable around me. Of course women are lucky that when they experience such a physical reaction it is not as obvious.''

Physical reaction? She couldn't be flat-out referring to his...

Shit. She was. He did *not* intend to stand here and discuss hard-ons with this woman. "I have work to do."

Like beating his head against a wall until he passed out and woke up to find this conversation never happened. He executed a sharp military pivot and started back toward the light.

"It is okay, you know." Her voice dogged him. "There is no need to worry I expect anything long-term from you. I understand that men can not control when it happens for them."

What the hell did she know about men with no self-control? The light faded until he saw red. Thoughts blasted into his head, harsh images brought on by too many years of seeing the worst so-called humans could inflict on the helpless.

Hand on his military-issue side arm holstered on his hip, he charged back to her. His other hand thumped the side of the metal hangar beside her as if already erecting a wall between her and any threat. "Has someone hurt you?"

"Hurt me?"

Anger blew away his frustration, gelling into a cold-core call to protect. "Assaulted you? Sexually."

Her eyes widened with her gasp. "No! No."

Tension unwound inside him. His arm fell back to his side.

"But thank you for your concern for my well-being."

Her smile kinked that tension right back to an overwound spring.

"I'd be concerned about anyone. It's all a part of my job description to protect." He barked the words gruffer than he intended, but for the best.

She winced. "I realize that."

He'd hurt her feelings, and he ignored remorse. Now maybe she would back off. He could have some peace of mind and overlook the fact that he'd started searching for her every time he stepped away from his room.

Or a meeting.

Or another bowl of goat slop.

She relaxed against a metal beam. "I think you must have been very young when you had your daughter. How old is she again?"

"Twenty-one."

She smiled. "So I am older."

"By only two years. Now this conversation is over." Why didn't he tell her he was a grandfather?

"Men in my country have many wives."

The W-word.

A curse in his vocabulary he'd given up long before becoming a grandfather and a conversation he knew damned well to avoid. "So I hear around the water cooler."

"My mother was my father's fourth wife. Some say being the first wife is the most honored and important position. My mother always said being the last was best because it meant my father wanted no one else after having her."

He refrained from making a comment about monogamous marriages since that would lead him deeper into a discussion he wanted finished. "Well, rest assured, I can control myself, and having had one wife, I now have absolutely no intentions of taking another."

Yasmine studied him silently. Wind tugged at her silly scarf, revealing a hint of silken black hair. And just that fast, the attraction blindsided him again.

She tightened her scarf against the tearing gusts. "You loved her that much?"

Hell, no. But he knew an out when he saw one, so he kept his yap zipped and let her think what she wanted. Damned persistent woman would, anyway.

"How tragic for you." A frown ribbed her brow. Then she smiled. Man, did the woman ever know how to smile, creasing dimples in her smooth skin. "But also fortuitous for our situation. There are no worries now since I never want to marry, either. Once I am in the United States, I will be my own woman. No relatives to claim me and what is mine as their own."

Her mouth snapped shut abruptly. What was she talking about? He needed to listen but he couldn't stop looking at her smile lighting her brown eyes. It had been a long time since he'd seen anyone smile without reservation.

Her energy was contagious.

"Which brings me to why we are having this conversation."

"Well, thank you, Lord, at least the woman has a reason for tormenting the hell out of me."

"I torment you?" Her dimples deepened with an old-as-time Eve feminine confidence.

Contagious like a rash. "I don't have time to play tour guide for you."

There. That sounded logical.

Yasmine-Eve just kept smiling her sage womanly smile. "These feelings you have for me are not a problem since I am not after a green card. I don't need a tour guide, either, only your protection until I leave here."

Great. He had the hots for her and she didn't give a damn about more than the M-16 over his shoulder. "This is supposed to reassure me how, Sheba?"

Eve evaporated into something more like a miffed kid with a rejected gift. "I thought you might be concerned that I would take advantage of your...reaction to my closeness."

Back to that reaction issue again. Damn. And just

when he thought his fly buttons might get a reprieve from being strained to the limit around this woman.

Girl, he reminded himself. She was just a girl. Nineteen damned years younger than him and a refugee under his command. Must be some midlife crisis when he no-shit thought he wasn't upset about the grandparent thing. Other than regretting he'd never felt like a parent first.

Some men combated middle age with a sports car. Others, with women. Damn but he hated being so cliché as to lust after a nymphet, and would have sworn he wasn't the type.

He wasn't a monk, but he chose his lovers selectively. Mature women his age, women focused on their careers and in search of companionship with mutual physical release tossed into the mix.

Yasmine's hands fluttered up to her scarf again, resecuring the drape over her shoulder with butterfly grace. Still he could see the tip of her widow's peak, just a hint. More than enough since he was long past the adolescent days of ogling overt displays.

Age taught a man to appreciate the understated nuances of pleasure. The sensuality in the glide of a woman's hands as she touched silk. The beauty in the subtle suggestion of her hair begging to be revealed.

Good God, he was in a shitload of trouble here.

No, it wasn't a simple midlife crisis. More like

temporary insanity and he intended to recapture his grip on reality. Starting now.

He leaned down, nose to nose, and stared straight into her eyes while ignoring the silken hint of hair inches above. "Little girl, do you not realize I am a colonel in the United States Army? I have served combat in more conflicts than you have years. I have stared down the barrel of enemy rifles and pulled my own to shoot before being shot. I am the man in charge of your fate and yet you keep right on with this campaign of yours that you have to know is guaranteed to… Piss. Me. Off."

Yasmine stared back, unflinching as he unleashed tones that made even hardened warriors wet their pants. Damn, but he could use her cool under fire in his regiment.

She blinked slowly, a glimpse of Eve returning with wisdom beyond the young woman's years. "So why have you never called for one of those military police persons to take me back to my quarters?"

Huh?

He stood with his boots planted and his brain on stun. He wondered for a second if his M-16 had slid from his shoulder and shot him in the foot. Because sure as hell, *pop,* he was busted. And busted meant dead in his world.

This woman was dangerous for more reasons than he ever could have guessed.

She backed away toward the gaping hangar opening, taking all the air with her. "No need to call for them now. I will leave."

With a sweep of her arms, she twirled toward the tarmac with more of that subtle grace he didn't want to appreciate but now couldn't deny. She stepped out of the dim enclosure. Sunlight glinted on retreating daisies, declaring him almost in the homestretch.

Then Yasmine paused, glanced over her shoulder, a glimpse of vulnerability teasing through her poise. "Although I have to confess I am pleased you can not quite subdue your reaction to me. It would be a very sad thing for me to think only one of us was suffering from this attraction."

Waiting for Jack before his flight, Monica felt as transparent as a teenager loitering by the quarterback's locker.

Or worse yet, like her mother. Ruled by hormones and lacking in common sense when it came to men.

The life-support area bustled with activity from Rodeo and Tag picking up equipment before flight. A small back office that opened onto the flight line, the room was now jam-packed full of helmets and gear for the fliers.

Guilt stung Monica yet again. She should be focused on Sydney. Yet what was wrong with needing to see Jack before he took off to drop the SEALs? She just wanted an update without others listening in. For all his insistence that he intended to stay close to her, time alone together had sure been scarce since she'd thrown herself at him a day and a half ago.

Monica fingered the survival vests hanging from hooks alongside shelves of helmets. Rodeo smiled, nodded, but didn't initiate conversation as he and seasoned loadmaster Tag preflighted their helmets and NVGs. Thank God. She wasn't up to crew dog ribbing tonight.

Of course their silent acceptance of her presence said a lot for her and Jack's inability to keep things low-key. Yes, she wanted him, but there had to be more to a relationship than attraction. She knew that. Apparently, Jack knew it now, too, since he seemed to be keeping his distance. She should be relieved. Instead, frustration kicked through her.

The door swung open seconds before Jack entered from the corridor. The room seemed to fill with broad shoulders stretching a tan flight suit to the limit beneath the body armor they'd all begun wearing since the shooting.

Her hormones went on full alert as they always did around this man. At least her armored vest provided better coverage to her reaction than those pageant Band-Aids used to mask her reaction to the cold. Except now her reaction had more to do with something hot. Very hot. Her breasts definitely weighed heavy and needy and *in* need of closer contact with Jack right this moment.

His eyes found her. Held. He angled his dark head toward Rodeo and Tag without looking away. ''Go on ahead without me, guys. I'll catch up in a minute.''

The copilot and loadmaster pushed through the second door outside to the waiting truck, leaving her alone with Jack and an airman deep in paperwork at the desk.

Jack moved toward her with a loose-hipped strut, the black M-9 pistol in his web belt bringing gunslinger images to a Texas girl's mind. The weapon also engendered insidious reminders of danger when even noncombatant medical personnel like herself needed to be armed—at Jack's insistence.

He stopped in front of her, crowding her space just by being him. ''You should be in bed.''

She wasn't so far gone with her feelings that she couldn't scavenge a face-saving excuse for waiting for him. A valid one at that. ''I wanted to make sure everything's okay. I heard you moved up the flight.''

''Because of bad weather. Heavy winds expected later tonight. Only a couple hours change.'' He checked out his helmet and survival vest from the airman behind the desk.

''I thought there might be signs of moving the hostages.''

''Nope,'' he answered without even sparing her a glance. He shrugged into the webbed survival vest. He unhooked his pistol belt and transferred his M-9 to the side holster in the vest, before shifting his attention to preflighting his helmet. His hands skimmed the oxygen hose, searching for breaks or cracks, then checked for frays along the communications cord wrapped neatly around the hose.

"Jack?" she prompted, unsure whether to be worried or pissed.

He tugged the gray helmet over his head. "The possibility of the hostages being moved is always a concern, but not so much now that we're over here since we can be in the air and there before they clear the perimeter."

Crossing to the counter with the oxygen regulator check machine, Jack worked the metal bayonet snaps into the catch until the oxygen mask fit securely around his mouth.

Well, that sure as hell was one way to avoid talking.

He plugged in the regulator hose and adjusted the setting up to 30,000 to check air pressure forced through the hose. Then cranked it back down again.

She waited. He'd have to take the thing off sometime, damn it. Which he did. Only to disappear seconds later into a closet designated for testing his NVGs.

Finally he stepped out. "Monica, I don't have time for this tonight."

A valid—and obvious—excuse to dodge her.

What more did she expect? She'd set the limits and made the appointment with a divorce attorney.

Now wasn't the time to discuss more, anyway. Jack's mission was dangerous enough without a big confrontation before takeoff. She swallowed back the need to ask him if he was as confused as she was by a simple kiss when they'd done so much more in the past.

Much more. Her body reacted with a will of its own.

Yep, the Kevlar vest definitely served her well tonight.

Following him to the door, she watched him walk out into the night, not that Jack ever simply walked. Heavy combat boots ate the distance between him and the humming truck with a lazy arrogance and assurance she once would have found annoying. Yet now she knew enough about these zipper-suited sky gods she treated—knew enough about Jack— to understand that unshakable self-assurance allowed him to place his body in the line of antiaircraft fire in only an aluminum can.

Her stomach pitched. "Jack!"

He glanced back without answering, and though he looked powerfully alive right now, her job left her all too aware of mortality.

"Be careful."

"Piece of cake, babe." He vaulted onto the truck bed with the rest of his crew and the sixteen waiting SEALs.

Backing into the room as the dark soaked up the moving truck, she reminded herself that tonight he would be flying too high for antiaircraft fire to reach him. A reassurance, if it weren't for the fact she also knew his flight involved a no-lights takeoff and landing with night-vision goggles.

A flight skill only about ten percent of fliers in the squadron were qualified to perform. More medals.

More risk.

As if flying in Rubistanian airspace alone didn't provide enough cause for caution. Too many fanatics hauling shoulder-held missile launchers crept around this stretch of the Middle East, as a recent downing of one of their planes could attest.

Sure the crew had returned home alive. Eventually. After being "detained" in Rubistan until diplomatic channels cleared. Even straightforward humanitarian flights were fraught with danger.

This was not a straightforward flight.

Nodding to the airman, she strode into the hall. Night stretched out long and empty in front of her like the quiet corridor leading to her room. No matter what history she and Jack shared, or how little future they might hope to share, she knew she wouldn't be getting any sleep tonight.

She rounded the corner toward the stairs. Hairs at the base of her scalp pulled tighter on her braid. The sense of being watched tingled over her. Too strong to ignore.

Pivoting, she scanned. Looked. Found no one.

Just as she started to turn back, a shadow flickered through the yellow light. A dark form darted.

Adrenaline tingled. Monica slid her hand to her web belt. She unsnapped her military-issue 9 mm side arm.

Sleep would definitely be delayed.

Chapter 8

Monica's fingers tightened around the grip of her M-9. She considered calling out for backup, but a shout would alert the person lurking through the halls.

Slipping out of sight. Time and opportunity slipping, as well.

Flattening her back to the wall, she padded sideways. Careful not to let even a squeak of boots on tile give her away. The figure moved faster. Monica closed in until she could discern a hunched female in black garb.

"Stop and identify yourself," Monica ordered.

The woman straightened. Spun.

Yasmine. Cradling a bundle in her hands. Relief quickly faded to suspicion.

Monica abandoned stealth and confronted her sister, keeping her gun aimed on the woman she didn't know all that well. A woman ordered by Colonel Cullen to stay in her room. "What are you doing?"

Her sister's hands whipped behind her back. "Tactful as ever, sister dear."

"Drop the humor unless *you* want to be dropped." Monica leveled her weapon, not realizing until just that moment how damned much she'd wanted to believe Yasmine's request for asylum was genuine. Monica forced her 9 mm to stay steady. She would kill in defense of her country. Knew she would kill in defense of Jack.

But good God, she wasn't sure she could live with herself if she had to pull the trigger on her mother's child staring back at her with eyes in a face much like her own. "Show me what you're holding."

"You do not trust me?"

"I can't afford to." She pointed the gun. "Show me or I *will* make you. There's no doubt here but that I can."

Yasmine's hands slid around. She thrust them forward to reveal...a dress?

"I only have one change of clothes with me." Defiant pride bathed her words. "I could not hide

more when I came to work here, or people would
have been suspicious.''

''Why sneak around at night?''

Pink tinged her sister's cheeks. Yasmine blush-
ing? The brazen chick who'd been chasing poor
Colonel Cullen seven ways to Sunday?

''I only have one set of underwear. Stupid over-
sight, I know. But I was more than a little anxious
when I left. I wash at night for everything to dry
before morning. It would be...uncomfortable...to
walk around this way during the day, even if no
one could tell. I would know.''

So her sister was running around sans bra and
nobody would have guessed it? Figured Little Miss
Perfect would have perky breasts, too.

Illogical laughter tickled. ''No Band-Aids for
you, huh, kid?''

''What?''

''Nothing.''

Awkward silence blanketed the stale air between
them, minimal noise outside, a truck, the low hum
of airplane engines just prior to takeoff.

Would Yasmine recognize the sound and question the timing?

A lone voice drifted down the hall through an
open office door, Crusty patching through his
nightly call home to his family. Hopefully that
would distract Yasmine from the other echoes. His
dry laugh, jokes about the crummy food and questions to his wife about Trey's asthma, Austin's

training wheels, everyday family concerns seemed so at odds with the distance and stakes of where they were. But if they stopped life, emotions, even happiness every time their country called on them lately, there would never be time to live. A notion that made her feel slightly less guilty for wanting Jack while Sydney was suffering.

What would it be like to have a normal life alongside the high-tension existence of her job? She'd worked hard at her last relationship before Jack. For four years she'd tried with Hunter, a civilian doctor with whom she'd shared much in common. But then he'd demanded she choose between him and her job that kept them apart. The decision was heartbreakingly easy to make.

"Uh, Monica?"

She blinked clear the foggy memories. "Yes?"

Yasmine nodded toward the gun still raised and aimed. "Could you please put that away now?"

"Oh, of course. Sorry." She reholstered her weapon. Still, Yasmine didn't leave. Monica couldn't bring herself to walk away, either. The swelling rumble of jet engines outside echoed the roaring tension within her. Three hours until Jack landed.

Yasmine nodded toward the open office door. "How sweet that he calls his family. He must be very proud of his sons."

"They're actually Crusty's half brothers. His father and stepmother are dead." Monica watched for

Yasmine's reaction, some sign that her sister already knew of Crusty's connection to the assassinated ambassador to Rubistan.

Sympathy furrowed her brow. "Those poor boys. Losing both parents is…difficult…even when you're older. What happened?"

Monica shoved aside the twinge of compassion for Yasmine she couldn't afford. "Auto accident."

Assassination by local terrorists. The Rubistans definitely wanted the heat off them for that one, something that wouldn't happen if they didn't get their underground factions in control. The war on terrorism might be different from any other in history but the Rubistans knew they were skirting dangerous territory with the U.S.

"Do he and his wife have other children? What a full load that would be to take on the two young brothers, as well."

"No. They don't have any other kids." And never would due to his wife's medical condition, but that was more information than Miss Nosey needed. "Why are you so curious?"

"Just making conversation."

Chitchat? Well, hell. If her sister could try, so would she. Besides, she'd lose her mind in the next three hours, anyway, if she didn't stay occupied. For once the pesky little sister in front of her actually posed a welcome disturbance since she needed watching, anyway.

Monica waved a hand. "Follow me."

"Why?"

"I can't help you with the bra situation, but I've got some extra toiletries if you're short."

Her sister's shock almost made Monica laugh— if it wasn't so sad since she and Sydney shared everything.

"Come on," Monica ordered, bossy-big-sister authority coming in handy for once.

Up the stairs and two rooms down, Monica stopped in front of her quarters all the while trying to keep her eyes off Jack's door a few steps farther. Yasmine stood to the side, ill-disguised suspicion stamped on her brow. Monica swung the door open. "Come on in. I'm not going to put green dye in your shampoo."

Yasmine inched inside the room. Monica brushed past to her bag while her baby sister stood in the middle of the room, so still except for the slow move of her head as she looked around the converted office.

Riffling through her stacks of clothes, Monica snagged the empty Ziploc left over from sealing up her conditioner and carried it with her. She stuffed a handful of cotton balls and a tube of cherry Chap Stick inside. Digging for an extra pair of socks, her fingers brushed a box.

Of condoms.

Hell. No real need to pack them, but being the responsible one in the family was tough to shake. Given the way Yasmine was chasing Colonel Cullen, a few of those square packets might be wise. The last thing she needed was a pregnant sister on her hands.

Monica slid a handful inside before crossing into the cubicle bathroom. From the counter she plucked duplicate minibottles and dropped them into the bag.

Yasmine hovered in the open bathroom doorway. "This is very nice of you."

"It's a tube of Crest and some travel shampoo. No big deal."

"I mean nice that you thought of it." Yasmine leaned on the doorframe.

Monica's hands hesitated over an extra travel toothbrush. She always brought two in case she forgot one in the packing and unpacking from various stopovers.

Of course she never forgot.

She dropped the toothbrush inside. "You can return the favor for somebody else one day."

Monica reached for an extra comb, her eyes meeting Yasmine's in the mirror, the two sister faces framed together like the annual sibling photos their mother insisted on.

But with one face painfully absent.

For three silent seconds Monica considered confronting Yasmine, demanding to know whether she had any clue about their sister's kidnapping. Or even to try a few subtle questions...

The temptation was strong to reassure herself that

Yasmine was being honest. Logic was stronger. She couldn't afford to risk tipping Yasmine off about the rescue effort just because of a personal need for reassurance her baby sister wasn't a monster.

Yasmine cocked her head to the side. "Our mother always kept a school picture of yours," she said, her mind obviously traveling the same path. "Mother would place a new one in the frame each year. My father did not like that much. But she insisted. Just as with the visits every year."

And she was supposed to be grateful for this?

Monica pinched the Ziploc closed airtight on the first try, one of the many skills she'd picked up early keeping house on her own so people wouldn't talk about those poor motherless Hyatt girls and their trampy mother who'd run off with an oil sheik. "My relationship—" or lack thereof "—with my mother isn't your concern. In fact, it's a moot point now, anyway."

Her sister stared back silently without wincing, then continued as if Monica hadn't even spoken. "She especially liked that photo of you in the pageant. She showed everyone her beautiful daughter."

Monica couldn't contain the snort this time.

"What?"

"At least somebody found a use for those pictures." She shoved the bag toward her younger sister.

"You weren't proud of your accomplishment?" Yasmine took the bag, clutched it to her stomach.

When had a trip for toothpaste turned into a gory gut-spilling? Monica sidled past to find a sleep shirt for Yasmine. "I did it for the money. I needed it for college."

"But Mother sent you money, very much."

"I gave it all to the American Cancer Society." Prideful, sure, when it well could have cost her an education. But at the time it had seemed symbolic of cutting cancerous emotions from her life. She simply couldn't accept her mother's money. Not even her mother's actually, but from the man she'd married. The man who'd stolen another man's wife.

"That was really impractical."

"You're so damned young." Monica dropped an Atlanta Braves' T-shirt on the office chair beside her sister.

"So I keep hearing quite often these days," Yasmine mumbled, scooping up the overlong shirt.

"I understand what you're trying to do here with mending fences, and it's…nice." As much as she resented admitting it. "But you are not helping. I don't hate her, but she made a decision not to be an active part of my life a long time ago. Collecting pictures and taking a kid to the mall once a year does not make a person a parent. I respect that you love her. But you really need to back off on this subject if we're going to have any kind of civil discussions."

Snooty Yasmine returned in full force. "Am I free to go now?"

So much for the sister sharefest. Monica tried not to think of how she and Sydney would have sat cross-legged on either end of the cot sharing a bowl of popcorn while they talked about man troubles.

Monica waved her sister by without answering. Yasmine walked past, so damned quietly it was spooky sometimes. The tail end of her turquoise scarf fluttered gently.

Memories, unwelcome but persistent, nudged through of Yasmine as a child running down the airplane gangplank, whipping off her scarf and trailing it behind her like a kite.

"Yasmine?"

Her half sister turned. Waited. The scarf settled along with memories. "Yes?"

"I want to believe you about why you're here. Really I do." God, she was already in danger of losing one sister and Sydney would tell her to be kinder. Of course, Sydney always had been the bleeding heart in their family. "But I don't want it bad enough to close my eyes."

"Is that supposed to frighten me?"

Regret nicked that walls were so high between them. Yet as much as she wished they could be closer, wished they could cry together for Sydney, Monica couldn't risk doing anything that might expose the rescue mission. "It's not like we have that much history for some deep bond or sisterly trust. I don't know you. You don't know me. As long as you're straight up, there's not a problem."

Yasmine tucked the bag and shirt closer to her chest. "I guess that means I will not be bunking at your place when I get to the United States."

A scary thought. Regret scratched deeper. "Did you plan to?"

"No. After I arrive, I will call Sydney." Yasmine turned and left, scarf fluttering defiantly behind her.

Monica accepted the emotional stab delivered with Sydney's name as a reminder of priorities. And dealing with emotional baggage from Yasmine just couldn't be a priority with life-and-death stakes in the balance.

Blake drew heavy hits off the oxygen mask plugged into the C-17 cruising at high altitude out over the gulf. Chuted up and ready to roll, he regulated his breathing in time with the steady drone of engines. His fifteen SEAL buddies sat in file beside him.

Red lights bathed the metal tunnel with a hellish glow. Figures blotted the image. Dark. Moldy. Like in the countless caves in Afghanistan where he'd worked SSE—sensitive site exploitation. Then the endless tunnels under Baghdad. Constant risk of cave-ins and booby traps whittled away at nerves until a man finally figured out how to shut down feeling altogether.

A skill he longed for now.

The metal walls threatened to close in on him, to

fill his brain and nose with cobwebs until it shut off air. He forced oxygen in. Out. Routine.

How many times had he done this? Flown in countless cargo holds of C-17s, C-130s, even dropping out of the bomb bay of a B-52 once for a HALO.

Today's agenda: a HAHO—high altitude, high opening, on oxygen while they cruised. Guide the chute for over an hour for a covert insertion. Land a couple miles shy of the terrorist compound.

He breathed. In. Out. Always remembering their axiom.

Quitting is not an option.

His head fell back and he stared up at the tangle of cables and wires tracking the ceiling. If only he could recapture the numbness. Instead, memories stalked him, slipping past his defenses...

He didn't want much from the afternoon at Virginia Beach. Some beer. Sun. Maybe luck into a woman's smile directed his way.

After five months of no sex, no alcohol and a belly full of MREs mixed with SSE cave crawling in Afghanistan, he was due a little R and R during his two weeks of leave. And Virginia Beach's annual Neptune Festival seemed the perfect place to start.

Weaving through the crush of tourists at the outdoor booths, Blake walked silently alongside two of his team buddies while Carlos talked and scoped babes in bikinis. Silence suited him fine. Always had. Sometimes he and his uncle could go days without saying a word during the summer. Work on the farm. Eat. Read. Go to sleep.

No need for conversation.

Sex, on the other hand. He sure as hell wouldn't mind some of that in the near future.

Twins with matching belly button rings glided by on Rollerblades. Hoo-ya.

And apparently, from his buddies' conversation, they wouldn't mind, either—both recently divorced. Military deployments wreaked hell on relationships. A guy was better off not expecting the sex to turn into anything more, only to find out he'd been dumped while deployed and didn't even know it until port call.

He wasn't in a hurry to settle down, and when he did it would be for keeps. White picket fence, wife, kids, a forever haven.

Blake fished in his front pocket for more tickets to buy another beer, and came up short. "Be back in a minute," he called as he tugged his wallet out of the back pocket of his jean shorts.

Pulling out a twenty, he tucked sideways past a family, sidestepping back to avoid being hit by their wagon with a toddler inside.

His butt bumped a booth. Turning to apologize, he found a woman at a fund-raising table with her head bowed while she cracked open a roll of quarters on her cash tray.

She looked up. "Can I help you?"

And that was it. He fell hard and fast in spite of three seconds earlier being certain happily-ever-after was at least five or more years away once he quit active field ops. He could almost feel the hammer in his hand as he nailed pickets into the ground.

He'd seen prettier. He'd had hotter. But never had he met someone so damned sexy and perfect.

Her short brown hair lifted around her face with the wind blowing in off the ocean. Even sitting, she didn't seem too tall or too short in comparison to the older woman working next to her. Average height, slim body with hints of understated curves in khaki shorts and an Earth-Day T-shirt. Brown eyes and brown hair.

She was maybe a couple years older than him, with even features in a slim face. Nothing out of the ordinary. Yet, here he stood like an infatuated dork checking out her bare ring finger while sweaty tourists jostled past him.

"Can I help you?" she repeated with a smile.

Her lips weren't particularly sultry, but somehow that just made him want to kiss them until they plumped.

He made his move. "Go to lunch with me—" he paused to glance down at her name tag "—Sydney."

She blinked fast, startled but not outwardly offended. Hoo-ya. He had enough challenges on the job. For once, he wanted something in his life that was simple. Straightforward. Uncomplicated.

She emptied quarters into the tray. "I don't know your name."

"Blake Gardner. I'll even leave ID and a blood sample with your friend."

She laughed, a light gliding sound that blew away cobwebs. "I have to work the booth. I only just got here."

"When does your shift end?"

"At four."

Three hours from now.

The older woman in a soccer-mom shirt next to Sydney leaned closer. "Or when she sells out her roll of tickets."

"Fair enough." Blatantly canvasing or not, the woman had offered him a three-hour reprieve.

Blake emptied his wallet of two hundred dollars and thanked the sweet Lord in heaven for credit cards or this would be a bust date from the get-go.

Sydney shoved his money back to him. "This is incredibly generous, but I would feel bad. We can just meet at four."

"What kind of fund-raiser for the—" he glanced down at the plastic drape over the front of her table and read "—National Wildlife Fund are you, lady?"

He turned to his soccer-mom ally and passed his money, garnering himself a roll of tickets that he promptly gave to a young mother standing behind him in line with two children.

Sydney laughed away a few more of his cobwebs. "You're good."

He sure hoped so. "Where do you want to go for lunch?"

She shoved to her feet. Hoo-ya. And snagged up her purse. "How about I treat you to lunch and we can both watch the air show together since you just gave away two hundred dollars' worth of chances to win a new truck?"

A truck? Ouch. But well worth it for a chance with Sydney. "Sounds great."

Filing in beside her, he knew they wouldn't go home together tonight, but would one day soon once they knew each other better. Something he intended to accelerate as fast as he could.

"Texas?" he asked her as they neared the hot dog vendor's cart.

"Pardon me?"

"Is that Texas I hear in your accent?"

"Red Branch, born and bred."

"I'm from a small Midwest town, too, a little more north. Missouri."

"Are you vacationing here, then?"

"No. I live here, and I sure as hell hope you do, too."

Again she laughed, filling his brain with a sound he would never forget. "I do. My job's here. And what is it that you do?"

* * *

An elbow caught Blake in the belly from his swim buddy. Carlos flashed him a thumbs-up with a questioning look. *You ready?*

Wordless communication came easily after so many missions together.

Nodding, answers stuck under cobwebs in his throat, Blake shook off the past and stood, the boulderlike weight of his gear not nearly as heavy as the weight in his chest. He disconnected from the plane's oxygen and opened his own.

What did he do? she'd asked. He was a Navy SEAL. Always. To the core. Something he should have made clear to Sydney from the start. But mentioning the full extent of his occupation to strangers wasn't safe. He'd simply told her that he was in the Navy and changed the subject while gathering up their food and popping a French fry into her mouth.

Not that he'd wanted to talk about it then, anyway, his brain still cobwebbed full of the intense months in Afghanistan.

Blake filed in with the rest of the SEALs, straddle-walk waddling under the weight of their gear. The load ramp lowered, gaped to reveal inky night sky. Four abreast in rows, they stopped at the top of the ramp. Dark sky, roaring wind and turbulence waited to swallow him.

He was a SEAL. Something he still believed in, cobwebs and all, even if somewhere along the line he'd forgotten how to believe in white picket fences.

* * *

Jack piloted his empty plane back to base, SEALs offloaded. That much closer to finished. A good thing, but also a reminder time was running out with Monica. He was making progress in getting to her by being patient, keeping some distance.

But would it be enough?

He clenched the stick, easing it forward to descend as they put miles between themselves and the parachuting SEALs. That left another half hour to relax with clear flying into the night sky before strapping on NVGs for the no-lights landing.

Rodeo flipped through pages in his flight data log before finding the correct one and pulling his clipped pen free of the ring. "You okay, man?"

"Yep."

"Uh-huh." Rodeo grunted an unconvinced response while jotting in the book. "I'm here, ya know. If you want to talk."

"You've been watching too much 'Dr. Phil' when you're TDY. There's nothing to talk about." Frustration swelled in the dark cockpit.

"Well, now we both know that's not true. You can't let it weigh you down in the workplace."

"I'm doing my job. Back off."

"Can't do that."

Anger at life overflowed toward Rodeo. "You're a helluva one to talk about spilling my guts here. You wanna talk about screwed-up relationships? Feel free to start."

Rodeo continued to write without looking up. "Since we're friends—and twenty thousand feet in the air—I won't punch you."

"Try later, if you're so moved. I haven't been in a good bar fight for at least seven months." Since Monica came into his life and he had a reason to clean up his act and better things to do with his time.

"You want me to talk first, hell, I'll talk." Rodeo stopped writing, hooked the pen on the edge of his data book. "Thing is, my situation is a no-go. No chance. I think you may have a window to fix this mess you're in if you'll try."

Jack kept eyes front on the opaque sky. "Who says I'm not trying?"

"Is it working? Are you two back together?"

"Hell, no."

"Gotta be tough working in the same place, watching each other move on."

"Like hell," Jack muttered. "She won't be moving on anytime soon."

The plane's rumble filled the silence for a five count before Rodeo said, "Run that by me again."

"Nothing."

"Not gonna wash, man."

Finally, Jack let three and a half months of hell out. "A divorce takes time."

"Divorce?" Rodeo snapped the binder closed. "Good God, Korba, that 'wife' thing back at the

Warrior Inn in Nevada was true? Holy crap. You weren't just holding out details on a little argument here. You two eloped and then… What?''

Monica would have his ass if she found out he told, but damn it, he needed a sounding board and his crew mentality rebelled at the whole solo act. A guy had a wingman for a reason. He trusted Rodeo with his life on a regular basis. Why not on this, too? ''We didn't exactly elope.''

''Exactly what, then?''

His memory of the surroundings might be hazy, but his determination that night to tie himself to Monica before she slipped away remained clear as water. ''Downed a bottle of tequila and ended up shit-faced in an Elvis chapel.''

Rodeo's cheeks twitched with restrained laughter.

''Go ahead and laugh. Hell, I've laughed at my own dumb-ass self often enough the past three and a half months.''

''Three and a half months? You've held out telling me that long?'' Rodeo slapped a hand over his heart. ''Man, I think I'm hurt.''

''It's easier to talk about crap that doesn't matter.''

The copilot's hand slid from his chest along with the humor from his eyes. ''That it is, my friend. That it is.''

Engines droned. The radio chatter crackled in his

helmet. The night sky scrolled ahead and for all the confiding, nothing had changed. No answers, and he couldn't dodge the feeling he'd betrayed Monica.

He switched back to work mentality, instructor mode. Training never ended. Fewer land mines waited there, anyway. "Hey, Rodeo, time for a little training. If we got hit right now, where would we land?"

Thank God Rodeo took the hint, not that he really had a choice as the junior crew member. He twisted in his seat, reaching for a chart. "I'll have the answer for ya in a second."

"A second isn't good enough. You should already know at any given time." He always needed a lock on the best place to land and evade until pickup. Even in "safe" Rubistan, local tribes could still nab them first. "And, Rodeo, the answer is Thumrait. We'd land there."

If only the answers with Monica were as easy to calculate.

Yet hadn't she kissed him? Waited for him? Her clean aloe scent teased into his memory along with the taste of her when they'd kissed. Progress? Maybe, but then he'd realized how much more he wanted for her, all or nothing. Win or lose, no in between, in what promised to be a tough-as-hell battle without much of a foundation to withstand the storm in the making.

No trust either way. He realized now that it

hadn't been there to start with or they would have told each other more.

Easier to tell crap that didn't matter.

In a splash of further realization as blinding as a floodlight for a guy wearing NVGs, it hit him why she hadn't told him about Yasmine. Because it mattered. It hurt too damned much.

Exactly the same reason he hadn't told her about Tina.

He would have sworn he was over losing her. God, it was fifteen years ago. Yet right now he could almost feel the pinch of a bandage being ripped from an old wound only to find the whole damned thing had festered under the protective covering.

Froot Loops. Things from the past dogged a person no matter what. He wasn't over Tina's death. The cut-off-at-the-knees pain of it burned all over again from being exposed, leaving him in need of somewhere to hide out alone to lick his wounds until he could put himself back together again.

And in that one-second flash, his problems doubled to a pair of women in his head. And no one in his bed.

Chapter 9

Knowing she should be in bed didn't stop Monica from waiting for Jack. She'd met with Crusty about Yasmine, checked in with the command post about the drop, even watched Jack's plane land. He was fine, the mission a success, not that she expected anything less from him.

Standing outside his room to catch him after debrief, she told herself she was waiting around to tell him about Yasmine. She knew better.

She needed his level steadiness to settle her world after the conversation with her youngest sister. While Jack's I-don't-give-a-shit attitude often drove her crazy, other times she envied his ability to shrug things off. He didn't dwell or let stuff out of his control bother him.

Froot Loop memories. He accepted life's quirks, banging back a handful of cereal while acknowledging he didn't like little planes. No apologies or mad dash for a shrink to analyze for possible claustrophobia. Adapt. Move on.

He knew how to let go of his past.

She needed that now. So much. God help her, she was slowly beginning to wonder if she needed Jack.

And there he was, all wide shoulders and hard angles, with the sweaty swirl of dark hair along his brow. Jack strode down the hall, Rodeo behind with a pensive frown marring his normally suave, unflappable demeanor.

Jack turned to his copilot. ''Go ahead without me and you can have first dibs on the shower.''

Rodeo thumped him on the back. ''Take it easy, man.''

The copilot skated one more curious glance Monica's way before circling past and into the two-man room.

Jack didn't move, making Monica come to him, an odd sensation after so long of always finding him in her face and space. As if drawn by a magnet, she stepped closer, closer still until she stopped short. Intensity radiated from him, something dark, alien, even a little mean and so unlike Jack. His stand-back vibes created boundaries around him until the magnet feeling suddenly shifted poles to propel her away.

What the hell was going on? "Is everything all right?"

"Just fine." He swiped a hand through his sweaty hair creased from a serious case of helmet-head. "You could have just hung out in the command post to hear how things went."

"I already did that."

"Then why are you here?"

His abrupt tone acted like a cold splash over her. Was the thrill of the chase gone? She'd started to weaken so now he didn't care anymore? Damn but that possibility bit. Even while she'd predicted it might happen, she couldn't stomach the thought that the past seven months had meant that little to him.

Still pride was difficult to subdue. She refused to be like any of the ex-live-ins her father had gone through, red-eyed, weeping women jamming possessions into a suitcase once her father booted the woman out for becoming too needy. "I found Yasmine wandering around the halls after you left."

"Was she coming out of the Colonel's room?"

"God, no."

"Then I wouldn't worry about it. She can't leave, and everything important is sealed tight." He shuffled from boot to boot, eyeing his door, obviously wanting the hell away from her ASAP.

Damn him. Well, he could just sit tight for five

freaking seconds and answer her questions. She wasn't going to bolt off into her room next door like some intimidated rabbit. "What if she's not being straight up?"

"She's being watched. There's really not much more we can do than that except shunt her back into the Rubistanian community after we're through. Which of course could put us in sticky diplomatic waters because of her mother."

"I realize all of that, and I'm trying like hell not to let my bias against her affect the way I'm thinking." She mentally counted to cool her temper at Jack as well as Yasmine. "She said she was washing her spare set of clothes."

"Anything else?"

She crossed her arms under her breasts. "Not anything important."

His eyes fell to her chest. Interest flickered. "Okay, I'll mention it to Keagan and Crusty at the next briefing."

"Thank you."

He pivoted away. Double damn him.

Then his shoulders fell. With a sigh that sounded more like a snarl of self-disgust, he turned back. "What's wrong?"

"Don't put yourself out on my account," she couldn't resist muttering.

"Mon, I'm in a shitty mood. Doesn't happen often, but that's how it is tonight. So if you have something else to say, spill it now before I turn into a really surly son of a bitch.''

Kind of felt like he was halfway there already.

Her arms fell back to her sides. ''Why do I feel like such a grown-up tattletale?''

He leaned so close she thought for a moment he might kiss her. Instead his face blanked of emotion. ''It's all about the Froot Loops, babe. And how the past has a helluva way of coming right back to cut us off at the knees when we least expect it.''

Jack strode three paces past her to open the door to her quarters and waited for her to step inside. Standing in her gaping doorway, she watched Jack pivot, disappear into his room.

Babe. Pushing her away. Leaving her alone. But wasn't that what she'd asked for over the past months? For Jack to leave her be and quit pushing her to give more because she wasn't ready. She wasn't sure. She didn't trust her judgment around a man who scrambled her brains until she couldn't think. And without her reason, what was she?

Alone.

Her mama's voice whispered in the vented air wafting down the empty hall. *Watch out what you wish for, sugar. You might just get it.*

Life seemed to be granting her wishes in double doses these days.

Yasmine tipped her face to absorb the warmth of the midday sun, strolling across the cracked cement, ever aware of not one but both of her latest escorts. Crusty and his OSI friend walked a discreet but undeniable distance behind her.

She had wanted safety. Too bad neither of them was the escort she preferred. She was not sure whether to blame the Colonel because of their chat in the hangar the day before. Or if the escorts came due to Monica and their late-night run-in. Either way, she couldn't breathe even with a wide expanse of uninterrupted desert stretching in front of her.

Refusing to allow anyone to destroy her brief respite from the steaming kitchen, she resolved to soak up every remaining moment of what could be her final days in her homeland. Not that she actually had to work anymore according to the intelligence persons. But she was afraid of stirring talk among any of the other hired locals in case one might be spying for Ammar.

She shuddered in spite of the heat. No question, leaving this place was the right thing to do, but still an odd homesickness already tore at her soul. There was much to love about Rubistan, rich in ancient heritage and stark beauty.

Unlike the sweltering kitchen. Ugh! A detestable place.

Adjusting the drape of her favorite rose scarf, Yasmine stole a covert peek at the OSI officer with Crusty. Intelligence officers in her country certainly never looked like this man. Other intelligence personnel visiting her country either wore suits or, in more informal settings like this, wore khakis with a nondescript shirt. This man paired his pants with a shirt in outrageous colors, lime-green today, as if he did not mind drawing attention to himself. With his sun-bleached, spiked hair he looked more like a beach boy than an operative.

Excellent disguise. She could take lessons from him.

Her feet carried her farther, toward the buzz of voices. Toward one voice in particular she tried to tell herself she did not recognize right up until the moment the man came into sight.

Colonel Cullen's closeness back in the hangar had left her off balance. Surely if she watched him from a distance that would not be so obvious. And truth be told, she did not know if she was ready for another such conversation with him.

She had expected to trust him. She had not expected to like the sound of his voice. The rasp of his wit. The touch of his hands.

Did he sense her presence as she did his? She certainly could not tell from his attitude. He didn't even glance her way while he talked to his fellow officers.

Irritation itched more than her air-dried dress. Surely the clothing washed in harsh detergent and dried over a chair in her room had to be the reason her skin suddenly chafed, oversensitive to each brush of fabric.

She stopped. Two pairs of feet behind her stopped, as well.

How ridiculous to pretend they were not there. Why not speak to them? Yes, they could sit here in the sun and talk. Nothing wrong with that, even if it happened to be close to where a certain rugged colonel met with his men.

"Gentlemen?" she called over her shoulder.

She could almost hear their confusion. She stifled a laugh. "Come walk with me and save yourselves the trouble of trying to keep up."

"No trouble, ma'am," Crusty answered, ambling forward, the ever-present wrinkles in his flight suit rippling as he walked. "No trouble at all."

Because she had not tried to make trouble. She may not have been able to lose them, but most definitely could have made them work.

However, her survival instincts recognized these men were not to be toyed with. As much as she told herself they would not resort to painful measures to subdue her, she was not willing to take the risk she might be wrong.

Suspicions did not fade easily. Getting to know her jailers would be wise.

Yasmine trailed her fingers along the rough exterior wall, flecking paint free, moving nearer to the end of the airport building. Nearer to voices. The Colonel's voice rode the wind toward her as he talked to two other men while four soldiers climbed to the one-story roof, a line of a hundred more filing alongside the building.

The four men…ran toward the edge?

Yasmine gasped. "Why are they doing that?"

Crusty tipped up his sunglasses and searched. "Doing what?"

She pointed toward the four lunatics hurtling through the air toward the sandy earth. Landing. Rolling to their sides. Ouch! "Jumping off the building. Falling down."

Laughing, Crusty dropped his aviator shades back into place. "Parachute training. Practicing their PLF—parachute landing fall. They're using the one-story, flat roof as a makeshift PLF platform."

"Fall? That seems silly. Why not land on your feet?"

"Because you might shatter your ankles or knees. Falling to the side in a controlled manner helps absorb the shock of the landing by distributing it out among different body parts." Crusty reached into the leg pocket of his flight suit, pulled out a small pack of peanuts. "Ever lay on a bed of nails? Same principle."

He proffered the snack bag her way in an obvious attempt to change the subject. "Want some?"

"No thank you." She watched the soldiers roll to their feet again and dust sand from their uniforms. "I thought these soldiers were only here to distribute food and medical aid."

"We all need to stay up on our parachuting skills." Crusty pitched back a handful of peanuts while the OSI officer silently pierced her soul with all-knowing, sea-green eyes.

She kept her gaze steady on Crusty, a man who never seemed to stop eating. Perhaps she could pry information out of him with a cookie—baked by someone other than herself, of course. "These are some of your Airborne Rangers, then?"

Crusty walked alongside, crunching peanuts, assessing her with narrow-eyed suspicion before answering. "Soldiers other than Rangers can be airborne qualified. Regardless, we always train. Always. What we do is dangerous even if it's a simple humanitarian run. And of course we're always working to be mission ready for the worst."

Her gaze locked on the Colonel's broad back in mottled tan camouflage as she wondered how shoulders that seemed so invincible seconds before now had mortality etched across them. "What if one of them breaks his leg and can not work?"

"Better his leg than his life from lack of training."

"But can't they die in training, too?" How many odds had the Colonel defied over the years?

"It happens. A reality of a dangerous job. But training hard under controlled circumstances keeps our casualties lower, and ultimately keeps far more of us alive in combat."

"Are not the higher-ups in service like Colonel

Cullen exempt from these dangerous training exercises?''

''Well, no doubt a commander becomes valuable for the overall knowledge he has, the cohesiveness his leadership gives to a unit. But he still has to perform in the field.'' Crusty pointed his half-eaten bag of peanuts toward the Colonel. ''The Regimental Commander over there, for example. Above all, he's still an Army soldier. Airborne qualified. No different from an aviator wing commander staying current on his flight status. He may not fly as often—or in this case, jump—but he still has to be qualified. And he'd better not screw up in front of his men or his credibility is shot to hell, which means there goes the unit cohesiveness if they can't trust their leader.''

Which meant her colonel still threw himself out of airplanes, an image that thrilled and scared her all at once with how much the man already affected her emotions.

And she didn't even know his first name.

What a stressful way to live. ''Your wife is all right with this?''

''She's a special lady.''

This man was definitely taken, and happily so until it almost stirred envy. ''Did you have a nice conversation with your wife and little brothers last night?''

Crusty's smile fled. The bag crumpled in his hand. Brown eyes hardened to a lethal flatness of a predatory male who would kill to protect his own. "Yes."

His protective urges were admirable. Once he and his wife had babies of their own, they would never be left vulnerable.

Of course his territorial manner was dangerous for her at the moment. There were many things she would consider doing to protect herself, but endangering a child did not number among those alternatives. Of course he did not know that and she would have to reassure him if she expected any further conversation. "I know Monica and her major told you about my midnight walks. I heard you on the phone."

His stance relaxed slightly, but not totally. "With the time change, it's easier on my wife if I call during the night here. I don't like to disturb her sleep."

"That is very thoughtful of you." Not all men were as sensitive to a woman's comfort. Was his wife ill? Or was he genuinely that considerate a husband? She continued to stroll in an effort to give her questions a less obvious air. "And your boys would be awake then, too. Children can be so grumpy when their schedules are disrupted."

As she had well learned during her annual childhood flights to America. Just when she lost the foggy feeling, she found herself on the return flight to Rubistan.

Crusty swept a palm branch out of the way for her to pass. "Do you have children?"

"No." A fact she mourned would never happen, but did not want a husband that would come with the baby.

Since Crusty did not seem likely to budge on his tight-lipped protective stance in talking about his family, she shifted her attention from the rumpled pilot to her spiky-haired escort from the OSI.

"What about you? Do you have someone at home to call?"

At her question, Max Keagan jerked, his sea-green eyes widening. Like a man being stalked, he stepped back from the perceived predator.

A giggle bubbled, but she suppressed it. "No need to worry." She angled closer. "I do not have designs on your neon-green shirt."

No, sir. Her attention gravitated toward desert camouflage these days. Surely only in her imagination could she distinguish his deep rumble from the collective swell of masculine voices drifting from a hundred yards away.

"I have a fiancée."

"Congratulations." She sagged back against a palm tree trunk. "When is the wedding?"

"No firm date, yet."

Not a chatty man, and she could not hide from the fact she wanted an excuse to stay out here where she could see the Colonel.

Crusty stepped into the conversational hole. "His

fiancée is also in the military." He offered bare essentials. "Scheduling is hell. My guess is we'll all get about ten minutes notice that they're ready to get hitched."

Crusty's comment elicited the first grin from the spiky-haired man. "There are plenty of folks who would pay good money to see me in a tux. Wonder if they make pineapple-patterned cummerbunds?"

Yasmine laughed, couldn't help herself after so long of holding back from any kind of emotion. With restraints lowering, thoughts of opposites blending filled her mind, uniform and unconventional, different worlds coexisting.

Silk scarves and starched uniforms mingling.

A shiver tickled through her at the sensual image. And for a moment in the middle of a stark airfield, she let herself dream and laugh.

Drew planted his boots to prep himself as more of Yasmine's laughter drifted in the gritty wind. Sure as shit, that tinkling sound slammed into him with all the force of a grenade.

Watching her flirt with the two younger men while he tried to listen to a captain detailing a duty roster, Drew told himself he didn't give a damn. He reminded himself this should be exactly what he wanted, hell, had even asked for since telling her to take her scarves and all-out smile elsewhere.

She hadn't stopped turning up anywhere he found himself, but she no longer spoke to him. A whole twenty-four hours and he was already pouting like a kid.

He closed his eyes, pressed his forefinger and thumb to the bridge of his nose. If only he could stop seeing a rose silk scarf in his head.

Rose? The sun must be cooking his brain, a common enough occurrence around this woman.

Since when had he started noticing what women wore? And pink was pink, damn it. Not rose. Next thing he knew, he'd be watching the fashion network and whipping out a credit card for a *fuchsia* scarf.

He may not be the most creative Joe Sensitive on the planet, but he knew his job and his place. He nodded to whatever the hell it was the captain just said, eyes on the four Rangers flinging their bodies through the air, landing. Damn near perfect.

Except damn near wasn't good enough.

Next thing he knew, his boot jammed itself in the porch latticework while he hauled himself up. "Follow me, boys."

He might be getting old but he was *not* going soft.

"Break your ankle practicing and you won't be any good to anybody. Break your ankle out there in the field and you're gonna be a liability to your fellow soldier who'll risk his life to carry you out." He jerked a thumb toward young Santuci. "Keep an eye on the private here."

Santuci beamed like a star pupil. Kid wasn't much older.

Drew lined up beside Santuci. "You ready, Private?"

"Uh—" his Adam's apple bobbed "—you're gonna jump, too, sir?"

"I have done this once or twice before."

"No disrespect meant, sir."

"None taken." Sometimes a commander had to remind his troops he'd been in the same trenches. Walked the same walk. He wasn't doing this to impress some woman.

"Anytime, sir."

"Hoo-uh." Two sets of boots pounded the roof, nearing the edge, flat desert sprawling ahead through hazy heat waves.

Airborne!

Launching himself, he focused on the horizon, on her scarf. And God, but it sure was rose and pretty and called to him like a beacon as he flew through the muggy air, a sensation of freedom as damned incredible as it had been the first time he launched himself over twenty years ago.

He landed, instincts carrying him through the PLF to absorb the shock of impact—balls of the feet, roll to the thigh, the ass, up the arm to the shoulder.

He sprung to his feet. *Hoo-uh!*

His knees shouted back in response.

Shit, that hurt. He schooled his features and suppressed a wince as the pain shot from his time-battered knees all the way to his teeth.

And then his men gathered around him blocking Yasmine from sight. Smiles and backslaps, hoo-uhs and grunts jam-packed the air.

Hell, yeah. This is what it was all about, how he liked his life, and he needed to remember that. The camaraderie. Unity. Not about posturing like some young stud on the make for a woman he wasn't even interested in having.

Didn't want?

Damn. All right. He wanted her. But that didn't mean he'd left behind rational thought.

Drew dug in his pocket, found the LifeSavers and thumbed one into his mouth, sucked back a curse and the throbbing in his knees echoed by a far more painful one a few inches north of his knees. He definitely wasn't twenty-five anymore.

And if he were twenty-five now? Newly divorced, with a solid set of knees and a recklessness time hadn't had a chance to beat out of him. What would he think of Yasmine if they'd met then? A damned ridiculous thought since she would have been six, for God's sake.

But what if?

The answer rushed in without hesitation. If they were closer in age, he would already have her scarf off and his hands in her hair, working his way toward persuading her to let his body be inside hers.

The applause faded along with hoo-uhs as his

men resumed their training exercise. But Yasmine hadn't moved. Wasn't laughing.

Wasn't talking to her two young escorts anymore.

She stared straight at him, breathing faster in rapid bursts that lifted the gentle curves of breasts against her dress in a passionate rhythm of arousal. Damned if the ache in his knees didn't fade right that minute and it was all he could do not to climb back on the roof.

And double damned if he didn't feel a little like he was already flying, anyway.

Damn but he wished he were flying.

Parked in a seat at the mobile command center, Jack twitched his boot against the metal underpinnings of the console on a pallet down the belly of the plane. Close-up intelligence gathering from the SEALs for the next couple of days was crucial, though, so he would just have to cool his jets.

His shitty mood from the night before simmered on the back burner. Only completing this mission would clear his mind enough to deal with it. Three screens hummed in front of him, just like at the other eleven stations manned by military representatives from each service in the joint mission, maintaining databases, ensuring comm links remained up and working.

Colonel Cullen sat across from him, slowly

drinking from a coffee mug with the words "It's All About the Hoo-Uh" stenciled across.

Jack's dual flat-screen color monitors contained intel on one side, maps on the other. A smaller six-by-six, black-and-white monitor perched above with continuous feed from the Predator unmanned spy drone.

Monitoring went on pretty much 24/7 now to make sure the hostages weren't moved, but the daily walk time was of particular interest. They logged with interest the one time of day they were assured the hostages still lived.

That Monica's sister still lived.

Dusk approached. Predator images scrolled by, over the locale where coordinates indicated two SEALs lay completely camouflaged in their desert ghillie suits—strips of tan cammo and mesh that resembled a desert swamp thing monster. Effective as hell. Someone could pee right on them and never know.

The rest of the SEALs were holed up two miles back in a bunker dug out of a knob dune. Once the sun set, the pair—Blake and his swim buddy Carlos—would start recon along the compound's perimeter for intel. But now they waited silently with their handheld parabolic satellite dish sending back any sound from the compound.

Unusually little sound.

"Control," Gardner's voice echoed through, "the place is too damned quiet."

"Hold steady," Jack answered. "I show a human target at your two o'clock. Looks like a sentry. He's lighting up a smoke."

"Roger that."

Lighting a cigarette screwed with night vision for valuable seconds, crucial info to be exploited for a point of entry on a recon run after dark.

"Predator three-seven," Jack called to the pilot and his sensor operator flying the unmanned spy drone by remote from Indian Springs Auxiliary Airfield in Nevada, "how many do they have stationed around the northeast guard tower?"

"Only the one," the sensor operator answered, his job being to interpret data and adjust the pilot's remote-control flight path accordingly.

Catching some fresh movement on the screen, Jack keyed up the mike to transmit to the SEAL pair. "Check your six o'clock. Truck moving toward the front gate. Looks like…just a dump truck. Gravel and some rocks in the back."

An airman at the end of the console chuckled. "Maybe they're going to build themselves an outhouse."

"Hey, not bad," an Army lieutenant answered, "or some kind of Zen rock garden to spruce up the place."

As much as Jack couldn't find the laugh within himself, he knew these guys needed the release from stress. Everyone was tense, ready to roll, in need of an outlet for all the pent-up energy. Hell, the Rangers were even jumping from rooftops.

"Truck's clear of the gate," Jack informed the SEALs, then straightened sharply. "Okay, heads up, people. We have some serious activity."

The SEAL pair stayed silent except for louder breathing, heavy, but steady.

On the screen, figures poured from brick and cement buildings, men, women, at least a hundred, most armed with machine guns and rifles carried as casually as a businessman's briefcase. "We've got some kind of gathering in the works. Not the regular afternoon walk."

The dump truck rumbled down a central dirt road until it reached the compound's main square. A groundbreaking ceremony?

Another door opened from a small cement outbuilding. Three stepped out. Two men. One woman covered in a burkah from head to toe. Jack shifted in the unrelenting seat, not liking one damned bit the bad feeling creeping over him faster than a debilitating rapid decompression.

And liking even less the gaping pit dug in the center of the town square.

"Oh, shit," the young airman at the end of the console whispered.

"What? What the hell's going on? Over." Gardner's voice demanded an answer and carried an edge that made Jack leery as all get-out of giving him the obvious one.

Someone was about to get stoned. A woman, because only men in this region were sometimes granted the faster execution of beheading.

And there wasn't a thing they could do to stop it. With chilling horror, it would unroll before his eyes, his mind already three steps ahead because of all the briefings he'd received on the region in the past.

There wouldn't be a mob-frenzy-style stoning like movie dramas perpetuated. Reality was far worse. Far more calculated. Coldly barbaric. A token stone was thrown, usually by an old man, and then a dump truck unloaded rocks and cement onto the condemned up to her neck until she was crushed to death.

Who would be placed in that pit?

Sweat iced on his brow. He'd tried to prepare himself for the possibility Sydney might die. But, God, he couldn't stomach it being this way. Not Sydney. And damn it all, not this hell for Monica to have to think about for the rest of her life.

He and the Colonel exchanged glances over the console, then back down again to their screens. The image continued of two men hauling the woman toward the pit, bound her hands and feet, then dropped her in.

The crowd roared. No way would Gardner and his partner miss that, too far to see or help, but damn well close enough to hear even without the parabolic dish.

The dump truck rolled to a stop, jerked, shifted into reverse and repositioned until it idled, butt facing the pit. Gardner's insistent questions gained speed while an airman stalled with excuses of interrupted satellite feed.

Jack couldn't escape the cold sense of kinship with Gardner, since he knew too well the nightmare of being helpless while the woman he loved died. Even if this wasn't Sydney, there would still be an endless wait until the Predator could pick up fresh footage of her or the SEALs risked slipping in to check.

As much as he tried to tell himself that Tina had been fragile and Monica was the strongest woman he'd ever met, the current situation unfolding in front of his eyes reminded him everyone was vulnerable sometime.

And women were most especially vulnerable here.

"Damn it, Control," Gardner's words grated through, "do you read me? Update needed. Now! Over."

Jack clicked computer keys, typing a chat room message over to the Colonel that wouldn't be overheard by Gardner. *Your call as the senior officer in charge, sir. But Gardner's gonna go ballistic.*

Something they all knew would happen, anyway.

Meanwhile their only hope of containing him came through reason, the truth, and the hope that his partner Carlos could restrain him.

Colonel Cullen nodded, slowly replaced his mug beside him, steady, rock-solid in spite of the tight cut of his clenched jaw, and keyed up his mike. "People, this is Alpha. Everyone settle. It appears they're about to hold a public execution."

Chapter 10

Execution?

The response popped through Blake's earpiece. Landed in his stomach like a cold stone as he lay flat on his belly in a shallow desert trench.

Stone.

Damn poor word choice. Shut down emotions. Quitting was not an option.

"Man or woman?" Blake grunted into the small boom mike at the corner of his mouth even though he already knew the answer because of that dump truck full of rocks.

"Female," Colonel Cullen answered.

The confirmation burned hotter than the setting sun.

Gaze jerky, Blake scanned the desert to the chain-link fence with concertina wire barbs spiraling the top. About two football fields away, he could discern the crowd. Barely, but he was mostly at the mercy of visuals supplied by command post with his team buddy sweating beside him in his desert tan ghillie suit until his streaked face paint slicked.

"Is it one of ours?" Blake forced the question out, refusing to let his mind create the image of Sydney dropped into a stoning pit in the center of some godforsaken backwoods town square.

The moment's hesitation from the stalwart colonel scared the shit out of him.

Finally the headset crackled. "We can't tell. She's completely covered."

He swallowed down grit-laden dread and the memory of Sydney's pretty smile the day they'd met. It wasn't her. He wouldn't let it be.

His parabolic dish picked up sound, threw it to the satellite and bounced it back through transmitters into his earpiece. The roar of the crowd. A declaration in Arabic.

He tried to tell himself they wouldn't carry out the barbaric punishment. Many governments in the region had outlawed the practice.

This wasn't a government.

The need to charge ahead built. Surged. Pressed. He could all but feel her presence somewhere in that crowd. So damned close. Not close enough. "Plan of action?"

"Hold steady," the Colonel commanded quietly. "Direct action is not called for."

Like hell. Quitting was not an option. Blake exploded from his low pit and scrambled forward before he finished forming the intent.

Weight tackled his back. Two hundred and thirty pounds of Carlos sandwiched him against the hard-caked sand.

"Oof." Blake reached behind him, twisted a fistful of ghillie suit. "Get the hell off me!"

Voices bombarded through his headset from around him.

"Pin him."

"Contain him. Now."

"Gardner, no direct action. That is an order."

"Screw your goddamn orders!" The hoarse response ripped through Blake's throat. "I'm going in."

"Gardner?" Korba's voice cut through the chaos. "Man, I know where you are right now but don't blow this. Think! It's probably not her. And there's nothing you can do. Nothing."

Nothing? Then he'd die trying before he risked anything happening to Sydney. He punched, bucked, adrenaline giving him the edge to reverse position to his back, staring up at Carlos.

His swim buddy's forearm slammed down

against his throat. "Don't make me knock you out. Listen to the Major."

Sweat trickled along the streaked face above, dripped down. Splatted on him.

"No matter who that is," Korba continued, "there's not a damned thing you can do. You're too far out. You'll just get yourself killed. Your buddy, too. Do you hear me? And if it's not her, you'll have killed her by going in. If it is her, there's nothing you can do. The other hostages will die and no one will pay because with advance warning, they'll scatter before we can get there. We gotta make them pay and keep them from doing this to anyone else."

Slowly, reason trickled through his rage one drop at a time like the sweat streaming off Carlos's face. Blake forced his tensed muscles to ease. Even as his breathing regulated, his vision narrowed, returning him to the caves of Afghanistan. The bowels of Baghdad. No light at the end of the tunnel. Just cobwebs and a goal.

Make them pay. His rules. His game. Quitting was not an option.

Time to quit for the day, except Monica couldn't shake nerves enough to sleep.

Walking the halls likely wouldn't help, but at least she might eventually exhaust herself. She would rather talk to Jack, sink into one of his foot rubs while she tried to figure out what set him so on edge. They hadn't shared a moment alone since his flight last night, and now he was finishing up his shift in the command center.

Her feet carried her down the stairs to the first floor. Given the low hum of music swelling from the end of the corridor, apparently someone else couldn't sleep, either. Their schedules were all turned around with the time change compounded by night flights.

She followed the music, rock songs, tunes about fifteen years younger than her thirty-four years, but a welcome slice of America so far from home. Maybe that was the reason portable CD players seemed to be standard issue for soldiers these days with more time spent overseas on cots than in their own beds.

Rounding a corner, she moved closer to the luggage return terminal housing the Rangers. The music increased until it boomed to party level.

What should have seemed incongruous with the gravity of their mission somehow felt right. Life asserting itself as the boys let off steam. Like with Crusty's calls home to his family.

Sydney of all people would approve. No matter how down things got at home growing up, Sydney always smiled, danced through mud puddles, insisted everything would work out so why waste life worrying. Please God, don't let this place have crushed that out of her.

In honor of her sister, Monica walked forward as

if being a little like Sydney tonight might bolster her sister somewhere else.

The open archway revealed the high-ceilinged room pulsing with noise. Santuci perched on the luggage return belt, using it like a disc jockey dais. A small boom box rigged into the ancient, crackling P.A. system blasted Foo Fighters. Stripped down to only his BDU pants and a concert T-shirt, Santuci was jotting requests on a notepad.

Others danced, some stretched out and read. A few even slept, the reverberation of music nothing compared to the concussion of combat.

Leaning against the archway, she watched, listened, losing track of time until a shadow stretched past her. Jack. She smiled over her shoulder.

He didn't smile back, simply moved across from her to lean against the opposing side of the archway. "I told you when we left Nevada I wanted you to stick close whenever we can. This place isn't safe."

She frowned, studied him, the stress lines fanning from the corners of his dark eyes. His "shitty mood" after the night flight had increased to something darker, intense and so unlike the easygoing lover she'd come to know the past months.

Scowling, he reached down to check the BlackBerry—wireless handheld e-mailer—attached to his web belt.

"Jack? Everything okay?"

He dropped the handheld back in place, then

twisted open a water bottle. "Just finishing up my shift in the command center."

"And everything went all right?" she repeated. Was he dodging her question? "Is there any news I should know about?"

"No messages. Nothing to tell you. Everything's on schedule." He braced a boot behind him, tilting back his bottle, effectively ending conversation for a few seconds at least.

"I thought for sure you'd be over there with Santuci ordering some Elvis tunes."

He grunted, drank again. A hungry glint overlaid the edginess with a new intent she recognized well. Sultry tension pulsed from him much like after a dangerous flight when he needed the ultimate physical release. Sex.

Her mouth dried right up as too many memories bombarded her. She snatched the water bottle from him and moistened her lips, the rim still warm from him.

Uh-oh. She rolled the bottle between her palms and searched for safer ground. "Sydney would like this. She always loved music, even as a kid. Music played and her feet would start moving. She never cared who was watching." Monica passed back his water. "You have that same comfortable-in-your-skin air. I envy you both that."

"You do okay. It's tough to hold your own in a squadron of crew dogs, but you fit. Hell, they even gave you your own call sign. Not all flight docs get 'em.''

The heat in his eyes combined with his compliment warmed her insides into soft chocolate. ''You've never told me how you got your call sign.''

He drank again, studying her over the bottle, visibly reining himself in. What churned in his head? And could she handle this darker Jack, anyway, when they barely survived in his easygoing days?

Finally he lowered his bottle. ''I used to be 'King,' the whole Elvis theme. Before long, 'King Korba' shuffled to 'King Cobra,' and then just 'Cobra.'''

A deep chuckle sounded from behind her. She turned to find Rodeo looming over her.

He leaned one shoulder against the wall. ''Don't let him bullshit ya, Hippocrates. It's a snake joke from the time he lost his wallet at a bar in California and the manager offered to comp his tab if he dropped his flight suit.''

Jack winced. ''I had on shorts.''

''With big hearts on them, I seem to recall.''

''You don't have to tell all my secrets.''

Laughter faded from Rodeo's face. ''Well, sometimes secrets can be toxic.''

Monica's eyes flicked back and forth from Jack to Rodeo, unspoken communication so heavy there almost seem to be a visible thread linking the air between the two men.

The last strains of a Rolling Stones' classic dwindled. Santuci raised his megaphone to his mouth and shouted, "This next one's a special request from Captain Derek 'Rodeo' Washington going out to his pal Major Korba. Let's hear it for the King!"

Three notes into "Hunka, Hunka Burning Love," suspicion niggled along with memories of Vegas vows serenaded by music from the King. There had been all those pointed looks from Rodeo lately. Now Jack's glare at his best friend. Sure, everyone knew he liked Elvis, but somehow this went further.

By the time Elvis started wailing, she knew just how far. "God bless it, Jack Korba! You told him, didn't you?"

Damn him, he didn't deny it. Or even apologize. Just stared back at her with one slow blink before shooting another glare at Rodeo that stated clearly the guy was dead meat.

Did everyone know their marriage secret? She darted a quick look at the other fliers sprinkled in the crowd. No one was staring their way, which boded well. For now. Gossip flowed faster than air through a squadron.

Crew dogs were bad enough about teasing with little or nothing for fodder. Now her most painful mistake would be paraded in front of her for the rest of her Air Force career in the form of endless Elvis dedications.

As if she wasn't already going to have enough

trouble getting over Jack Korba. Heartbreak *and* no sex. Now wasn't that a sad tune in the making?

Anger and betrayal strummed through her in four-four time. The music built along with laughter and dancing, all seeming to mock her with the mess she'd made of her life.

So much for warm chocolate and tender feelings toward Jack. "I specifically made it clear I did not want this discussed with others. You agreed."

God, she couldn't think right now, felt selfish enough for worrying about herself when Sydney was suffering.

She spun away, sidled past a small cluster of soldiers, ignored Jack's voice for five steps until she plowed into another body. Yasmine. Could this day get any worse?

Her sister nodded past her to Jack standing a couple of feet away. "Trouble with your boyfriend?"

Boyfriend? The word grated, although husband didn't sit too much better right now. But calling him a blabbermouth bastard would require an explanation she certainly didn't want to make, especially to Yasmine. "Everything's fine, thank you. Could you step aside please?"

"Fine? Really? He certainly does not seem happy."

"Aw. Too bad." And she felt petty and small for finding comfort in the notion he hurt, too. She started past her sister.

Yasmine stopped her with a fluttery hand on her

arm. "Maybe if instead of storming off you went back over and smiled, talked."

Like a flood of gas on fiery anger already alive and well inside her, Yasmine's buttinsky advice incinerated the last vestiges of pretended civilities. "And you're a fine one to pass out love life advice after all your great success chasing Colonel Cullen down every hall."

Yasmine gasped. "That was flat-out hateful."

"And your sisterly advice wasn't solicited."

How five hundred Army Rangers could go completely silent, Monica didn't know. But a roomful of men crowded the portal, eyes all trained on her with her sister like randy men ready to watch a wet T-shirt catfight.

Yasmine definitely looked mad enough to hiss.

Instead, she pulled herself up with inherent regality, the calculating gleam giving Monica all of a two-second warning that this woman would fight a helluva lot dirtier than eye scratching or hair pulling.

"Well, my goodness," Yasmine crooned, her lilting voice somehow filling the entire luggage return hangar. "No wonder you did not win Miss Congeniality in the Miss Texas Pageant."

A hand clamped over Sydney's mouth tighter than a Texas lasso around a neck.

She swallowed down her scream mixed with bile. Hollering would only bring trouble to her friends.

God, she'd thought this part of the nightmare was over. Facing another sexual assault was more than she could bear. Especially after the horror of being forced to watch a public stoning. If they discovered her pregnancy, would she be executed in the same way?

Nausea roiled. But the will to live burned.

She allowed herself to breathe. Exhale before she passed out. Inhale.

Her nose twitched. She smelled—

"Shh."

Blake. Sweaty, stinky, just-out-of-the-field Blake. Oh, God. So amazing and perfect.

"Is it really you?" She muffled against his hand.

His face lowered closer until he whispered against her ear, "Don't talk. Just listen. Okay?"

She nodded against his wonderful, warm, American hand.

"Are you all right?"

She nodded again.

His hand clenched, twitched, then slid free. "Soon, I'm going to get you out of this hellhole. I promise. I'm here to give you instructions so you can be ready."

Not now? No! Agonizing regret poured acid over her relief. Followed by stark reality and reason. He was giving her hope rather than making her wait in ignorance. She needed to be grateful for that. He trusted her with information about a possible escape when she hadn't even been willing to share with her dearest friends her pregnancy and plans to run.

Oh, Blake. Her eyes blinked against the pitch dark, the side of his face a near indiscernible blur.

"Hang on just a little longer, not more than a couple of days. Hopefully this will go fast and easy. But there's a chance we may have to set explosives and mouse-hole in. If you hear the whippoorwill call I used to make when we went hiking, I want you all to flatten against the south wall. Okay? The south wall. Hang in there. Help is on the way."

Big help. Serious help. Wipe-these-bastards-off-the-face-of-the-earth help.

"Thank you," she mouthed, the words a mere brush of air.

"Are you really okay?"

No. Hell, no, she wanted to cry and vent and finally let down and grieve over what had happened to her.

Except she couldn't. If he knew, he would scoop her up now and ruin the plan. The temptation to leave immediately was agonizingly strong, but not strong enough to risk his life.

"I'm all right," she dared to whisper, prayed she was convincing.

A shudder ripped through him just before he pulled her close. Fast. Too fast for her to think or react to hide the telling bulge. And then her torso was flush against his.

Would he guess? She was only three months

along, and he was a bachelor with no experience about pregnant women. Maybe he wouldn't notice. Maybe he would have forgotten what she felt like before. Maybe she could will him not to know if she just kept quiet.

He stilled against her.

His heart pounded so hard she could feel it against her own, so loud she feared its echoing bounce through the cell would wake the others. A shudder that could only be realization raced through him.

"Oh, God, Sydney." His hoarse whisper stroked her ear into her hair. "Is there any possibility it could be…" *Mine.*

The lone word stayed unspoken but easily understood.

He had to know the chances were next to nil given she wasn't showing much and they hadn't been together in four months. Four long months ago—their last time together followed by a fight in bed about her decision to leave for Rubistan when he wanted her to quit, to get married and start a family with him. He wanted a baby of his own so damned much.

She couldn't lie to him. "No."

The truth burned her throat. She couldn't even allow herself to dream what it would be like to carry his child instead.

She heard the catch in his throat. A quiet primal

groan from his soul sounded as he accepted what had happened to her in this place.

His arms slid under her.

"Blake? Wait."

"Shut up," he growled low.

"But—"

"You're out of here. Now."

"What about Kayla and Phillip? I can't leave them behind." Hope mingled with fear, panic.

He hesitated. "All right. We'll take them, too."

"Are the rest of your guys outside?"

No answer, just the slow lift as he hefted her from the cot.

Of course they weren't. Why would they have sent a whole group to give an advance warning when one person could slide in more easily?

A sneaking suspicion niggled. Did they even know he was here at all? Had he gone commando to check on her?

Her vision adjusted until she could see determination glint in Blake's hazel eyes peering from his painted face. The strength of his will almost persuaded her to let him try. His training could haul her as well as her friends out. He had military survival skills beyond her imagination. He'd told her before that whatever a SEAL wanted for weapons or training, a SEAL got.

The darkness of his job that unsettled her more than once would save her. God, she longed to get out. Now. Her teeth chattered as an innate need for

An Important Message from the Editors

Dear Reader,

Because you've chosen to read one of our fine romance novels, we'd like to say "thank you!" And, as a **special** way to thank you, we've selected <u>two more</u> of the books you love so well **plus** an exciting Mystery Gift to send you — absolutely <u>FREE</u>!

Please enjoy them with our compliments...

Pam Powers

How to validate your Editor's
"Thank You"
FREE GIFT

1. Peel off gift seal from front cover. Place it in space provided at right. This automatically entitles you to receive 2 FREE BOOKS and a fabulous mystery gift.

2. Send back this card and you'll get 2 brand-new *Romance* novels. These books have a cover price of $5.99 or more each in the U.S. and $6.99 or more each in Canada, but they are yours to keep absolutely free.

3. There's no catch. You're under no obligation to buy anything. We charge nothing—ZERO—for your first shipment. And you don't have to make any minimum number of purchases— not even one!

4. The fact is, thousands of readers enjoy receiving their books by mail from The Reader Service. They enjoy the convenience of home delivery...they like getting the best new novels at discount prices BEFORE they're available in stores... and they love their Heart to Heart subscriber newsletter featuring author news, horoscopes, recipes, book reviews and much more!

5. We hope that after receiving your free books you'll want to remain a subscriber. But the choice is yours— to continue or cancel, any time at all! So why not take us up on our invitation, with no risk of any kind. You'll be glad you did!

GET A *Free* MYSTERY GIFT...

SURPRISE MYSTERY GIFT COULD BE YOURS **FREE** AS A SPECIAL "THANK YOU" FROM THE EDITORS

Yes! I have placed my Editor's "Thank You" seal in the space provided above. Please send me 2 free books and a fabulous mystery gift. I understand I am under no obligation to purchase any books, as explained on the back and on the opposite page.

PLACE
FREE GIFT
SEAL
HERE

393 MDL DVFG   193 MDL DVFF

FIRST NAME   LAST NAME

ADDRESS

APT.#   CITY

STATE/PROV.   ZIP/POSTAL CODE

(PR-R-04)

Thank You!

The Reader Service — Here's How It Works:

Accepting your 2 free books and gift places you under no obligation to buy anything. You may keep the books and gift and return the shipping statement marked "cancel." If you do not cancel, about a month later we'll send you 3 additional books and bill you just $4.74 each in the U.S., or $5.24 each in Canada, plus 25¢ shipping & handling per book and applicable taxes if any.* That's the complete price and — compared to cover prices starting from $5.99 each in the U.S. and $6.99 each in Canada — it's quite a bargain! You may cancel at any time, but if you choose to continue, every month we'll send you 3 more books, which you may either purchase at the discount price or return to us and cancel your subscription.

*Terms and prices subject to change without notice. Sales tax applicable in N.Y. Canadian residents will be charged applicable provincial taxes and GST.

survival rocked her, trying to hold back the words that would send immediate rescue away.

No one would fault her for leaving instead of waiting.

But she would fault herself. It would be more dangerous for him to try solo. She couldn't do that to Blake when he'd done nothing more than self-lessly risk his life for her and two people he'd never met.

Her teeth chattered again. The urge to run swelled. Deep inside her, scared, flighty Sydney who let her big sister fight her battles and keep track of her forgotten lunch box still lived.

She just needed to be stifled for a few minutes longer.

"Blake. Stop. This isn't right."

Still no answer. But no movement, either.

"You have to go. *Without* me."

His breaths grew heavier, louder even though she knew holding her would in no way test Blake's stamina.

"They don't...hurt me anymore." He didn't have to know about the slaps or punches, nothing compared to the humiliation of the first days at Ammar al-Khayr's mercy. Specifics were better left unspoken. She sensed too much information would snap what control Blake had left over his rage. "Do you understand? But I want them—" *him* "—to pay. I don't want them to be free to do this to someone else. They need to be stopped, and that won't happen if you take me now. You have to leave me behind.''

Pain pulsed from him in an agony that rivaled her own. She hated that she'd brought him to this. For months before their breakup she'd seen the darkness swallowing his soul and blamed it on his profession.

This time, she could only blame herself.

He tucked her tighter until the corded muscles in his arms bit into her flesh. Then his grip loosened, gentled into the man who'd won her heart on a crowded Virginia Beach by giving away two hundred dollars' worth of raffle tickets to a tired mother.

Blake lowered her back to her bed as gently as any piece of spun glass. Because she was pregnant or because she was simply herself, she didn't know. Either way, his tenderness after so much violence touched her with reminders of all the things that had drawn her to Blake before the rest pulled them apart.

His lips pressed to her forehead. "I'll be back for you. Never doubt it." His vow caressed her skin. "And I won't ever let anyone hurt you again."

Her spine met the unrelenting cot, Blake's arms sliding from beneath her. She clamped her jaw shut until her teeth hurt from holding back the urge to call for him.

As silently as he appeared, he slipped away. Leaving behind a churning mix of hope and tears.

Music blasting around him, Drew stood with his officers, keeping track of the impromptu Ranger party, and waited for Yasmine to start pumping out the tears in the argument with her sister.

Something that never happened.

Damn but the woman had grit and fire, pulling no punches when it came to battle. Drew chuckled low like most of the rest of the room. That little pageant piece of history on Major Hyatt would rain more hell on the flight surgeon's head than anything else Yasmine could have tossed out there. Hyatt would no doubt have a crown painted on her helmet by sunrise.

Steam all but blew from Major Hyatt's ears, yet Yasmine stood down her sister from seven inches less height. His Sheba had regal down to a fine art.

His Sheba? Shit. Where the hell were LifeSavers when a guy needed them?

Doc Hyatt pulled back her shoulders with a long-suffering breath, plastered a smile on her face before turning back to the clump of fliers standing nearby with goofy-ass grins on their faces.

"All right, gentlemen, I want to clarify something straight out of the gate here. You have exactly one hour to razz me about the pageant gig. And after that, if anyone touches my tiara, I can guarantee his annual physical will include a most *uncomfortable* and cold-handed hernia exam.''

The group of flight-suit-clad warriors groaned. More than one covered his groin as coughs echoed even from the Rangers.

''That's right, flyboys,'' Hyatt crooned. ''Turn and cough. Just turn your head and cough.''

Apparently fighting dirty ran in the genes for these women. Doc Hyatt would be just fine. Yasmine, however, he wasn't so certain about. Her smile didn't come close to reaching her brown eyes as she turned with a snooty little sniff and strode away unnoticed by everyone—except Special Agent Keagan keeping watch.

Drew waved him away and started after her himself.

Huh?

His boots kept moving toward her, anyway, dragging his body right along. Hell, he didn't know why except that a monosyllabic fella like Keagan wouldn't be much help to Yasmine. And he simply couldn't walk away, not with hellish images from his shift in the command center still hammering in the back of his mind, of the stoning, of just how few rights a Rubistanian woman had around here.

No way was he letting her walk *anywhere* unprotected.

Tracking Yasmine down the hall, Drew followed, kept enough distance so she wouldn't hear him and turn until they were well away from the crowd. She stopped in front of her closet-room, twisted the knob and disappeared inside.

Okay, safe and set for the night. He only needed to call for a guard. Let her cry her eyes out in her pillow or whatever it was women did to vent frustrations. Personally, he preferred a trip to the gym or shooting range. But, oh well. To each his own.

And still his feet wouldn't carry him away.

He just wanted a few more minutes with her to reassure himself. To blast away the image of her face superimposing itself over that of the condemned woman earlier. Yasmine was getting to him, no question, and at the moment he couldn't recall a single reason why he should leave.

He surrendered and knocked.

"The door is unlocked as ordered."

Twisting the knob, he swung the door open to find her sitting on the edge of her bed, scarf in her lap. Gleaming black hair streamed down her back.

Lust rolled over him like an M-1 tank charging across a flat stretch of undefended desert.

Yasmine stared up at Colonel Cullen filling her doorway. Finally he was with her. Of his own will. Alone. Now, when she looked foolish and felt far too open.

She could almost hear her mother whispering in her ear. *Watch out what you wish for, sugar. You might just get it.*

Yasmine considered covering her hair, even if she couldn't quickly twist it into a knot again. But of course seeing a woman's bare head was nothing special to this American man. She twined her favorite rose scarf around her fingers.

She resorted to sarcasm, better than crying. "Well, this is certainly a change, *you* following *me*."

He hooked his hands on his gun belt, standing in the open doorway, half in, half out. "Would you rather I call Keagan?"

"You know better and I find it spiteful on your part that you would make me say it."

Laughter rumbled in his broad chest.

"I would prefer that you not laugh at me."

He shook his head. "I'm not laughing at you, but you do amuse me, lady."

Lady? Not little girl. Something warm unfurled inside her like the scarf loosening around her slackened grip. "How do I amuse you?" she asked.

So she could figure out how to do it again.

He stepped farther inside, leaving the door open in a respectful gesture of propriety that touched and stirred her all at once.

"Well, Sheba, I expected to find you bawling your eyes out and instead you're spitting fire."

"Spitting fire? That is not an attractive image."

His eyes made a subtle shift from light blue to intense gray, deep gray, draw-a-woman-in-and-make-everything-else-fade gray. "I disagree."

Her breath caught somewhere between her lungs and her throat, right around that tender spot at the base of her neck where her pulse throbbed faster. Louder in the already small room growing smaller by the heartbeat.

He knelt in front of her on one knee, forearm resting on his other bent knee. "Thing is, I know some of us spit fire because tears are just too damn silly-looking. And I'm thinking you don't like looking silly."

"You would be right there."

"It's safe to say neither you nor your sister came across looking anything less than fighting mad."

Shame still burned her face over behaving like such a brat. "We have never gotten along. She resents our mother and I never could stop feeling defensive because Monica hurt her." She held up a hand to forestall the answer she already knew. "I know. I know. Our mother hurt Monica, as well, and it is not my place to solve their issues."

She glanced up through her lashes and found the corners of his blue-gray eyes crinkled with intensity as he listened. Really listened to her when most men would have no use for what her mother would have called "chick issues."

Yasmine searched deeper in those beautiful eyes until she found genuine caring wrapped around a pragmatic soul.

She let herself indulge in the warmth of safety, being free to talk with another person and to share a piece of herself. "I have eleven other sisters here from my father's other wives. It should not matter to me so much that this one sister hates my guts.''

''Eleven sisters? No brothers?''

''No brothers,'' she confirmed. ''Apparently my father did not produce that Y chromosome when making a baby.''

Drew coughed on a laugh.

She liked that, making this rugged man find the laughter he buried too deep.

Yasmine draped her scarf over her knees, the gift from her father draping comfort over her battered nerves, as well. ''We were spoiled, all of us. Sons are undoubtedly prized in my culture, but my father never made mention of disappointment in front of us. He called us his treasures. I think, though, that perhaps he adored all of the attention from a houseful of females.'' She smoothed wrinkles from the silk. ''I am sure you think it is a strange practice for a man to have four wives.''

''I guess it's more important what you think of the practice.''

Oh, she could get to like this man who not only listened but also valued her opinion. ''I believe Monica would tell you I am selfish. And she would be right.'' Yasmine looked up from her scarf. ''I could not share a man with anyone else.''

For a weak moment she let herself dive into those beautiful eyes of his and even permitted him a peek into herself. Quiet fell between them, stretched with only the low thrum of the bass beat from the music below.

Or was that her heart?

He glanced away, down, connection easing yet not breaking. "You still miss your father."

"Of course." Understatement of the century.

She missed both her parents. How easily she had taken for granted something like a cruise with them to celebrate her graduation from the university.

Tears burned after all. Much more talk of her parents and she would start blubbering all over this man who already found her childish enough.

"Um—" she tried to sniffle up her tears "—I think I would like to spit some more fire now if you do not mind."

A whisper of air brushed by her cheek a half second before his hand fell to rest on the back of her head. His fingers cupped the base of her skull with firm comfort.

No movement. No stroke. Yet the heavy touch of his hand against her hair was so alien and sensual. Forbidden, which made it all the more arousing. She held still and savored the moment because undoubtedly once she looked up, things would change forever. Either he would jerk away and scramble for his nice safe distance from the woman who seemed determined to chase him down hallways.

Or he would kiss her.

And that scared her all the more because then her lies would someday send this honorable man running faster than any meaningless age difference.

Chapter 11

He should run. Drew knew it deep in his battle-seasoned bones that insisted a wise man who wanted to live to fight another day understood when to retreat.

Right this moment with his fingers buried in Yasmine's dark hair and her exotic scent drifting all around him, he wasn't feeling particularly wise. As a matter of fact, he was feeling downright reckless and unable to stop staring at a perfect pair of lips. Perfect lips on the face of the most exasperating woman he'd ever met.

With her jet hair caressing her face, she looked more American, less foreign, more approachable. Drew cupped the back of her skull with a firmer touch, nudged her forward and, God help them both, Yasmine didn't need much persuasion. If she'd shown any resistance, he could have scavenged the grit to pull away.

Instead she drifted forward into his arms with more of that fluid grace that sent lust hammering through him until he couldn't think about anything but getting naked with her. Taking the release his libido demanded with sex, long, hot, physical sex, her hair tangled around their sweaty bodies as they both worked through whatever the hell insanity twisted them inside out.

Lust. It had to be lust along with the sense of the forbidden. He refused to consider it could be anything more. Once he kissed her, she would become like any other woman in his mind, and therefore easy to walk away from. The sooner he kissed her, the sooner he could forget her.

Yeah, that made sense.

His mouth met hers partway, slanted over, found the unique feel of her. Taste of her. Mint toothpaste and pure Yasmine.

His other hand slid up to grasp her arm, his fingers wrapping around the delicate give of womanly flesh. In a world of hard dirt beds and harder decisions, he'd forgotten anything could be this soft. Brushing another kiss over her lush mouth, he tried to stay gentle, to remember this woman was half his weight. Half his strength.

Half his age.

Damn, but he didn't want to remember that just yet with her lips moving under his. Parting with enough encouragement to assure him he hadn't misread a thing here.

"Well, Colonel, I never would have expected a big, bold man like you to be a shy one." Her warm breath and challenge washed over him and washed away the last of his restraints, as well.

A growl rumbled in his chest. His fingers tightening in her hair, his other hand dropped to her waist, pulling her nearer. She leaned into him, breasts to his chest and, ah, shit, but he'd never hated the bulk of his Kevlar vest more. The bulletproof protection shielded him from the feel of her softness giving against his unyielding chest, a sensation that surely would have knocked him on his ass faster than any bullet.

As if he wasn't already falling. The warm velvet inside of her mouth had him harder than hell and in need of more. More of her.

Her hands feathered over his head, through his close-shorn hair, down his neck, teasing him with the sensation and notion of having those soft hands all over him. He explored the warm recesses of her mouth, more softness, and wondered how hot and soft the rest of her would be.

At the hesitant touch of her tongue to his, he discovered the answer to a question he damn well didn't want answered right now. *Innocent.* The word blazed through his mind.

She might talk a good game about her informed decisions, but her information leaned more toward book knowledge. Her in-the-field experience was definitely limited.

Her enthusiasm, however, seemed boundless. She wiggled closer. Ah, hell. What now, Cullen?

While her untutored enthusiasm wasn't a turnoff, it sure as shit brought a splash of cold water reminding him he had no business doing this. With her. To her. She would have to find another man, another day.

Another man? Drew's grip tightened. Primal possessiveness snarled through him. What was it about this small bit of a woman that had him twisted in knots until he forgot who the hell he was, even where he was?

Where he was. In front of an open door.

He tore himself away from her. "Shit."

Swaying, she blinked. She dropped her hand to his chest to steady herself. "Shit? Well, thank you very much, Colonel. I do not believe I have ever been so prettily romanced after a kiss before."

Not too steady himself, Drew gripped the edge of her cot. Beside her hip. A hip his hand itched to explore. Irritation throbbed in time with his erection. "Lady, if you were looking for romance, you picked the wrong man to hit on."

She straightened away from him. Hurt or embarrassed or just plain pissed? He couldn't tell for certain. But look out, she was spitting fire.

''To hit on? And I assume little, defenseless me hauled a big man like you right into this room and forced a kiss.''

''Anyone who calls you defenseless is an idiot.''

And he was acting like an idiot himself. Funny as hell and yet not funny at all that frustrated hormones turned a man cranky at any age.

The fact that he had no business taking a test run with this woman made him crankiest of all. Twenty years in the field had taught him well that live fire exercises sometimes left a guy taking a bullet. And he sure felt gut-shot at the moment.

None of which was her fault. ''But yeah, you're right. No one forced me to kiss you.''

He let himself touch her hair again, to reassure the innocent part of Yasmine that he wanted this. Wanted her. And yeah, because at the moment he was a weak-willed man around her.

Drew hooked a silken strand behind her ear. ''You're a damned pretty woman and I let myself get caught up in the moment. I'm madder at myself than I am at you. Hell, anyone could have walked by. The talk would have been…bad. For both of us.''

To say the least. His hand fell to his knee.

Scooping her scarf from the floor, he started to push to his feet so he could get the hell away from her before he repeated his mistake. Or made a worse one. ''Which is all the more reason I should—''

"What is your name?"

She stopped him half rising with just her voice.

His hand fisted around the scarf as silky as her hair. "What does that have to do with anything?" He lowered back to one knee, jabbing a thumb to his chest, which had his last name stitched on. "And I know you can read English. Cullen. My name's Cullen."

"No." She stroked her finger over the name tag. Her slim finger seared right through Kevlar more effectively than shrapnel from a mortar round. "I mean, your given name. Everyone calls you Colonel Cullen or simply by your rank. You do not wear tags that I have seen with your complete name."

Something done for battle-time safety. The less information the enemy had about a POW, the better. Many of the fliers opted not to wear anything that gave away crew position for just that reason.

Now she wanted his full name. The request stirred suspicions he didn't want with the taste of her still filling his mouth. He stayed silent so long he could feel her anger growing in a power struggle of wills.

Almost as powerful as the one going on inside himself. The soldier within him shouted warnings to stay on guard. The man inside demanded he was honor bound to a few things because he'd kissed an innocent woman.

A damned pissed innocent woman. "Have I

overstepped, Colonel Cullen? Silly me, but I thought since you had your tongue in my mouth a few moments ago, it would be all right for me to know your name.''

God, she made his head hurt. And turned him on all at the same time.

She folded her hands in her lap, a prim contrast to her lips still full from kisses stirring a whole new host of fantasies.

''Having your name does not equate with some grand commitment. I realize that while you are attracted to me, Colonel, you are not interested in anything more. Territory well covered and understood. And of course you also believe we have nothing in common because of our differing ages and cultures, and you are too honorable to offer a fling.''

The buzzing in his ears quieted. Was she propositioning him? If so, her blush at a simple word like ''fling'' made ''flinging'' with her even more out of the question. Although flinging her on her back was a mighty damned enticing prospect.

With his hand clenching around her scarf still in his fist, he focused on her blush instead of her words.

''But even if nothing more happens, we did kiss.'' Her all-out smile tipped her mouth and his world. ''Quite wonderfully at that. And after we have left here, I would like to know your name when I think of this moment.''

Her words trickled through with images of her reliving what they'd done because it moved her, as well. The woman might be innocent, but she was a seductress with simplicity. Like the understated allure of her scarves hiding her hair. Damn but she got to him.

"Drew. My name is Drew."

He waited for her to say it, prepped himself for the inevitable impact of hearing his name softened by her lightly accented voice.

Instead she watched him, chewed her bottom lip. "Would it upset you or break some sort of rule that would send you running if I say your given name aloud?"

"You make me sound mighty damned wimpy."

Yasmine slipped her fingers through the waterfall drape of her scarf trailing from his hand, twined it around her wrist, linking them without touching. She tugged. "Wimpy? I think not."

She was playing him. He could feel it with every stroke to his masculine ego, and still she made him smile.

"When have you ever sought permission or followed my orders, Sheba?" he asked, as close as he could come to telling her that hell, yes, he wanted her to say his name. The higher he climbed in the ranks the less often he heard his given name and right now he wanted to hear it on her lips more than he wanted a regular bed and a real U.S. of A. meal.

"Thank you for following me instead of sending the spiky-haired intelligence officer who only answers in grunts." She looped the scarf tighter around her wrist until their hands met, held. "You are a sensitive man, Drew Cullen."

Oh, yeah, good thing he'd prepped because his name sure as shit sounded good coming out of her mouth. Then her words smoked into his mind. "Sensitive?"

Her smile turned downright wicked. "In a completely non-wimpy sort of way."

He laughed, which broadened her smile, which made him smile again, too. Which sobered him. "I'll think about you, too, after I leave this place. You make quite an impression on a man, Yasmine." He allowed himself to say her name and even let it hang in the air between them for an extra second. "If things were different…"

"If-onlys are a waste of time once a choice has been made, and you have obviously already made yours." Her eyes pinned him as she lobbed the verbal grenade.

One he couldn't afford to touch.

At his silence, she untwined their fingers he hadn't even realized were still linked. "You may leave my room now, Colonel."

Not Drew. Colonel. And already he regretted that he wouldn't hear her say his name again. "I'll have someone stationed outside your quarters shortly."

He turned his back and left, closing the door be-

hind him. She'd told him clearly enough that she
wanted him, too, and didn't want marriage. Good
God, most men would jump at the no-strings opportunity. What the hell was wrong with him?

Must be sleep deprivation screwing with his
brain or he wouldn't even consider turning the knob
on her door for round two. He needed to get the
hell out. Check on his men. Then land on his cot
for some shut-eye before he did something irrevo-
cable.

Drew stepped away from the door, his hands fisting at his sides. Closing around something in an
odd déjà vu moment from when he'd first found her
note in his hand.

This time, his fingers closed around rose silk he'd
somehow forgotten to give back.

Taking in Monica's tight-lipped smile as she
fielded another "tiara" joke from the crew dogs,
Jack could tell she'd hit her limit. Sure she was
holding her own with the fliers. She'd saved face
after the hissing match with her sister, even if Monica would spend the rest of her career with the call
sign "Tiara" now that Hippocrates had been overturned. But he could see the strain on her face after
months of stress from Sydney's capture, a drunken
wedding.

An impending divorce.

The Yasmine confrontation had been the spat that
broke the camel's back. Which cinched it for him

regarding whether or not to tell her about the stoning ordeal. The last thing she needed was anything else to worry about. Odds indicated it wasn't Sydney, anyway, and he didn't intend to worry Monica until they had firmer intel on the incident. He flipped the wireless e-mailer clipped to his web belt again to check for an update on Sydney and…

Nothing. Shit.

He needed to get Monica away from here and leveled out, just in case the worst came around later. He ignored the damned voice of reason in his head that insisted he was concocting excuses to be with her. To reassure himself she was alive in a place where women were killed all too easily.

Jack angled sideways into the circle of fliers and gripped Monica's upper arm, tugging her toward the hall. "Time to go."

The feel of her under his hand sent a jolt of hunger through him that he was too damned raw to fight tonight.

Her smile pulled tighter, leaving high cheekbones prominent. "I'm okay."

"I know you are. But things are winding down anyhow. I'm tired, but I won't be able to sleep if I'm worried about you. We had a deal when I let you come here. You're not walking around alone when there's an option otherwise." Especially not while the images of that woman being crushed to death under thousands of pounds of rocks and cement pounded hard and fresh in his memory at a time when Tina had decided to crawl back into his head.

Yeah, Monica wasn't the only one about to snap.

She quit resisting his grip. ''Of course. You're right.'' Monica turned to the makeshift disc jockey stage on the luggage return belt where Private Santuci prepared to fire up his next tune. ''Thanks for a great party, Private. It was good to have a piece of home here.''

''Yes, ma'am.'' He spun a CD on a finger, concert T-shirt with BDU pants declaring his heavy-metal preference. ''We're on the road so much these days, why put life on hold? Gotta be 'me' and live my life even in a crisis or I'd never get to be 'me.' Know what I mean?''

Monica stilled under Jack's hand. ''Yes, Private. I've been thinking the same sort of thing myself lately. Thanks for the affirmation.'' She turned to Jack. ''All right, Cobra, let's blow this pop stand.''

Whoa. That sounded a little like the old Monica who didn't shut him down with defensiveness. She stared back at him, frenetic need scrolled across her green eyes with streaks of hot amber. Just like during sex.

With his defenses already blasted to hell, memories ambushed him—of those eyes flashing while she was under him. Beside him. Less soft and more demanding over him.

He wanted more from her. But at the moment he couldn't remember why he wasn't willing to settle for sex while he waited. "Okay, then. We're outta here."

Jack made tracks for the hall. She started up the stairs ahead of him, controlled military steps with her hint of a sway that always sucker punched his libido.

He followed. Caught up. Beside her. Silently as they passed a security cop patrolling the halls. Colonel Cullen hauled ass past them on his way back to the Ranger party to check on his men, so intent on his destination he barely nodded.

Around the corner, closer to her room, Jack kept pace, prayed like mad his conscience would quit yapping at him until he could bury himself in Monica and find the reliable release they both wanted and, hell yes, *needed* tonight.

She unlocked her door, stepped inside and turned to wait. Invitation obvious.

Conscience nipped again. "Monica, if I step into your room, we won't be talking. I want you to be absolutely sure—"

Monica jerked him into her quarters and slammed the door. "Quit talking and start acting."

"Yes, ma'am." He flattened her to the flimsy metal panel, squashing his conscience in the process.

Then he couldn't think at all, just feel Monica's mouth open, hot and hungry under his. Her hands clamped him closer, harder against her as if trying to crawl into him when he knew damned well she'd gotten under his skin long ago.

It had always been this way with them, intense. Immediate. Explosive sex with guaranteed blow-your-mind satisfaction beat the hell out of the tougher prospect of talking.

She yanked his zipper down, farther along the full length of his torso until she could unfurl the length of her hand to his throbbing erection. Throbbing? Hell, what an ineffective word to describe his pounding need to have her.

If there just weren't so many clothes between them.

The flight suit offered easy access for her to get to him, but damn it, the uniform impeded him from getting to her. Into her. Where he needed to be now, because he was seconds away from screwing her where they stood.

He might be far gone—hell, he *was* far gone—but he wanted her still speaking to him afterward. Unlike the last time she'd been this upset.

Jack inched back, sucked in air. "If you don't want to finish right here against the door, say something fast. I've got about one minute's worth of restraint left in me to throw your sleeping bag on the floor for us."

"Here suits me just fine." She slid her hands from him, clasped them over her head in a sensual arch that notched his blood pressure. "Take off my clothes. I want to feel your hands against my skin when the clothes are falling away. I want to be able to watch you as you see me.''

No mistaking that. ''I like it when you get bossy.''

One hand slid from above her head to scratch down the open vee of his flight suit, deeper, a hint too hard. ''I am not bossy. Just assertive and damned determined to be in control of my destiny.'' Her finger trailed lower until she snapped the waist-band of his boxers.

He knew there was a reason he should stop to analyze what she'd just said, but she grabbed his wrist and molded his palm to her breast. Her full-ness filled his hand, dragging his other hand up for more.

Air thickened in the room. Breathing became op-tional. Touching, however, became essential.

Her hand roved lower. Her fingers tucked inside his boxers, found, cradled the weight of him in her hand, stroking again and again, her thumb gliding over the head with a familiarity of just what brought him to the edge until he almost came in her hand.

Jack clamped her wrist. Her other hand slipped past and he stopped it, too. Pinned both to her sides against the door.

''Not yet.'' His mouth found the crook of her neck where it met her shoulder. ''You're always in such a rush and I'm not ready to finish yet.''

''Then we'll start again.''

Start again. With Monica. His mind pushed

thoughts through the red haze of lust almost blinding him. Almost.

Damn it, but the brain was an annoying-as-hell organ battling for control with another organ that seriously wanted jurisdiction over this moment.

He looked down at her, so vulnerable in his grasp in spite of her bossy ways and take-no-shit attitude. Passion took a nosedive.

A man kicked ass for women. Protected them. Honored them. And he'd been lying to her by omission about Tina, as well as about the stoning incident.

Monica chose just that second to capitalize on his weakening grip and slid her hands free, brought them down, into his gaping flight suit and into his boxers again, gripping his ass and guiding him. Her nails bit an arousing urgency into his skin.

Three more seconds and he would be inside her.

Her teeth grazed his bottom lip.

Two.

The press of her body jammed the e-mail pager against his hip with an uncomfortable reminder of all the lies between them.

One.

Damn. Damn. Damn.

He manacled her wrists again and tore himself away from her, the toughest thing he'd done since his first spin recovery in pilot training. "I can't do this."

Chapter 12

Mission accomplished. Belly to the ground, Blake crawled back toward his sandpit outside the terrorist compound.

Gunshots echoed across the stretch of desert with more night maneuvers and training for al-Khayr's operatives. And the perfect distraction when he'd slipped in and out to check on Sydney. An even better cover to obliterate any sound from the faint Predator drone unmanned spy craft gathering additional intel and monitoring to ensure the hostages weren't moved.

She was alive.

Finally he let his brain wrap itself around that fact. The knowledge filled him like Sydney's scent still clinging to him, overriding the dank must of the sand under him.

He should be relieved. Grateful. But he couldn't feel anything more than the scrape of the desert floor against his skin and the dense haze of something too violent even to call anger.

His hands clawed at the ground, propelling him forward. He'd known the bastards would rape her. Knowing it, and facing the tangible reality were two different beasts.

Blake inched across the last patch of ground. He landed in the hollowed trench still empty of his partner who'd been monitoring guard patterns for him, feeding possible threat info through the small boom mike headset.

He stowed the briefcase-size UWB sensor—ultrawide band motion detector—that could track the movement of people through walls in 3-D. The cutting-edge technology should have kept him from risking going all the way inside to see Sydney.

Except nothing could have kept him away from her.

He forced himself to lie flat, breathe, hold back the urge to slip into the compound again. He could do it, too. Easily. See her one more time before his shift ended when he and Carlos would swap out with another pair before sunrise to snag some sleep.

But he shouldn't risk it. Less than forty-eight more hours. Hang tough.

Some other poor bastard had lost a sister, girl-friend, wife to the stoning today, but not him, and he forced himself to remember to be grateful for that much and not think about those goddamned bastards brutalizing Sydney.

Pricks of light popped from the training field. Shouted orders in Arabic echoed, muted to unintelligible by the wind and distance.

He forced breaths in and out. He would uplink and give his report back to the command post in a minute. First, he needed to let his body switch gears and taper off the adrenaline buzz from stealthing into the compound. A few seconds more and his hands would stop twitching.

And what would he say when the time came? If he told command post about her being pregnant, they would know he'd gone in against orders. Not that he gave a shit about much of anything right now except getting Sydney out of here. But the information had no bearing on the rescue attempt.

She wouldn't want him to tell. He knew that. So he would keep his mouth shut and not broadcast it over the radio waves. He wished he could prepare her sister, but there would be too many listening ears over the frequency.

God, things had been easier when they hadn't known everything about each other. When he and Sydney were still in those early days of discovering…

* * *

Sydney snuggled close to him, soft, warm. Her contented sigh purred up her throat and vibrated against his bare chest.

Even hoo-ya or words like "great sex" didn't sum up their first night together. Never before had a morning after felt so...mellow.

He stroked his knuckles along her back and up again. "Tell me about Red Branch, Texas."

"Not much to tell." She tucked her head under his chin, her tousled, toffee-colored hair tickling his nose. "It's just a wonderful sleepy tiny town. Nothing you'd be interested in."

"You came from there. I'm interested."

She tipped her face to smile up at him. "You're too sweet."

"I'm trying, lady, I'm trying."

She stretched to skim a gentle kiss over his mouth before nestling back against his side. "Like I said, sleepy town, small."

"Family? Parents?"

"Mom and Dad met in the auto parts factory where they both worked. Settled down. Had some kids. Got divorced."

"That must have been tough."

"At first maybe, but everything worked out okay. Being in a little town made things easier on my dad, I think, with all the close-knit feel, and my big sister is a whiz at keeping things organized."

He couldn't miss her positive spin on life, ad-

mired that, needed it in a world that was showing him the dark side of humanity far too often lately. "You stayed with your dad?"

"Yeah, my mom moved overseas, so legally she couldn't take us."

"But she wanted to."

"Of course."

He waited for her to volunteer more, but apparently he'd landed in bed with the one woman who wasn't into post-sex chitchat. "You mentioned a sister. Any more? What about brothers?"

After such a solitary childhood, he vowed to pack his house with kids and noise, a haven after he quit active field ops.

Or sooner maybe.

"I have the older sister I mentioned, my best friend actually." She paused. "And another younger half sister, too."

"You're lucky to have siblings."

"Living the American Dream."

God, he liked her upbeat attitude. Sure she'd come from a broken home, but focused on the positive. Her small town. Her father. Her best friend sister. With everything he learned about this woman, he became all the more certain he wanted to keep her and her light in his world.

Her soft thigh tucked between his and already he was plotting how he could convince her to move in—her with him or him with her. He didn't care *where as long as they shared a bed and a breakfast table.*

Morning rays through the blinds played on her pale skin. His hand rested on her side, his thumb tracing a small strawberry birthmark on the right side of her flat stomach.

She squirmed, laughed lightly. "That tickles."

Another discovery about his new lover, a passionate woman who liked to take things slow. Who enjoyed long, gentle lovemaking.

And so many more things about her left to uncover. His hand smoothed around to cup her bottom as he rolled her onto her back...

An explosion shook the ground.

From his head or in the compound?

Blake blinked. Tensed. Cleared his mind.

A bloom of smoke puffed from the terrorist training field. Nothing to worry about now.

And later? The bastards weren't going down easy. But they *were* going down, even if they hadn't dared touch what was his. Even if they hadn't done the unthinkable to the gentlest human being he'd even known.

A woman with a strawberry birthmark right over the small, undeniable bulge of her belly.

A soft whistle cut the night. Carlos. His partner whistled once more to announce his return a second before he crawled into the trench. "Everything okay?"

"They're all three alive." He repeated the essentials to Carlos. "And they're ambulatory."

Carlos settled beside him. "You went in, further, to see her, didn't you?" He held up a hand. "Wait. Shit. Don't answer that."

His partner knew him too well. More of that wordless communication from working ops for years filtered back and forth. He couldn't tell Carlos the worst, but the man would no doubt feel the fallout radiating off him. Only Sydney understood him as well.

Gunfire sputtered, sparked the sky. Carlos thumped him on the back. "Are you okay with all this?"

"Don't worry. I can do my job. I'm not gonna get you killed."

"I know that. I'm more worried about you getting yourself killed."

Blake forced himself to be light. "Won't happen, dude. Not now that I know she's okay. I've got everything to live for, right?"

He couldn't let himself think about what had happened to her or he'd turn into some berserker opening fire on everyone in the compound he could find and damn the consequences.

Patience. Steady. Like through the caves in Afghanistan. Hold the nerves together. Because he sure as hell did have a reason to live.

Blake reached for the cammo case with the comm equipment. "Let's get the update called in and our shift over."

Once he had Sydney safe, he needed more than revenge. He would have vengeance. And no one knew better than him how to make it happen.

Monica angled closer to rock-hard Jack and knew she had seconds left to make something happen before her husband turned honorable. After chasing her for months, what a helluva time for him to decide he wanted to take the high road.

"What do you mean, you can't do this?" She needed him. A scary thought, but true. Private Santuci's words from earlier kept echoing through her head about living now or risk never getting to live at all because there was no guarantee their lives would ever get any easier. "Sure as hell feels like you *can* to me."

She shaped her hand to the length of him.

He laughed. A pained, choked sound. "I almost wish that was the problem."

Her fingers crawled up to his chest. "Then what's going on here?"

She arched into him, closer, even though the e-mail pager on his hip bit into her skin as much as his steely erection. Just when she thought he might answer her, the pager buzzed between them.

Relief splashed across Jack's face so damned obviously she wanted to punch him. Did he have to be that pleased about the interruption?

He nudged her away, yanked the handheld e-mail

pager off his web belt. His thumb scrolled down as he read.

Unease itched along her already oversensitized skin. "Jack? What is it?"

His hand clenched a second before his forehead thunked to the door. Hot puffs of breath fanned down her neck, into her gaping flight suit.

"Jack? Damn it. Talk to me."

"Hang on a sec." His throat moved with a long swallow. "Nothing to worry about. Just a little good news for a change. A report from a SEAL recon run. The hostages are all where they should be. Sydney's where she should be."

"You had doubts?"

His eyes opened, fell away from hers then back. "There are always doubts until the minute we have them out of there."

Too many emotions churned inside her, faster, searching for a release. With Jack. "Then let's take comfort in this bit of good news right now, for heaven's sake, and let's celebrate, because there has been little enough of that lately."

"I want to be with you so damned much it hurts." He bit the words out through gritted teeth. "But it's still not right."

"I heard what you said about needing more from me, from us. I'm trying here, Jack."

He hit his head against the door. Once. Twice. "I know you are. God, this would be so much easier if we could go back to simple. I have to be straight up with you. There's something I haven't told you.''

Her doctor mind-set immediately started clicking through horrific possibilities…

She grabbed the collar of his flight suit, twisted her fingers in the fabric until he met her face-to-face. ''You're scaring me, Jack. I don't know what to expect. Stop stalling, okay? Just go for the Band-Aid yank approach and get it over with. Quick.''

''I was married before.''

Talk about stunned stupid.

Shock hit her first, followed by a stab of disillusionment. Jack had been married before? And he hadn't told her.

Never would she have guessed that would be his confession. Jack, the squadron player. The man who never got serious about anyone. His reputation had kept her at a distance for a long while. She might not have been searching for marriage, but didn't want to be a bedpost notch. Now to learn he hadn't shared even such a basic part of his past with her?

It hurt.

She'd condemned Jack for his cheeseburger-and-Elvis definition of love, but she'd thought at least it was open and honest and full-out. Now she knew otherwise.

''I realize I was wrong not to tell you. That's probably the only thing that kept me from exploding over the Yasmine deal. Still boggles my mind how we ever ended up in that chapel.''

His regret slapped her. He'd chased her so hard and fast she hadn't considered his second thoughts. Her numb fingers unclenched from around his flight suit and she couldn't will enough feeling back into them to yank up her own zipper.

She tucked past him and dropped on to the edge of her cot. "Why did you two get divorced?"

"Divorced? Thanks for the vote of confidence on my staying power." He sagged back against the door, his flight suit gaping open, his black T-shirt rising with a ragged breath. "She died."

She couldn't stop her gasp. Or the ache. The pain etched on his face spoke volumes.

He wasn't over losing his wife. Easygoing Jack, who never let anything bother him, was still mourning the woman. The proof of that stained his endlessly brown eyes, overwhelming her with how much grief he'd been holding inside that he'd never shared.

So much emotion. For someone else. Something that shouldn't have bothered her this damned much after she'd spent three and a half months shoving the man away.

"Oh, my God, Jack," she whispered, "I'm so sorry. When?"

She could see his reluctance to talk. The shutters closed down on his eyes and only now that she'd seen into his soul did she realize she'd never been let inside before. But she had a right to her questions, and something within him must have known that, too, or he wouldn't have opened this door she suspected hadn't been so much as cracked for others. "Jack, is this what your 'shitty mood' has been about?"

He jolted. "You know me pretty well even when I don't tell you everything."

"Us being together—" she swallowed "—getting married has made you think about her?" Come on, Jack, talk. She needed a lifeline, some order restored.

He hauled his hands through his hair, still sweaty and swirled from hours in a helmet. "We were young, got married right out of high school. We were working our way through college. Two years before graduation—" he paused, cleared his throat, studied the top of his boots "—she had one of those fluke heart attacks and slipped into a coma."

The doctor within her couldn't help but question, "A heart attack? So young?"

"In childbirth. The baby didn't make it." His foot pounded back against the door. "And damn it, she shouldn't have even been pregnant. We were going to wait until after we both graduated, when I would be on active duty… Shit."

His foot rammed back again.

Nothing about his words or stance invited her closer. A scowl slashed his face. For an easygoing guy, he did brooding damned well. Which left her imagining how much practice he'd gained while alone.

"A month later, we had the doctors take her off life support." His booted foot slid to the ground. "*I* had them take her off life support."

Loss hardened his face. Jack wasn't a traditionally gorgeous guy by any stretch with harsh angles and a nose a little too big to be classic. But he was all man and somehow his grief cut through her with a jagged-edge tenacity because it had brought down someone so strong.

Hints of insecurity scratched over the vulnerable, open part of her, and she resented that most of all. It hadn't escaped her notice that Jack didn't share his first wife's name or even whether his child had been a girl or boy. She didn't want these vulnerable feelings that were so very selfish in light of what he was feeling.

Monica gripped the edge of her cot. Tighter. She hated being anything other than in control of her environment and emotions. So she did what she always did when the world around her spun out of control.

She found someone to heal.

Jack watched Monica's knuckles whiten with her tightening hold on the edge of her cot, her restraint evident in the increasing bloodlessness of her fingers. He waited for her anger. Or even tears. Anything. What he'd kept from her was far worse than failing to mention some half sister she rarely saw. He understood that. Accepted his guilt.

He deserved her anger and almost welcomed the idea of a confrontation so he could storm out, crawl back to his room, shut his eyes. Reestablish his blank wall of forgetfulness.

Jack started to zip his flight suit, all the while in tune to the sound of her shifting on the cot, standing, her footsteps coming closer.

Her arms went around him.

Surprise stilled him half-zip. He'd expected any number of reactions from her. Except this one. "Aren't you pissed that I didn't tell you?"

Her cheek fell to rest on his shoulder. "It would make things easier for you if I got mad, wouldn't it?"

A harsh laugh scraped his throat. "Oddly enough, yes."

"Well, I am…more than a little upset about what you've told me, and the fact that you didn't tell me before." She stroked the nape of his neck, soothed.

"And hurt?"

Her fingers paused, resumed. "Oh, yeah."

"Then why aren't you booting me out on my ass?" Hell, he married her and she kicked him out. He lied to her and she hugged him. When would he ever understand this woman?

She eased back to stare up into his eyes. "Because you're hurting more."

Monica arched up and pressed her mouth to his.

No doubt she meant it to be a tender, comforting kiss. She didn't move or even mold herself against him.

She didn't have to.

The ever-present combustible emotions and passion between them flamed to life, still barely banked from their earlier kiss. What damned inconvenient timing with the past scrambling his brain and wrecking rational decisions, the ability to strategize.

Her lips parted under his and he threw away rationale, took the healing forgetfulness that she offered. Warm, hot, moist Monica, and still he wanted more, had missed her, missed this so damned much. He banded his arms around her back and she melted against him with a familiarity and intensity that numbed his brain.

Hell, yeah. Immersing himself in Monica's soft curves and needy sighs seemed like a mighty good plan at the moment. Except the past three and a half months had taught him the hell of losing her. He didn't know what to do to keep her, or if he even deserved to have her.

Nipping once, twice on her bottom lip, he eased back, guided her head to rest on his shoulder. "It was easier when it was just about the sex." He anchored her to him. Anchored himself with the feel of her lush body against him, her aloe shampoo scent rising to greet him as he buried his face in her hair. "I'm a mess right now, Mon."

"So am I." Her lips moved against his neck,

inching him closer to the edge of total loss of control. "I was a mess before we met, and no doubt I'm going to be a bigger mess after all this is over."

Over. Them or the rescue? His arms twitched possessively around her.

Monica cupped his face in her cool hands. "I know all of that, but I also know we're married, for God's sake. Will we be tomorrow? Who knows? But today this is legally our right. Yes, our lives are screwed up. And yet I just keep remembering what Private Santuci said about how there are so many crises lately. Do you remember?"

"Something about losing his troubles with the Goo-Goo Dolls in concert?"

She chuckled against his mouth. "Close. He said we have to live life even in a crisis. We can worry about regrets later, and you know me well enough to know I certainly will. But right now I'm hurting so damned much for you and over you and over a thousand other things I don't want to think about. Let's make it stop for at least a while."

Damn but he wanted to believe her. "You're sure?"

Hints of amber streaked her green eyes, eyes wide open and not hiding a vulnerability that threatened to level him. "Jack, I only have one question. I need to know you're not using me as a substitute for her."

Christ, how could she even doubt him on that?

Because he hadn't been up front with her. And now he had to make that right. Even if he didn't end up in her bed now, he had to reassure her he'd known exactly who he was with in the months before.

He stared down at this proud woman who'd knocked him flat since the first time he saw her at a squadron cookout and knew what it cost her to ask that question. "You turn me inside out with the way you've taken up residence in my head. I'm confused as hell about a lot of things when it comes to us. But you can be damned certain I know exactly who it is I'm with right now. No substitutes. You're an incredible one-of-a-kind woman. I wish I could come up with better words to reassure you that I need to be inside you, with you right now...*just you.*"

He let his knuckles glide along the side of her face and wondered if he'd said the right things so this wouldn't bite him on the ass later.

"Hell, Mon. This deep-water stuff is new for me. I'm not good at reading nuances and don't know if I've given you what you need here. I'm already being a selfish enough bastard by not walking out the door. The next move has to be yours."

A slow smile eased over her face in time with her fingers pulling his zipper tab all the way down. "Then just so you're clear on any nuances, how about I be bossy and tell you exactly what I need?"

Chapter 13

The stunned look on Jack's face was priceless. Any other time and Monica would have laughed.

She refused to feel guilty about needing Jack tonight. Her carefree lover had offered her more of himself in the past five minutes than he had in seven months. And now, by God, she was eagerly embracing the mantra of Private Santuci. Live, even in the midst of a crisis.

Yes, it hurt that Jack had held back something so vital from her. Thinking of him loving someone else was somewhere she damn well didn't want to go. She focused on the fact that he had told her the truth when he could have so easily had her flat on her back.

Or against the door.

Giving herself a second to gather her tattered control, Monica turned away, facing the room, searching for the perfect setting in her sparse quarters. Flat surfaces were limited with only a narrow cot, the tile floor, the desk completely covered with her gear. No nifty hot tub or queen-size bed. But if she waited for those...

Her eyes landed on the oversize office chair. Not flat, but with definite possibilities.

She gripped the back of the chair, wheeled it out of the cluster of furniture in the corner and spun it around to face Jack. "For you," she ordered. "I want you...here. Now. Will that do for a clear enough first move?"

His shock faded to a scowl, not that she was fooled. Instead she read his wariness.

She'd certainly given him cause with all her talk about needing a definite understanding of how they would work through their problems. Yet only a few days spent back with Jack and he'd already filled her life and mind again to the point where the thought of just quitting knotted her stomach with as much tension as the notion of pressing ahead on faith.

"Well, Korba? Are you ready to let me be in the driver's seat for a change? Because I definitely have some plans to fill the next hour."

"I'd say that's one helluva move, Mon."

She held out her hand, heart thudding. Three

lazy, loose-hipped steps brought him to her. Chair between them, he cupped the back of her neck and sealed his mouth to hers. Her knees went wobbly, her control not any steadier.

Which of course was what Jack was telling her with the heat of his kiss. His submissive stint could evaporate at any moment. A power play that stirred her all the more.

He pulled away, slowly, sank into the chair. She circled around to face him, his arms splayed on the rests, his knees wide enough apart for her to step between them.

She brought one of her booted feet up to rest on his thigh. "Remember when I said I wanted you to undress me?"

Masculine approval rumbled low in his throat an instant before his fingers set to work on the long laces on her desert-tan combat boots. With expert touch, he freed the knots, constraints loosening, pressure releasing around more than her foot.

The boot thudded to the side and before the echo finished, Jack had one hand up the leg of her flight suit. Strong fingers caressed past her ankle. Without once looking away from her face, he lowered her sock, peeled it away in a sensual massage over her calf that left her swaying long before he repeated the ritual with her other boot.

He rubbed from her heel to her arch. "You have the sexiest feet."

"Feet? Korba, I think you're losing your touch."

Bold, calloused fingers played over her skin, behind her knee to linger on a sensitive patch of skin that threatened to buckle her other knee from under her.

As always, Jack rose to the challenge. "Really?"

"Keep on convincing me."

"This bossy gig of yours is starting to grow on me." His hands stroked up her thighs, over her quivering belly to cup the undersides of her breasts, tormenting her with the knowledge that too much fabric kept them from skin-to-skin contact. "I seem to recall your saying something about wanting my hands on you, undressing you, watching me see you."

He skimmed her flight suit down over her shoulders, loosened the Velcro around her wrists with expert hands until the uniform slid, pooled around her feet. "And I do enjoy seeing you, Mon."

His eyes scorched every inch of her bared skin, heating through the pale cream cotton of her sports bra and high-cut panties.

She knew he was subtly reassuring her without blatantly throwing the former wife issue out there like a bucket of ice water. Even thinking about the subject on her own was chilling enough. So she refused to think. Only feel. Take this moment.

Take Jack.

Monica canted forward until her mouth met his. The chair wheeled backward across the floor. Jack's hands clamped around her waist, steadying her with broad palms against tender flesh.

Without breaking their kiss, he lifted her while she brought her legs up to kneel, straddling his thighs. The snug confines of the chair pressed her flush against him. The chair bumped to a stop against the desk with her bag and gear.

After three and a half months without him, Monica indulged herself to the fullest with the breadth of his shoulders under her hands, the musky scent of him around her, the taste of his salty skin as she nipped his neck.

Jack peeled her sports bra over her head and sent it fluttering to the floor like a white flag of surrender. He filled his hands with her breasts, lifted, dipping his head to draw on the hardened nipple already sensitive, needy, while his thumb brushed, circled attention on her other.

Greedy for the feel of more of him, Monica crawled her fingers down his chest and yanked up his T-shirt. Since she couldn't get him naked without standing, she thanked heaven for the long zipper on his flight suit that still gave her easy access to him. All of him.

She freed him from his boxers. His fingers twisted in the fabric of her panties, the power play of restraint continuing. Who would give first? She stroked down, slow, up again.

His clenched fingers tugged, pulling cotton tighter along her hip, almost cutting into her skin until…her panties snapped. He tugged, tore and flung away the underwear along with any remaining barrier between them.

Her aching breasts rubbing against his chest, she took his mouth, ready, needy for more. She flung one hand out to the side, to her bag, searched by touch through the stacks of clothes, flinging T-shirts aside until her fingers closed around…oh, yes…the box of condoms. With fumbling fingers, she filched one free and smacked it against Jack's chest.

He looked down, smiled. "Maybe you weren't so sure you could write me off after all."

"Jack."

"What, Mon?"

"Now's not the time to talk about how damned weak I am around you."

She rolled the condom down his erection in a tantalizing swipe that left them both panting.

Conversation over.

Monica positioned him, stopping just shy of penetration, teasing herself against him, her slick readiness already working to welcome him even as she rocked the tip of him against her. She needed to hear him frantic for her after all the times she'd begged him to take her. To finish. But he'd always continued with his measured pace, dragging out the tension.

Suddenly she realized what had bothered her earlier. He'd always held back emotionally, as well, the physical restraint being a symbol of that. She'd wondered if life simply wasn't that deep for Jack Korba. Now she knew better. He just hadn't allowed her admittance into that part of his life.

She didn't doubt he wanted her and enjoyed the hell out of sex with her. But at least once, she wanted to make him feel as over the edge as he made her feel. This time, she wanted to torment him.

Monica eased herself down, just an inch, no more regardless of how much her body screamed at her to take all of him. She eased up again. Then back down, no farther. Never looking away from him as she repeated the teasing partial entry for endless seconds, minutes, she lost count and was close to losing the battle...

"Enough," he snapped. Not a litany of begging but the need in the one word, the near-painful clench of his fingers on her hips sent a bolt of satisfaction through her.

He guided her down and met her with an upward thrust of his hips. The fullness, the thick pressure held her still, him as well, until her body became accustomed to him again.

Jack moved, moved again, and oh, how he moved with driving possession, faster, deeper. The familiarity of it all swept over her with a rightness tinged by a new edge—the knowledge of what it felt like to lose this. The undeniable sense that they could still lose it all if they couldn't figure out how to be together without tearing each other apart.

And damn, but the pleasure building inside was threatening to tear her apart right now. She held back. Stemmed the tide of her orgasm already clawing deep inside her for release. His hand dropped between them, found the pulsing bundle of nerves. The battle of wills stormed and, damn him, he was going to win.

The pad of his thumb circled harder, more insistently, until—

He stopped.

His fingers left her to be replaced by the cool brush of air.

"Jack," she gasped, biting back her cry of frustration that would lead her to beg him to finish when she wanted him to be the one weak with want.

Splaying his one hand along her waist, another under her bottom, he stood, taking her with him, their bodies still joined as fully as their mouths. She swung her legs around his waist, her arms hooked around his neck.

He sure as hell wasn't weak at the moment.

"Um, Jack? What are you—"

He walked. Pleasure rippled through her.

Oh, my, how he walked. Something she would never be able to watch him do again without thinking about this moment and the sensation of Jack's hips rolling with every step, nudging him deeper. Tantalizing her, increasing the building pressure then easing off without granting release, only to start the hip-rocking process all over again.

Sweat slicked her body. Or his. She wasn't sure, only knew the familiar musky scent of them together swirled around her, arousing.

"Where are we going?" Not that she particularly cared as long as he had a destination in mind for this endless torment.

She should have known he would outlast her as he always did, damn him. Her eyes fluttered open. Restraint pulled his jaw tight, turned his eyes hard.

Yes. This was costing him every bit as much as it was her. There was some victory in that at least.

He crossed the threshold into the bathroom cubicle, gently lowered her to the vanity. Cool porcelain met heated flesh. The damp warmth of his skin peeled away from her as he knelt in front of her.

Enough incentive to close her eyes again. Her fingers twisted in his hair, his hands clasping, supporting her legs, spreading her wider to accept the first tantalizing flick of his tongue.

Thank heaven for the bracing support of his shoulders against her thighs or surely she would have melted off and to the floor in a boneless mass of languid pleasure.

Her fingers fisted tighter along with the thready need to finish. Enough dragging this out, her game of enticement had turned on her. Jack's infinite patience always stretched her beyond her comfort zone into a pleasure that bordered on painful need.

More insistently, firmer, he worked her. The

knowledge that she couldn't do more than moan
softly without risking the intrusion of an entire security force drove her insane. A scream of release
built, swelled, fuller from being repressed.

Jack, no more.

She wasn't sure if she groaned it aloud or simply
thought it. Before she could reason enough to decide, he stopped.

He stood, her legs sliding to wrap around his
waist. His palms flattened to the sides of the mirror
behind her head before he drove home. Hard, deep,
insistent.

Once. Twice.

Enough.

She bit his shoulder to stifle her scream of release. Her fingers groped for a firmer hold along his
sweat-slicked back, dug, held as he bucked against
her, pulsed, muffled his shout in her hair.

Aftershocks rippled through her, through him and
back again to her, triggering another release. Muffled moans mingled with her name, his, until they
both sagged back against the sink jabbing into her
skin.

She dusted a kiss across his shoulder over the
reddening patch already purpling where she had
nipped him. So much for controlled emotions
around Jack.

With Monica's body draped against his in the
shower, Jack wondered when this woman in his

arms would quit surprising the hell out of him. She'd sure knocked him on his ass with her "bossy" scenario.

Finally he'd gotten her into the shower, his original destination, but he'd been too overwhelmed to make it beyond the bathroom sink. And then overwhelmed all over again in the shower stall.

Just the memory of her hot mouth wrapped around him minutes ago left him aching to have her again. But first he needed to find his footing. He hadn't expected the night to end this way once he'd started telling her about Tina. No shit, he wasn't lying about being new to this deep-water stuff and he wanted some lighter ground back ASAP. "So what was your talent?"

"Huh?" Monica stared at him with dewy-dazed eyes, droplets clinging to her lashes from the spray beating against his back.

"For the Miss Texas Pageant. What was your talent?"

Smack. She swatted his wet butt. "Not funny, Korba."

Oh, yeah, lighter ground and familiar territory. "I knew you'd get around to spanking me eventually."

Her laugh floated on steam. "You can be such an ass."

"Flaming batons? 'Beer Barrel Polka' on the accordion, followed by the chicken dance?" He danced her right against the tile wall.

Her hands gripped his buttocks. "Are you mocking my scholarship pageant experience?"

"Not a chance. Just trying to satisfy my burning curiosity." He rocked his hips against her, something else entirely burning hot. "Yodeling? Because if fifteen minutes ago was anything to judge by, you yodel mighty damned good."

Smack.

"Please say you worked world peace in there somewhere."

Her cat eyes narrowed. "That was number two on my platform, right behind having all fliers neutered."

"Ouch! That one hurt worse than a spanking."

"Serves you right." She settled against him again, steaming water streaking over their well-washed bodies. "Do you really want to know?"

"Yeah, Mon, I want to know everything about you." Uh-oh. Seriousness slid in like a bogey from his six o'clock.

She hooked a finger in his dog tags, tugged him down, closer, until they stood nearly nose to nose. "I gave a demonstration on how to organize cabinets."

"Really?"

"No, you idiot." She released his dog tags to clank against his chest.

He traced the path of her dog tag chain down the side of one breast, up the side of the other. "But I'm an entertaining idiot."

"That you are." She kissed the base of his neck, sipped away a taste of the water with a flick of her tongue. "I needed money for med school. I've always wanted to be a doctor. Always. The military part came later and I'll thank God for the rest of my life for the fact that I ended up in an ROTC recruiting office all because I tripped on the hem of my dress during the evening gown competition. First runner-up only gets enough scholarship money for books along with a one year's supply of beef jerky."

No self-pity for this lady, she always met life head-on, made her own way. A veritable mountain of will.

The damned persistent bogey slid in with a memory of the strain stamping her face back at the luggage hangar. He kissed the side of her brow. "Sorry Yasmine spilled it all out there."

"It's done. And there certainly are worse call signs than Tiara."

"Amen to that. Just ask poor ole Booger."

Her light laugh caressed his neck. His arms looped around her waist, hers around his. If only things could stay this warm and simple, he'd be a happy man.

"I'm sorry about your wife."

Well, hell. So much for wishes. He wasn't going to get away with light and easy any longer, not that Monica had ever let him take the easy way out. His hopes for an uncomplicated relationship like with Tina were as gone as she was.

"Me, too." His chin fell to rest on Monica's damp head and he let the water beat some sense into him. "And for what it's worth now, I'm sorry for not telling you sooner. I could make excuses, but when I line them up now, they all sound lame-ass and I owe you better than that."

"Where do we go from here?"

At the moment he was so damned glad to have her back in his arms again, he didn't want to worry about the rest. Of course, that hadn't worked with Monica in the past. "I still don't understand why the hell we have to make permanent decisions now, but I get that you need a clear plan."

"Progress." She smiled against his chest.

He crooked a finger under her chin to tip her face up to him. "But I'm not going to let you lead me around by the nose for four years like you did with that wimpy-ass Hunter while you make up your mind if you like the plan or not."

Shit. Where had that come from? Probably the same damned place as the jealousy chewing his hide.

"By the nose?" She stilled against him. "Are you trying to make me remember why I want to sign those papers or does being a bastard just come naturally to you sometimes?"

"Naturally. No doubt. And that's something else we'll have to deal with, isn't it?"

He'd had a belly full of deep-water talk for one night. Turning, he shut off the shower.

He swiped aside the plastic curtain, reached to snag two towels, passed one to Monica. Sawing the towel across his back, he forced himself not to look at her, not until he figured out where the hell his jealousy had come from.

"You know that's unfair." Her voice drifted over his shoulder.

"What?" he shot back while retrieving his clothes.

"About Hunter. Every time I postponed the wedding plans I had a TDY. You know we can't always get out of those."

Great. So she really did have a thing for the guy? He yanked on his boxers. "Whatever you want to tell yourself. How many times was it you canceled wedding plans with him? Four or five?"

Her footsteps stalled. "What was her name?"

He should have remembered she didn't fight fair.

"Tina," he answered, yanking his T-shirt over his head. "She was twenty years old, liked sci-fi movies and mushrooms on her pizza, and had just declared her major in electrical engineering before she gave birth to a stillborn son who she never even got to look at."

Monica wrapped the towel around herself, her wet hair clinging to her neck in clumps. "And you loved her. Your son, too."

Apparently, jealousy ran a two-way street, and

yet the thought didn't make him feel one damned bit better. "Yes."

This time her arms didn't go around him, no talk of who was hurting, just the two of them standing near-naked with barer souls.

"How is it that by getting closer, I feel like we're further apart?"

Couldn't they even enjoy one damned night of afterglow? "I guess that means you're not going to invite me to sleep over for another round of Mistress Monica."

"There's the Jack I know, using laughs to avoid any tough talk." She unearthed an overlong jersey from her bag and jerked it over her head, towel falling to her feet.

Of course she picked it up and made tracks to hang the damned thing on the rack. God forbid she should just let it lie there growing musty while she talked to him.

"Well, Mon, the way I see it, things don't always have to be so goddamned complicated."

She didn't answer him. But she didn't snap back, either, a positive sign he needed to capitalize on before things exploded.

"Time out," he said. "Let's stop before either one of us says too much. Okay, before *I* say too much and you haul ass the other way. How about I throw some of those blankets on the floor and we sleep the day away until it's time for my night shift in the command center."

Still she stood at the towel rack with her back to him, and he was feeling every bit as predictable as her. Instead of calming her, he had them both off center and heading for a crash if he didn't maneuver a recovery soon.

"Damn it, Monica, you have a way of getting to me. I sure as hell didn't mean to lose control just now."

She glanced over her shoulder, a strand of wet hair swinging, clinging to her cheek. "I make you lose control?"

"Hell, yeah."

She stepped into the doorway. "Sleep?"

"Seems smart." Better than talking.

"Together."

He shrugged. "Not so smart."

Her stance softened. Striding past him, she reached over to her cot and snagged the quilted sleeping bag. "I guess I'm not feeling all that smart today, either."

Again she'd surprised him. One side benefit to the complicated relationship deal.

Together, they silently spread the sleeping bag on the floor and stretched out together, Jack using Monica's pillow and Monica using Jack's chest for hers. Her damp hair soaked his T-shirt, not that he cared.

"I sang."

He pulled a wet strand off her cheek. "Sang?"

"For the talent competition. I sang a really, really

bad rendition of that Lee Greenwood song, 'God Bless the U.S.A.'"

"Ah, those soldier bones of yours begging to be set free."

"That, and probably a subconscious slap at my mother for leaving."

He hooked an arm around her waist and pulled her flush against his side. Saying nothing seemed wiser than shoving his size thirteen boot in his mouth.

Her arm slid around to hug him back. "I haven't had much experience with making a relationship work."

Saying nothing definitely seemed wiser since the truth hammered in his head loud and clear that he didn't have any more experience than her with the long term. Tina had died so young. And his bachelor days were no testament to commitment, either.

The smart woman in his arms nailed it dead-on. Somehow by getting closer they kept ending up further apart.

Jack settled onto the hard floor to sleep with his wife for the first time since the night they'd said "I do" to an Elvis impersonator nearly four months ago.

Drew pushed through the flap on the sprawling tent, a two-pack stretch of canvas holding tables with computers and the comm radio. A far sight different from the music-filled hangar of the night before.

His men were out in the desert readying for live-fire exercises, a practice run of taking the compound's airfield including everything but the jump.

While he orchestrated from the cushy-assed tented command center. In the rear with the gear, listening to radio calls being manned by the RTO—Radio Telephone Operator.

Hell, he'd worked his ass off to get to this point in his career. Damned silly to want to be out there in the field instead of sitting in here with an over-size sand-tray model of the battlefield.

Of course he *would* be in the field when they took the compound. His command center then would be nothing more than the radio and a smaller mobile comm set up in the middle of the battle.

Still, part of him itched for the time when he humped through the field for days on end, when a hot meal meant an MRE warmed on the engine block of a Humvee. Just thinking about it gelled that sense of unity, family, in him again. He embraced the feeling of pride at being a part of a hardcore, elite unit. Conditions sucked, and anyone who couldn't handle it wasn't man enough.

Drew settled in a chair behind his intelligence computer. Their practice maneuvers involved a fairly straightforward battle tactic. Once the hostages were secured by the SEALs, the support platoon would fire into the objective to get the enemies' heads up. The heavier armed attack platoon would launch a sneak approach from the other side. A flare would alert the support platoon at the correct time for a lift and shift—lift fire up and shift away so as not to shoot into the attack platoon.

They should have been launching the real deal tomorrow night, if not for the weather forecast of sandstorms. Now they would have to wait an extra day. At least they had confirmation that the three hostages were alive. Sydney Hyatt was alive.

Yasmine's half sister.

Damn, but he still couldn't believe he'd kissed Yasmine. Really couldn't wrap his head around the fact he wanted to do it again and was starting not to care how things looked.

Well, hell. Didn't he want a return to his old days when it was all about the hoo-uh? The tough choices. Easy was for the weak.

Maybe he would check up on her after they returned to the States. See how things played out on neutral ground. Take it slow since she was more innocent than he ever recalled being.

Dating? He popped a LifeSaver into his mouth.

No way could he envision himself with flowers and candy in hand on her doorstep. But he could see himself taking her to his favorite restaurant, sitting on the deck, wind in her hair and smile on her face enticing him to shake some sand off his boots.

None of which would happen if he didn't get his

mind on his job here. He shut down emotional crap and focused on the operation at hand.

Time passed in the tunnel-vision focus on his mission, the familiar sounds of radio calls and orders mixing with the pop of gunfire in the distance.

Support troops full-out. Flare. Lift and shift.

"Cease fire!" the radio crackled. "Cease fire! Cease fire!"

The tunnel vision broadened. Adrenaline and dread splashed like light exploding into his vision. Both training and instincts already predicted the next words that would bark over the radio.

"Friendly fire."

Quiet echoed through the waves, that cavern of silence during the realization of a no-going-back moment.

Drew shot to his feet and took over the radio controls. "Alpha, stat-rep to my locale ASAP."

"Will-co." Will comply.

He waited for the status report while platoon sergeants ran out to take accountability of their men. Then for the information to trickle back up the chain—company to battalion, to brigade and finally to the regiment.

"One down. Medic on the way."

Drew's thumb slid off the button. "Shit." One breath later, he ordered, "Expect me in five."

Hauling ass out of the tent and into the pitch dark toward the closest Humvee, he shouted the order to enter the field. With each slamming yard during the mile toward the glow of too many headlights and flashlights, he told himself the injury would be no more than a bullet to the leg. As if he could command it so.

The Humvee jerked to a halt. The minute his feet hit the ground, he heard it. A moan. Gurgle. The unmistakable sound of blood in the lungs.

Not a simple shot to the leg.

He knew he spoke and others answered, was certain he said the right things because training always overrode in a crisis. The very reason they trained so hard. Just as intellectually he knew how the hell this happened. Training accidents occurred because training hard also kept them from losing more in battle.

And none of that meant shit to him as he stared down at the body of one of his men on a litter having his blood-soaked uniform cut away from a sucking chest wound. His men were closer to him than his own goddamned family.

The medic finished stabilizing the private for transfer to the Battle Aid Station, two clicks behind them. A physician's assistant there would either treat him…or make the decision for more intense treatment.

Drew stared down at the bloody mess of the concert T-shirt from a boy who had barely lived half as many years as he had. As they loaded the private into the Cracker Box Army ambulance, the scent hit him. The smell of blood and war that a man never forgot.

The smell of mortality.

Chapter 14

The smell of freedom. It was so close Yasmine could almost sense it even in her dank, stuffy closet. Soon she would be out of Rubistan and away from Ammar.

So why wasn't she turning cartwheels in excitement? Or sleeping away the hours with blissful dreams?

Shuffling restlessly on her cot, she kicked the sleeping bag free, the quilted fabric too hot. Of course, no cover proved too chilly. One more reason she couldn't drift off. The erratic schedules of these military people had her sleeping patterns all flipped, leaving her cranky, restless, with too many lonely hours to remember one kiss that should not have changed so much.

The true reason for her insomnia.

Barren walls stared back at her, their monotony broken only by the hooks holding her drying underwear, daisy scarf and spare dress. Soon she would have a closet of clothes again. She would be leaving shortly, they assured her. Only a couple more days for the impending sandstorm to pass and apparently red tape would be snipped cleanly with the State Department. She would be away from Ammar's constant threat. Except she would also be away from Drew.

Drew. Rolling to her tummy, she punched her pillow, smoothed it, hugged it to her. She'd never met anyone like him. Someone so strong who did not use strength to overpower those around him into submission. He took the time to be gentle.

She'd been out with boys at the university and sometimes on trips with her mother away from Rubistan. She'd even flirted a bit on her graduation cruise, coming close a time or two to going further than a few kisses, curious as to what would make her mother leave her country and first family. What would cause other women to risk being publicly ostracized? Or worse.

But she had always stopped short because her practical nature held her back from risking all for something that was simply…nice.

Kissing Drew Cullen was way beyond *nice*.

He'd stirred more feeling with that one simple encounter than all of those *boys* combined. Could it simply be his experience, his age?

Maybe.

Regardless, she suddenly understood why women risked everything. Because right now, she would risk all to have more than just one kiss to remember Drew Cullen by.

A door slam jarred her back to the present. Feet thumped, picked up pace, pounding down the hall. Urgently, faster than the regular nocturnal activity of this never-sleeping group.

Curious, she crossed to the door, peered outside left, smiled briefly at the poor guard stuck watching her. Then looked right. Monica double-timed toward her.

Yasmine slid out into the corridor. "Is something wrong?"

Her sister slowed only briefly, tucking a wayward strand from her braid behind her ear. "Nothing for you to worry about."

Yasmine gripped her arm. "Then why are you running?"

"Work." Monica pulled free and sprinted past.

A niggle of concern tickled. Why would her sister, a doctor, be running? Yasmine trailed Monica and let the guard worry about keeping up. Breathless, she caught her at the stairs. "Since you don't have time, I will run alongside while you talk."

Monica's exasperated sigh hissed through her

teeth. "Something went wrong on a training exercise."

"Training accident? A flight?" The tickle turned to a painful pinch, but she kept pace.

"No. The Army. A gunshot wound, one or two. There are too many damned stories coming through for me to get anything straight but that they need me at the medical transport before the ambulance brings in the wounded."

"Will you have to leave?"

Monica stopped, sighed. Ill-disguised anger snapped from her eyes. "If it happens that someone is so mortally wounded that we have to fly out, I'll be sure to put in a good word for you to get a spare seat."

Her sister's words smacked over her. "That's not what I meant."

"I'm sorry, then," she acquiesced, backing away. "But I don't have time to talk."

Monica pivoted and jogged toward a door opening onto the parking ramp.

How long would she have to wait for answers?

Not as long if she followed her sister. Yasmine crossed, paused in the doorway, searching for a benign place to wait where security would not drag her back to her room. Wind lifted her hair.

Her hair?

Her hand drifted up to her bare head. She'd been so concerned about Drew she'd abandoned twenty-three years of training by leaving her scarf behind.

All because of a man she'd known less than a week.

The wind whispered her mother's voice over her. *Ah, sugar, five seconds after I set eyes on your daddy stepping out of that Mercedes, I knew. He was the one.*

As much as she loved her mother, she wasn't sure she wanted the kind of emotion that made a woman do reckless things. But. what if she never had the chance? What if the ambulance speeding in the distance held Drew?

Yasmine's feet carried her a step farther outside, as far as she dared. She did not want her escort hauling her back inside where no one would care to give her answers to the questions already tumbling over themselves in her head.

She watched her sister sprint toward the open end of one of the planes. Light poured from the gaping back ramp, people massing into a clump of desert-tan uniforms. She would have thought she could recognize Drew anywhere, but there were too many, too far away.

A military ambulance streaked across the cement. Stopped. Unloaded, the mass of uniforms blocking her from viewing the patient.

Who?

Night wind whipped all around her as it had her first night cooking the goat stew. The chilly gusts were nothing compared to the icy fear stinging through her veins. Only a handful of days before she had stared into intensely beautiful blue eyes and everything changed.

She inched deeper into the biting wind's path. Time was precious. She should have remembered after her mother's and father's deaths too early in life from a fluke flu epidemic.

Just as the unrelenting gusts tore away facades with brutal force, she felt her own self-delusions strip away. She wanted more than just a memory to take with her when she left. She craved the freedom to be with Drew.

Jack threw away his half-full paper cup of coffee and charged down the side stairs of the mobile command post now that the Army ambulance had arrived. Not that he would be able to do a damned thing for the injured private.

His boots pounded pavement toward the open ramp of the medivac plane—fully equipped for surgery. Shouldering through the crowd at the base of the plane, he worked his way into sight of the mayhem inside. He didn't know who the page had found, Monica or one of the other deployed doctors. Either way, he hoped to find the physician doing nothing more than setting some bones or stitching up an arm.

Instead he found Monica covered in blood.

He didn't do blood well, odd thing for a military guy, but there it was. Since Tina's death, all he remembered about that night was blood from the emergency C-section as they worked to save the baby while trying to save her. All the while dragging him out of the room.

To this day he couldn't even get a vaccine without breaking into a cold sweat.

For the most part his job didn't involve a lot of blood, and that was fine by him. Monica's job was all about blood. But even as his head went a little light, he couldn't look away from her involved in something so much more intense than a routine flight physical.

IV bags dangled from poles, some with clear fluid, another two dripping blood into the tube. Even with the olive-green surgical drapes, Jack could still see enough—the young man's boots, his head with an oxygen mask over his nose. A medic stood to the side, suctioning out the soldier's mouth. And in the middle of the orders and bustles and suctioning noise he heard wheezing.

Gurgling.

Death sounds of a lung deflating.

The magnitude of what was happening hit him. A kid was in there dying. Someone he had brought here. Jack braced a hand on the side of the C-17. Constricted breaths pinched inside his chest.

Monica flipped up the field medical card and scanned the contents, face unemotional. Her fingers tightened momentarily around the card.

She spoke succinctly, her firm unshakable voice somehow piercing the echoing clatter of feet and jangling equipment. "ABCs, people. Airway. Breathing. Circulation."

Her gloved finger swiped his mouth, pulling free a J-shaped device that had secured his tongue flat. With quick efficiency, she slid a tube down his throat, setting up oxygen and suction into one system while the flight nurse took vitals and called out updates.

Monica peeled back the bandage.

"Damn." The word hissed from between her teeth, her only hint of emotion before she began to flush out the wound.

Monitors squawked a half second before the flight nurse called, "He's crashing."

"Paddles."

The cavernous aircraft filled with activity. Equipment rolled from offstage closer to the litter holding their patient. Medical staffers moved around each other at breakneck speed, all focused on the patient yet never impeding one another's momentum. An absurd ballet of life and death. Organized pandemonium.

"Switch to 300. Clear."

The body jolted.

Silence.

Twice more she repeated the routine until defeat slowly filtered onto every face. Except Monica's.

"Two minutes down, Doctor," the flight nurse called.

"Get me the rib spreaders," Monica called.

A brief hesitation.

"Spreaders." No shouting, just an irrefutable order that elicited instant results, her complete control essential when seconds counted. Her assertiveness, that bossiness he teased her about, took on a new complexion, a forgivable trait in light of what her job demanded.

She leaned over the private with the oversize tongs.

He would never forget the sound. Like cracking open a chicken carcass.

Blood splurted.

He heard gagging behind him, followed by retching fading with running feet heading to the side of the plane. He didn't turn, immobilized even as his own supper knocked around inside his gut.

Never leave your wingman.

She reached her hand inside the prone man's chest. Looked up. Closed her eyes. He watched the gentle ripple of muscles flexing under her sleeve while she held the man's heart in her hand and squeezed, again, again.

Silence.

Stubbornness and confidence stamped on her features. No wonder this woman gave off the air of never needing anyone.

"Four minutes," the flight nurse said.

Her jaw tightening, Monica kept squeezing.

"Dr. Hyatt, it's been six minutes."

Her eyes closed tighter for—hell, he didn't even

know how long—before her chest deflated with a sigh, eyes opening.

Her bloody hand slid out of the chest cavity.

The roaring pandemonium stopped. Short. Quiet. Nothing but blood, hanging tubes and still people remained.

Shit. Jack's fist clenched against the metal of the plane. His eyes closed.

"Time of death…" Monica checked a watch, continued the pronouncement of calm facts riddled with bitter undertones.

This woman did not accept failure well. Being responsible for her family, her patients—feeling the weight of someone's life in her hands—had to be one helluva load to carry.

Jack looked down, saw a pair of boots beside his, not even sure when someone had joined him. He glanced up, found the Colonel, not looking much steadier than he felt.

Monica tore off her gloves. Snap. Fling. Restrained anger and frustration filled the belly of the plane.

He started to go toward her, but realized she wouldn't be ready for comfort. Not yet.

At least he'd learned something from the Vegas mess.

Backing away, he left Monica to her patient, the Colonel to his troop. Jack cleared the ramp, pivoting back toward the mobile command post, the death gurgle still echoing in his head.

A shadow snagged his attention.

Across the cement, near the main terminal door, a lone female figure stood with a military cop a few feet to the side. Yasmine. What the hell was she doing here? Regardless, the last thing Monica needed was round two of a hissing match with her sister tonight.

Here was something he could do to help her. Jack strode across the open tarmac toward Yasmine, his steps heavier than just ten minutes ago but no less determined. Slowing but not stopping, he gripped her arm to guide her through the door. "You need to be inside."

She dug in her heels with far more strength than her size or weight would dictate. "Who?"

"What?"

"Who was hurt? How bad is it? Monica wouldn't tell me anything."

What did it matter to her? She knew her sister was fine and she'd only just met the rest of them. Could she care that much about the Colonel after only a few days?

Of course, he'd been knocked on his ass five seconds after seeing Monica for the first time.

Jack gentled his hold on her arm. "One of the troops—a private—was injured during a training exercise."

He left out mention of the death until the rest of the deployed soldiers could be told. Still couldn't quite wrap his brain around it himself yet.

Yasmine blanched, flinched. Then undeniable relief flooded her face. "But Colonel Cullen is all right?"

"Yes, he's fine. I saw him myself less than a minute ago." How odd that she hadn't waited to ask Monica. He knew Yasmine was scared spitless of him, but she'd opted to question him rather than her own sister.

Her sister.

Yasmine was his sister-in-law.

What a strange damned thought right now. But after a life spent in a tight-knit family, the connection niggled at him. This woman wasn't just a pain in the ass, she was also at least temporarily his family, which made her his pain in the ass, too. His responsibility, even if things went to shit while she was here, the woman's connection to Monica was permanent.

"Thank you, Major Korba, but maybe if I stay a while longer they will have more information."

"Come on, Yasmine, you really do need to be inside before one of the security police makes a scene none of us needs tonight." He reached for her arm again.

She almost managed to suppress her fearful wince. Just as proud as someone else he knew. But she wasn't leaving without more of an answer.

"Physically there's not a mark on him. Colonel Cullen is as all right as any commander who just had one of his troops injured can be. But yeah, physically, he's fine.''

She backed away from him, toward the door. ''Thank you.''

He thought about saying more, but what? Like her sister in more ways than one, it seemed Yasmine would only tolerate help and comfort in small, measured doses.

Jack glanced back at the plane. Monica needed his distance for now. Fine. But she had to come down off her hill sometime and she would need him then whether she wanted to admit it or not.

Even under all her calm, he hadn't seen her this rattled since the news about Sydney. God, if that was the case, then he probably shouldn't set foot anywhere near her.

Thing was, he'd learned long ago with Tina that he didn't always make the rational choice.

Gut-weary, Drew reached for the doorknob to his quarters. He needed sleep. He needed peace.

Above all, he had to get himself together if he expected his men to recover morale. Officially announcing PFC Santuci's death had been beyond hell. No matter how many times he performed that task, it always sliced away a piece of him he would never get back.

He swung his door open. And stopped short.

Yasmine sat at his desk, elegant, ramrod straight.

Her uncovered hair gleamed in the lamplight, her daisy scarf in her lap.

"How the hell did you get in here?" He slammed the door shut behind him before anyone saw her in his quarters.

"People were preoccupied with the tragedy outside, which made it easy enough to slip my guard." She shrugged. "I am very quiet."

"All right. Fine. I get the picture." He pinched the bridge of his nose, not that it did a damned bit of good easing the remorse biting the edges of his brain, hampering his thinking, impeding his already-compromised ability to be rational where Yasmine was concerned. "What the hell are you doing here?"

"Waiting for you. I was worried. I needed to see that you were not hurt on the training exercise."

"Are there no secrets in this place?"

She pleated the daisy scarf between her fingers, her only sign of nerves. "I am sure there are many."

Unhooking his M-16 from his shoulder, he wondered why the hell he didn't just throw her out.

"Who was injured?"

"One of my men." He shrugged out of his flak vest.

"I know that much."

He glanced over his shoulder, questioning.

"Major Korba told me. Will your soldier be all right?"

"No."

"Oh." Her fingers stilled their quilting. "Is he—"

"Yes." He turned his back to her and resumed the reliable routine of cleaning and stowing his weapons. "Now get the hell out of my room so I can write the report."

"Do you have to write it tonight?"

"Before tomorrow. Yes. I do. That's my job." He emptied his pockets, his hand closing around a roll of LifeSavers.

A whispery rustle sounded behind him, his only warning that she approached until she eased close enough for him to smell her. A man could lose himself in that smoky sensuality.

And damn but did he ever need to lose himself tonight.

Anger, frustration and a pile of other emotions he didn't want to label popped through him like gunfire until he snapped at her, "Are you dense or just that pushy to stay where you aren't wanted?"

She stared back unflinching, her hands loosely clutching the scarf. "If I only went where I was wanted, I would not have anywhere to be lately, now would I?"

He would not allow himself to feel sorry for her. "Well, lady, at least you're alive."

Her clasped hands inched forward until she hooked one soft finger over his clenched fist. "I thought perhaps you might be upset by what happened. You do not like for others to know you are sensitive, an understandable thing for a man in your position.''

"Upset?'' He jerked back. ''Yeah, I'm upset.''

He stared down at the roll of candy in his hands. His fist clenched tighter until the fire of emotions inside him built into a collective blast. He hauled back. Flung the candy with a curse.

The roll exploded against the wall, raining lemon- and cherry-flavored fury on the floor.

Yasmine flinched, but didn't pull away or even speak.

''If you had any sense, woman, you'd get the hell away from me right now.''

Still she didn't move or answer.

He wanted to punch his fist through the wall, which would break his hand and put him out of action. Damn it, he needed an outlet for the rage bellowing inside him.

More than that, he needed Yasmine to leave his room before he lost what little control he had left. ''What do you want from me? I'm not in the mood for games. Damn it, I'm not even sure you know what you want.''

Although she'd made it clear not too long ago with her supple body draping all over him in a kiss that seared from the inside out. Even remembering brought heat, desire, darker feelings from a side of him far from sensitive. Shit, yeah, he was weak right now. One nudge and he'd fall over the edge.

She stepped closer, bringing all that smoky sensuality with her. "No games. And believe me, Drew, I know exactly what I want from you."

Her fingers went to the top button of her dress. Ah, hell. He knew he should stop her, but his battered brain went on stun. She couldn't actually be about to...

Black linen slid from her shoulders, hooked on pert breasts, before gliding free to pool around her ankles in a dark cloud. And she wasn't wearing a damned stitch of clothing underneath.

More than a nudge, she'd packed a full-out shove to a man already standing on the edge.

Chapter 15

Yasmine willed herself to stand still as Drew's shocked gaze locked on her naked body. If he laughed at her, she would die. Or kill him.

She hoped she had not misjudged. She was so certain he desired her and would welcome comfort. Her comfort.

Stay resolved. She wanted this and perhaps she was selfishly taking advantage of a weak moment, but then, ultimately they would both be glad. Yes, she was being greedy, but she also saw the pain of loss in a man who looked out for everyone and had no one to look after him. For tonight at least, that would change.

Drew scrubbed a hand over his face. "Please tell

me you haven't been like that under your clothes all the time."

She shook her head. "Only at night. Only for you."

His blue eyes flecked with molten steel. There was something a little ferocious about him tonight in his grief, but she kept focused on his eyes. She knew he would never hurt her.

Then he exploded into action. She forced herself not to flinch.

"Shit." He yanked his sleeping bag off his cot and threw it around her shoulders. "You don't know what the hell you're doing."

"You are wrong." She stepped closer, kicking her clothes aside.

"Wouldn't be the first time, and I'm not going to let it happen again. Not tonight." He scooped her dress off the floor and thrust it toward her. "Now get dressed. And for God's sake, find some underwear."

Embarrassment burned her chilled skin but she was not the type to quit. She released the sleeping bag.

"Damnation, woman!" Her dress fluttered to the floor again as he grabbed the quilted blanket and folded it around her.

Which brought them chest to chest, his fists between them securing the sleeping bag. The heat of the backs of his hands branded the sides of her breasts. Immobilizing her.

Him as well.

Yasmine peered silently up into eyes muting from flecks in the deep blue to that total silvery gray of arousal. His chest expanded and she knew he was catching her scent. Emboldened, she sidled nearer, flush against him. The rigid heat of his erection pressed against her stomach even through the fabric between them.

She smiled, slow, sure.

"Shit." Drew cursed low.

Yasmine clasped her hands over his. "You really need to quit saying that every time we are together."

"Then maybe you need to quit driving me insane."

Any fears of being rejected melted to warm butter in her veins. "I do that?"

"You know damned well you do."

Yasmine wiggled against him, longed to toss aside the blanket to feel the undiluted sensation of his hands on her flesh. Her skin cried out for his touch, for contact. For so long she had gone without the most basic of physical affection from even family. Her half sisters from her father's side resented her because of her mother. Her sisters from her mother resented her because of her father.

She was lonely and aching and so very alone. She'd been denied freedom and choices for too long. This moment was hers. Theirs. "Is it so wrong for me to want to comfort you right now?"

To steal some comfort for herself?

"Do you make it a practice to dole out comfort this way to any man?"

His harsh words sliced her. But then she had brought this on herself with her behavior. Even if he had guessed at her limited experience, he might not know just how limited.

Intuition whispered through her. Was he trying to push her away? "Take me and you will have your answer as to whether I have 'comforted' anyone before."

"All right, Yasmine, you can cut the crap. I've had worse days than this. I can assure you I'll survive without your virgin sacrifice."

A smile welled inside her but she stifled it for fear of angering him more. Of course he knew how innocent she was. He had kissed her and would undoubtedly have recognized her inexperience. "Before you can roll out any more excuses…" She paused, snaking a hand loose to reach down to fish in her dress pocket, tugging free a small packet to press into his palm. "I brought protection."

He stared down at the condom nestled in his hand with more shock than when he had found her note in the same place. "Where the hell did you get this?"

"From my sister."

He choked on a cough. "You talked to your sister about us?"

She couldn't help but laugh as she slid back

against him. "No, although now I wonder if I should have sought advice from her after all. Apparently the fact that I am standing naked in your arms and you are doing nothing must mean either I am not attractive to you or I am too inexperienced to do this right."

"You're doing damned fine." His eyes strayed down to the hint of cleavage showing above the clasped material. His throat moved with a long swallow before he forced his eyes back up. "I just can't figure out why the hell you're doing this. How does a woman who's held out for twenty-three years make the decision to lose it with a guy she's known about a week?"

"Would you like to hear the whole list?"

"Yeah, I think I need to."

If he wanted to hear her list, then he wanted to be convinced. Yes.

"Number one, the opportunities were rare before." She counted down on her fingers. "Two, I am finally free to make my own decisions and three, I like you. Four, you are a sexy, fascinating man. And why am I so quick to decide? Well, women in my culture often end up married to men they've met only a few times after always being chaperoned prior. We've spent more time together than that, and this certainly is not about marriage. Which gives you five solid arguments right there."

All of which did not appear to be swaying him.

She would have to bare a little piece of her soul, far more daunting than baring her body.

"But the real reason?" She stopped her countdown and tapped his temple. "Your eyes. I trust from your eyes that you are the man who will treat my first time with care. So much of my life has been chosen for me. Right now, I choose. I want you. And as long as you want me, too, then as two consenting adults we have every right to this."

His stance adjusted, a slight shuffle of his boots that brought him even closer, his legs bracketing hers. She was not even sure he consciously realized his action of his body beginning to accept the feel of her against him.

"Are you a lawyer? Because you sure do argue like one."

With his warm thighs pressing against hers for encouragement, she allowed herself a laugh, surprising even herself with the low, husky sound that came from her throat. "No, I am just a woman very determined to have exactly what she wants, and more than anything, I want to make more memories of you to think about once we leave this place."

She left unspoken her desire to erase the torment in his eyes and repeated, "I want you, Drew."

The instant his name caressed the air between them, she saw his resistance evaporate. With deliberate hands, he eased the sleeping bag from her shoulders. The nip in the night air warmed under the heat of appreciation in his eyes.

Her hand glided to cup his face as she arched on her toes to press her lips to his. The freedom of touching him loosened threads within her tangled so tight from years of restraint she unraveled against the hard-muscled strength of him.

"Touch me," she whispered against his mouth.

His growl of surrender vibrated through his chest, against her skin, the coarse fabric of his uniform rasping an arousing abrasion against her nipples. His arms rose from his sides, his hands falling to rest against her back and stirring a low moan deep inside her. Her eyes slid closed at the strong warmth of his arms along her skin.

If his muted heat through his clothes felt this exciting…

He kissed her thoughts silent. How could she do anything but feel with his intensity poured on her, her mouth? Sensuality long denied flooded her. Too many emotions, sensations, jumbled through the waves sweeping away control.

She fumbled with the top button of his uniform, but her fingers shook. His hands fell over hers, brushed them aside, and just as she began to protest, he started down the row of fastenings.

The long overjacket went first, leaving him in just a brown T-shirt stretched taut across his broad chest, tapering down to trim hips encased in camouflage pants. Her hand itched to press against the flat expanse of his stomach, but she feared slowing him.

Or worse yet, doing something to jar him into turning away.

So she watched and soon realized that her undisguised appreciation apparently pleased him. And oh, but she was mesmerized by the honed cut of him as his T-shirt swept up and off to reveal an expanse of tanned muscle, defined pectorals.

And a toned stomach she vowed she would explore soon.

Some vaguely rational part of her brain also realized he was using this time to give her a chance to adjust to the newness of this moment. To the newness of a naked man's body in front of her.

His boots settled beside the chair next, followed by his pants until he stood only in his military-brown boxers. Impatience jabbed like hundreds of tiny needles against her skin. No more of his slow adjustment time. She wanted to see all of him. Now.

His thumbs hooked in the waistband. "Last chance to walk away, Yasmine."

Instead she walked toward him, clasped her hands over his to urge his shorts down and off. Then she really looked, followed the broad bare chest down to where his skin lightened with a tan line. Lower.

Her breath hitched in her chest. Nerves increased the pin-prickly sensation. Okay, apparently there would be some serious adjusting going on for her soon.

He flung his shorts and uniform pants over a

chair. A flash of color snagged her eye. She used the distraction to steal a moment to steady herself.

Rose silk? She reached past him, hooked her finger on the hint of pink fabric peeking from his pocket and trailed it free, inch-by-inch, like the magic show on the cruise she'd taken with her parents…

Her scarf.

Her mind raced back to the last time she'd worn it, how she'd linked their hands while they'd kissed. He'd kept it.

A heady rush pulsed through her, something alien, exciting. Powerful. Her insecurities vanished. ''You kept my scarf?''

''I guess it's a good thing this attraction is two-sided.'' He echoed an altered version of her words from before.

''That it is, Colonel.'' She draped the length around his neck, tugged his head down to hers. ''That it most definitely is.''

He did not speak, but the presence of her scarf secreted away in his pocket was reassurance enough. Interesting how being desired heightened her own desire all the more.

Drew stared down at the unmistakable passion smudging Yasmine's near-opaque eyes and knew he was being a selfish bastard to allow her to give up her first time in the crap confines of cramped military quarters with a guy old enough to be— Hell, he didn't want to think about that.

And damned if he could walk away from her now.

All the rage and loss from a hellish day demanded release. Hard. Fast. In a warrior's roaring need to conquer. Win.

He might be selfish, but he wasn't an animal. He could, would, rein himself in enough to make sure she received the gentle treatment she deserved. He might be taking, but he would damn well make sure he gave her something in return.

Backing her toward the cot without breaking the warm drugging draw of sweeping her mouth with his tongue, he reached behind her to snag the pillow, fling it to the floor on top of the discarded sleeping bag. He cradled her to him, lowered her, dropping to one knee, his hand extended past to slow their fall until he guided her to rest in the fabric folds.

Never had an Army-issue bedroll looked so damned good. As a backdrop for Yasmine's dusky-naked beauty it was goddamned masterful.

Control inched further away with a painful throb.

She stared back up at him with trusting eyes, her fingers twisted tight in the splash of pink from her scarf. Her hair pooled around her, glossy dark on the white pillow.

Kneeling over her, he worked the silken length free from her grasp. He might not be much with pretty words, but he sure as shit understood a thing or two about the subtle nuances of pleasure he would like to teach this woman.

He hooked her scarf on one finger, the two tails trailing. Slowly he grazed the edges over her shoulder, along her collarbone in a gentle never-ending swipe that raised goose bumps on her skin while she watched him. No objection came from her mouth, just the soft rush of a contented sigh that rippled silk.

His path continued, lower to skim the tip of one hardened nipple the exact same deep rose color of the fabric between his fingers. He repeated the scarf's trail further, over her belly, down one leg and up the inside again until he stroked to the vee of her legs. Even as the all-over blush spread across her, she didn't tell him to stop.

Then he retraced his course with the scarf, followed by the caresses of his free hand. And once more. This time with his mouth skimming, nipping just after the gentle swish of silk against silkier skin until he found his way back up to her lips again.

One elegant arm stretched up around his neck, languid, her fingers gliding along his shoulder, tracing every muscle, following down his arm…

To steal the scarf from him.

Her Eve-smile gave him all of three second's warning before she stroked down his chest, her hand covered in the scarf. Down. Down. Until…oh, yeah…damned if she didn't drape the scarf over his erection, deliberately, wrapping the silky length around and around.

She folded her fingers over it, encircling him, stroked. "Am I doing this right?"

His head fell to rest on her shoulder, his breath ragged. "Yeah, I think you've got the right... Yeah."

A woman with intuition and imagination like this could rob a man of his will to breathe. The combination of her hands on him and the smoky, exotic scent all around him stirred him too much, too fast, for a man his age, damn it.

Scooping the scarf from her along with control, he rolled onto his back and positioned Yasmine over him.

Hints of maidenly embarrassment, a sense of awkwardness flickered across her face. "Uh, Drew, isn't that uncomfortable for you—"

"After twenty years in the Army, I've grown accustomed to hard ground." He made fast work of tearing open the condom and sheathing himself. "Hell, the sleeping bag makes this downright cushy compared to some gigs."

"But I'll squish you." She fidgeted against him until he gritted his teeth to combat the sensation.

"Lady, I've jumped out of planes carrying gear heavier than you."

He stroked from her breasts to clasp her waist. Her muscles tensed beneath his hands into a sheet of nerves in contradiction to her encouraging smile.

"Trust me." He massaged gentle persuasion

along the slight flare of her hips until she relaxed under his hands.

His hold firm, he guided her down. Stopping. The first touch of her moist heat against him battered his better intentions. Her impatient wiggle threatened to send him deeper, faster, when he knew well they needed to take this initial entry slow, careful. Excruciating.

His muscles trembled more from the effort of holding back than from holding her until finally he breached the thin barrier. Her wince, followed by instinctive tensing of internal muscles had him tensing in return, clenching back the surge of pleasure from her vise grip around him.

Again he forced himself to wait until she relaxed under his caresses before moving, thrusting, all the while watching her watching him and finding in her eyes an echo of what he felt certain scrolled across his own.

Heat. Need. *Pleasure.*

He moved with her as she discovered her natural rhythm and grace here, as well. Then they found the pace and style unique to the two of them together. Moving with and against each other in the darkened room until perspiration sheened her smooth skin, sweat beaded along his brow. And he knew that soon, damned soon, he wouldn't be able to hold back any longer. But he wasn't going solo.

Reaching between them, he stroked her where

their bodies joined. Her head lolled forward, her hair sliding past her shoulders in a black curtain.

He increased the pressure, allowed himself to thrust harder, quicker, until the increasing rise and fall of her rose tipped breasts reassured him she was seconds away from finding her...

Release.

A moan built, swelled up from her mouth in a torrent of foreign words as a fresh wash of goose bumps swept her flushed skin. She trembled beneath his hands, and again until slowly her lashes slid open and she peered at him through her curtain of hair with astonishment.

He stared up at her staring back down at him. What did she see in his eyes now? Her hand glided from his chest to cradle his face. She smiled and she moved, some sort of instinctive womanly roll of her hips against his. *Hell.*

His restraints tore, sent him plummeting hard and fast like tripping out of an airplane into the wide-open sky, all the more surprising since he damned well should have more control at his age. But who the hell was he to argue? Instead he let the all-out force whip over him like the wind against his body in a free fall that just kept pulsing over him because of this woman.

Yasmine.

His hand still between them, he stroked high against her slick folds again, intense, deliberate until she joined him this time. Her spine bowed, her head falling back until the tips of her hair swished along his other hand bracing her waist, sending another jolt of pleasure shuddering through both of them.

Finally she crumpled onto his chest with a purr, as well as an exhausted sigh that stirred masculine satisfaction. Along with a hefty dose of confusion over how one woman could shift everything so quickly.

He'd set his course long ago when Glenna walked out on him, dragging their daughter and any sense of family along with her. Sometimes when a man heard a calling as strong as his, he had to choose. And he'd opted for the Army and nights camped out on nothing more than packed earth rather than the comfort of a wife's bed.

With the hard ground under him and soft Yasmine over him, he wondered if maybe a man could have the best of both worlds after all.

Monica rested her head against the shower wall and watched the blood-tinged water swirl down the drain. Any residual hold over her shredded emotions spiraled away, as well.

She'd lost patients before. Not many. But it happened and it was never easy. Yet this one tore a new hole in her heart.

Rocked her confidence.

Her grasp on the threads holding her world together was slipping away faster than the water down the drain when she prided herself on controlling her destiny. Her science, scalpel, boots, it was all about being in control of her world on every front.

What a joke. She controlled nothing. She couldn't save Santuci. She and Jack were still a mess. She might be here for Sydney, but she sure as hell wasn't saving her. Jack was taking care of that. She hadn't ever felt this out of control, except when Sydney was captured.

Or had she?

Water chilled on her body. She'd felt exactly like this the day her mother left. The day Cheryl Lynn Hyatt clicked off Saturday morning cartoons to explain to her girls why she couldn't be their full-time mama anymore.

Anger steamed through Monica hotter than the water scouring her skin. Strange, but she hadn't felt even a fraction of this much rage when Hunter had issued his final ultimatum after her job wrecked their wedding plans for the fifth time.

Was she truly unable to commit as Hunter had accused her of? Had she led Hunter around by the nose for four years as Jack said?

She shut off the water, sagged back against the wall and tried to scavenge the energy to step out.

The shower door popped open instead. Jack filled the void, wearing a flight suit and a face full of worry. How had she missed him entering her room? Some warrior she made today.

A big towel in hand, he waited, not a normally expected wisecrack in sight. She was too soul-weary for modesty. A ridiculous notion around him, anyway.

He backed to give her room to follow, then wrapped the towel around her, pulled her against him while the fluffy cotton soaked up the water on her skin.

Her cheek rested against the steady percussion of his heart. "Jack, I can't have sex with you. Not tonight."

Not now when she was so out of control.

Oh, hell. Had even sex with Jack been about control for her? She'd controlled the relationship in the early days since he was chasing her. And heaven knew Mistress Monica had been in control in the chair.

Still, she couldn't think about sex with Santuci's blood, his death, still all over her. "I wish I could, Jack. God knows I'm wound tight and could probably use the release. But I just…I can't."

"I know." He walked backward, leading her into the room. Holding her firm with one arm, he reached with the other to pull a sleep shirt out of her suitcase. He tugged the jersey over her head, tugged one hand through, and then the other. "Sleep."

Her eyes strayed to the floor where they'd slept tangled in each other's arms before and wasn't sure she could even open herself that much without revealing too many wounds right now. "Is this really such a good idea—"

Jack scooped her up, strode to her cot and set her down. He lifted her feet and slid in under them to sit before dropping her legs into his lap.

Not sleeping against each other. He'd offered her an out, a way she could keep her distance so she didn't fall apart, while still being there for her.

She sagged back into her pillow. "Thank you."

For being here. For understanding she was so damned messed up she couldn't even accept the comfort of sleeping in his arms.

He started a firm massage along the arch of her foot. "There's nothing more you could have done."

"I know. He bled out. That simple."

His strong grip worked her ankle in a slow rotation, and damned if he wasn't peeling back layers of protective covering until her eyes prickled.

She flung her arm over her face as a barrier against tears. Instead her blank eyelids provided an empty canvas for memories of picking up the patient's field medical card to check his prior treatment. Seeing the name. Recognizing it. Looking up to the blood-covered face she'd been unable to identify before, and back at the card again.

"Oh, God, Jack, his name was Pete. Day by day, he was Private First Class Santuci. But right now, all I can remember is that his mama named him Pete."

"Doctor or soldier, we both work in jobs that

take too many lives too young. Hearing their names is what keeps us human.''

And also tore her apart.

Jack kept rubbing, and while her ache didn't ease, at least it was back under control. Thanks to Jack. He wasn't an easy man to be with, but she couldn't deny there was so much wonderful about him. If only she could open herself up enough to accept it.

Instead she cinched her pillow tighter and simply remained grateful that she hadn't lost all grip on her world. Her emotions.

Self-knowledge was a huge pain in the ass. She was scared of failing with Jack, of being abandoned again and having her grip slide away for good. Of course, she was already alone in her rigidly ordered little world. But then being alone by choice was a helluva lot easier to face then being left alone if Jack walked.

Foggy edges of sleep thinning, Yasmine blinked against the disorientation. And found herself staring into deep blue eyes looking back up at her as she sprawled over a decidedly male and naked chest.

''Good morning.'' Drew's gravelly greeting vibrated under her.

''Good morning to you, too.'' She stretched against him, worked out the kinks and slight ache in well-loved muscles, Drew's body making the most wonderful mattress. She arched forward to drop a quick kiss on his mouth, then on his furrowed brow that worried too much.

Had he even slept? She couldn't see him lowering his guard to rest. And of course he had every reason not to trust her.

Already the niggling truth diluted her morning-after euphoria. She tucked her face against his bristly chest to keep him from seeing the fears that likely flickered through her eyes. What would he do when he discovered the truth? Maybe he would never have to know. How easy to latch on to that notion.

His fingers stroked along her back, continually, as if he sensed her need for contact. "Yasmine, the next few days are going to be hectic. And then you'll be tied up with inprocessing and questioning once you make it to the States."

A chill iced through her skin to her bones. "Are you giving me the brush-off?"

"Do you want me to?"

She shook her head against his chest and listened to the steady thump of his heart.

"What's your plan once you're there?"

The thought that he might offer more... She tamped down even the idea. "I had hoped to stay with one of my sisters until I find work."

"Don't you have a pile of your daddy's oil money stashed away somewhere?"

"Not if I leave here."

His arms tightened around her protectively. "If you need anything…"

She smiled against his chest. How like a man to assume she was helpless. "Thank you, but I will be fine. Of course I have to pass licensure boards in the United States, but then I plan to find work."

"Licensure boards?"

Worries took a momentary back seat to the immediate pleasure of surprising him. "I am a nurse."

He didn't disappoint. He hefted her shoulders up far enough where she could see his shock—and pride. "A nurse? No shit?"

"No shit."

They laughed together as she cuddled back against his chest. "I graduated from the university last year." Took a cruise with her parents, so happy and carefree only weeks before her world exploded into hellish mayhem. "My bachelor's degree may not be as prestigious as my flight surgeon sister's medical degree, but I can support myself anywhere I choose to live."

"Anywhere?"

Had she pushed too hard for a sign from him? These man-woman dances were new to her. "But of course first I will need to take care of those licensure issues. So I imagine I will be spending some time with my sister in Virginia."

His chest rose and fell under hers and she could almost hear the thoughts shuffling around inside his head. Finally a deep sigh lifted her higher before he said, "Virginia, huh? I know this restaurant I like to go to whenever I am up in D.C., not too far away from where you'll be."

Her fingers convulsed against his arms with hope that maybe she could hold on to this moment after all. Have another such moment with this man. "A restaurant?"

"On the water. I think you'll like it."

He fell silent again. She sensed he would not be offering her any more just yet, but recognized the wealth of commitment in that simple statement coming from such a stark man. He kissed her hair, toyed with a lock. And just that fast, that simple, her heart tumbled.

She loved him. Truly loved this man.

She let the notion settle. Where was the joy? Instead she was terrified because the flash of love showering through her illuminated hundreds of tiny flaws and lies within her, leaving no unexposed corner to tuck them away.

Selfish wishes had no place here between them. This was no longer about her keeping her secrets. It had become about him, and being worthy of him, because somehow one day this man would see into her soul.

And she desperately wanted a someday with him.

There was only one way to have it. Tell him the truth now. She would have to pray that his innate sense of honor would understand she really had no choice before and that he would forgive her.

"Drew," she repeated, savoring the feel of his name on her lips in case she never had the right to say it again. "I need to tell you something I have been keeping hidden."

Chapter 16

The daylight exposed everything.

Sydney closed herself in to hide from the bright sun's rays, her arms wrapped around her stomach. She hunched ever so slightly during her brief walk within the small fenced area. Changes in the schedule unsettled her. Why a lunchtime walk when they always, always, walked after supper during the cooler part of the day?

The high-noon rays baked her skin and the top of her head until sweat trickled between her breasts. Kayla and Phillip strolled a few feet ahead, side-by-side most of the time these days. Their growing bond seemed so obvious to her she feared their captors might see it, too. Exploit it. Soon, she wouldn't have to worry any longer.

Stored heat from the ground saturated up through the soles of her sandals. Still, she didn't dare complain or sacrifice the too brief taste of freedom.

Today more than ever she wanted to be outside, that much closer to Blake.

Scanning the stark stretch of rocky desert broken only by high, barbed fences, she marveled that he had made it in, stayed hidden even now. Where was he? She shifted left, right, tried to sense his eyes on her. Craved the connection.

For the first time in nearly four months she dared dream about afterward. She wasn't naive enough to imagine she would escape this hell without some emotional scars. She wondered if it would be easier to move forward with someone who understood the nightmare as Phillip and Kayla had done. Or would any relationship need to be a fresh start with no connections or reminders of…everything.

Of course, she would have one very tangible reminder in the baby. She wouldn't abort it. And even as she considered adoption, she just as quickly abandoned the notion because it smacked too much of her mother's leaving. As much as she tried to put a positive spin on that one, it still hurt.

Deeply. It had taken her a long time to share her real feelings about that with Blake.

She squinted into the rippling heat waves distorting the horizon. Could he see her? Focus in on her more clearly now than he had in those early months of their relationship when she'd kept so much hidden. Out of his reach. She tried to remember what sort of equipment he mentioned using on other missions. But then before long they'd avoided talking about work. Hers and his.

Until finally there hadn't been anything left to talk about *but* their jobs...

"If you quit, I will, too." Sydney delivered her ultimatum with hope, even while deep within her a voice much like her practical sister's insisted she'd just dealt the relationship a death blow.

Blake turned his head on the pillow. "What?"

"If you quit the Navy, I'll resign my position with the IFB. I won't go to Rubistan."

He leaned to kiss her, inching the patchwork quilt higher to combat the Virginia winter chill. "You know I can't do that. I owe time. I can't walk away without risking a court martial."

"Then stop being a SEAL. There are other things you can do in the Navy that won't take you into the same dark pits you've seen lately."

He stopped adjusting the quilt around them. Morning sun glinted a halo off his golden hair, highlighting the swirl of his boyish cowlick so at odds with the honed man. "You're not really serious. You just want me to be the one to say no so you're off the hook."

"Try me."

"Fine, then." Rare strains of anger tightened his jaw. *"I'll make this easy for you. Quitting is not an option. I'm a SEAL. It's who I am and if you can't live with that then apparently you can't live with me."*

"Why can't you see the same applies for me, as well? The very things you want from me are the things that make it impossible for me to walk away from what I do."

"Bullshit. At least I protect myself."

"We have protection. Escorts."

He snorted.

"More of you are injured and killed in your profession than mine. The only real difference I can see here is that you're a man and I'm a woman."

His eyes shut tight. Exploding into motion, he rolled away from her and buried his face in his hands. *"Damn it, Sydney, you don't know what I've seen over there. What they can do to you."*

Because he wouldn't talk to her. Instead he let it swallow him whole until she knew one day he wouldn't come back even if the shell of his body walked in the door. *"I love you, Blake."*

Muscles flexed and rippled across his back, twitched in his arms. *"You know I love you, too."* His hoarse answer scratched the air.

"I'm not so sure love is enough anymore if we can't accept each other." She sat up, pulled her knees to her chest, the gulf between them widening by the second. *"You tell me all the time I'm your*

*haven. Well, you know what? You don't want me
so much as somebody to save you the same way I
save homeless kids in a Third World country.''*

How damned ironic that now Blake would be the
one saving her.

She stared out at the hard-caked sand and winged
her thoughts toward him. *I'm sorry.*

If only she'd thought to say it then.

Sydney walked as close to the edge of the camp
as she dared and talked to Kayla and Phillip in case
Blake could hear with all that equipment they never
discussed. The sound of his voice had brought her
immeasurable comfort two nights ago. She hoped
hers, if he could hear her, would do the same.

''Who won the last game of spades?''

A hand clamped around her arm. ''Come with
me,'' the guard ordered in guttural English. A flut-
ter twinged in her stomach. Nerves. Again. Stronger
until she realized…

Oh, God. Not nerves. The baby moved.

Before she could wrap her mind around the land-
mark moment in her pregnancy, the guard tugged
her again, dragging her toward the center of the
compound until they stopped in front of a stark,
cement, one-story building beside her barracks cell.

Like all the other buildings.

Inside, down the hall they walked. His knock
elicited a brusque command. The voice. Too familiar. She fought the urge to run.

The door swung wide, bringing her face-to-face with her worst nightmare. Her baby's father.

Ammar al-Khayr sat behind a desk like any businessman on a lunch break, plate in front of him. His dusty khakis and loose, linen shirt rippled with gusts from the fan in front of a window, the same fan wafting spices into the air, gagging her. She remembered too well the smell of them on his breath inches from her face, over her.

She forced herself to blink and breathe evenly. He was just a man. Quite ordinary in appearance actually, average height and weight.

Deceptively so.

God, but he was strong. Fearfully strong even when he had to be nearing fifty. Fanaticism defied age. He might harm her, but he wouldn't win. She just had to stay alive a little while longer.

His gaze roved her, but not sexually—it had never been sexual. She knew without question he hated her simply because of what she represented. He didn't lust after her, in fact, found her disgusting, to be used. Abused.

Still he continued to evaluate her while she struggled not to fidget in spite of the creepy feeling spidering up her spine. Had she somehow given Blake away? Or had they been found out? Bile burned hot in the back of her throat. The stifling heat, stench, and memories wreaked havoc on her already queasy stomach.

"Have a seat, please, Ms. Hyatt. It seems we

have a problem on our hands and since you are the senior member of your group, I decided to bring it to your attention first.''

He definitely knew something. And between Blake and the baby, she carried two colossal secrets that could cost her life. Or worse—theirs.

Jack hated dreams because there were no secrets.

Dreams attacked with a no-holds-barred approach while a guy's defenses were down. Everybody had to catch some Z's eventually and dreams' agendas were patient. Even as he tried to wrestle himself out of the nightmare of the moment, he wasn't having a helluva lot of luck.

This particular one had its claws in deep, submerging him in a skyful of blood and wives with life-and-death stakes. His dad kept chanting over Jack's headset about how a man kicks ass for his woman.

Jack understood he'd screwed up that lesson. He turned over control of the jet to Rodeo so he could crawl down into the cargo hold and ask his brother Tony for absolution.

And crap, but his dreams always seemed to enjoy digging those claws deeper with irony and humor as if to pay him back for his own smart-ass ways. Because then damned if Tony didn't deny forgiveness with a resounding rendition of ''Don't Be Cruel'' before hopping into Grandma Korba's Pinto and driving off the back load ramp into a wide-open sky.

Shit, he *was* trying with Monica. This time he had his uniform and M-9 and military airplane. He was doing his best to kick ass and take names, to save her sister. Keep Monica safe. He wouldn't screw it up again.

He had himself reined in. Always, slow and easy. No losing control like some reckless college kid who was so horny that half the time he forgot to walk across the room for a condom when making love to his wife even though they had both decided to put off kids until after graduation.

Hell, no. He held it together with Monica.

But still she was standing beside him with blood all over her uniform and he knew it was hers. Except he couldn't find where she was bleeding from. And if he couldn't figure out what she needed from him, then he would lose her. He would have failed again.

He didn't have much longer left. The load ramp was shutting, cranking up, almost there, soon would shut off all the light and he wouldn't be able to see where the blood was coming from. Closing. Darker.

Thunk.

Thunk. Thunk. Thunk.

Jack jolted awake, Monica's legs heavy in his lap, the room dark from her blackened window.

Thunk. Thunk. Thunk.

The door. Someone was knocking on Monica's door.

Her legs stirred against him. She flung an arm over her face. "Jack?"

"Shh." His hand rested on her feet. "It's okay. Just someone at the door. Go back to sleep. I'll take care of it."

She bolted upright, jerked her feet from his lap to the floor. "For God's sake, this is my room. I'll get it."

Swiping a hank of dried-wild hair from her face, she padded to the door, cracked it open while blocking the view inside with her body. "Jesus, Rodeo. Do you know what time it is?"

"Uh, sorry to bother you, but, uh, I'm looking for Cobra."

Jack strode up behind her, rested a possessive hand on her shoulder. "This better be important, man. Your timing sucks."

"Sorry, bud." Derek winced. "I wouldn't come here unless it was serious and I figured better me than someone else. The Colonel's looking for you two. There's a…situation…with Doc's sister."

Drew didn't need to see outside the office window to feel the sandstorm brewing. The blocked window prohibited view, anyway, since being boarded up after the looting peasant incident.

And again here he stood, Yasmine on the wrong

end of an OSI inquisition about her presence at the airfield.

He focused on the impending sandstorm and its implications instead. If it weren't for that damned storm due to start rolling in right around midnight, they'd be prepping to leave and finish this whole operation. He and his men never would have been out in the field last night running training maneuvers, making use of the extra time to perfect their battle plan just a little more because of the bad weather predictions.

PFC Pete Santuci would still be alive.

Which brought him right back around to Yasmine again, anyway, as she answered endless questions. When the hell had he thought about anything but her since she shoved that note in his hand?

He felt like an old fool.

Old being the operative word for a man stuck smack-dab in the center of some damned midlife crisis. She'd read him and played him right up to the moment she stared down at him with those bottomless brown eyes, her nubile, naked body fogging his brain.

Drew, I need to tell you something I have been keeping hidden. Ammar al-Khayr sent me here to find out the truth about your mission.

Everything inside him had shut down at that point.

He didn't remember much afterward other than that he'd hauled her up, barked at her to get dressed while he'd yanked on his own clothes. No turning his back on a woman who might knife him. No, he'd kept his back to the wall and watched her stoically drag her dress over her head.

Then he'd led her here to let Max Keagan and Daniel "Crusty" Baker do their work because apparently his objectivity was shot to hell. She'd concocted some story about their maps of the terrorist compound being incomplete. Helpful guidance? Or a deadly trap?

Drew crunched a LifeSaver since he'd already been through every other goddamned letter in the alphabet over the past hour. Sure, she'd 'fessed up, right after she hooked then reeled him in. Did she expect to play him as her sympathy card? Think again, Sheba.

Fool me once, shame on you. Fool me twice, shame on me.

His involvement with her already put him in a sticky-as-hell situation. From here on out, it was by the book.

Anger sparked from her eyes as she repeated answers to questions already asked. Tough shit. This was how the game was played to check her story. Let her get mad.

Or was she spitting fire to keep from crying? Damn it. Damn it. Damn it! He would not fall into that trap of hers again.

Her spine straight against her chair, regal as ever,

she insisted, "I genuinely want to go to the United States. So when he—"

"Ammar al-Khayr," Crusty Baker interjected from beside the window, his voice tight, "a known terrorist responsible for targeting Americans around the world simply because of their nationality, a man directly linked to assassinating our ambassador here."

Who also happened to be Baker's father. The interrogator had more cause for his anger than even Yasmine knew.

She paled, dark circles from her night with little sleep staining a deeper purple. "When he offered me a way into your camp, of course I said yes."

Keagan stepped in to take over the questioning from Baker, stopping by the desk. "This would have all carried more weight if you'd told us straight up."

She looked down, displaying a stretch of daisy scarf along her head. Her hands in her lap twisted around her rose scarf. Damn her. "I did not know who to trust."

"And now you do," Keagan prompted.

"I hope so." She didn't even glance Drew's way. She didn't have to. "I will tell you whatever you want to know about him if that will help your people."

"Why would we be interested in this man?"

She raked her best haughty gaze over the uncon-

ventional OSI officer's spiky hair and bright yellow
polo shirt. "You must really think I am stupid."

The clock on the wall ticked. How much did she
know and how had she found out?

More important, who had she told?

Keagan hitched a hip on the desk corner. "Now's
the time to prove to us just how smart you are."

She pleated the scarf in her lap faster. Nerves?
Or lies? "It is obvious you are here for more than
dropping off food for starving locals. Ammar al-
Khayr has escaped justice in the States once. I sin-
cerely hope you are here to dispense it now so he
cannot appropriate the funds of every orphan who
happens to share a distant relative with the man. I
am not the first he has tried this with. A simple
search will tell you that. As you so eloquently put
it, your own unfortunate ambassador here was assassinated. And only because the ambassador's wife
was related to Ammar who wanted control over the
man's wealth through his children."

She paused, frowning. "Or maybe you already
know that."

That and more. Baker's father, the man's wealth
and political influence was far spread and well
known in the States. The very damned reason Baker
and Jack Korba together had been able to land
themselves on this mission.

"All I want is to get out of this country. You
can listen to what I have to say or not. Your choice,
Mr. Keagan."

"What about the hostages in the compound?"

"Who?" Her fingers stilled on the silk. "Which ones? Ammar is always holding somebody. Snatching people for bargaining influence. You seem to think I am making an easy choice in telling you because you can offer me military protection. But you do not seem to realize how far his reach extends. I risk much more by talking than by staying silent."

Finally, Drew let himself ask, "Then why do it?"

She met his gaze directly for the first time since she'd sprawled naked on top of his chest. "Because I want people to look in my eyes and see honor."

Damn but she fought dirty. All the more reason to keep his guard up around her now more than ever. She knew him, had used her time wisely to find the chinks in his armor.

A knock sounded. Snipped the tension between them.

Baker swung the door wide to Monica Hyatt standing tall and pissed, Jack Korba scowling just behind her. Both wore rumpled flight suits and barely combed hair.

Apparently, Yasmine had wrecked everyone's sleep.

Keagan closed the door behind them. "Seems we have a situation here."

Hyatt's eyes stayed locked on her sister. "So Rodeo informed us."

"Do you have anything to add, anything that might vouch for her character so we can all breathe easier today?"

That sure snapped Hyatt's attention off her sister. "You're joking, right?"

The OSI officer nodded to Jack and stepped toward a far corner of the room. "How about taking a look at the compound map."

The question of the hour. Was Yasmine's input about the layout genuine? Or a trap. Baker, Keagan and Korba huddled in a corner while Drew did his damnedest to stare at the file in front of him instead of looking at Yasmine and her rose scarf. Because then he wouldn't have to see that slight quiver on a mouth that used to smile at him.

She damned well had reason to be scared.

Hyatt walked with calm deliberate steps toward her sister, stopping. "You little bitch," she said low.

Drew kept his head down. He had to give Yasmine credit, she didn't blink, kept her regal calm and took what her sister doled out.

"How dare you use me, use all of us like that? But then I shouldn't be so surprised. You're no more loyal than the bitch who gave birth to us."

"Please do not hold back your feelings, sister."

Hyatt all but snorted. "I'm not too worried about you. I figure we're pretty much evenly matched, you and I." She leaned closer, controlled rage vibrating through her body and even her voice. "But if you've done anything, anything at all to put Sydney in more danger than she's already in, I swear to God I'll make it my personal mission to ensure you rot in jail for the rest of your life."

"Sydney?" Yasmine's poise slipped.

"Cut the innocent crap, little sister." Hyatt's words trembled with impatience and rising volume until heads started to turn toward her. "Your lies this week pretty much negate the act."

Yasmine's brows pulled together, her attention skipping from person to person in the room. She blinked faster, then her eyes widened, brows relaxing apart again. "She's one of the hostages?" Her voice grew louder, higher with each word. "Is she?" She directed the question at Drew, at the trio of Air Force officers in the corner. "Did Ammar take my sister Sydney?"

Silence echoed a loud affirmation.

"No." The lone word held more pain than any speech. Her hand clamped against her mouth just before she doubled over.

If this was still an act, it was a damned good one. He stomped the spark of sympathy even as he wanted to believe her horror was real. Damn, but did he ever need it to be true, for her, for himself so he wasn't the same dumb-ass fool he'd been all those years ago with Glenna. And for some reason he refused to let himself analyze, the betrayal cut deeper this time.

It had to be because stakes were higher now,

more people depending on him not to screw up. By God, he would not let himself go soft.

Once Yasmine straightened again, Hyatt cocked her head to the side and continued. "It sure would be all nice and pretty if you're telling the truth. But you know what? Even if you're not lying this time, you understand what Ammar al-Khayr is capable of. You put everyone in here who was helping you at greater risk by keeping silent."

Hyatt's composure deflated. Her shoulders sagged, dark circles under her eyes matching her sister's in an ironic sibling resemblance of grief. "Yeah, getting Sydney out of here is personal for me. But what about the hundreds of other people here who've never laid eyes on her and are selflessly willing to die for her? For you, too." Her voice cracked. "What about the young man who died last night?"

Hyatt's teeth clamped together on a hiss and she spun away.

Keagan shoved up from the desk. "Okay, people. Let's take a breather, grab some coffee from the mess hall, shake off the dust and start again."

The Air Force officers all banded together around their own, leading Hyatt out into the hall. The doorway stood open, an Army guard to the side, an unspoken message that Yasmine wasn't free to leave.

Drew hooked his thumb in his M-16 strap, but didn't move. Why the hell hadn't he made tracks out for java, as well? God knows he could use some.

Shit. Damned women. He snagged another file off the desk from beside his Land Mobile Radio and buried his face in weather report data.

"I am sorry." She spoke softly, her meaning clear enough for him but vague enough if the guard happened to overhear.

"I'm sure you are," Drew answered without looking up. "But it's too little, too late."

"You don't believe I want to leave here?"

"Oh, I absolutely believe you want to leave." He clapped the file closed. "But you should have listened to what your sister had to say about why we do what we do."

Drew leaned closer, to keep their conversation private as well as to make his point while proving to himself he could be near her. Smell her. And *not* take her. "You didn't have to waste the energy playing me. I would have fought to the death to help you escape here even if you'd been a ninety-year-old woman with only three days left to live."

The fire in her eyes died. Tears pooled. The first all-out ones he'd ever seen from her.

Fool me once…

He pivoted away from her and her tear-filled eyes, pitching the folder to skid across the desk to rest beside his LMR.

On cue, the radio crackled with an incoming call for him and he returned his focus to his job, something that grew increasingly difficult with every day he spent with this woman. "Alpha, here. Over."

"Sir, there's some activity going on you need to check out. Looks like the camp's packing up. Intel indicates they'll be on the move anytime now."

Chapter 17

Dusk. Not dark. Damn it.

Helmet bag in hand, Jack strode toward the pickup trucks that would carry the crews out to the airplanes. As much as he wanted to get this mission under way, he would give his left nut to be taking off a few hours later. Deeper into the night as originally planned for the maximum element of surprise. But with an impending sandstorm and camp activity indicating a move...they would just have to pray like hell that the evening would be dark enough and that everyone turned in early to rest up for their big moving day.

The door creaked open behind him, likely more crew dogs filing out to fill the two waiting trucks.

''Jack!'' Monica's voice stalled him in his tracks. ''Jack, wait.''

He turned to find her rushing toward him. Breathless. Not her normal composed self. Her caramel hair swished along her shoulders, down and in defiance of military regs. Unease boxed around in his gut. She'd been through hellacious stress the past months and now faced the most tense of times in her own profession. Had he made the wrong decision in letting her come? Not that she'd left him any choice.

Monica stopped short, hair whipping all around her face in the wind, stray strands reaching out to brush his face. ''I just wanted to say goodbye. Good luck. Kick some serious ass out there for me.''

''You know I will.''

Only an hour from now and she would be entering preflight briefs herself, readying for takeoff in the medivac. Then landing at the terrorist compound's airfield to treat and load hostages and wounded.

Monica. In a combat zone. All the more reason to make damned sure the place was secured and locked down tight. He understood intellectually that military husbands and wives now entered combat together. The new face of the modern military. That didn't make any of it one damned bit easier.

Big picture war plan, this would go fast, efficient. Once the SEALs secured the hostages, the Rangers would be dropped in and have the whole place secure in twenty minutes. Tops. But there was still the wild card of the lone straggler hiding out in a hole, ready to pop a passing soldier or to launch an infrared missile at a landing plane, refusing to surrender even with certain death staring him in the face.

Shit. He had to quit thinking like this and get his mind on his job. "Go grab something to eat. It's going to be a long night and who knows when you'll get another chance."

"I'm heading to the mess hall after this." She nodded, but didn't move.

"I'll see you soon." He tore himself away from the temptation of hanging around for more of Monica.

"Jack!"

She wasn't going to make this easy for him. And he needed easy today or he'd never make it through worrying about her. He couldn't go deep with heavy thoughts tonight. Stakes were already high enough for him when it came to this woman.

He pulled a smile and pivoted back to her. "Come on, Mon, this Casablanca stuff isn't your style."

Biting wind plastered her flight suit to her body, streaked her hair behind her, leaving everything about her there for him to see. Her shape. Her face.

Her fear.

Still, she boldly strode toward him. "I just figured since the secret's out about us being together again, there's no reason to hide anymore.''

"Hide what?''

"This.''

Looping her arms around his neck, she urged his head down to hers, kissed him, full, hard, thorough, with open mouth and open emotions, all that fear and worry for him pouring from her into him. And just that fast—or was it longer but simply never long enough with this woman—she pulled away.

Monica backed from him, gusts lifting her hair and her words. "I could really love you someday, Jack Korba. So cover your ass and make sure you're still around for us to find out.''

She hesitated at the door, her eyes all over him as if to imprint a last image before she slipped inside, her hands already gliding up to start securing her hair. The door eased shut, closed her away from him.

"Hey, uh, Cobra?'' Rodeo's call from the back of the military truck yanked him back to the present. "You about ready to roll, dude?''

Hell, how long had he been standing around like an idiot? Jack jogged the last few feet, the truck chugging exhaust into the dusky night, and vaulted into the back to sit beside his copilot.

"Damn, Cobra.'' Rodeo inched over on the bench seat. "That was one helluva goodbye. Guess she forgave you for spilling the beans to me about the Elvis chapel.''

"Seems so."

Rodeo frowned. "Uh, are we okay? You and me? I really didn't mean anything with the dedication. That lady of yours must have read something on my face or whatever. Chicks have a way with that laser look. It's like they've got some kind of interuterine lie detector."

A smile twitched Jack's face. "Monica would pin you in a heartbeat for a sexist comment like that." The truck jolted forward. "But, yeah, man, we're okay. Although I figure you owe me a beer next time we're in Ireland."

"Done deal. And for what it's worth, I swear I haven't told a soul about, you know, the Elvis deal." The truck jarred along potholes and ruts. "But even if folks don't know all the details, I'm glad at least you've quit trying to hide your relationship."

"Yeah, great to have things out in the open now." Great, my ass.

"Isn't love grand?"

Love? Of course, right. She'd said she could love him. He should be punching the air with a victory shout. This was exactly what he'd hoped for with his strategy of using their time together. He'd won.

Oh, damn. Realization hit. He hadn't said it back.

He scoured his memory and...no. He really hadn't said it. Dumb ass. Hell, he'd told her he loved her at least a hundred times before they'd tied the knot in Vegas. But he'd held the words inside ever since.

Because she needed space, right? He didn't want to scare her off. Okay. Logical. So why not say it now when she'd opened the door wide?

The answer nailed him nose-on like a missile hit. Their marriage rocked him as much as it did her.

He hadn't held back the words for her. He was doing it for himself. He'd denied any deep-waters crap because he was scared as shit of risking a repeat of losing someone he loved.

Damn it all. He did not need these kinds of thoughts seconds before flying into combat. Thank God none of the other crew members could peek in his head or they'd be booting his butt off the truck onto the tarmac.

Plane drawing nearer, he worked to get his head on straight. All right. So he loved her. Really loved her.

The hell of it was, acknowledging the emotion didn't make him feel one bit better. But it sure made the prospect of flying into combat a lot less daunting in comparison.

"You gonna eat that?"

Monica stared across the chow hall table at Crusty already scooping up her chocolate-chip cookie. "Not anymore."

Not at all, actually, since her stomach was turning flips, but Captain Junk Food didn't need to know or he'd clean her out of even the things she might be able to choke down tonight.

"Thanks," he said as he jammed the whole cookie into his mouth.

Sitting beside him, Max Keagan ate silently, moving his cookie to the far side of the tray away from Crusty while the rest of the medivac crew and medical staffers took their seats in the nearly deserted mess hall. Quiet that should have been peaceful only served as an echoing reminder of crews and Rangers in the air. Monica shoved her tray aside.

Across the room, a lone figure peeled away from the food line with her meal. Yasmine stood solitary, holding her tray with her guard three steps behind her.

Did she have to look so damned pathetic searching for which of the hundred empty seats she would select?

Ah, hell. Monica sighed long. Hard. "Yasmine."

Her sister turned.

"Come on and have a seat with us."

"Is that an order or a request?"

Ungrateful brat. "It's a request."

"Thank you." Yasmine moved with that spooky silent walk of hers and glided into the seat beside Monica. At least she had the sense not to talk.

Crusty tore into another roll, his third. "So, Tiara, what're you going to do after we get out of this shithole—'' He paused, glanced at Yasmine. ''No offense.''

''None taken.''

Monica tamped down the irritation over the Tiara comment and answered honestly, ''Sleep. For two days straight.''

Cancel the divorce proceedings.

Then what? She'd finally given Jack the green light and he hadn't said he loved her back. A man who'd said it so often in the past hadn't dredged up a single word now—much less those important three. Because of the upcoming battle. Had to be. Which still didn't make Jack's omission hurt one damned bit less.

Crusty chewed through his roll. ''Hey, Max? You got plans?''

''Darcy and I are going to head out to the beach cabin for a while, get away from the world. We haven't been in the same country together for more than a week in two months. What about you?''

''Disney, dude, for five whole days.''

Keagan tossed his napkin on his tray. ''A blast for the boys. Take lots of pictures to show us.''

''The boys? Sure. But I'm already dreaming about Space Mountain and the food. Oh, baby!''

Monica forced a laugh. The image sounded perfect. Normal. A couple enjoying alone time. A family going on vacation. Something she would have loved growing up and found she actually dared dream about having now.

"You should have a houseful of children, Crusty," interjected Yasmine.

What a time to try to be social.

Awkward silence settled like a toxic cloud while everyone looked anywhere but at Crusty whose wife couldn't have children. Of course, to be fair, Yasmine had no way of knowing that since she'd only heard Crusty didn't have other children yet. Not why.

"We will someday." Crusty snitched the cookie from Yasmine's tray. "No rush. My brothers can use some more time to settle in." He jammed the pilfered dessert into his mouth.

Before Crusty finished chewing, a staff sergeant from Keagan's force protection counterintelligence team entered the chow hall, stopping at their table.

Keagan shifted round in his seat. "Problem?"

"We've got a situation outside," the burly staff sergeant hurried to explain. "A worker from one of the NGOs that helped us pass out the supplies just arrived with a local. Apparently there's a medical emergency in one of the villages. Said she's gotten help from our military before."

"Yeah, that's true. American forces send out medics and docs to help treat locals, but we're tapped out now. Everyone's either been sent forward into the field or is heading for the medivac in an hour."

"All right, sir. I'll let them know."

Yasmine canted forward. "What is the problem?"

The sergeant glanced down at Keagan for permission to answer. Keagan nodded the go-ahead.

"A woman's having a difficult labor and their resident midwife is ill, doesn't want to risk infecting the mother and baby."

Monica shoved to her feet. "I'll write out instructions for the NGO worker to translate and pack up some supplies, things to keep the field sterile. We could send one of our SPs. Security police have some basic medic type training."

"Wait," Yasmine interrupted again.

Monica forced herself not to snap. Fighting wasted minutes. "Time's short, Yas."

"I can help her."

"Run that by me one more time?"

"I am a nurse. I can deliver her baby."

Shock glued her boots to the floor. "You're a nurse?"

"The woman is not going to let your military man—or any man—treat her. I am trained and speak her language. Send me."

Shock gave way to suspicion. "I thought you wanted to leave here? If you want to stay in Rubistan after all, you really don't need to be so elaborate in your escape."

"I have no wish to stay. Send your security man along to guard me."

Crusty leaned forward on his elbows. "She'll

need a military escort, anyway, for safety. Max? Security's your call, dude.''

Keagan studied her long and hard, then speared a hand through his blond-tipped hair. ''There's no reason not to send her if she wants to go. Nothing she could do or say will change anything or harm anyone at this point.''

They continued to bat plans and specifics back and forth while Monica stood with her feet stuck to the floor and worked to wrap her brain around the changing image of her sister. A nurse, not just a spoiled trust-fund girl. And if Yasmine was truly trying to leave Rubistan, stepping outside the compound was a brave thing to do.

She'd spent so long associating Yasmine with their mother, how many feelings had been unfairly transferred? And what else about her sister would she have to rethink?

How strange that Yasmine had never opened her mouth to say anything about her training. If positions were reversed and Yasmine had implied her older sister was a leech on society, Monica would have flashed that education like a neon sign under the offender's nose. So much for assumptions. Yasmine's cultural orientation gave her a different way of moving through the world, not necessarily wrong or bad. Just different.

Monica reassessed her proud baby sister perched like a princess beside her. And then the clock on the wall gave her no more time to mull anything over.

Crusty tapped his watch. "Max, good luck settling this one out and handling the home front. We gotta roll for preflight."

Ready to roll.

Blake crouched beneath the guard tower, below where the guard now lay crumpled and dead in his perch. Sweat burned salty trails into his eyes. Adrenaline kinked muscles tight, ready to spring into action.

C-17s circled five minutes out, waiting for the all-clear that the hostages had been secured so they could offload the Rangers. No more waiting.

"Go!"

The order through his headset unleashed him into action, noiseless, fast, lethal, like a bullet through his silencer. Under the stealth of night, he moved in. Not as dark or late as he would like. But hopefully confusion from the camp loading up to leave would give him a new edge.

They all fanned out in pairs. A movement flickered on his right. M-4 hip level, he popped the terrorist sentry, silencer hissing. Another hiss sounded behind him. Carlos shooting. Blake swallowed. Damn. What had he missed?

For the first time he questioned the wisdom in his being here. He would die to save Sydney. He would take a bullet for Carlos. No question. But what if he screwed up? Carlos would take a bullet for him, too.

Shit. Get it together.

He ducked, dodged, wove around parked vehicles. Three steps through the open, then behind the cover of a one-story building. Back flattened to cement, he sidled.

Almost there. The next barrack-style building. Blood thundered in his ears.

Six would go inside to secure hostages. Ten would guard outside the building through seizing the compound. One company of Rangers had been specifically tasked to sweep past this particular building first. Fast.

He scanned the UWB along the wall. One heat source. Two. And… Nothing.

There were only two people inside the cell.

Intensity upped the adrenaline. Rekinked his muscles. He prayed to a God he wasn't even sure existed anymore that Sydney would be inside that building.

Time to go in. No alert from the compound, so no need to set explosives and mousehole through for speed. Only seconds more and he would have her safe.

He made eye contact with the other five team buddies heading in with him. *Go.*

Adrenaline surged. Two shots, he double-tapped the guard outside the door.

By mutual consent, he was first in. No one questioned his right. Unhooking the key off the dead guard, Blake stepped over the lifeless body, opened the door...

A man. A woman. Both familiar faces from hostage profiles. Neither one Sydney. The hostages Kayla and Phillip stared up with shell-shocked surprise from a cot and card game.

Blake's brain sparked with miniexplosions. Embers flecked his vision.

Carlos spoke first. "U.S. Navy, we've secured the building. We'll be holding position until the rest of the compound is in our control."

Blake charged in. "Where's the other hostage? Where's Sydney?"

Kayla cowered closer to Phillip. "They took her for questioning during our walk this afternoon. She never came back."

No. His mind refused to accept it. He'd seen her walk earlier, could have sworn she looked right at him, but then she'd left, returning to her cell, he'd assumed. "Where?"

"Barracks next door."

He'd walked right past her.

Blake spun, charged around. Carlos clamped a hand on his arm. "Hold on."

"Get your goddamned hands off me. I'm going in."

Carlos's grip stayed firm. "I know. I'm going with you."

Blake nodded, the thanks understood between

them. Leaving the two hostages with the other four team buddies, Blake swept past without a word. He retraced his steps. His feet hammered sand in time with his heart. He resisted the urge to blast in. Reconned the perimeter instead. Found a window.

And there she was. Pale, but alive. Relief surged so strong he almost vomited.

He swallowed down bile, reined in emotions, scanned the UWB across. Found one other person in the room.

Blake held up his pointer finger to signify his find to Carlos. *The bastard's mine.*

Carlos nodded.

It was almost too easy. The door was even cracked open. He could see Sydney just beyond the man even though she was still oblivious that help was on the way. She stood, unwavering, seemingly unharmed, wearing the dirty brown jumpsuit given to prisoners. Still alive and being questioned.

Blake shifted his attention to the target. Medium height. Dusty khakis and a stained linen shirt. Ammar al-Khayr?

He hoped so. Burned for it to be true because in seconds this man would die.

How? A shot would be risky, could go through and hit Sydney. He never even considered missing. He eased the door open farther. A garrote would be too messy and horrific for Sydney to see.

His fingers closed around his knife. There was

no other way. And no way to shield her completely from watching the man die.

He allowed himself one second to look at her before he would have to spring into her line of sight to attack. He absorbed the image of her...just in case this went to shit and he died. And damn but she was something. Small signs showed her fear, the twitch of her pinky at her side. Her lips pressed slightly too tight. But overall she was standing as tall and brave as any warrior he'd ever seen.

A warrior.

How many times had she told him she had battles to fight just as he did? She understood the risks but insisted she couldn't simply sit back and hope someone else would take care of problems.

Her work put her in the line of danger in hopes of erasing the danger for others. Just like his job, except he wasn't called in until all other options failed. Sydney tried to fix things before they went to shit. Before the military was left with no choice but to pull their knives and take out the enemy with force.

Why the hell hadn't he seen that before? His need for vengeance faded by a few degrees as blending Sydney's perspective with his own blew away enough of the cobwebs for him to see clearly again. He only needed an end to this camp and Sydney back in his arms. Not vengeance.

His haven wasn't a house and white picket fence. It was this woman. Yet he'd tried to make her deny the very things about herself that made him love her.

And in seconds he would kill a man in front of her. Blake accepted the inevitable. Once she saw the total darkness of where he existed, she would never come back to him. A price he had to pay to keep her alive.

He moved in. Fast. Silent.

Sydney's eyes widened for a flash. Long enough for the man to stiffen, but not long enough for him to turn before—

Blake clapped a hand over the man's mouth and slid a knife between his ribs. The man jerked. Blake shoved deeper. Twisted. Hot blood surged over his hands.

The body went limp.

Sydney's tear-filled eyes held Blake's over the dying man's shoulder while blood puddled on the floor.

Blake flung aside the corpse. Stepped forward and caught Sydney already flying into his arms. He pressed her face against his neck, shielding her from death at their feet.

Shielding himself from seeing death in her eyes.

Behind him, Carlos called in, "Hostages secure. Ready for the Rangers."

Chapter 18

"Five minutes," called the jumpmaster at the aft door.

"Five minutes," Drew repeated, passing the call to the next Ranger in line seated beside him in the cargo hold.

The echo telegraphed down. "Five minutes, five minutes…" Waking, rousing, readying. Soon this would be over, mission complete, Rubistan in his past.

Calls mixed with the roar of engines and tension filling the metal cavern along with the sound of shuffling bodies, some praying, others snoring. Yet his mind was blank. Training, right? Hell, yeah. Not because thoughts of Yasmine Halibiz pissed him off. Made him fighting mad. Spitting fire instead of...

Shit.

Yeah, he believed her. She wanted asylum. She'd probably even convinced herself she felt something for him to justify her actions. But how the hell could he trust her, forgive her? He'd lived in a world of clear-cut routines, precision, right and wrong for too long.

He was better off doing what he did best.

Drew focused on the two aft hatches. One directly beside him. As the colonel, the commander, he would be first out. In charge.

At least here, anyway.

"Stand up," the jumpmaster shouted, his order rippling back.

Focus. Routine. Clear-cut. Drew stood.

"Hook up."

Reaching up, he hooked his lanyard to the static line, which would trigger his chute to deploy on time. He checked the static line. Clean. Straight. Not looped around to rip off an arm when he jumped. He inspected for the man next to him, a routine that mirrored down the row just like the calls. By rote, his hands checked his Kevlar helmet, both buckles.

Focus settling. Hoo-uh.

"One minute."

Shifting, he made his way toward the open hatch, suited and geared up as he had a hundred times before. Eighty pounds of rucksack. Chute weighing thirty-five pounds. Reserve chute adding fifteen more. And he wasn't even carrying near as much as the medic behind him.

Sweat poured down him from the weight and adrenaline. Welcome familiarity. Nothing throwing his world off balance like...

Nope. Not going to go there in his mind.

He stepped into the open hatchway, assumed the position. Pitch-black void waited.

Clear-cut. Absolutes. His dependable life. He could already feel the exact timing of what would happen next, a precise replica of times before—

"Go!" The jumpmaster signaled with the traditional slap on the ass.

Jump out the door and count to four...three... two...one.

Whoomp.

The chute deployed. Streaked. Filled. Jerked.

Drew pumped his feet in the air to spin himself and untangle the cords. Even though visibility was next to nil, he watched for others in the air, checked the chute for a line streamed over, creating a Dolly Parton or a Mae West as they used to call it. Hell, the new recruits were probably calling it a Pamela Anderson.

He'd been around a helluva long time.

And in the middle of all the familiarity he was always stunned anew by the silence, the peace after the roar of the airplane. With a sneak attack, it wasn't like being dropped into a hot zone rife with gunfire below.

Just opaque, silent sky. The calm before the storm to come. He could lose himself in that sensation.

Just like he'd lost himself in Yasmine the night before.

Hell. He wanted the sky back. He owned it. And now she was even here. He could almost see her damned daisy scarf calling to him on the horizon.

Thank God, his body worked on instinct. She hadn't stolen everything.

Fifty feet to go. He pulled release straps on his rucksack and grabbed his risers, pulled toward his chest, changed the drift of his parachute. Listened for the reassuring *thump* of his rucksack hitting the ground, his eyes on the horizon. Pulled in harder. Harder. Arms straining. Drawing risers in until by landing his fists met.

Feet and knees together. Fall to the right, M-16 strapped to his left leg.

He hit the release straps on his chest, cutting the top half free to deflate the chute. Lightning-fast, he outrigged from the harness. He whipped out his 9 mm, ran a function check. Unstrapped the M-16 from his leg. Repeated function check.

Troops ditched chutes and converged in preplanned groupings, spreading. And even as he hooked up with his RTO for radio transmissions, threw himself into full battle mode, Yasmine trickled into his thoughts. As much as he told himself she was nothing more than a mistake in his past, he couldn't stop the soul-deep relief over knowing she was safe at the airbase.

Plaster raining from the ceiling, Sydney slid farther under the desk, hugging her knees to her chest and praying the roof wouldn't collapse in on her. Gunfire stuttered outside. An explosion. Light splashed through the window. Brighter.

Closer this time.

Blake's arm slid over her shoulders to tuck her against him, a tight wedge for them both under the desk, but the safest place in the room until the battle passed. Carlos guarded outside the door as the first line of defense, Blake keeping her secured inside while the fight for the compound unfolded.

She tried not to tense in his arms. This was Blake touching her. Breathe. In. Out. Relax.

Plaster and dust from the dank interrogation room clogged her throat. Great. Ugh. She coughed. At least she didn't have to look at the dead man. Ammar's henchman.

She shuddered.

Blake's embrace tightened. "Hang in there. This will be over fast. I swear."

She wanted to believe him but couldn't imagine how a compound that held at least a couple hundred trained terrorists could fall so soon.

Although the U.S. military had certainly started

the operation quickly and silently enough. With Ammar and his men already preparing to move the camp, she'd been terrified Blake would be too late.

And then there he'd stood. Taking down her interrogator—Ammar's right-hand man who'd continued the questioning after Ammar had been called away to prepare the camp for moving. If Blake had been just an hour earlier…

But there would have been two men with her then, both Ammar and his second in command. Somehow she knew that wouldn't have stopped Blake. "How long do you think it will take?"

"Twenty minutes at the most, and they'll have the compound under our control. There may be some stragglers to gather up, some outbuildings or escape routes to secure, but we'll be on the watch for them. It'll be over."

God, she wanted to believe this horror would soon be past, but knew an end to the nightmare would probably take a little longer for her. "I still can't believe you're here."

"I should have come sooner," he said, words punctuated with gunfire, another explosion.

"You shouldn't have had to come at all. I'm sorry." For so many things.

"You don't have anything to apologize for." His chin rested on the top of her head to fit under the desk, his hands firm on her back but unmoving. "Your sister's here, too. Well, not right here, but close by. She'll be landing in a medivac C-17 once the initial hostilities have passed.''

Tears prickled, joy a welcome emotion after months without it. ''Monica? Oh, my God, is it totally selfish of me to be glad she's in the middle of all this?''

''Once she found out the mission was in the works, nothing could stop her.''

Memories of neatly sealed lunches came back to slug her hard. ''Sounds like my take-charge big sister.''

''She thought it was important to be here for you, that maybe all of this would be easier if she was the one to check you over rather than a doctor you've never met.''

''She's right. I can't imagine telling someone else…'' She swallowed down acid. Monica would be devastated when the medical exam revealed the full impact of what had happened in this place.

Rat, tat, tat. Gunfire. Shouts. Running feet and a scream. Mayhem reverberated outside while inside she heard the anger in Blake's heartbeat, his labored breaths. Would he blame her after all? Be disgusted by her? She waited, wondered what he would say.

''Do you want to talk about it, being taken and…after? he asked with a calm contradicted by his tensed muscles.

''Not yet, if that's okay.''

His arms relaxed a notch, if not totally. ''Probably better we hold off on that until we're both leveled out.''

''I think so, too.'' Details would trigger his tightly leashed rage. She knew this as well as she knew him.

She knew him.

Understanding flooded at least a trickle of peace. His rage was directed at those responsible. Not her. This man's innate sense of justice, his unfailing defense of anyone attacked, would help him wade through it all. But later. Not now.

He shifted against her, his hand falling away from her back.

''Blake?'' Even as she'd winced at being touched, oh, God, she couldn't bear to be left. She gripped his arms, jolted, bumped her head on the underside of the desk. ''Where are you going?''

And then she smelled—spearmint. She smiled. Blake's chewing gum, a habit he once told her he'd picked up after he stopped dipping at eighteen when he joined the Navy.

''Want some?''

''Yes, please.''

He pressed a stick in her palm, papers rustling as he unwrapped one for himself. She folded the gum in her mouth. Spearmint saturated her taste buds.

She chewed out her tension. So this was why he enjoyed the stuff, always chomping double-time after returning from a deployment. She embraced the familiar flavor in the midst of a foreign world and slowly felt herself relax a bit more against him.

Like many times before. Normal. And, oh, how she wanted everything to be the way it was before. Except the past couldn't be erased. Would she ever be completely okay again? Would she and Blake ever return to those lazy afternoons of tender lovemaking and spearmint kisses?

His arm curved around her waist again, his hand settling on her belly. An accident in the dark? Or deliberate?

The baby fluttered inside her, not that Blake would be able to feel it yet. God, she wanted to cry, but if she lost it, all of this would be harder for him and damned, but wasn't life hard enough for both of them right now?

"Marry me."

The taste left her gum. She'd expected the proposal from him, just not so soon. "Because I'm pregnant?"

He flinched and she wanted to cry all over again.

"Not because you're pregnant."

She needed to believe him. Certainly they'd talked about marriage before—not that they'd made it through the discussions without fighting about her quitting her job or him quitting his. And things were even more complicated now. "I'm sorry. Sorry that you have to be here. Sorry that we even have to think about whether or not you're proposing because I'm pregnant."

"Good God, you don't have anything to apologize for. It's not your fault." Sincerity rang clear.

Months of holding it together shattered, the shaking deep inside threatened to rattle her teeth. "I was afraid you would think maybe it was because I came here in the first place."

"Hey, stop that kind of talk." His cheek pressed to hers, slick with grease paint and sweat, but emphatic. Familiar. "I may not have agreed with your coming here, but I understand your reasons now for doing it. And, hell, you gave me an out when we talked that last time and I didn't take it."

He couldn't possibly blame himself. Could he?

Of course he did. He was a man. They thought they were responsible for everything.

She shrugged off her own fears quaking deep inside and wrapped her arms around his waist, her elbow bumping a half-open desk drawer, the stab of pain nothing in comparison to the ache that swirled between them. He stilled for a second before a sigh shuddered through him. She felt his eyes squeeze shut tight against her skin. He needed her forgiveness every bit as much as she needed his.

"It's okay. It's going to be okay, Blake."

He nodded against her, and they sat, curled up under the desk and wrapped in each other's arms through three more window-rattling explosions splashing light through the room...then fading.

"So, Sydney, does this mean you'll marry me after all?"

''It's not that simple anymore. You need to know I'm going to have this baby.''

''Okay.''

''That's all you have to say?''

''If you want to have the baby, then I'll love it because it's yours.''

''How can you be so certain?'' She had to ask because, God forgive her, sometimes she wasn't sure how she would manage it herself.

''I just am. You know I've always wanted a big family since growing up alone with my uncle. We'll just start earlier.''

''What if…'' She pushed free words she'd never spoken aloud, barely allowed herself to think. ''What if I gave it up for adoption? Would you think I'm an awful person for walking away from my child?''

His fingers wove through her hair, the gesture so gentle, so familiar, she could almost ignore the sound of the popping gunfire and shouts outside. ''Is this about your mother?''

He knew her as well as she knew him. Too well. She didn't even bother answering.

His forehead fell to hers, bringing them nose-to-nose even though they couldn't see each other. ''You don't always have to do the opposite of your mama just to be different from her. Giving up this baby for adoption to a good home is not the same as leaving your kids behind to run off with some rich guy. You are a good, strong woman. Whichever way you decide, you're going to make the right choice for the baby.''

He wasn't going to tell her what to do. He just assumed she would make the right choice for her. For them. She wasn't Sydney, the absentminded dreamer.

In Blake's eyes, she was a strong woman.

His words shuffled around inside her mind with reason and sense and healing. So often he'd told her she was his haven, his saving grace. She'd believed him, in fact embraced the role of herself as saving him just like one of her causes, determined not to be the dependent little girl who let her sister fight her battles.

Yet in doing so, she'd denied Blake his equal role, his contribution to the relationship. Finally, all the components of Sydney Hyatt came together within herself. It was okay to be saved, and she would be saving him right back. ''I know it's not the same as her walking out. I know.''

Now, thanks to Blake, she really believed it, too.

''That's my Sydney.'' He smiled against her skin, the smile even held for a minute before he turned serious again. ''Just so we're clear here, if you change your mind either way, I still want to marry you. And I believe you want to marry me, too.''

God, she couldn't lie to herself anymore. ''I do. So much.''

Relief rocked through him, rebounding into her

with reassurance. His tight hold around her eased. "Well, hang on to that thought until we land and can find a preacher. Because I'm not holding off and letting you get some idea about waiting until after the baby's born. I want to be there with you through this. I *need* to be there with you. For you."

It was okay to save and be saved right back.

"You're not going to get any argument from me on that one." A giggle snuck up and free, her first in four months since she'd walked away from Blake. She laughed some. Cried some. Laughed again. Relaxed a little more against the hard wall of his chest.

His chin fell to rest on her head again. "I guess I need to know you're okay with who I am, too. With what I do."

Her laughter faded, but not the sense of security, an odd-as-hell sensation in the middle of a war zone. But true. As real as his arms around her.

"After what I've seen here, the lack of basic compassion for another human being...God, Blake, it would be so easy to lose our humanity. To rage and throw off civilization in the name of revenge. The fact that all of this sent you to dark places in your mind just means you're human. I should have been more worried if it didn't affect you. Now more than ever I realize how important it is to have people like you making decisions on how these operations unfold. People who won't lose their humanity or compassion when faced with inhumane acts."

"It isn't always this clear-cut-and-dried, Sydney, the rights and wrongs and how things play out for me."

And still he was trying to be fair with her. How could she have ever doubted this man's compassion? "Life often isn't fair, something I didn't understand before, either. So we meet somewhere in the middle?"

"I'm thinking that's the way it's supposed to work, the whole checks-and-balances idea." His broad palms bracketed her face. "I've learned my haven isn't a place with a white picket fence. It's you. Just as you are. I was trying to change the things about you that made you perfect for me all along."

Another explosion rocked outside, flashed light into the room. Illuminated Blake's face streaked with cammo paint. His golden blond hair darkened with sweat and dirt, his stubborn cowlick in place and undaunted by all the grime. She saw the warrior. She saw the man. And loved them both.

"Oh, God, I love you so much, Blake." The words fell free with a new ease and rightness.

"You know I love you, too."

Four months ago she'd been wrong to doubt the power of love. When faced with the worst the world could offer, love was everything. The most important thing. "It *is* enough."

"It has to be, because I can't live without you."

Her hand on the back of his neck, she gave a

gentle nudge forward. Her consent. Slowly he leaned closer, brushed his mouth against hers. Careful. Cognizant and considerate of all she'd been through.

The kiss wasn't passionate or deep, but the familiar connection with Blake and spearmint warmed her cold soul. A flicker of something more tingled wonderfully through her. Just a flicker, and not anything she was ready to explore yet.

But so damned reassuring.

She would be okay. Not today, and probably not tomorrow, either, but someday. Because this man who had the patience and strength to crawl through tunnels and cobwebs to face hell could crawl into the dark place where she'd been taken and hold her hand all the way back.

"Alpha, this is Budweiser two-one." Jack updated via the radio from the cockpit while his C-17 circled the seized terrorist compound. "The aeromedical evacuation team is two miles out."

Two minutes out.

Monica's plane approached, dimly visible through the night and approaching sandstorm.

"Runway secure," Colonel Cullen responded. "All clear for them to continue."

The Rangers had taken the airfield and the compound with no fatalities on their side and minimal injuries. Now Monica's plane descended below

him, neared the dirt runway, ready to treat the
wounded and to assess the freed hostages.

Meanwhile he flew the mobile command post
over the airfield. His comm equipment in back on
pallets provided radio relay for the short-range information transmitted from the ground. He'd just
tool around up here in the sky until the AWACs
arrived to take over communications.

All was hunky-dory, right? He'd flown through
hotter zones than this. Still he couldn't shake the
fear that some Gomer a few miles out with a
launcher on his shoulder would pop Monica's plane
with a missile. Something even the Rangers
couldn't control.

Hell. At least now he acknowledged his fears
were a screwed-up backlash from losing Tina. Acknowledging didn't do much for making those de-
mons go away.

Probably for the best that he had at least another
twenty-four hours to get his head level before talking to her again. Monica would land and he would
leave. No chance for chitchat until the sandstorms
passed and she headed back to base. Not that he
was a hundred percent certain how he would make
up for his obvious omission just before takeoff.

Three important words left unsaid, dumb ass.
Damn, but he wanted to thump himself upside his
head.

Whoomp.

The plane shuddered. The thump too close on the

heels of his thought stunned him silly with confusion before he realized...

Something was seriously wrong.

"What the hell was that?" Rodeo's voice snapped through the headset.

Wind whipped over him. From the side. Tiny holes peppered the plane.

Jack twisted, looked out the windscreen. Found. Flames streaming from his left wing.

The inevitable conclusion nailed him. The Gomer with a missile launcher on his shoulder had hit him instead. And Monica's plane was already descending toward the runway. A pop to her craft would be fatal without the altitude to recover.

Dread pinging over him, he keyed up the private interphone. "Rodeo, we've been hit."

And so have I. Words he held back.

Stunned numbing eased. Reality seared through his skin. Hot. But he couldn't think about that. Later, he'd worry about the shitload of shrapnel lodged in his thigh. Right now, he didn't have the time to waste on extra words.

Anticipation tingled through her. From her jump seat behind Crusty piloting the medivac, Monica watched the dirt runway come closer. Closer. Back wheels touched down, then the nose, buildings sprawling in front of her.

One holding her sister.

Only a few more minutes and she would see Sydney. The hostages were all safe and accounted for, the airfield and compound in American hands. And she had Jack to thank.

They had problems, but they weren't quitters. Some things in life were worth fighting for and she was beginning to trust in herself enough to let down her defenses.

She was finally learning to trust Jack. If only she didn't have to wait so long to start her campaign to get him to expose his feelings to her.

The open-frequency channel crackled. "This is Budweiser two-one, we took a missile in the number two engine."

Jack? His voice echoed over her headset. A buzzing started in her brain. Loud. Like someone let loose a hive of bees. This wasn't supposed to happen. Jack, of the jokes and killer smile, was invincible, damn it, and they all knew it. His cocky arrogance was obnoxious as hell sometimes, but everyone believed in him.

"This plane's pissing gas out all over the place," he continued with more of that calm confidence. "We're gonna have to put her down here. Alpha, is the runway clear?"

"Hold, Budweiser two-one," Colonel Cullen replied over the radio waves. "We have a plane on the active runway—Budweiser two-seven."

Crusty reached for the throttles. "This is Budweiser two-seven. I'll be clear of the active runway in thirty seconds at the south end."

The engine whine increased, almost as deafening as the buzzing in her brain. The plane surged forward to taxi out of the way. A tight turn in the parking area cranked the C-17 around to face the incoming craft.

She'd wanted to see Jack today, but God, not this way, peering powerlessly through her windscreen as he came in for a crash landing.

Fire streamed from the left wing, trailing out into the night sky. The hulking gray plane screamed toward them.

Helplessness screamed over her just as thunderous. ''Tell me what's happening,'' she asked Crusty as if that gave her control, some kind of active role. ''What's he doing? What's he thinking?''

''He's fine, Tiara. Trained. In control.''

''Tell me, damn it.''

Crusty angled toward her while facing forward. ''He's losing fuel fast out the hole in the left. Losing weight. Which screws with the center of gravity because of all the gas still on the right. He'll be shifting fuel to the left even though it drains, too.''

''He's feeding the fire to stay upright?''

''Basically. He needs to land quick. As long as he's going fast, the flames are behind him.''

But when he stopped to land…

She listened to Crusty beside her and Jack's voice over the headset, absorbing the words of both men.

Crusty depressed the mike button. ''Cobra?

Dude, you'd better plant this one. There's threat on the right. And you can't turn left into that dead engine without crashing. You're not gonna make it around for a second approach. You need to throw it into an inflight thrust reverse.''

The C-17 was the only plane in the world that could perform that maneuver. She'd once heard Jack brag about it. But was now the time?

God, it sounded insane, on fire and slowing while still in the air. Once he lost speed, the flames wouldn't be streaming behind. If the plane ignited, he would have nowhere to run. But Crusty was infamous for jerking the plane around, knowing its limits after years as a test pilot.

Please, please be right now.

And suddenly the speed slowed. The plane seemed to hiccup midair. Hard, steep and fast, the C-17 descended, landed.

Lights sparked in front of her eyes as if all those bees in her brain had become lightning bugs. She swayed, grabbed the back of Crusty's headrest to steady herself.

He patted her arm. ''Breathe, Major. Breathe.''

''Oh. Yeah.'' She exhaled, gulped in two more breaths until her world steadied and she remembered to listen.

To Jack. On the ground. Alive.

''Alpha, which way do you want us running?'' Jack asked.

Oh, God, to think he could sprint out of the plane

into enemy territory. She tried to envision where the Rangers might be now.

"Haul ass toward the medivac plane," Colonel Cullen instructed. "I'll have some of my guys cover your six."

Monica gripped the headrest harder, her world flipping all over again, with relief this time. She would see him in minutes. She needed to hold him, warm, solid and alive. Time to quit running from the fact that she loved Jack Korba. Fully. Completely. Not someday, but right this minute and forever.

"Will-co, Alpha," Jack answered. "Heading for the medivac plane pronto. In fact, that works good for me. 'Cause I believe I've been shot in the ass."

Sweat making tracks through the grit on his men's faces, Drew issued orders in person and over the radio. Sand rode the night wind, thicker by the minute. He inched the Ranger wrap cloth higher over his mouth and nose.

The battle had been won but their work wasn't over. The airfield was secure. The compound taken. Korba's crew was safe in the medivac.

Gunfire only echoed in his memory now instead of his still-ringing ears. Fast, furious and efficient, they'd implemented their attack plan. Reports of wounded trickled in, but so far no KIA—killed in action—on their side. All their preplanning paying off.

Drew issued orders to begin SSE—sensitive site exploitation—for booby-trapped buildings and uncaptured stragglers. Still no sign of Ammar al-Khayr yet. But they would find the bastard.

Something they needed to do fast with the sandstorm rolling in. Once the storm hit, they would have to lock down tight until it passed, which gave those stragglers who were too damned accustomed to sandstorms a chance to maneuver.

He checked his watch, looked up at the opaque sky.

"Colonel!" called a lieutenant from a cement outbuilding twenty yards ahead at the perimeter. "You're going to want to come check this out."

Al-Khayr? God, he hoped he was seconds away from seeing that sadistic son of a bitch.

From the open door, a sergeant escorted someone down the cinderblock steps…another Army sergeant? A man he thought they'd left at the air base.

"What the hell are you doing here, Sergeant?"

"I was ambushed, sir," he answered while shrugging off the last of the knot binding the rope around his wrists. Apparently he hadn't gone down easy if his split lip and torn sleeve were anything to judge by.

Shit. "On patrol?"

"No, sir. A request came in from one of the NGOs for medical assistance for a woman having a tough labor. The officer in charge back at air base assigned me to escort the nurse."

Nurse? A bad, bad feeling spidered up his instincts. "The nurse? One of our military nurses?" he asked, already knowing damned well they would have all been loaded up to go or already out in the field with his group.

"No, sir. We had a volunteer—"

"Colonel," shouted one of his Rangers from across the path. "I think we've got someone over here, too."

Drew charged across, heart thumping in his head as loud as the wind pounding against his ears. *It wasn't her.* The bad feeling increased with every step closer to the cement outbuilding. *It wasn't her.* Closer to muffled sounds growing louder.

He would not let it be her.

Hiking his gun up and ready, Drew booted in the door to dark and dust. And a muffled moan. Weapons from his men clicked up and in place.

"Light!" Drew ordered. "I need some light here, damn it."

On command, flashlights arced beams into the room. Streaking across. Landing on a woman clothed in a black dress. She twisted, jerked against the wall without moving forward. Illumination flicked up to...

Yasmine's face, a gag in her mouth, her wrists manacled above her head.

Chapter 19

Yasmine's arms burned in the sockets. She resisted the urge the arch closer to Drew. Wonderful, big and right-there-alive Drew with his beautiful blue eyes watching her above a camouflage cloth tied over his mouth and nose. During the thundering explosions she'd prayed he would be all right. Prayed he would come to her.

Prayed his men would not level the building first.

"Shit!" Drew charged across the dank cell, kicked over a chair on his way toward her. He reached up, unlooped her tied hands from the hook over her head.

Her arms fell like lead over his helmeted head to land across his shoulders, her hands still bound.

Forget being strong. She sobbed against his chest, from the fear of the past hours of being ambushed and interrogated, from the burning pain in her numb arms with nerve endings shrieking back to life.

From the excruciating thought that she might never see him again and have the chance to find forgiveness in his eyes. That he might be wounded. She'd heard so many cries of pain intermingled with the gunfire. Did not know who...

Drew's gloriously healthy hands worked behind her head to untie the gag.

She gulped in gasps of clean air filled with the scent of him. Sweaty, musky and yes, yes, yes, alive. "You are really all right, Drew? Nothing happened to you tonight?"

"I'm fine." His gruff answer from beneath his camouflaged face wrap didn't reassure her. "Not a scratch on me, ma'am."

Ma'am? How cruel he could be.

But he was rattled, too. She knew it. Believed it. Embraced it as firmly as she wanted to embrace him.

He ducked from under her arms, careful not to jostle her, then looked back over his shoulder at the soldiers standing wide-eyed. "Check the perimeter around this building, make sure it's secure before sight lines go to shit in the sandstorm. You've probably got about five minutes tops."

Once they cleared the doorway, he tried to untie

her wrists. Puffy flesh swelled over hemp. Blood soaked the rope, pulling it tighter.

Drew's curse cut the air a second before he whipped out a knife. Large hands so gentle, he sawed through the binding, massaged feeling back into her fingers while she stared at the top of his helmet as he bent over his task. She bit back an instinctive cry of pain just to keep his hands on her again.

"How is my sister?" she finally dared ask. "How is Sydney?"

"She's fine, secured and under guard. Both of your sisters are safe."

Relief left her dizzy.

"Are you okay? They didn't—" his hands continued the tender touch in spite of his icy tones "—assault you, attack you in any way, lay one goddamned finger on you."

"No. No. They did not assault me."

The big man in front of her swayed. Then his eyes snapped open, snapped with anger, as well. "What the hell are you doing here?"

Tender time over.

"They set a trap for me, lured me out with a concocted story about a pregnant woman in labor. Please, please say the sergeant who accompanied me is all right."

"He's fine. Right across the path with my radio operator."

Drew swiped down his face cloth until it fell like

a bandana around his neck. He picked up the radio from the floor. When had he dropped it? Perhaps when he'd reached to free her. Her eyes skittered to the hook. Shuddering, she wrapped her tingling arms around her waist and turned her back on the image.

Striding across the room, Drew barked orders into his radio. He opened the door. A blast of wind yanked it from his grip, slammed it to the wall. Sand exploded inside in sheets. So quickly these storms came, something she knew and even still it took her by surprise.

"Damn it!" Drew grabbed for the door, braced his shoulder on the back and forced it closed again.

Click. The door closed. Sand settled.

They were alone.

Drew continued to keep his eyes off her, his attention glued to his radio. "Pass the order down the chain. Take cover. Do your damnedest to enter only sites that have already been through SSE. Bottom line, get the men out of this shit, but maintain perimeter security."

His flashlight cast strobe effects as he walked and talked and surveyed the dark, cement room. Finally he placed the radio on a ledge, voices and different frequencies squawking through.

He turned toward her, sweaty, streaked with soot, mud. Blood. His poster-worthy face seemed more like something that graced a dark and sad war flick.

The Colonel. The battle-hardened soldier. She should have been scared.

Instead she wanted to hug him, give him somewhere soft to sleep. But their last parting had been full of hurt. Final. She waited, watched.

He closed the last five feet between them. She held her breath. Wanted. What? Everything.

Drew hitched the flashlight high, shone the beam down on her face. His knuckles skimmed her bruised cheek. "You're sure you're all right?"

She stared up into blue eyes still full of distrust. Anger. Hurt. "Ammar slapped me around a bit to see if I knew anything about your plans. He was suspicious since I had not reported in."

"You could have told him and saved yourself a lot of pain." His fingers fell away along with the blinding beam.

She blinked to adjust. "I knew I would not have to wait long."

"I appreciate your confidence."

"Thank you. Even if you would have done the same for a ninety-year-old woman with three days left to live. Thank you."

"You're welcome," he clipped, pacing around the near-empty cell like a caged tiger with his flashlight checking every corner for…what?

She stood in the center of the room and pivoted in a circle, watching him while rubbing her chapped wrists. "I am sorry."

He righted the chair he'd kicked aside when charging to unhook her. "Uh-huh."

"Do we have to be miserable in here together?"

Drew stopped, faced her, scowled. "Sorry, but I'm not much in the mood to drop my pants and keep you occupied with more scarf play."

He retrieved his radio off the ledge and dropped to sit on the floor. Back against the wall. Facing the door with his rifle resting against the wall beside him.

Hurt slapped across her harder than Ammar's hand ever could have. Hurt over Drew's careless dismissal of what they'd shared. Over the notion she might never feel the excitement of his hands on her bare skin again. "There is no need to mock me."

"Why not? You've been making a fool out of me since day one."

She shuffled across the dusty floor to him. "Is that what you think I was doing?"

"Think?" Flashlight propped beside him, he studied the radio clasped in his hands between his bent knees. "No. It's exactly what you did."

"That was not my intention." She stemmed a torrent of emotional, defensive words that would only shut him down. She needed to be logical. This could be her last chance to talk to him.

Be reasonable. So difficult when she wanted to curl up against him and forget the fear of being questioned.

Instead she lowered herself to sit beside him. He'd used the word "fool."

Ego.

Ah, how could she have forgotten the power of the male ego? This man's ego just needed to be stroked with reason rather than her hands right now. Hopefully hands later, too. "As you said, I had security in place back at your air base. Why would I have slept with you then unless I wanted to?"

"Insurance."

"You know me better than that."

"No. I don't."

That stung. She knew this man in her soul and he called her a stranger.

Or was that ego again? Defensiveness? How ironic that the biggest, bravest of men could have the most tender hearts. Not that she would dare risk mentioning that to him.

She *had* hurt him, which meant he cared after all. But instead of rejoicing, she could not get past an ache in her heart and the need to cry all over again. "My name is Yasmine Halibiz. I am a twenty-three-year-old nurse who—"

"This isn't necessary—"

"—who was spoiled by her mother growing up because her mother somehow seemed to think that she could make it up to her other two children for leaving if she paid all the more attention to this daughter. And this daughter spent all her life being as bratty as possible to test her mother's love because she was certain that if her mother could leave her children once, she might do it again.''

''Yasmine—''

''I am spoiled.'' She let her pride slide a bit and a lifetime of defenses along with it. ''And insecure.'' An even tougher thing to admit. ''I do not…trust…easily. But I am also very determined and decisive. And while I may lie to protect myself, I would never, never, knowingly harm another person for my own benefit.''

''Enough, okay?'' The flashlight cast dark shadows up the tight set of his square jaw. ''I told you already that I believe you really want out of the country.''

Yasmine hitched up onto her knees to face him. ''I also want you. And I wanted you enough to risk my freedom. That a selfish person would do so should tell you something.'' She fisted her hands on her thighs to keep from touching him. ''I have fallen in love with you.''

''Stop.'' He cut the air with his hand. ''You're twenty-three years old. It may have been a helluva long time since I saw twenty-three, but I remember it well. People think they're in love all the time and it's fickle bullshit.''

''Your first wife taught you this?''

''I taught myself.''

''During your first marriage.''

The storm wailed the only answer.

Drew stretched his long legs out in front of him,

hooked one booted foot over his other ankle. "I'm a grandfather."

Where had that conversational leap come from? And what did he hope to gain? "How wonderful. Congratulations. A little boy or little girl?"

His head turned along the cement wall toward her. "You don't get it, do you? I'm a goddamned grandfather and you're twenty-three years old. There's just too much time between us."

This worn-out argument again that did not mean a damned thing to her? She stifled the urge to stomp her foot over him being an idiot. Instead she bit back what she really wanted to say to this man who'd just thrown her love in her face. "A baby boy or girl?"

"Shit, Yasmine, are you listening to me?"

"Yes, I am listening." And trying to figure out what was really going on in his thick head before she lost the chance forever. "A *grand*son or *grand*daughter? There. Does that let you know I heard? You are a *grandparent.* Now answer my question, please."

"A granddaughter," he barked right back.

"Named?"

"Damnation—"

"Not a pretty name."

He sighed heavy, belabored, before conceding, "Isabella."

"Oh, that is lovely." And he was talking. Even

more lovely. "Isabella's mother? What is her name?"

"My daughter's name is Emily."

She pushed further to what she really wanted to know and did not want to know all at once. "And *her* mother's name?"

His eyes narrowed. She blinked back innocently to wait him out, an art well worth cultivating around this stubborn man.

"My ex-wife's name is Glenna."

Progress. Yasmine stretched her legs out beside his. "I will likely think of her as 'the bitch.'"

He choked on a cough. "Pardon me?"

"If she has made you this bitter about love, then she must be a bitch."

"Maybe I was a bastard."

"Were you?"

He was so close the heat from his solid body warmed her aching arms, tempted her aching heart.

"I was married to the Army. She said she felt like a second-rate mistress." He pinned her with gray-blue eyes that carried desire and no trust. "I'm still married to the Army."

"Of course you are. That is one of the things I most admire about you, your honor."

The gray of desire in his eyes edged out some of the blue. "For what it's worth, if I was in my twenties again this might be different."

"What if I was forty-two?"

That threw him for a second. "What the hell has that got to do with anything?"

"You seem to think you are ancient. Would you find me less attractive at forty-two?"

"You'll be hot as hell at forty-two and we both know it. Moot point. When you're forty-two, I'll be…sixty-one. Ah, shit, Yasmine. You're not helping your case here."

"Will you find me less attractive when I am sixty-one?"

"This is ridiculous."

"Well, then, can we have an affair?"

"Hell, no!" He shot five inches to the left. Away. The flashlight toppled.

"Why not?" She resisted the urge to crawl toward him. "I, of course, think you will be an oh-so-sexy, sixty-one-year-old in my forty-two-year-old eyes. But since you disagree, I will take what I can today. How is the age difference a problem for a short-term affair if you are not considering us being together when you are sixty-one?"

No answer. The flashlight rolled on its side and as much as she wanted to see Drew's face—his eyes—to gauge his reaction, she did not dare pause.

"Because you *are* considering what it would be like for us to be together then. And I am so very glad since it would be a sad thing if all of these feelings I am having were one-sided."

She allowed herself to move closer, to touch him, her hands on the solid deck of his shoulders. He flinched but did not pull away or tell her to go. She explored the roughened texture of his skin along his neck, the rasp of late-day beard against her finger-tips. Skimming up, she traced his tight jaw, the scowling line of his brows. "Just so there is no misunderstanding. I fell in love with your eyes. With the man I see inside those eyes. That will never change. Never age."

She leaned, pressed her lips to his. Prayed. Please, please, that he would kiss her back, or touch her. Just a simple fall of his wonderful hands to her waist.

Nothing happened. And she could not even take comfort in the fact that he did not pull away since he had a wall at his back.

She sagged onto her heels. "You can relax. I do have on underwear and I am not going to drop my dress. In fact, that is the last time I will throw my-self at you. If you ever want to kiss me or hear me speak your given name again, Drew Cullen, you will have to come to me."

Dignity intact, her heart in shreds, she backed to the corner, curled her throbbing arms around her knees and began her vigil to feign sleep through the sandstorm. The wind howled. Drew manned his ra-dio. And she fought sleep for fear she would miss him coming to her. Or dream of his strong arms around her and mistake it for reality.

The wind howled on. The radio continued to crackle.

He never came.

"All right, flyboy, you can pull up your pants now," Monica instructed.

Sitting on a litter in his boxers with his flight suit around his ankles, Jack struggled not to wince at the sting. More to his pride than his thigh, since the numbing shots were still in effect.

He stood. Shit. Not totally numb. His leg hurt like a son of a bitch. He hitched his flight suit back up, zipped.

Gusting winds from the sandstorm battered and rocked the C-17. Engines had been shut down, covers sealed over to keep the sand out. Which left them without major power for lights. Only small, battery-powered lights and chem-sticks offered a hazy dim glow that hinted at a privacy negated by the other medical personnel and crew members milling around them.

But at least they knew Sydney was all right, secured safe with Gardner. Although hearing Yasmine had somehow landed in the camp, too, still boggled his mind. He'd been so focused on keeping one of Monica's sister's safe, he hadn't considered the possibility something could happen to the other one. A tactical error on his part.

Damn. What a night.

"You know, Jack—" Monica pitched away bloody gauzes "—it would have been helpful if you'd given me your correct medical status regarding your thigh instead of going for the laugh line about being shot in the ass.''

Jack yanked his gaze off the bloody bits of shrapnel glistening in a silver pan. ''Just trying to lighten the mood, bring everything down a notch.''

''Not funny.''

''What are you going to do to me? Feed me crappy goat stew and shoot me in the ass?''

''Hmm, did I remember to give you your tetanus shot?''

''Yes!''

''I'm not so sure. Maybe you need another.''

She cleaned up with steady hands. He would have thought her calm except for her tight lips. Pale face.

Contrition tweaked. ''Sorry. Guy thing, you know, joke instead of whimpering like a baby.''

Worry pulled her chalky skin taut across her high cheekbones. ''You need to lay down.''

''I'm fine.'' Definitely a male thing. No way was he going to be a wuss in front of everyone.

''Of course you're fine. But I also know that very shortly you'll be working your not-shot ass off. You should take advantage of this time when there's nothing to do and give your body a break.''

Irritation nicked harder than the shrapnel. His body was revved for battle, not napping.

''You'll be more efficient later if you do.''

Score one for the doc. ''You're good at maneuvering flyer egos.''

"Practice." Crossing her arms over her chest, she smiled her victory.

A flight suit never looked so good as it did drawn taut over Monica's full breasts. God, she was hot, leggy with curves and a sensuous mouth. Oh, yeah.

His revved body found another target for all that adrenaline. "How about this? I'll head up to the crew rest compartment and stretch out…if you'll come talk to me."

Yes. Yes. Say yes, damn it, before the top of his head exploded.

"And you're getting good at maneuvering the flight surgeon."

"I'm only interested in convincing you."

He led the way up the narrow stairwell, wincing at each tug to his leg working its way through whatever numbing shot Monica had given him before digging out the bits of metal and stitching him up. And he couldn't afford to take mind-mussing pain pills.

Clearing the last step to the cockpit, he found Crusty sprawled in the aircraft commander's left seat eating a handful of chocolate-chip cookies by the hazy neon glow of a chem-stick.

"Take a hike." Jack jerked a thumb toward the stairwell.

Crusty looked from Jack to Monica, back to Jack. "Seat's comfy here and there's nobody around to snitch my food. What's in it for me if I leave?"

Not getting pounded for yanking my chain? "I

could pull the senior officer gig and order you out, but since I'm a nice guy and a little off my game after being shot in the ass—''

''All right! All right.'' Crusty rolled to his feet. ''No need to play the sympathy card.''

''Thanks. And, hey, Crusty, if you keep anyone else from coming up, there's a bag of licorice down in my flight bag that's all yours. I need to talk to Monica.'' *Talk* being the euphemistic understatement of the century. Oh, yeah.

''Licorice? Consider me a Berlin Wall between you and the rest of the folks down there.'' Crusty disappeared into the stairwell.

Jack pivoted toward the bunk area. Fire flamed through his thigh. He chewed back a curse before Monica whipped out her doctor credentials and grounded him. All he needed was a few minutes off his feet and something to distract him.

And he knew just the perfect distraction.

Sweeping an arm for Monica to precede him into the small sleeping compartment behind the cockpit, he waited until she sat in one of the two seats across from the bunkbeds built into the bulkhead. He jerked the privacy curtain closed.

Total darkness blanketed the tight quarters. Slowly his eyes adjusted and he made his way to the bottom bunk. For good measure and added isolation, he secured the curtain across the viewing window, as well, before he stretched out on his right side. Flush against the wall. Not much room, but then, he wanted her close. "You know what would make me rest better?"

"Not a chance, Korba." Her chastisement sparked through the inky darkness. "No way are you and I going to get busy. Your doctor says no because of your leg. And your wife says no because of all those people downstairs. I thought you wanted to talk."

"You overestimate me if you think I can do it after flying combat, crash-landing with shrapnel in me, followed by getting stitched. My leg hurts. I'm tired. I want to hold my wife."

He could almost hear her melt. For a tough lady she always did like those sappy-soft words when spoken at just the right moment. He'd have to dig deep for a few more.

Rustling sounded seconds before her aloe scent washed over him, his senses heightened by the absence of sight. Would it be the same for her?

All her senses, touch most of all.

She dropped to the edge of the bunk. "There isn't enough room."

"Sure there is. Lay on your side." He reached, found her back and guided her down.

He heard her surrender, sigh as she sagged against him. She was right. There wasn't really enough room. If either of them so much as sneezed, their tangled bodies would flip off and onto the floor. But he couldn't bring himself to let her go now that he had her in his arms.

The whole damned night clobbered over him. How near death had come to truly biting him on the ass. How close he'd come to leaving this woman a widow. To never holding her again.

Wind howled outside, not too far off from the howling adrenaline rush in his veins. He understood all about combat aftermath and the body's instinctive reaction. Understanding didn't stop the feelings. Through the ache in his thigh, arousal stirred to life after all.

And no way would Monica be able to miss it as close as they were flattened together.

"Jack," she warned.

"Shh." He shushed into her hair. "I'm not going to risk having those clowns downstairs find either of us with a flight suit around the ankles. I respect you too much for that."

Truth. Which earned him more of that Monica-melting. If only he had more words, but with testosterone and adrenaline searing paths through his brain, rational thought got tough.

Monica's face shifted against him. Her lips skimmed his ear. "Kissing's okay, though. Right? Your doctor says that wouldn't hurt you. And as your wife, I know everyone downstairs already saw us kiss earlier before takeoff."

"I think kissing would be okay." He palmed her hips to rock against his while holding himself still. "As long as we didn't enjoy it too much and start moving around."

Her husky laugh ended short, captured by his mouth. In his mouth. Pent-up adrenaline, edgy battle aftermath channeled itself into drugging desire for the sexy, pliant woman in his arms.

Who the hell ever said they had to get naked to get busy? Or for at least one of them to get seriously busy, anyhow, because his leg did hurt like hell and he couldn't risk putting himself out of commission.

His hand skimmed her hip, forward, between her legs to cup her hot mound in his hand. He rubbed gentle circle massages of his palm against her. Her breathing sped, her reaction to his touch as instandamn-taneòus as always.

Her oh-so-getting-busy fingers skipped between them, onto him. Adrenaline aftermath was working its magic on both of them. His hard-on leaped in response and if he didn't stop her soon, the rest of him would be grinding against the cradle of her hips.

He clamped her wrist. "I meant it when I said I don't think I can right now. If I flex any muscles—" one major muscle in particular "—I'm gonna whimper like a baby for real. But it would bring me immeasurable pleasure to pleasure you. Call it a macho ego kick if you want, but it gives me such a rush hearing you come and knowing I brought you there."

Her panting moan of consent, insistent urging, split his restraint.

By touch in the dark, he located the zipper on her flight suit, traced its path down her belly until he located the tab between her legs. Lucky for them, flight suit zippers opened both ways, up as well as down.

He inched it up, not far, but far enough to slide his fingers inside to cotton bikini-cut panties. Damp cotton. Thank you, yes. He scooched aside the crotch, tucked in to find...

Immeasurable pleasure.

Her breathing snagged, picked up pace, pressing her generous breasts against him, faster, harder with fuller breaths. With her free arm, her hand fluttered over him in restless patterns that lacked control. Her hands fisting in his hair. Clutching his shoulders. Skimming around to his buttocks before sliding up again to his back.

He parted her, slid two fingers into moist, tight heat. Her hands stopped moving altogether.

Deeper he dipped, crooked his fingers with a beckoning twitch until he found—

"Oh, yes," she whispered. "Right there. Don't stop."

The roaring storm outside echoed the adrenaline storm in his head, rushing with a pounding need to feel this woman come apart in his arms. Elemental forces raged outside and in. Nature at its most basic.

He accepted that his feelings right now weren't pretty or even civilized. Combat did that to him. Her, too, apparently.

Driven, hungry, he thrust his tongue into her mouth, swept, searched, mimicking the motions with his fingers. He needed Monica to unravel for him. Needed to mark her as his, to claim her and to prove that at least on some level they connected.

While he guided her with his fingers inside, his thumb worked gentle torment outside, coaxed until he felt her muscles tighten, pulse around him. So damned responsive, fast and ready. Now. He captured her sighs of completion with another kiss until finally she relaxed against him.

If only things could always be this simple between them. In the past he would have said something funny right about now, make her laugh, his gift to her. She might be sarcastic, but rarely lighthearted.

Great. He gave her knock-knock jokes and orgasms. What piss-poor offerings for this incredible woman.

I-love-you stuck in his throat again.

"Jack?" She snuggled closer now that his hand was no longer between them and nestled her face against his chest with a sated purr of contentment he recognized well.

"Yeah, Mon?"

Her fingers played with the short hair along the nape of his neck. "Why is it you always need to be in control of things, here, like this, between us in bed?"

In control? He would have laughed his ass off if

it wouldn't hurt and pitch her onto the floor. He wasn't in control of squat these days. "I'm not sure what you mean."

"You're such an easygoing guy day by day. I've never understood why you're so emphatic about owning the bedroom. Don't get me wrong. I thoroughly enjoyed myself. You're a generous lover. Actually, I feel a little selfish sometimes. Like what have I given you back?"

If she didn't realize his shortcomings, he sure as hell didn't feel much like cluing her in. "Do you hear me complaining?"

"Well, no. But I don't think you would." Her doctor hands roved his body, his arm, back, soothing him in the only way she could at the moment.

"What do you give me? Christ, Monica, you're smart. You challenge the hell out of me. I could get off watching the way your brain wraps around things. You're loyal to your family, and that means a lot to me because family is important." *Dangerous territory, pal. Kids and family and forever.* "And you drive me crazy in bed. You always have. Does that answer your question?"

"I drive you crazy?" Her soft snort of disbelief gusted through his clothes and to his chest. "So damn crazy you're always in control."

No way could she not know how much he wanted her. No damn way. Or not? *Dig deep for the right thing to say, Korba.* He was running out of chances to get his head out of his ass when it came to this woman. Monica melted over...the truth.

Guess he'd have to dig with a scalpel to pry that out. "Remember how I said Tina died?"

"In childbirth."

"Right." He bled a little more inside with each word picked free like bits of shrapnel from his leg. "Except she never should have been pregnant. She should have been thinking about choosing her classes for the next semester."

"Did you two have to get married?"

"No." Flashes of their wedding poured alcohol over his wounds, their big church ceremony packed with family, flowers and smiles. "We'd been married over a year before she got pregnant even though we'd both agreed to wait until after graduation to start a family. I got slack with birth control. And, well, there we were..."

"Oh, Jack," she sighed over him, rubbing more soothing circles across his back. "It's horribly unfair that anyone should die that young, and especially during what should be a time of celebration. But you can't really blame yourself for making love to your wife."

"I can't?"

"There were two of you in that bed. Birth control is the responsibility of both partners."

His ever-practical Monica.

"You're a woman. I don't expect you to understand."

"I would slug you for that sexist comment, but you're injured, so my Hippocratic oath prohibits me from harming you."

"Okay, so I grew up in an old-fashioned home, maybe a little behind the times. But my dad hammered it into my head from day one. A man takes care of his responsibilities. A real man protects women. His woman in particular. And I can't get past the sense that I failed on that one."

Monica went silent. Dangerous. She always could outthink him. He'd be ambushed and on his butt in a heartbeat.

"Is that really all you believe you have to offer a woman?" Her hands slowed on his back.

"I'm not following."

"Is that really all you think you give me? Tantric sex and protection, whether it be with a condom or your 24/7 escort through a war zone?"

Trick question alert. He kept his yap shut. No answer had to be better than a major screw-up response.

"I carry my own condoms and gun." Her voice filled the small chamber, soft but firm. "If that's all you think you have to offer me in a relationship, then we really are toast."

Something he'd known from the start, but just kept hoping if he dazzled her enough...

"I love you. No maybes or someday about it." Her sad laugh drifted over to him. "It's strange how you used to say those three words all the time and

I never thought you meant them. But now, when you're keeping quiet about your feelings, I sense more emotion coming off you than before. Not—" she pressed her fingers to his lips "—that I'm hinting for you to say anything. Those three little words that carry such a big commitment should only be said without reservation. Otherwise, it's damned cruel when they're taken back."

This line of argument, at least, he knew how to combat. "Don't confuse me with your mother. I would never walk out on a commitment. You know I'm not going to leave you."

Still missing those three words, Korba, logic taunted.

"I'm not just a commitment or someone to protect, Jack."

Damn, this was getting out of control. *He* was feeling out of control, something he sure as shit didn't need right now in the middle of a combat zone. Jack nudged her back until she had no choice but to sit up as he swung his legs off the bunk, a maneuver that hurt like a son of a bitch. "What the hell are we fighting about?"

"Nothing." She rushed to stop him, her hands falling on his shoulders to keep him from moving. "We're not fighting. You're resting."

"Then we're canning this conversation now or I'll be doing all my best Greek dances from the cockpit out the load ramp."

The fight seeped from her hands. "God bless it, Jack, I'm pissed. Don't make me laugh right now."

Yeah, he was good at that. Lob a joke at life when things got rough and leave the deep stuff to more sensitive dudes. Hell, he'd already dug so *deep* inside himself for what to give this woman he was damn near bleeding out.

And just that fast, an image of his dream slammed over him. Of Monica bleeding out. Time passing. Him not able to save her.

Now he knew. Her wounds weren't outside, but rather inside. Insecurities inflicted from her childhood. An elusive enemy he couldn't fight with weapons, but would have to look in himself for weapons he didn't possess.

This was his brother's territory, damn it. She needed substance that Jack was afraid hadn't been issued him by the big man upstairs along with a sense of humor and a cache of knock-knock jokes.

A whistle sounded from below. Crusty. Jarring Jack as well as Monica beside him.

"Hey, Korba," Crusty shouted up the stairwell with plenty of notice for anyone needing a chance to straighten clothes. "The licorice is all gone and the sandstorm is easing up. So roll your lazy ass out of the bunk and let's get Tiara to her sister."

A flashlight gained brightness as Crusty climbed the stairs. The beam increasingly illuminated Monica's face as she expected…what? Jack stared back. He didn't have a clue what to offer her other than finishing this mission. Hell. It seemed they both agreed that's all he could do.

Chapter 20

It was all Yasmine could do not to duck and run.

Perched on the top step of the building that had first been her jail and then her haven with Drew, she watched and waited with the others for the sister reunion. Finally, Monica and Sydney would see each other. Certainly she did not begrudge them one moment of the impending closeness or joy, what they had all been working toward.

She just hated feeling on the periphery of it all. She wanted to be invited into the circle of hugs and to rejoice with them, but knew she would not be welcome. No one had even bothered to tell her Sydney was being held hostage, instead leaving her to discover it in such a painful way.

Early morning sun poured over the crowd of Rangers parting as Monica plowed past, her pilot lover firmly at her back for support. The possessive stance stabbed at Yasmine, reminding her too much of what she could have had with Drew.

She focused on the throng of Rangers instead, studied their grit-covered faces and uniforms, sand from the now-passed storm caked in their sweat. For some, it caked in blood. Jack Korba limped ever so slightly as he followed Monica. What had all of these people been through during the night? Her eyes skittered along the group again, searching for Drew just to reassure herself he wasn't hurt and hiding it.

The mass parted on the opposing side. Sydney stepped through. Alive. Yasmine snuck a hand behind her back to steady herself against the cement wall while she searched her sister for signs of mistreatment.

Sydney walked slowly, but then she always did, their dreamer sister never rushing for fear she might miss something or someone. And yet this woman who already gave many of her days to others had been robbed of months of her life. Her normally short caramel hair now grazed her shoulders after so long without a cut, attesting to those lost months.

Monica and Sydney fell into a hug. There was no other way to describe it as both stumbled the last steps. Reaching. Laughing. Crying. Unrestrained emotions and so much love mixed with grief.

The solid block of cement behind Yasmine wasn't enough to steady her. She couldn't imagine what would be.

Rage and shame scoured her. If only she had loosened her hold on her pride enough to communicate with her family, she might have known her sister was in Rubistan, then held hostage. Perhaps she could have sought information. Helped. Brought an easier end to the situation so all these battle-weary faces might have seen less blood today.

So young Private Santuci might have lived.

Self-examination stunk. Yasmine slipped her other hand behind her back for a double dose of steadying against the bullet-pocked wall.

Monica and Sydney eased apart from their hug. Tears streaked tracks down their dusty faces and slid into wide smiles.

"Are you okay, kiddo? God, I've missed you." Monica hugged Sydney again, pulled back. "Look at your hair. It hasn't been this long since you were in the second grade. Are you okay?" she asked again in an un-Monica-like jumble of words.

Sydney's hand tucked into the clasp of the grubby oversize soldier beside her. "I am now. I just want to go home. Sleep. Eat a whole pizza. Sleep some more."

"Soon. Very soon. Just a few more hours. And,

hon, that pizza's on me." Monica's smile held firm, but her hands shook as she hooked her sister's hair behind her ear, eyes searching, sister and doctor in tandem seeking reassurance. "I need to check the three of you over while the rest of the medical team treats and loads up the wounded. And these folks need to check airfield security. Then we're out of this place."

Monica looped an arm around Sydney's shoulders and began retracing her path through the crowd. Closer to where Yasmine stood.

Would Monica gather her up with relief, as well? Before she could discover the answer, Sydney gasped. Locked eyes with Yasmine. "Oh, my God! You're here, too?" She bolted up the stairs and hugged Yasmine with typical Sydney openness. "This is too wonderful. I don't even care how it all happened. It's just so awesome to see you both."

Monica paused at the foot of the cement steps. Climbed up, peering at Yasmine with a more caged expression. "Are you all right?"

Yasmine stiffened for recriminations.

Monica reached. Yasmine waited for a rebuff after the frosty way they'd parted last. Instead, Monica straightened the trailing end of Yasmine's scarf.

Affection? Or restraint?

"We need to head over to the medivac." Monica's hand fell away. "See you there later? I'll need to check you over, as well."

The old Yasmine would have only heard the subtle nudge that Monica wanted a few more moments alone with Sydney. Now, Yasmine stuffed aside her pride and reminded herself the invitation to join them would not have been issued at all in the past.

Yasmine nodded. "I will be right with you."

She stared out over Drew's world while her sisters ambled down the steps. Monica's words from earlier washed back over her, caking the grit into her skin with more guilt as thick as sweat. She'd taken their protection and given nothing in return.

So what that she had not known Sydney in particular was being held hostage? She *had* known Ammar snatched people, and thought only of her own escape. Of a freedom she had not earned any more than she had earned her sisters' affection.

Drew, Monica, they were all correct. Freedom did come with a price—the responsibility to safeguard it for others.

Monica and Sydney walked away, both shadowed by the men in their lives. Yasmine's gaze landed back on Drew. His head dipped as he listened to one of his soldiers beside him while talking on his ever-present radio. What was her freedom worth if she had no one to share it with?

Drew had told her he did not really know her. She had been so quick to question how that could be possible when she knew him so well.

The answer unfolded clearly. Because her defensiveness and pride had kept her from showing her true self. Trust had to be earned. And love had to be nurtured.

She would not give up. Now was not the time to push him, but thanks to Drew she had forever in a new country to make the effort. Once she had her American nursing license, she would find a job close to his Ft. Benning Army post. There was no reason at all why she could not work in Georgia, and she would still be close enough to see her sisters in South Carolina and Virginia.

And her ride out of Rubistan waited a short stretch away.

Yasmine started down the first step. Stumbled. A hand steadied her from behind with a firm grip to the arm pulling her upright. Albeit a bit brusquely until she landed back in the doorway. She glanced over her shoulder to thank her rough savior.

Her blood iced in her veins. Ammar al-Khayr stared back at her.

Before she could do more than gasp, he yanked her inside, clapped a hand over her mouth. His other hand lifted to thrust a machine gun in her line of sight. "Not one word or I will open fire on the crowd outside and your colonel will be the first to fall."

Drew? Her heart stuttered like a machine gun already in motion as Ammar tugged her into darkness, deeper into the cement building that had been her prison. How could he know about her connection to Drew? And how in the world was he here…

Blinking, she noticed the pit waiting open in the corner of the floor. A trap door gaped.

Tunnels. Of course Ammar had secret rooms and tunnels out. Her memory even niggled with Drew's words into the radio to his men about how they had to take cover from the storm in places that had already been checked. Yet, she had led him right here, to the area that hadn't been cleared. Where Ammar had hidden just below them until the storm had passed.

He hauled her down into the pit. Shadowy. Full of cobwebs and Ammar's gross stench of garlic and body sweat. She gagged under his bruising grip over her mouth.

"Do not worry. We will not be in here long." His fanatical eyes bit into her through the hazy dark as sharply as his hands grinding into her skin. "Only long enough for me to plan. Since the Americans collapsed my escape route, I will need to devise an alternate means of getting away. And what better hostage than the Colonel's woman."

Her sister was pregnant.

Monica called upon every molecule of doctor calm. The toughest thing she'd ever done. But she would hang tough because, damn it, she'd come here to support her sister, not to curl up and cry like a baby.

Baby.

Oh, God. Monica rolled her latex gloves off

while her sister adjusted her clothes. Military-green privacy curtains offered a modicum of isolation from the rest of the noise and bustle in the medivac aircraft, exams in progress, wounded being treated.

She reminded herself to be grateful that her sister was here. Healthy. Alive. The rest, they would deal with. Hyatt girls stuck together no matter what the world threw their way.

If only she didn't feel like such a failure. This time, there would be no Barbie Band-Aid that could make her sister's hurts go away.

Monica reorganized her supply tray, gauze rolls, tape, alcohol swabs. Intellectually, she understood this wasn't her fault. But that didn't ease the brain-searing sense that she was responsible for watching out for Sydney, a duty that had been ingrained in her since childhood.

Ingrained.

Hadn't Jack said something close to the same thing about the way his father expected him to kick ass for women? Of course Jack knew his wife's death wasn't his fault, but that wouldn't stop the guilt or pain. How odd to find a common ground in this.

At least something made sense in this whole crazy day. She couldn't stop the snarl of emotions tangling tighter inside her, as never-ending and convoluted as the cables along the C-17's ceiling. But for her sister's sake, she would contain herself a little longer.

Her sister didn't need her falling apart right now. Sydney had enough to worry about with Blake crawling around in tunnels working SSE to reestablish airfield security so there wouldn't be a repeat of what happened to Jack. The tangle knotted tighter in her stomach until the threads began to fray.

Rustling sounds of Sydney dressing slowed. Monica turned, hitched up onto the edge of the litter to sit beside her sister. "Whatever you need, I'm here."

"I know. And thank you. I'm trying not to make too many plans yet. I want to take the next few months off from work, spend time with Blake, get my head together. Heal." Her mouth lifted into a sad, one-sided watery smile. "Have a baby."

The smile creasing Sydney's sunburned face clenched the snarl around Monica's heart. Her sister's pale complexion never could tolerate more than fifteen minutes at the beach without sunblock. How damned silly to obsess over the fact that no one gave Sydney sunscreen when so much worse had been inflicted upon her and the other two hostages.

Monica slung an arm around her sister's shoulders. Sydney slid one right back around Monica's waist and they simply sat, heads tipped and touching, connected by blood and bonds years in the making.

The raveling emotions inside Monica multiplied

until they strained against her Ziploc-seal control. Damned if it didn't feel like Sydney seemed to be propping more than being propped.

Sydney slipped a fresh stick of gum into her mouth. "How wild is it having Yasmine here?"

Monica snorted, let the dry humor ease the tangle a bit. God, what she wouldn't give for one of Jack's jokes right now. "She's not quite so obnoxious, anymore."

"She never really was except around you." Sydney's smile dimpled both sides of her face below wise eyes. "You two didn't bring out the best in each other."

Instinctive defensiveness eased as more perceptions shifted. "I guess not."

Sydney studied the tops of her dusty sandals, her toes flexing and relaxing while the hum of activity beyond them droned into an indistinguishable blur of noise. "Part of the reason I came here was to find some peace about her."

"Yasmine?"

"Our mother."

Apparently she wasn't the only one keeping emotions, fears and unanswered questions locked tight. "You always seemed okay with things growing up."

"No one is okay with their mother walking out on her kids for some rich dude." Sydney snapped her gum in a minibubble.

"I guess not." The million-dollar question

knocked at her brain. "Do you think she really loved him?"

"God, I hope so. I would hate to think she left us just for the money. But I guess we'll never know for sure. Maybe there aren't any answers here for us." Her hand curled protectively over her belly.

How damned sad to think there would be no answers since they'd both come so far and hurt so much to find them. Would they ever be able to move forward?

Were they both fated to a life on hold?

The noise faded around her. Her mind focused inward. Her world levered sideways until it righted when she hadn't even realized how off-kilter it had been.

She didn't have to stop living life while waiting for her answers. Just as Jack had said. Santuci, too. They didn't need the full picture or a total plan to forge ahead as long as they knew they were on the right path. And she'd almost thrown away their relationship because she hadn't fully understood the importance of living in the moment. "I'm learning we don't have to know all the answers about our childhood right now. We found some new pieces of the puzzle, and we're putting it all together. We're getting there. Making progress. That's good."

"What's this laid-back attitude?" Sydney cocked a brow. "Who are you and what have you done with my sister?"

Monica laughed because Sydney needed it. But the emotional tangles were still multiplying with illogical but real guilt over her sister's pain. Over the pain she'd caused Jack during the past months.

Sydney gave Monica's waist a gentle squeeze-hug while the privacy curtain rippled with the drift of a muggy breeze blowing into the open aircraft. "Thank you for being here."

"Nothing could have stopped me." And wasn't that the truth? Only a week ago she'd been waiting in Jack's VOQ room in Vegas still reeling from what they'd done nearly four months ago in a wedding chapel on the strip. They'd known so damned little about each other, sharing only a killer attraction and a love of Atlanta Braves' baseball.

But the time had come to accept responsibility. Nothing could have stopped her from coming to Rubistan. And not even a whole bottle of tequila shots could have made her marry Jack if she hadn't wanted to.

Sydney pulled her arm free from Monica's waist. "I don't know if I could have made it through an exam from a stranger."

And yet Sydney sat tall, radiating far more peace than Monica could find within herself. God, she'd made a mess of things all the while deluding herself that just because her medical trays and suitcases were organized, she had control over her life.

Her little sister was the stronger one today. Wounded but not broken.

"You would have held it together. But I'm glad I could be here to make it a little easier for you."

"Me, too." Her arms crossed over her stomach. "I'm thinking about giving the baby up for adoption."

"You can come stay with me," Monica answered instinctively.

"Blake and I are together again, for good this time. That's one decision I'm certain about. As hellish as all of this has been, we understand each other better now."

Not only was Sydney stronger, but Monica's little sister wasn't so little anymore. Roles shifted and shuffled some more. How strange she'd never thought to look to Sydney for advice, far more comfortable in the role dispensing it. "I'm so glad for you and Blake both. You deserve happiness more than anyone. But the offer stands. If he's TDY, you could drive down. I'll drive up when I can. We're family."

"I'm really going to be okay."

"Maybe I'm not." Well, hell. Way to go with the support.

Sydney blinked, wide-eyed. "Excuse me?"

Okay, she would hold it together enough not to sob her eyes out, but maybe some truth was good, too. "Call it a part of my puzzle and journey— acknowledging I'm not okay yet. God, hon, you know I was worried as hell. I need to see you're all right. Often. And I suspect that's not going to ease up for a while."

"Of course." Sydney pressed her sunburned cheek against Monica's, then pulled back. "I figure we're due some major gab fests with lots of pizza and popcorn because, God, I'm craving popcorn these days so much I can hardly stand it."

The Ziploc seal strained close to breaking even with her newfound respect for her sister's wisdom and strength. Tears burned the backs of her eyes and no way was she imposing the full extent of her pain on Sydney.

"Popcorn. You're on. Lots of it, with extra butter." Sliding off the litter, Monica pulled a smile and wondered if her other sister liked Jiffy Pop. After twenty-three years, maybe it was time to find out. "I really should see what's keeping Yasmine. And I'll check on Blake while I'm out there."

"Thank you."

"No problem." No problem at all, because it gave her the perfect excuse to run from the plane before her Ziploc seal ripped.

Ripped stitches hurt like hell, and Jack was pretty sure he'd pulled one free while checking in with Blake about SSE.

Jack worked not to limp, but damned if it wasn't taking all his energy not to wince with each step closer to the medivac plane. His crash-landed aircraft loomed like a wounded soldier off to the side, the left wing mangled at the engine port. Once stripped of computer equipment, the battered aircraft would be blown up to keep it out of enemy hands.

Damn, but that hurt more than the shrapnel. And he wouldn't even be around for its destruction since he was being sent back early in the medivac. Monica wasn't budging on that edict. She'd even backed up her diagnosis with one of the other docs. Married service members flying together wasn't an issue today since he'd been injured.

And when she found out he'd messed up her handiwork... Damn. He would get an ass-chewing to go along with the ass-shooting.

Sooner, rather than later, since Monica stood outside the plane with her back to him. She braced a forearm on the side of the aircraft. Her forehead fell forward to rest on her wrist.

And then...hell. Indomitable Monica's shoulders slumped.

Fiery pain in his thigh faded and he picked up his pace toward her. The notches in her French braid had loosened over the hours, straggles teasing free with the bulk of her hair still contained enough that the vulnerable curve of her neck showed in the midmorning sun.

He cruised to a stop beside her, careful not to startle her. "Everything okay?"

She didn't move. Didn't speak. Didn't acknowledge his arrival. But since she couldn't have missed

his words, he let his hand fall to rest between her
shoulder blades, inched up to work a light massage
at the base of her neck.

"Are you all done here? They should be finished
securing the airfield soon and we can leave. Gardner and his team buddy checked in a few minutes
ago. So far as they can tell, all the tunnels out have
been blocked. Now they'll start searching them
from the inside."

Was she asleep on her feet?

A shudder quivered through her, then echoed into
another, continuing into a trembling akin to someone freezing to death in spite of the rapidly rising
desert temperatures.

Screw distance. He gripped her upper arms,
turned her toward him, not that she put up much
resistance. She sagged against him, no tears, but
still shaking with a grief that went beyond crying.

He rubbed soothing strokes over her back, mur-
mured shushing and it's-okay platitudes that didn't
mean shit, but since she wasn't pulling away he
decided he must be doing something right. He tried
to sort through the morning to figure out what must
have...

Her sister's physical.

Damn.

How shortsighted of him to imagine finding Sydney would bring instant smiles and partying. Facing
what her sister had been through must have been

hell for Monica. It was hell for him right now and he didn't have the details.

But he could damn well imagine.

"She's pregnant, Jack. It happened here."

He hadn't expected that.

His hands stopped. Rage blindsided him faster than that missile. He'd been prepared to hear Sydney was raped, but... This was too much. "Ah, hell, Monica, I'm so damned sorry."

She didn't answer the obvious, just kept shaking in his arms while he held her tighter and absorbed the trembling. He wished he could soak up her pain, as well. Finally she stilled in his arms, limp against him, spent.

His chin rested on her head. Light hints of her aloe shampoo drifted through the air of sweat, dust and war. "Does Gardner know?"

"Yes, and he's okay with it. Well, as okay as anyone can be with what happened here," she said, her hot breath saturating through both his flight suit and T-shirt. "She's going to have the baby, maybe give it up for adoption."

"Do you want us to offer to raise it?"

Where had that come from? Somewhere deep. And hell if he wasn't surprised all over again. Although maybe he shouldn't be, considering Monica always inspired him to dig deeper even if he fell short of the mark sometimes.

She eased back to stare up at him with stunned wide green eyes. "Us?"

Well, she didn't have to look quite so damned surprised. "There is an us, you know. Unless all that talk earlier about loving me was bullshit."

Her shock melted with an irreverent snort. "You're such a romantic."

"Yeah, well…" He shrugged, his quota of sensitive stuff to say already depleted. "You know me."

Her hand snaked up from between them to caress his face. "Yes, I do and still you surprise me sometimes. Thank you for the beautiful offer."

"She's family."

Monica melted again, but in the good way that let him know he'd done something right. Three cheers for digging deep.

"God, Jack, how could you ever doubt yourself?"

Okay, now things were getting deeper than he was comfortable with standing on a flight line in the middle of a war zone with people milling willy-nilly everywhere.

He dropped a kiss on her forehead. "You need to head back inside. We'll be flying out soon."

Jack turned to guide her around and pulled up short for Colonel Cullen. How long had he been there?

The normally unflappable senior officer shuffled from one dusty boot to the other. "Is she okay?"

Monica stepped ahead of Jack to answer. "Sydney and the other hostages checked out fine physically. The emotional repercussions…well, those are out of my field.''

"I, uh, meant your other sister.'' He planted both feet, his gruff tones echoed by his frown. ''They slapped her around pretty hard during interrogation. I just wanted to be sure…''

Monica's curiosity must have been buried under doctor composure, because she didn't even blink. ''I haven't evaluated Yasmine yet, sir. But I'll make sure to get word to you. How much longer do you think it will be before your people escort her over?''

The Colonel's restless feet stopped. ''She's already here.''

''Where?'' Monica asked.

''Damn it, she's inside that plane.'' The Colonel's commanding tone stated it as if his will alone could make it so.

''No, Colonel, she's not in the plane.''

The seasoned Ranger winced, his eyes shutting tight. ''Shit.''

Yasmine wasn't here? A bad feeling itched up Jack's spine that had nothing to do with the sand in the wind.

Colonel Cullen's eyes snapped open as he yanked his radio up to his mouth, barking out orders for a search. And under all the Colonel's gruff, Jack saw clearly the gut fear, felt the echo of it slam right into his own chest.

Things were about to go to hell.

And just like a week ago when Monica had demanded her rightful place in being there for her sister, she would be in the thick of things now for this sister, as well. Already, he could see her shoulders bracing into battlefield mode. Her will strengthening to steel. This independent, incredible woman who never played life safe, would always be in the middle of things for others.

The hell of digging deep was that now he had to face just how deeply he loved Monica. And how deep it would slice if he lost her.

Chapter 21

Drew pounded sand with his boots. Each heavy step in his search for Yasmine increased the kinks in his muscles. Damn. Damn. Damn it! How the hell did one slip of a woman land herself into so much trouble?

Anger chugged in time with his pace through the compound. Yes, anger. He was just angry. He focused on that emotion and let it power him through his search of buildings so the fear wouldn't sink debilitating claws into him.

She was fine. Likely sitting in some building readjusting her goddamned scarf and thinking up ways to make his life hell. When he found her, he would shout the walls down around her ears until she realized how reckless she'd been and he could pretend he hadn't screwed up.

Shit. He'd been so concerned with keeping his distance, afraid of weakening around her, he hadn't kept track of her. Now she was missing. God only knew where. God only know who with.

And please, God, let her be alive.

He forced himself to stop. Think. Get his head out of his ass and figure out where she was. Where someone might take her.

Where had he seen her last?

His eyes landed back on the isolated cement building where he and Yasmine had ridden out the storm. They'd checked already, and she wasn't there.

But how thoroughly had they searched?

Since he'd already spent hours in there without anything blowing him up, they'd logged the building as secure. But was it? He strode closer across the gritty path.

"Colonel?"

The heavily accented voice snagged his attention left, to the echo from behind the building. He jerked his M-16 hip level. Ready.

A shadow slanted around the corner, large, long morphing as two shapes blended and separated and blended again until...

Yasmine stepped around the corner. A rope looped around her waist. Ammar al-Khayr—a face he knew from countless intelligence files and CNN reports—loomed behind her, bound to her. Too close for Drew to risk a shot. He refused to see her scarf askew in a way his Sheba never would have allowed had her hands been free.

Fear for Yasmine sunk those claws deep into his anger until he felt it deflate with a sinister hiss.

Swallowing back bile, he shut down a thousand images of this woman scrolling through his mind. Instincts. Training. He had to count on it now because his mind was one helluva mess.

Drew depressed the button on his radio so his RTO would hear what was going down and hopefully send reinforcements over. Fast. "You don't have to do this, al-Khayr. Hell, I'm sure you've got information our government would be more than willing to trade for some retirement villa. Just let the woman go."

"The woman?" Ammar laughed, dipped his head to brush his mouth against her temple. "You mean *your* woman, do you not, Colonel? What charming conversations the two of you had during the storm."

Tunnels beneath the building. Shit. He'd searched and missed it. Because of the dark or his messed-up mind around Yasmine? A weakness he couldn't afford now.

Movement sounded behind him, but he couldn't risk turning his back on Ammar. Damn but he hoped it was help and not an ambush.

Ammar's eyes flared with panic. Which meant

help for Yasmine. Drew allowed himself one heart-beat of relief.

Two shadows slid past him, footsteps closer, until Jack Korba and Monica Hyatt stopped beside him.

Ammar inched back. "No closer! Stay there or I will blow her up now."

He extended his arms on either side of Yasmine—a grenade clutched in each fist.

Pins pulled.

Fuck.

His beautiful Yasmine was seconds away from being blown up by a fanatic. Five seconds to be exact, once Ammar released the safety levers.

Unless somehow he made a Hail Mary save in a situation that twenty years of combat experience told him could only end in one horrible, explosive way.

Ammar's hostage plan would not work, if that was even his true wish. More likely the man planned to blow himself up and whomever else he could take along.

Logical answer? Bluff a while longer and let the sniper likely sliding into place take out Ammar. Hope the bullet wouldn't go through and hit Yasmine. Pray like hell somehow he could move forward fast enough to pitch both grenades after Ammar fell.

Too many variables. All ending with Yasmine dying, and God help him, as much as he knew he would do his damnedest to save anyone, this wasn't just anyone.

This was the woman he loved.

She wasn't Glenna any more than he was the same man from all those years ago. He didn't even bother to dodge the self-recriminations over having not figured it out sooner because that would have wasted precious seconds he could spend looking at her. He telegraphed his apology through his eyes that this woman swore she could read.

Why had he never thought to look in hers? Deep brown pools of an intriguing woman who challenged his world with her smile. Wise eyes that saw beyond his years to the man inside. Fearful eyes that believed he had turned his back on her.

Finally he saw *her.* The part of her that was timeless and not just a number of years. And now odds screamed she wouldn't see even another day alive.

Ammar raised his hands higher to showcase the grenades like perverted altar offerings. "So, Colonel, I see you understand my resolve. Now tell me, are you willing to let your woman die just so you can kill me?"

No, he wasn't. But this maniacal asshole failed to realize that Drew was more than ready to shield her body with his own and die in her place.

Oh, God. Monica sucked in sand-laden breaths that scratched all the way down her throat. She couldn't be on the verge of seeing her sister die.

Gritty gasps scoured her chest as she stood with Jack and the Colonel, all mentally scrambling for a way to save Yasmine.

Her sister. Another piece of the puzzle slid into a clean fit. Why had she waited so long to reach out? And now if they didn't stop Ammar from releasing the safety levers on those grenades, Yasmine would have five seconds left to live.

Pride radiated from her proud sister, along with a sure certainty that she would die. That no one would save her. And why shouldn't Yasmine feel that way? Had anyone helped her during the past year? Had she or even Sydney ever thought to check on Yasmine after their mother's death?

Resolve burned through Monica. This was her *sister.* Not a Hyatt, but her blood all the same.

And nobody messed with her sisters.

Options lined up in her mind, one by one discarded until she settled on the only plan with a chance of succeeding. The Colonel would tackle Yasmine, shield her, while Monica and Jack flew wingman at his sides to pitch the grenades.

In five seconds.

She looked left toward Jack, could sense his determination and understanding, as well. Like he'd told her earlier about Sydney: her family was his now. And along with that understanding, she saw his acceptance. He knew that she would do whatever it took to be there for this sister just as she'd fought to be here for Sydney.

Yes, she saw the acceptance. And, oh, my, she saw his love for her along with his fears. All there. Full-blown and just as real as any intense avowal. Steady, laid-back Jack who took life in stride with cocky declarations of how much he loved Elvis tunes, a good cheeseburger and his grandma actually carried around the same pain and baggage as the rest of the world.

And if she died, how much more would she add to his load?

Not an option, just as she refused to accept anything could happen to him, either. Not now when they finally had a chance. She had a few more pieces of the puzzle and looked forward to finding the rest. With Jack.

She held still, awaiting the silent order from their commander to—

The Colonel charged. Toward Yasmine. Monica sprung forward. She didn't need to look to know Jack was keeping step on the other side. The Colonel body-slammed into Yasmine.

Five. Four.

Monica landed on Ammar's left arm, Jack on the right. Scrambling for the rolling grenades.

Three.

Monica lobbed back her hand. Launched the grenade airborne.

Two. One…

Explosions rocked the ground beneath her. Sand,

rocks, shards blanketed the air. Rained down. *Tink. Tink. Tink.*

Her ears rang in the aftermath. A good sign, right? At least she was still alive. She opened her eyes.

"Jack!" she shouted, demanded. She rolled off Ammar's arm, to her knees.

"Uh-uh." Jack grunted, flipping to his side. Blood seeped from his thigh through his flight suit. But he was conscious. Whole. Relief, love and residual fear for her all scrolled across his eyes, his hands already reaching out to her.

Only then did she let herself check the others. Yasmine stirred, the Colonel already levering off her.

Ammar's eyes stared up unblinking between them. His head cocked at an angle. Neck broken. In the fall or by the Colonel?

One look in Colonel Cullen's cool eyes gave her the answer.

The Colonel began untying Yasmine from the dead man's waist with steady hands, but a tight jaw and possessive stance that broadcast well no one was getting near Yasmine anytime soon.

Apparently this sister didn't really need her, either. But that was okay. Because she knew someone who did need her…every bit as much as she needed him. Monica crawled across the jagged desert ground. She threw her arms around Jack's neck and damned well wasn't going to let go.

* * *

Almost time to go. Yasmine stood outside the overlarge cargo plane soon to be leaving for Germany before continuing on to the United States. Her new home.

No less than six military soldiers stood guard around her, so ordered by Drew. She would have preferred the company of one soldier in particular, but he stood in the circle of his officers issuing commands.

She understood the nature of his job kept him from having time to speak with her. Safety came first. Still, she wished for a chance to see him before she left. To thank him. To tell him to hell with her pride, she loved him and oh, how she hoped that her eyes were not deceiving her about what she thought she'd seen in his.

Her love returned tenfold.

And then there he was, marching toward her through the parting crowd. Her breath hitched somewhere between her chest and her throat. Late-day sun glinted off his helmet, fell to caress broad shoulders she'd once glided her hands across. Each steady footfall of his combat boots vibrated through the cracked cement and into her quivering belly.

He stopped in front of her without speaking, but he was there. He had come to her and for her gruff Spartan man, she read that for exactly what it was. A definite sign in her favor.

"Are you still angry with me, Colonel?"

Drew hitched his rifle on his shoulder, his gaze riding over her scarf before settling to stare straight into her eyes. "Almost getting yourself blown up may have put things into perspective for me."

A sentiment she shared. Never, even if she became that ninety-year-old woman with only three days left to live, would she forget the blazing fear when Drew ran toward her and she knew there was nothing she could do to stop him from giving his life for hers. Certainly this big and honorable man would do the same for anyone, which made her love him all the more.

She dared inch closer without touching. "Do you think you could hold on to that perspective even if I stay out of trouble?"

He shadowed her with his looming size that moved so gently against her while making love. He did not answer, merely stared back at her with those beautiful blue eyes in his poster-handsome face. New creases marked his features, ones she sensed she had placed there when she wished only to bring him laugh lines. Smiles. Somewhere soft to escape from his hard world.

Slowly, a smile crinkled his eyes. Only a half a smile if it had been on anyone else's face, but she searched blue and saw the joy. Even a bit of mischief twinkled at odds with the rugged exterior. "How about we discuss it over dinner? I know this great place."

Hope bloomed like a flower that found water hidden in the cracked desert. "That wonderful restaurant you enjoy near D.C.?"

"Actually—" He tucked her daisy scarf more securely over her shoulder, his knuckles skimming along the sensitive skin of her neck. "I was thinking about this place I know near post. If you're ever in the mood for a trip to Columbus, Georgia."

Relief trickled down her spine along with a shiver of awareness from his subtle touch to her neck, a touch that promised more to come. She relaxed into the flirty smile she knew drove him crazy. "Hmm. I have never been to Columbus, Georgia. Is it near Atlanta? Because I sense a serious need for clothes in my future and I hear Atlanta is a shopping mecca."

"It's close enough." His hand slid up to graze her cheek.

"Excellent." She teased her scarf into place, not missing for a second the way his gaze followed her moves with hungry intent. And for the first time she let all her vulnerabilities show because this man was far more important than her pride. "Perhaps we could do this to celebrate your return? You will let me know when that is?"

"I'll call you from my layover in Germany."

I'll call you. Simple words, but an unshakable vow from a man who honored his promises even to a country full of people he'd never met.

She arched up on her toes, skimmed his mouth with hers. Briefly, but he would understand the wealth of commitment from her to express herself so blatantly in public. His hand splayed against her back, a welcome, bracing security for her shaky knees.

Yasmine eased her lips away, pressed her cheek to the wonderful abrasion of his beard-stubbled face and whispered in his ear, "You are going to marry me one day, Drew Cullen. You know that, don't you?"

His hand pressed deeper, firmer into her back. "Yeah, Sheba. I know."

Wind twined around them mingling the familiar scents of her homeland with the now-familiar scent of her future. Tears filled her eyes and she blinked them away. She wanted Drew to hold a smiling image of her until they saw each other again.

She stepped back and found the tears tougher to combat than she had expected. "I will be waiting for you when you land."

"I'll be looking for you." Vibrant blue heated to total molten gray just before he winked. "And wear the rose-colored scarf. It's my favorite."

Her tears and smile were two parts of the same happiness. Yasmine backed toward her sisters for their return to America even though her journey was already complete. Because in this man's arms and honor, she had found the real meaning of freedom.

Jack watched the sun settle slowly into the sand and rocks of the Rubistanian horizon. Only ten more minutes until time to load up and leave, but he couldn't tear his eyes off the beauty in front of him.

His wife.

Fifty yards away, Monica stood with her back to him, a sister on either side as the three women linked arms and watched the sun sink. He didn't have to dig too deep to know they were saying their farewells to their mother.

The day unrolled in his mind. He could have lost Monica, a fact that still shook the ground under his feet. But that blast had also knocked some sense into him.

He loved her. Now and always. No holding back and wasting a minute more without her.

Two shadows slid past to bracket his. Colonel Cullen on one side, Blake Gardner on the other. Silently they stood together and waited for the women to finish finding what peace they could in the sunset. The last rays of the day melted mellow beams over Yasmine's modest black dress, Sydney's drab hostage-issue jumper, Monica's flight suit.

Without moving his eyes from his warrior wife, Jack asked the question that had niggled at him for the past few hours. "Colonel, how did you know Monica and I would take care of the grenades?"

"I didn't," the Colonel answered without missing a beat.

Jack nodded. Understood. Would have played the scenario out the same way had he been in the commander's shoes.

Together they stood and watched the women. Their women.

Cro-Magnon to be so possessive? Sure. But since it was just three guys hanging out, there wasn't any need to pretty up the emotions.

The Colonel reached under his Kevlar helmet, scratched his head. "Looks like we're going to be seeing a lot more of each other come family reunion time."

"Damn," Blake folded another piece of gum into his mouth, "just what every enlisted guy wants, senior officers sitting down with him for Thanksgiving dinner. A lifetime of 'please pass the mashed potatoes, *sir.*'"

"Mashed potatoes?" The Colonel shook his head. "Korba, is that what you were eating for the holidays last year? 'Cause it sure wasn't what I was served. Hell, last Thanksgiving I was chowing down on MREs in the desert while SEAL boys' exploits hogged the glory in the news and you were eating turkey leftovers."

Ah, the familiarity of service rivalry. Ooh-rah. Future Thanksgivings would be a blast. "You guys are just jealous because my idea of roughing it is no HBO when I'm TDY."

"Chair Force," Blake muttered on a cough.

"Hey," Jack groused, "last time I checked, I

was the one who got shot in the ass on this mission.''

Laughs rumbled low, back and forth. Yeah, Thanksgivings were going to rock, especially with the three women to rile up the mix. Regardless of whatever other flaws Cheryl Lynn Hyatt Halibiz may have had, she'd given birth to three daughters who sure knew how to kick ass in their own ways.

Willowy Sydney with an unbreakable spirit.

Petite Yasmine who could spit fire with the best of them.

And his warrior Monica with a tender heart and unstoppable drive to heal the world.

Ah, hell. Jack punted a rock with his boot. This was a little more in touch with emotions than he wanted to be. He cleared his throat, shifted his weight to his uninjured leg and turned to his two future brother-in-laws. ''Wanna go shoot guns or something?''

''Hoo-ya.''

''Hoo-uh.''

''Ooh-rah.''

The radio in the Colonel's hand squawked, yanking them back to the present and their jobs.

Jack pivoted to face the older officer, snapped to attention, popped a sharp salute and held. ''An honor working with you, sir. Cover your ass till things are wrapped up and I'll see you back in the States.''

''That you will, Major. That you will.'' He returned the salute, then to the SEAL, as well, before lifting his LMR to his mouth and answering the radio call.

Gardner strode ahead to Sydney. Once Yasmine was safely escorted with Gardner, as well, the Colonel turned his attention to the call at hand. Not that he left the sight line of the runway, something that Jack suspected wouldn't change until they were safely in the air.

Jack ambled over to Monica, and damned if she didn't meet him halfway. "You about ready to head out, Mon?"

"Whenever you are. Guess we'll be sitting together after all."

"Well, that's one way for a married couple to get to ride in the same plane together. Have the other plane shot out from underneath you."

Monica shuddered, that vulnerable soul of hers more visible now that he knew to look for the signs. He slung an arm around her shoulders, brought her close to his side, her heart slugging a double pace under his draped hand.

He kissed her temple. Let her lean on him. Discovered the surprise pleasure of leaning on her, as well. "When do you want to tell everyone about being married?"

"How about we tell our families first? Then we can cut the news loose in the squadron."

"I'm guessing that piece of gossip will likely

take the heat off you on the Tiara jokes for a while.''

Her light chuckle teased over him. He let himself join in. Laughing together, just being together, was a gift he didn't intend to take for granted again.

Five steps closer to the plane, the thudding pulse under his hand slowed to an almost normal pace. ''Hey, flyboy, I'm going to need you to drop your pants again once we're airborne so I can check out your injury. Looks like you popped some stitches.''

''You don't have to make up excuses to get me to unzip my flight suit around you.''

Her laugh vibrated against his side, her heart easing that last bit to a regular rate. Making her laugh felt good. *She* made him feel good.

''God, Mon, I can't wait to have you alone so we can get messy, noisy and really busy.''

''Uh, Jack, small problem with the noisy part.''

''Do I hear a challenge?''

She glanced up apologetically. ''I told Yasmine she could stay with me.''

''Shit. You did what?''

''Staying with me in Charleston is closer to Georgia and the Colonel than if she bunked with Sydney up in Virginia. Besides, I figured Blake and Sydney need the time alone more than we do.''

''And you want the chance to fix things with Yasmine.''

Her head fell to rest on his shoulder. ''Like you said. Family's important.''

Apparently she'd found more peace than she expected in this desert. "Between your family and mine, and all the crew dogs in the squadron, we're never going to be alone, are we?"

"Probably not." And she didn't sound one damned bit upset by the prospect.

Never alone. Definitely a good thing in his book.

Monica had been alone, taking care of herself and everyone around her for far too long. She might not need him to kick ass for her, but she did need him. Every bit as much as he needed her, this woman who challenged the hell out of him. Made him dig deep and give his all. Made him realize that, damn, his all was more than he knew he had inside him.

Of course tantric sex and knock-knock jokes weren't commodities to sell short. Monica also needed more lighthearted moments in her life. He knew his strengths and planned to capitalize on them to keep this incredible woman as head over heels in love with him as possible.

Stopping, Jack turned her to face him, looked in her dewy green eyes and realized...hell. He did have something else to offer her. Something she hadn't been given by her mother who'd walked, or her father who'd checked out emotionally, or her loser-ass ex-fiancé. Jack smiled back at his wife, and damned if his laid-back determined nature didn't make him just the right man to give her what no one had given this woman before.

Forever.

Monica stared straight into Jack's eyes and knew his words before he said them. But Lord have mercy, she looked forward to hearing them.

"I love you, Monica Hyatt Korba. And, God willing, I'll spend the rest of my life right by your side making sure you're never alone again."

His words melted her insides, melted her against him.

"Oh, yeah," he groaned against her lips. "Digging deep sure has an awesome payoff."

Jack cupped her face in his hands and kissed her. All-out. Full body press and fuller emotions. Monica flung her arms around his neck and quit trying to figure out what he meant by that last cryptic comment. Who cared right now, anyway, and who the hell cared about any regs on public displays of affection while in uniform?

She was kissing her husband and could have sworn she heard the strains of "Can't Help Falling In Love," what she now considered Elvis's best tune ever. A whimsical thought, whimsy being something she hadn't indulged in often. Until Jack. It felt as good as the rippling muscles and man under her hands.

She eased her mouth from his. "Jack, I love you so damned much and I intend to spend the rest of my life showing you." One last concern niggled her. "More than anything I want us to celebrate forever from side-by-side retirement rocking chairs

where we can talk about our children and grand-
children. But I can't promise you I won't die on
you before then. My job has taught me too well
how fragile life is. Your job does, too, for that matter. I'm careful. You know that. But is that
enough?''

How strange that when her ex-fiancé had pushed
her to the wall about quitting her job she couldn't
imagine backing down. Yet, she knew she would
do whatever it took to make Jack happy and give
him peace.

''I'd be lying if I said I don't want to wrap you
up in cotton and keep you as far away from this
kind of shit as I can.'' His arms banded around her,
loosely, supporting without constricting. ''But I
know you. I respect you. The last thing I want is
to change you. When push comes to shove, I'm
there for you. Whatever you need or want or
choose, I'm behind you.''

No wonder she loved this man.

And he *had* been there for her today. Even
though she'd sensed his fear of losing her, he hadn't
tried to stop her. Not even for a second, much less
the prolonged battle of wills they'd gone through a
week ago.

She wasn't naive enough to think they would
never argue or knock heads. But bottom line, they
now had unreserved love, and, yes, respect for each
other. ''What did I ever do to deserve you?''

''That's just it, babe. Things like trust and respect

are earned and deserved. But love? Well, it just exists of its own free will. What a damned fine thing, because otherwise we'd always have to worry about it being taken away the first time we screwed up. And the way I figure, it's a sure bet I'm going to screw up on occasion down the line.''

That simple and clear. He loved her. It made so much sense now that she'd stopped to listen to him instead of always telling him what he should be thinking and saying.

She toyed with the tab on his flight suit zipper. ''Making up is fun.''

''So I hear.'' He flicked her zipper tab right back.

Just because he was laid-back and loping through life didn't mean he wasn't very aware and always planning. She could learn more than a few things from this wise and oh-so-funny man she'd married. ''I really do love you, Jack.''

''I know.''

And she saw that he did. She'd been given the gift of his love, but she'd also won his trust.

A planeload of people waited behind them. Still she couldn't stop herself from taking a few more seconds to savor the moment. She glided her hands over his bristly face full of hard angles, strength and sun-bronzed laugh lines. Exhaustion carved a few extra creases around his eyes, reminding her he was her patient as well as her husband today.

''Okay, flyboy, as your doctor *and* your concerned wife, I'm telling you it's time for you to get in that plane and take a load off. You've been up for over twenty-four hours. Fought in a war. And been shot in the ass.'' She jabbed a finger toward the load ramp. "Move it."

He hooked an arm over her shoulders again, making his way toward the open load ramp. "God, I love it when you get bossy."

She wasn't sure if his leaning came from a need for support or a need to touch her. Either way, she wasn't complaining, not even when he grew heavier during the last few steps. "I'm not bossy. Just assertive."

"Uh-huh. Whatever you want, I'm game."

She pinched his side just as they reached the aircraft. "Zipper-suited sky gods and their egos."

"Mouthy and bossy." His boots thundered on the base of the metal ramp. "Babe, you're turning me inside out."

"Get used to it, flyboy," she whispered in his ear. "I've got ideas for what we can do in those retirement rocking chairs."

"Anything. Anywhere. Anytime. I'm your man."

Epilogue

Five minutes more and he could peel off his flight suit.

Jack hauled his weary body down the long corridor of the Warrior Inn toward his VOQ room at Nellis AFB, debrief for his flight completed before sundown. What a way to spend his one-year wedding anniversary. TDY alone in Vegas. Monica TDY elsewhere. But that was military life. They would just have a helluva celebration in Charleston in a couple of days.

Making tracks through the crew dogs packing the halls, Jack smiled, tossed nods, turned down invitations to head out to eat. He only wanted to find his bed and the telephone so he could call his wife.

He angled sideways around a cleaning cart, eyeing his door and already thinking up at least eleven different ways to romance Monica over the phone. Life was good.

"Sir," the uniformed maid called, steadying a tottering pile of towels, "I went ahead and let your wife into your room. I hope that was all right."

Wife? In his room? Life was about to get a helluva lot better. Anticipation punted exhaustion clean away. "Absolutely all right. Thanks!"

His double-timed steps thundered down the carpeted hall. A swipe of his key card and he swung the door wide to find, oh, yeah—his wife.

Major Monica Hyatt Korba reclined on his bed in her flight suit, her sock-clad feet crossed at the ankles. Crooked in the corner of her arm, she held his box of Froot Loops. "I hope the King's not too tired for a chorus of 'Are You Lonesome Tonight' followed by breakfast in bed."

"The King's very ready to step up to the mike for a performance. And more than one encore." Kicking the door closed, Jack sprinted across the room and fell on top of her. The bounce of the bed launched the cereal box and rained Froot Loops around them.

He captured her mouth with his. Breakfast at night never tasted better.

Caramel hair swirled around her shoulders, waves crimping it from hours spent restrained in a

French braid. His fingers combed through, couldn't get enough of the silkiness or the woman. "God, Monica," he groaned, rolling to his side, sweeping back her hair and enjoying the vision of her in his bed. "I can't believe you're here."

"It took some wrangling, but I worked it." She nipped his bottom lip, her eyes fluttering open to peer at him with emerald intensity. "I wanted us to have time alone together before all the family comes in this weekend for the baptism."

Quiet settled between them. Jack tucked her closer, brushed another kiss over her forehead, giving her the silent moment of comfort he knew she needed. Coming to grips with Sydney's capture had been an ongoing process for all three of the sisters, but they were women of grit. Perseverance. Slowly, healing came for all of them.

After a couple months of soul searching, Sydney decided for sure on adoption—an open adoption with Daniel "Crusty" Baker and his wife. Sydney and Blake had spent the last weeks of Sydney's pregnancy in Charleston with Monica so she could be on hand to assist with the delivery. Family pulling together. Finally, Sydney found peace in knowing her baby girl was being welcomed with undiluted joy by a couple who yearned for a child to cherish along with Crusty's two young half brothers.

Now Sydney and Blake were both ready to move

forward with their lives. A few more months and they would be celebrating their first anniversary, as well, in a rock-solid marriage. Sydney was back at work, but staying stateside for a while. Maybe permanently, now fighting her battles by slicing through red tape and political channels with a new-found fiery strength that had people listening—and even opening their wallets at fund-raisers. Her new favorite project was the Pete Santuci scholarship fund, her heart touched by Yasmine and Monica's story of the young man who'd given his life to save her.

"Jack?" Monica stroked aside the hair on his brow, damp from hours under his headset.

"Yeah, Mon?"

Her hands urged him back toward her and he forgot about family and thinking and anything but the feel of his wife's busy fingers working his flight suit off his shoulders, his T-shirt up. A cereal O inched into his shorts. Not that he cared since he was otherwise occupied, his mouth on Monica's lips, her neck, biting her zipper tab to expose the most awesome damned breasts ever encased in...

Champagne satin and lace? Ooh-rah. "Happy anniversary to me."

Monica's laugh vibrated under his questing mouth.

"Hmm." He nuzzled hot satin covering even hotter woman. "Where did this come from?"

She arched into the draw of his lips against a peaking nipple. "Shopping trip with my sister in Atlanta. Yasmine's really getting into this clothes-buying stuff." She gasped her rambling explanation between sighs and needy writhing over the cotton spread. "She should probably buy stock in Victoria's Secret for as much time as she spends scouting out new underwear to entice the Colonel with."

Jack winced, his face finding rest in the soft crook of her neck. "Okay, hon, that's more info than I needed about the Colonel's sex life."

Even as he razzed her, he couldn't stop the surge of pride over how hard she'd worked to establish a bond with her youngest sister over the past months. The effort seemed to be paying off if their shopping trips were anything to judge by. Yasmine and the Colonel even joined them for Atlanta Braves' games.

"Although—" Jack eased her zipper down farther to see if this bra was part of a matching set...and it was "—if shopping with your sister brings about more of this, maybe I can just plug my ears when it comes to discussing what she bought."

"There will be plenty more shopping in the coming weeks with her wedding next month. God, what a zoo it's going to be."

No doubt about that since Yasmine had insisted there would be no slinking off to hide their nuptials because of age-difference whispers. The Colonel had slipped a solitaire fit for a princess on her finger in record time, but then insisted on a long engagement to give her a chance to adjust to her new life. Ever fair, the Colonel wanted her to be sure.

And Yasmine Halibiz soon-to-be Cullen was damned certain.

Her job as an emergency room trauma nurse kept her busy while her fiancé was out in the field. That, and shopping jags for more gifts to spoil Drew's granddaughter rotten.

Monica snuggled closer. "And, oh, my God, you should see the veil she picked to go with her gown." She flopped onto her back. "It's a wonderful mix of her old country and new. Although the Colonel's going to have to fight his way through a lot of lace to get to her for the big kiss."

A question niggled at him. "Do you ever regret that we didn't have a big wedding?"

"Not a chance." She turned on the pillow to look at him. Her husky drawl rang with resolution. "We got the best of everything. A small family service when your brother blessed our vows. A big bash with our friends later. All that and an Elvis impersonator. What more could a girl want?"

He could think of a million things he wanted to do for this woman, out of bed as well as in. Luckily, somehow he'd convinced her to spend the rest of their lives together so he could work his way down that list. "What more could you want? I'm hoping you want me. Now."

"That's a sure bet." Her leg hooked over his hip.

His erection nudged her belly in response. This first time was going to be fast, intense, followed by long-drawn-out. Three cheers for tantric. "Did you bring condoms? Because God knows I wasn't expecting to get laid on TDY."

"Good thing, too, flyboy."

"So? Where the hell did you Ziploc those things up?"

"I brought them, but..."

"But what?"

She stared back up at him, intense, hopeful, her hair a toffee splash against the white pillowcase. "I was hoping I could convince you that it's time to stop using them." When he didn't answer right away, her hands glided over his back, soothing, but the longing in her eyes stayed. A primal wish for children together that stirred an answer within him. "I want us to be parents, Jack, and someday have grandbabies to talk about while we're in those retirement rockers. I got the idea lately that maybe now you're ready to start working on that, too."

Children with Monica. Hell, yes, he wanted a houseful of little Korbas with Monica's eyes. Sure he couldn't stop the twinge of fear in his gut when he thought about how he'd lost Tina. But he realized those fears were mostly illogical and just a part of loving someone so damned much. He was a lucky man to have found such deep love twice in a lifetime.

Deep. The word definitely did not scare him anymore now that he fully appreciated the payoffs. And what a payoff it was, being loved by this woman who honored his past while still demanding he move forward with their future. "Babies, huh?"

Monica skimmed her fingers over the bristle of his late-day beard. "I thought we could start with one for now. More later."

His mind filled with images of Monica with their baby at her breast. "I'm already working on the words for Elvis's 'Teddy Bear.'"

With a Texas-size cheer, she threw her arms around his neck. "I love you."

Three little words he never tired of saying or hearing these days. "Love you, too," he answered against her lips.

She arched up into his kiss as he sank down onto her lush curves. Cereal crunched under their writhing bodies. Fruity scent wafted up, almost managing to override the persistent itch from the mess, an itch that would be increasingly uncomfortable once he got Monica naked. Very soon, hopefully. They'd sure come a long way from his lonely cold shower in Vegas months ago.

And speaking of showers. "It was a long flight

and I really do need to wash up.'' He rolled off the bed and onto his feet. ''And, Monica?''

''Yes, my love?''

Amazing how those last two words coming from her mouth turned him on, and he knew that anytime, anywhere, they always would.

Smiling, Jack extended his hand. ''You're most definitely invited to join me.''

* * * * *

Catherine Mann has more
WINGMEN WARRIORS *stories to tell.*
Don't miss
JOINT FORCES,
available in May 2004
from Silhouette Intimate Moments.

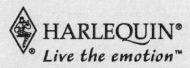

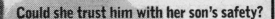
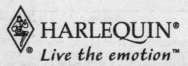

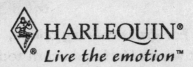